# VORPAL BLADE

# VORPAL BLADE

# JOHN RINGO
# TRAVIS S. TAYLOR

VORPAL BLADE

A Baen Books Original

Baen Publishing Enterprises
P.O. Box 1403
Riverdale, NY 10471
www.baen.com

ISBN 10: 1-4165-2129-1
ISBN 13: 978-1-4165-2129-7

Cover art by Kurt Miller

First printing, September 2007

Distributed by Simon & Schuster
1230 Avenue of the Americas
New York, NY 10020

Library of Congress Cataloging-in-Publication Data

Ringo, John, 1963–
    Vorpal blade / John Ringo and Travis S. Taylor.
        p. cm.
    Sequel to: Into the looking glass.
    "A Baen Books original"—T.p. verso.
    ISBN-13: 978-1-4165-2129-7
    ISBN-10: 1-4165-2129-1
 1. Physicists—Fiction. 2. United States. Navy. SEALs—Fiction. 3. Space flight—Fiction. 4. Technology transfer—Fiction. 5. Human-alien encounters—Fiction.
I. Taylor, Travis S. II. Title.

    PS3568.I577V67 2007
    813'.54—dc22

                                                           2007015781

10   9   8   7   6   5   4   3   2   1

Pages by Joy Freeman (www.pagesbyjoy.com)
Printed in the United States of America

# DEDICATION

~~~~~~

To Bob Heinlein, Andre Norton, Doc Smith,
Isaac Asimov, A. E. van Vogt and all the rest of the
greats who sparked a young man's imagination.

And to Jim Baen, for giving us both
the chance to pay it forward.

Last
As Always:
For Captain Tamara Long, USAF
Born: 12 May 1979
Died: 23 March 2003, Afghanistan
You fly with the angels now.

# 1

## A Plate of XXXX@ vhysw a7msyulhkreeee-eeeeeeeeeeeeeeeeeeerrrrrrrrrrrrrrrrrrrrrrrrrrrrrrr-rrrrrrrrrrrrrrrrrrrrrrrrrrrrrrrrrrrrrrrrrrrrrrrrrrrrrrrrrrrku with a Side of Muons. Please.

"You think I should hit the order again?" Bill said, looking over at the kitchen. Service in Adar restaurants was proverbially slow, but this was ridiculous. He and Sal had sent in their orders over thirty minutes ago and still they didn't even have their drinks.

Lieutenant Commander William "Doc" Weaver, RN, Ph.D., wasn't really happy about the lunch anyway. He'd known Sal Weinstein back when they both worked for Columbia Defense so when Sal called and asked if he was doing anything for lunch, he'd thought it was just a social call. He should have guessed that Sal, whom he hadn't spoken to in two years, wasn't going to drive down to Norfolk to chat.

"Won't work," Sal said, shrugging. "But go ahead if it makes you happy. Now, about the server . . ."

Bill flipped open the menu and hit the entry for *glangi* with extra *melaegl* sauce. The thing didn't even flash. He'd already ordered with this menu. One menu, one order. No tickee, no laundry.

"It's a damned Microsoft Vavala server with some code thrown

1

on top," Bill replied, hitting the entry again. The restaurant wasn't particularly crowded and now he knew why. Some of the Adar had started to catch on that humans didn't take four hours for lunch. Clearly the family unit running this place were right out of the Glass.

"We've got top Adar working on it," Sal argued. "Top Adar."

"You've got Fazglim and Dulaul," Bill said, not looking up. "Who are the only Adar I've ever met who fall into the description of credit-whores. And neither one of them knows diddly *maulk* about server tech. Fazglim's a natural processes philo and Dulaul is a micro-actions philo. So you're telling me you've got the best server on the market because you happen to have a tame biologist and quantum physicist who are willing to sign off on it. It's an MS Vav, which is one of the buggiest servers in the *world*, with code from Col-Gomo programming thrown on top. And that makes it buggier. Come on, Sal, don't try to snow me. I *know* Adar tech. I work with it every damned day."

The problem was, since the opening of the Looking Glasses, the whole world, and especially Wall Street, had gone nuts over Adar. Adar tech *was* light years ahead of human, but it wasn't magic. And a lot of stuff that was sold as being "Adar technology" was anything but. The Adar had been a philosophical race when they encountered humans. Which meant they were about as resistant to marketing as Native Americans to disease. So more and more of them were emigrating to Earth where "everything was prettier." And, by and large, they could command immense salaries because if a company had an Adar, even if the male, female or transfer-neuter was the training equivalent of a janitor, they could say they had an Adar working on their technology.

Bill had fallen for that scam exactly once, an "Adar-tech" shampoo substitute. Basically, it was a comb you were supposed to use in the shower to wash your hair. Guaranteed to do miraculous things for your entire head region.

He was still trying to grow the hair back.

He had to admit that there was some great stuff out there that was derived from *real* Adar technology. Forget brushing your teeth, all you had to do was pop a Nanobrush™ capsule, crunch it in your teeth and not only did your teeth turn lily-white but you didn't have to worry about halitosis for twelve hours. Then there was the entire electronic tech revolution. . . .

"Wait, got a call," Sal said, holding up his hand to the back of his head. "Yeah, Joe, Sal . . . That's great, man . . ."

Implants, though . . . Jeeze. Back when they were the "killer app," Doc had thought BlackBerry was a pain in the ass. The only way you could tell the difference between a raving street-guy and a raving corporate attorney was the quality of clothing and that one had a flashing blue thing in his ear. But since implants had hit the market, people really *did* hear voices. Now you couldn't tell the difference at *all*.

Of course, he was wearing a VeriNthal ear piece, which gave him pretty much the same look as an implant wearer. But you could at least see the damned earring.

He hit the menu again and was amazed to see an Adar exit the door to the restaurant's kitchens, bearing a massive platter.

That was the other thing about Adar cooking. The Adar approached their two daily meals with religious reverence. The most undertrained neuter home-cook had more passion for cuisine than a cordon bleu chef. Each meal had to be both satisfying *and* a work of art. They were worse than the Japanese about it.

So while Bill would have been perfectly satisfied with a platter of *glangi* noodles, what he got instead was a half a dozen dishes. Condiments, sides, little crunchy things, none of it was particularly identifiable. He'd been to dinners at the White House that were less elaborate.

"*Methmar*," Weaver said, nodding to the trans-neut waiter. The transfer-neuters were only semi-sentient and did most of the mundane tasks of the Adar. Far smaller than the males, much less the females, the trans-neut was about six feet tall with mottled brown skin and three eyes set over a wide, flat face that was mostly a mouth with wide, grinding molars.

Clashing with the standard Adar look, though, was its clothes. The Adar, when Weaver first met them, tended to wear something not much more complex than a loincloth. However, they had never dealt with marketing departments. While Adar tech had become the rage on Earth, human styles and fads had hit the Adar like hard liquor at a redneck party.

The Adar was wearing an electric purple skirt and a "blouse" that was basically transparent. Under it was a tank top of electric pink. It was sporting huge rhinestone-encrusted sunglasses with giant wings on either side that made it look like an Elvis Valkyrie.

It was also wearing an iPod. Given that it was assuredly implanted and the iPod was at best superfluous, it had to be a fashion device.

"Welcome, welcome, welcome," the trans-neut squeaked, a terribly high falsetto from something six feet tall and weighing in at damned near three hundred pounds. "Worship! Enjoy! Taking Care of Business! Nothing But Hound Dog!"

So it *meant* to be an Elvis Valkyrie.

"Thanks," Bill said as the being shimmied back to the kitchen. He sighed and picked up his tongs, scooping up some of the noodles.

Bill Weaver had been a peaceful little scientist working for Columbia Defense, coming up with solutions to problems U.S. national defense didn't even realize it had, when he got dragged over to the White House one rainy Saturday night to explain quantum physics to the National Security Council. A physics experiment gone awry had not only created a massive—on the order of sixty kilotons—explosion at the University of Central Florida, but it had left a strange anomaly behind. He'd just happened to be the nearest physicist the secretary of defense could lay his hand on who had a Top Secret clearance.

Subsequent to that he'd been blown up, ripped into other dimensions, killed he was pretty sure, resurrected he was more sure and generally had a "blast" stopping an alien invasion.

The anomaly had been a boson generator, a black sphere they still didn't have a theoretical handle on, that generated Higgs bosons at a phenomenal rate. What was worse, or better, take your pick, is that the bosons turned out to have the ability to "link" to other bosons and open up portals to . . . well, just about anywhere. Instantaneous transportation, even to other planets. The portals created mirrorlike openings that had been christened "Looking Glasses." They went some strange places, that was for sure.

The kicker was that some of those planets had sentient beings that were interested in taking over the Earth. Called the Dreen, the species reproduced via a mat of fungus that was programmed to produce various other creatures. Like big, howling dog demons that ate people—humanity's first contact with the Dreen—and all the way up to giant spider things the size of mountains. Presumably there was some sentient control behind the Dreen, but Bill had never seen it. All he'd seen was rhino-tanks and centipedes and howlers. Lots of howlers. The very name, Dreen, was an Adar rendition of the howl. *Dreeeeeeen.* Neither humans nor the Adar had any idea what the species called itself and didn't really care. All they cared about was avoiding them or, if necessary or possible, wiping them out to the last fungoid monstrosity.

The upside to the gates were the Adar. They had encountered the Dreen when they'd first started creating their own Glasses, had had similar problems and had figured out how to close a Glass. Basically, all it needed was a big enough explosion. Big. World-killing. Since there was no way to set it off in the middle of a transfer—the movement was as close to instantaneous as instruments could detect—you had to choose which world to set it off on.

The Adar hadn't wanted to risk it but when the Dreen were swarming through multiple portals the humans, specifically the president of the United States, had been willing to try anything. Weaver, with the support of a short division of mech infantry and a SEAL team, had managed to stick the explosive device on the far side of a portal in Kentucky. That was the second time he was pretty sure he'd died. But he'd been spit back out after a strange conversation with an entity or entities that might be God.

Shortly after they'd stopped the invasion, the Adar had given him another strange device. On first tests, it had appeared to be the world's most powerful nuclear hand grenade. Any electrical power sent to it, so much as a spark of static, and, well, there was a boom. A really big boom. "There should have been an earth shattering Ka-Boom!" boom. Putting three-phase on it had, in fact, erased a solar system.

The Adar didn't know what it was *supposed* to do but Weaver had basically *guessed* that it was, in fact, some sort of Faster-Than-Light drive. It took nearly a year of tinkering, and two more planets, to figure out that it was, in fact, such a drive. It had taken another year to create the first prototype starship.

By then, Weaver had switched sides in the ongoing sales war, leaving the Beltway and taking a direct commission in the Navy, which was the lead service in developing the world's first spaceship. He'd pointed out even before switching sides that the Navy just made more sense. The President wanted a presence off-world as fast as possible. They'd picked up enough intel in the brief war to know that the Dreen had some sort of FTL as well. Finding out where the Dreen were, whether they were headed to Earth through normal space, was a high priority. The only way to make a spaceship, fast, was to convert something. The obvious choice had been one of the many ballistic missile submarines that were being decommissioned.

So Weaver, while continuing to consult on engineering issues, was now the astrogation officer of the Naval Construction Contract 4144. Despite a couple of shakedown cruises around the solar system, the Top Secret boat had yet to be named. The 4144 had all the beauty and problems of any prototype. Most of the equipment was human, much of it original to the former SSBN *Nebraska*. Other bits were Adar or Human-Adar manufacture. The fact that it worked at all was amazing.

In two days, the still unnamed boat was going to be blasting off for points unknown. Well, actually, all the points were known. Bill had created the initial survey route. But what was there was unknown. Mankind was finally going "Where No Man Has Gone Before." And he was listening to Sal pitch the new Col-Gomo Adar 2007 to another unsuspecting client while picking at his ordundrorob beetle soup.

Most Adar food was incompatible with human systems. The Adar had, after all, evolved on a completely different planet. Even basic sugars were stereo isomers. Isomers were chemicals in which certain bonds could go in either direction. All the "sugar" isomers of Earth were so-called "left" isomers. Adar sugars were "right" isomers. Many Adar foods were so incompatible as to be poisonous.

But over the last seven years, humans and Adar had found a surprising number of dishes and drinks, starting with Coca-Cola, that each species could consume. Oh, it was usually the nutritional equivalent of eating sawdust, but the food was good. And since there was zero nutritional content it was *the* killer diet food. Bill, mostly due to spending all his damned time sitting at a desk lately, had started to pad on a few pounds. Given that he'd once been champion-class at mountain biking and karate, the tub was eating at him. Ergo, Adar food.

On the other hand . . .

"I've got a meeting at thirteen-thirty," Bill said as Sal finished his call, finally. "The answer is I'm not in that branch of procurement, I don't *do* procurement and I think your system sucks. If you're looking for me to say good words about it, look elsewhere."

"Bill. Buddy . . ." Sal said, shaking his head. "You don't have to be that way . . ."

"Yes, I do," Bill replied. "I'm a damned government employee these days, Sal. I'm going to have to do *paperwork* on this lunch, I'm going to have to pick up the bill or go Dutch and I've got a forty-minute drive back to the docks. All that to be pitched on a system we both know is crap."

"Okay," Sal said, holding up his hands. "Seriously. I agree with you. Fazglim and Dulaul don't know diddly about servers. We both know that. So . . . Do you know any *good* Adar that are in the market?"

"Why couldn't you just come out and say that, Sal?" Bill asked, tonging up another mouthful of noodles. "I don't, but I know who to ask. Good enough?"

"We really need a good Adar working in our code department," Sal said. "We're losing ground to LockLilug. They've got Gilanglka heading up their department. We can't compete with him."

"Whoever it is is going to want something like a CIO position," Bill pointed out. "You know that."

"I was told by very senior people to ask," Sal said.

"I'll ask around," Bill said. "Ring. Command. Bill."

"Your bill is twenty-nine, forty-seven," his earring phone replied. "Fifteen percent tip will be four, forty-two."

"Command: Add tip. Pay bill," Bill said, standing up. "Command off. See ya, Sal."

"Good to see you again, Bill," Sal said, standing up. "I should have gotten at least half."

"I needed to run," Weaver replied, shaking his hand. He'd gotten some *melaegl* sauce on his khakis and he wiped at it with the nannie nap. The napkin, which had active nannites that aggressively sought out and removed stains, should have swept the stain clean but all it did was rub it in. Of course, if they'd been *washed* too many times . . .

Weaver shook his head and walked out. What a day.

"You could have given me more warning," Mimi said acerbically to, apparently, nothing. "It's not like we didn't know it was going to happen. Yes, but you're not the one that has to convince Aunt Vera. Sure, but you *know* that she's going to *maulk* a brick."

Mimi Jones was fourteen, short for her age, slight of figure, with long brown hair. She currently lived with her aunt and uncle, her mother having died in the Chen Event, and was in the eighth grade gifted program at Dr. Phillips Middle School in Orlando, Florida. She was actually in two separate programs. Fortunately for Mimi, Dr. Phillips Middle School, which catered primarily to families that were upper middle-class in income, had a very open-minded approach to their gifted program. For most of the children in the gifted program there was a set schedule of classes with some electives and independent study. In Mimi's case, she was entirely in independent study. In fact, Mimi would have been, in earlier times, ready to graduate. From college.

You see, Mimi had a friend. And the friend was very smart. Smart enough and capable enough to take the child on adventures of the mind far beyond those of the classroom.

When Mimi was six she had lived on Mendel Terrace, Orlando, in a small two-bedroom apartment with her mother, Loretta Jones. Mendel Terrace was less than a half a mile from the center of the Event that destroyed the University of Central Florida and, on that particular morning, Mimi had been watching cartoons when everything suddenly went black.

Mimi's recollection of the subsequent period had been investigated several times. All that she could remember was being in a black space, then there was "someone," or more likely something, who was there, for some value of "there." The person, thing, entity or whatever, comforted her. And then she was back on Earth, in the darkness, lying in rubble with a new friend. The "friend" was a large brown spider thing that looked very much like a stuffed toy. It said its name was Tuffy, for values of "said." The best Mimi had ever been able to explain is that knowledge appeared in her head as if she had always had it.

Mimi had then gotten up and gone to the light. The light, Klieg lights in fact, had been set up at the base studying the brand new Chen Anomaly. Mimi's brief period in some otherwhere had taken most of that day and it was nearly midnight when she stumbled into a group that was taking a break from studying the enigmatic black globe that was Ray Chen's final legacy. Among those present was William Weaver, Ph.D., who at the time had no idea of the wonders he was about to experience. Already worried about potential biological contamination a deputy sheriff, against Weaver's advice, had attempted to relieve Mimi of her new friend. Tuffy had extended two of his ten legs, extended or extruded some claws and zapped the deputy with what was later suspected to be about four thousand volts of electricity.

After that, nobody tried to take Tuffy away from Mimi. Even her school had allowed the alien "friend"—the word "pet" was *never* used—to attend with her.

During his investigation of the Anomaly, Weaver had experienced some very strange events. One of them was either a vivid hallucination or a period of time outside the universe, a place that had no definition of "real" for anyone, even the most out-there physicist. In that time of untime he had either met other "Tuffys" or had hallucinated them. However, some of the revelations that had come from the sojourn indicated to him that Tuffys were real, for values of "real," and that the being that rode on Mimi's shoulder was from that unplace. In fact, there was an argument he occasionally had with himself as to whether Tuffy was, in fact, God, or at least some reasonable approximation.

Whatever Tuffy might be, he was definitely smart. And he had helped Mimi to become smart as well. There were very few researchers that Mimi, and Tuffy, trusted enough to let close. But a few had managed to ask enough questions of Mimi to get a feel for what was going on between the two. Initially, from the point of view of study, Tuffy had simply acted as a helpmate, expertly creating scenarios for Mimi that had assisted her in her own understanding of the work placed in front of her by teachers. However, as time passed, Tuffy had begun using that basis to take Mimi farther and faster than the teachers believed possible. By the time Mimi had left the third grade she was already exploring algebra, trigonometry and the beginnings of astrophysics with Tuffy. As she passed through subsequent grades she accelerated faster so that by the time she was in the seventh she was at a college level in all of the hard sciences with a massive knowledge, as well, of history, psychology, anthropology and even theology.

Mimi's aunt and uncle were very devout Christians and, in general, believers that the only book that people needed to read was the Bible. However, they had indulged Mimi's passion for eclectic reading, especially since a good bit of it was theological. Their minister, who had a Ph.D. in theology, had pointed out that knowing the details of other religions was not a sin and, in fact, vital for a truer understanding of Christianity. They had, however, drawn the line at certain texts on human physiology and aberrant psychology. So Mimi had just looked the data up on the Internet, easily bypassing the "child protection" programs with Tuffy's help.

Lately, Mimi had become more helpful with some researchers. The reason was simple: money. The Wilsons lived in one of the less affluent areas around Dr. Phillips, and Mr. Wilson was a carpenter whose income was enough to keep Mimi in relative comfort. But Mimi and Tuffy realized that in the near future they were going to need more money than that, if for no other reason than to keep up with Mimi's researches.

Mimi had, therefore, begun to contact some very senior researchers and offer to assist them in knotty questions they were stuck on. Whether it was Mimi or Tuffy answering questions like the seven *Millennium Prize Problems* was never quite clear. But the questions were answered.

The Clay Mathematics Institute of Cambridge, Massachusetts, or the CMI as it is known in mathematics circles, identified seven problems in mathematics that had eluded scientists and mathematicians for enduring periods of time. The CMI offered a one million dollar award for each solution. Mimi, more or less out of the blue, had submitted solutions to four of the seven unsolved problems. Although the solutions had been available for review for more than the two-year required "review period," the mathematics community did not consider Mimi as "a member of the community" so she was slow-rolled on the payment.

Specifically, and relevant to the Higgs bosons, the Chen Anomaly, and the gates, was her solution to the quantum Yang-Mills theory. Before the Chen Anomaly and the Dreen had come, the laws of quantum physics had been to the world of elementary particles what Newton's laws of classical mechanics had been to the macroscopic world for centuries: quantum physics had become the base theory from which to start in forming any new concept as Newton's laws had been a century before. Where Newton's laws described how things in the macroscopic world moved and reacted in general around mundane gravitational fields any odd things such as black holes required Einstein's General Relativity. Similarly, quantum mechanics described particle physics fairly well, until the Chen Anomaly.

In the mid 1950s Yang and Mills developed a method to describe the interactions of elementary particles using an approach that implements various structures also found in geometry, and they showed how to use the theory to predict particular elementary particle actions. Yang-Mills was more a description of particle actions than an explanation of them. The theory had been verified experimentally but there was no underlying model that supported the theory.

The theory itself is basically a *gauge theory*, like the Higgs boson theory that enables the prediction of particles which interact via the so-called "strong" force. The strong force interactions depend on a subtle quantum mechanical property called the "mass gap": quantum particles have positive masses, even though the classical waves travel at the speed of light, which is in contradiction, or at the least counterintuitive, to Einstein's Special Relativity. According to Special Relativity, a particle with mass can't reach the speed of light within the normal universe because it would take an infinite amount of energy, but some quantum particles appear to violate this. Hence, the "mass gap." Mimi's mathematical proof, finally, explained this violation.

Mimi, or perhaps Tuffy, had surmised that the fractal path the Looking Glass bosons—or the LGBs as they were now discussed in math and physics circles—took after the Chen Anomaly was through a dimension of the spacetime continuum that was *outside* those governed by even the multiple manifold dimensions of string theory but was a modified string theory that resembled the newer membrane theories. Interestingly enough, the new "field" required for the LGBs encompassed the Higgs field that "permeates" all of the universe at any instant and therefore the Higgs boson was a subset or actually an unstable relativistic version of the LGBs. For the first time humanity had an understanding of the "connectivity" of the LGBs and how it worked. Best of all, this new "field" required a mass gap at its fundamental level. Eureka! Yang-Mills theory explained!

Mimi had discussed this with her friend Dr. Weaver ad nauseum. Dr. William Weaver was first to surmise that the gates were Higgs bosons, which created an insurmountable amount of *maulk* from experimental particle physicists who assumed they knew everything and that the so-called Standard Model of modern physics was an end-all-be-all description of the universe.

In fact, the Standard Model was nothing more than matching experimental data with mathematical descriptions, not a true theory that could predict quantum actions. And Mimi, Dr. Weaver, and Tuffy were realizing that there were few scientists and mathematicians on Earth who would accept the subtle difference. Weaver and Mimi had used the analogy that describing light as photons or particles was still a "curve fit" to data and that light *is* light. That didn't go over well with the particle physicists either, as Feynman had told them all that light was a particle and therefore it must be. The Adar had often found this trait of human scientists who were supposed to be "open-minded" as an extremely hypocritical and humorous aspect of humanity.

So, Mimi at Weaver's request had actually stopped referring to these different Higgs bosons as Higgs bosons when in fact they both understood that that is exactly what they were. Or better yet, the Higgs bosons were actually a nonstationary and unstable version of what the LGBs really were. When it came to fighting the inbred physics community, Weaver had often told Mimi that he preferred fighting the Dreen. Tuffy usually kept quiet on the subject.

However, what Mimi actually did generate was the theoretical prediction of Yang-Mills. The theory that fell out of the math she had uncovered was not only the theoretical prediction of the Yang-Mills gauge but a whole heck of a lot more. It had become known as the "four plus one plus six formalism," where there were the four dimensions of space from membrane theory, one of time, and six other dimensions that varied between forms used in both string and membrane concepts. But it was Mimi's mathematical wizardry that tied them all together including the LGBs and that not only described the quantum Yang-Mills theory but predicted it.

The CMI had continued to slow-roll her in the payout until she had finally used one of her two ace cards. Her number one ace card of course was Tuffy, but she didn't go that far. Her second ace card had been Dr. William Weaver who, other than Mimi, was *the* planet's expert on the LGBs. Although Dr. Weaver had been spending most of his time of late learning the application of the LGBs and not the fundamentals, he was very politically connected—perhaps even more so now that he was a navy officer. When the director of the CMI received a phone call from the national security advisor—as a favor to Weaver—the CMI finally got off their dime and at least paid Mimi for the one solution. Mimi still puzzled over Weaver's remark about the "stagnant inbred not invented here eggheads." Weaver had also used several other "Southern" euphemisms and metaphors that Mimi's aunt wouldn't allow her to repeat. Tuffy had told her not to give it much thought.

The industrial complex, on the other hand, had no such "not invented here" problem. Clever entrepreneurs used any good source of information from which to make money and in Mimi's and Tuffy's cases they were crawling out of the woodwork to pay them. Mimi had been integral in the reverse engineering of the Adar miniature power supplies for communications implants, which left her with one percent of a patent that one of the major cellular networks owned, not to mention a slice of just about every battery being made in the market.

There was one armored glass manufacturer that asked her to help them decipher a problem with a new polymer manufacturing process. After a few months of her working with the company, a new patent for an aluminum, titanium oxide, and magnesium sulfide compound layered in precise alternating optical thicknesses was developed that ended up being as strong as aluminum or better and optically transparent. The company gave Mimi seven percent of that patent. Dubbed "aliglass" since "transparent aluminum" was too over-the-top, the material was beginning to replace glass in every skyscraper in the world, not to mention parts in most armored systems. It was a somewhat lucrative contract.

Each time Mimi and Tuffy would be involved with such solution endeavors Mimi always refused the aid of a contracts or patents lawyer or accountant. Tuffy seemed to have a preternatural knowledge of the actual value attached to a piece of information and the team was *very* good at writing iron-clad contracts. And when the negotiations were face to face, even the toughest corporate lawyer found negotiating with a soft-spoken fourteen-year-old—who just might have God riding on her shoulder—extremely disconcerting.

Some of the money they earned they gave to the Wilsons in thanks for taking care of Mimi. Most of it, however, was spent on books or put in the bank. At this point, Mimi had a bank account that would have made any accountant smile. The time had come, though, to spend some of it.

Which was why Mimi, wearing a light blue dress and dress

shoes, was sitting on her bed with her hands clasped in her lap, looking out the window and lightly tapping her thumbs together. At her feet was a packed suitcase.

Tuffy had changed over the years. Actually, most of the changes had occurred quite recently. His once stubby limbs had increased in length and now had definite little claws that glittered a silvery purple. His fur had also darkened to almost midnight black that flashed purple in the right light. In addition, he had developed eyes or eyespots that were a bright emerald green. Around the eyespots were patches of purple fur, sometimes blue, that were narrow and curved.

The changes had baffled most of the researchers who were trying to study him until one of them, a female, had pointed out that Tuffy now looked, "well, cool." When Tuffy had first appeared, and for many years thereafter, Mimi had needed comfort. She was a child and needed a teddy bear, or spider in this case, to hug and keep away the nightmares.

Puberty had changed that. Mimi had suffered few of the extreme mood swings of that period in life, but she *had* changed, none-theless. She had "put away childish things" and in keeping with that, perhaps, Tuffy had morphed to be more of what a young teenager, recently a child but now exploring the world of adult-hood, needed, somebody cool and Tuff looking.

Or he might just be aging. Nobody really knew. Except Tuffy and, maybe, Mimi, and they weren't talking.

"Okay, okay," Mimi said with an exasperated sigh.

She got up and walked into the living room where Mrs. Wilson was vacuuming with the TV on in the background.

"Aunt Vera," Mimi said over the sound of the vacuum.

"Mimi," Vera said, shutting off the machine. Vera Wilson was a heavyset woman in her forties, currently wearing a muumuu since the Wilsons kept the thermostat high to save energy. "You're dressed nice for school."

"I'm not going," Mimi said. "Tuffy has told me I have to go visit someone. Today."

"You're . . . what?" Vera Wilson asked, confused. Since taking Mimi in she had found her to be a very biddable and charming young lady, the daughter she'd never had. Mimi had *never* asked to skip school and had certainly never back talked or said anything this . . . strange. "What do you mean you're not going to school?"

"Tuffy has something that I need to do," Mimi said, calmly but definitely. "I need to go visit someone and then . . . well, I'll probably be gone for a while. But there will be adults who will talk to you about it. But I have to leave now, this morning; we have a transfer from the gateport at ten. And there's a taxi on the way."

"Young lady, you can't just walk out of this house . . ." Vera Wilson started to respond angrily.

"I don't want to make you mad, Aunt Vera," Mimi continued calmly. "But I really need to go. I'm not running away. Some adults will come explain, I'm sure, but I'm not sure what I *can* say to you about it. You remember when Dr. Weaver came to visit that one time and he said it was 'confidential.' It's secret like that."

"Well, if the government wants you to go, why didn't they tell *me*?" Mrs. Wilson asked, confused.

"They don't know I have to go," Mimi said. "But Tuffy says that if I don't, it's not going to work."

"What's not going to work?" Mrs. Wilson said, totally out of her depth.

"The thing I can't talk about," Mimi said as the taxi honked its horn. "That's my ride. I've gotta go. I'll write and I'll probably be back, maybe soon for a week or so, if you'll let me come back. But it's time for me to do the things I'm supposed to do. I think, it's sort of like being called by God, Auntie Vera. I have a calling. And the first place it will take me is San Diego."

Aunt Vera looked at the cool looking spider thing on Mimi's shoulder and sighed. She'd had a very confusing, but interesting, conversation with Dr. Weaver at one point when he visited Mimi to thank her for her help. After that she'd had to wonder: Do angels always appear in a cloud of light? Or, as Dr. Weaver had pointed out, "Well, we got the big light. And the city was certainly smited or smitten or whatever . . . I don't know exactly what Tuffy is, but from what I went through, an angel in heavy disguise is a pretty good description."

But God sure worked in mysterious ways. You just had to have the patience of Job and trust that it would all come out right.

"You write, you hear?" Aunt Vera said, tearing up. She and Herman had never been able to have children and Mimi had been, in a way, a gift from God. Now, it seemed, the time was come to lose the gift. She'd thought they'd have more years. She hugged the girl to her and sniffled. "I got the hang of that e-mail thing. You be sending me e-mails, you hear, girl? And come home when you got a chance. This is *always* home."

"I will," Mimi said, sniffling herself. "But where I'm going, well, I don't think there's e-mail."

# 2

## Welcome to the Space Marines, Please Keep Your Hands and Feet Away From the Monsters

Private First Class Eric Bergstresser parked his Jeep outside head-quarters and got out, stretching his back.

Berg's first intimation he was being transferred had been the previous day when his team NCOIC, a staff sergeant, had dragged him out of morning PT and told him to "get his ass up to battal-ion." Upon reaching the battalion headquarters he had been put through "the one fastest post-clearance in history" according to the gunnery sergeant from S-3 who had walked the private through, then handed him orders to proceed, via personal automobile, to Bravo Company, Marine Corps Force Reconnaissance, which was based, oddly enough, at Newport News Naval Base.

Berg hadn't even known there were any Marines at Newport News which, as far as he knew, was still in the process of clo-sure. He was more than surprised to find out there was a Force Recon company there.

Berg was a "Nugget," a NUG, the "new guy" in the battalion. He had volunteered immediately upon reaching the 1st Marine Division, his initial duty station after Basic. After taking the initial entry tests, mental and physical, he'd gone through the short hell

of Recon In Process and the much longer hell of Force Recon
Operator Training. After the Dreen War, Force Recon qualification had been revamped to concentrate more and more on
off-planet operations. It also had gotten harder to qualify; of the
sixty volunteers in the class with Berg, he had been one of only
four to pass the full course. While not quite as hard as Delta
qualification and training, it was equivalent to or surpassed SEAL
BUD/S. At least in sheer brutality.

Berg wasn't sure what was happening to the Corps he had
wanted to join for so long, but he was seeing changes that were
interesting. Unlike most troops, he paid a lot of attention to things
like the budget fights in Congress and current events. And in
the former, especially, there were some odd things happening.
After the Dreen War, and the closing of the various gates that
had permitted the Dreen to invade Earth, most of the forces
had suffered serious cutbacks. The still unexplained breakouts of
Dreen infestations in several Islamic countries had taken most
of the starch out of the Great Jihad and while U.S. troops were
still deployed around the world, mostly they were back to peace
enforcement or peace keeping missions; the War on Terror had
died along with several hundred thousand jihadists in the Bekaa
Valley, Mecca and Iran.

But while the Army and the Air Force were getting their bud-
gets slashed, most of the money wasn't being "reinvested." It was
going to the Navy and the Marines. And most of it was going into
black holes. The "black" portions of the budget were getting large
enough to cause some serious questions in the news media. The
only information slipping out was that the expenditures involved
"extraterrestrial military research projects."

He'd been directed to the windowless, block building by the
gate guard on reaching Newport News, one long ass drive from
Lejeune. Now it was time to find out just what this company of
Force Recon was doing and why it was hidden away in a secure
building in Newport News.

Entering the door marked "Visitor's Entrance" he found himself in a small room composed of mostly concrete walls. Directly
opposite the door was a plane of what he recognized to be aliglass
with a security station behind its protection. He knew that it was
technically transparent aluminum, but it looked more like transparent sapphire, ten times as strong as plexiglass and still expensive

as hell. A sheet of it meant somebody seriously wanted to stop
an attack. The inch and a half thick window would shrug off an
armor penetrator round.

"Bergstresser, Eric, PFC," he said, holding up his ID to the
guard behind the glass. The guard was a civilian, not a Marine,
but he was relatively young and armed for war with an MP-7 on
a three-point combat strap hooked into his chest, boron carbide
helmet and heavy body armor. "I'm reporting for duty."

"Hold your ID up to the scanner," the guard said, gesturing
with his chin. The guard checked his computer, then nodded.
"Hold there for escort."

"Aye, aye," Berg said, taking a position of parade rest.

"Nugget?" the guard asked through the intercom, smiling
slightly.

"Yes, sir," Berg replied. "I've only been in Recon for three
months."

"I used to be Recon," the guard said, glancing at his monitors.
"Welcome to Wonderland. Here comes your escort."

The heavy steel door to the room opened and a first sergeant
in Mar-Cam stepped into the small room. The first sergeant was
tall and slender with hair cropped so short it was hard to tell
the color, hazel eyes and a slightly oversized nose. His right jaw
was slightly protruding, the muscle clearly much larger than the
left's, a sure sign of a person who spent a *lot* of time in Wyvern
battle armor.

"Bergstresser?" the first sergeant asked. His name tag read
"Powell."

"Yes, First Sergeant," the PFC replied.

"ID?" the first sergeant said, holding out his hand. He checked
the ID and nodded. "Welcome to the unit. I'm going to handle
your in-brief then turn you over to your team NCOIC. Follow me."

"Yes, First Sergeant," Berg said, following the NCO into an
even smaller room. The first sergeant waited until the outer door
was closed, then cleared his throat. "Clearing Fourteen."

The inner door, marked with a large red numeral 14, slid
aside revealing a corridor. They took a right and headed down
the highly polished tile floor, passing several doors. Unlike at
Berg's previous station, none of the doors had titles on them,
only numbers. And most of them were sliding doors similar to
the ones he'd entered the building by. For that matter, every ten

feet or so there was a black pod on the ceiling that indicated a security camera. The interior of the building looked less like a headquarters than a prison.

The first sergeant stopped about halfway down the long corridor and cleared his throat again.

"Entering Seven-Six."

"Seven-Six, opening," a robotic voice replied as the door opened. "Five, four . . ."

"Come on," the first sergeant said, stepping through quickly.

At "Zero" the door slid closed with Bergstresser barely clearing it.

"Hate that system," said the Marine behind the desk in the office they'd entered.

"So do I," the first sergeant replied. "But it's there for a reason. Come on, Berg," he added, opening the door marked "First Sergeant."

The first sergeant took a seat behind the desk and looked Bergstresser up and down. The PFC had come to parade rest again, legs spread shoulder-width apart, hands folded behind his back, and was staring at a point six inches over the first sergeant's head.

"Rest," Powell said, ordering him to keep more or less the same posture but the PFC could talk. "I've read your service record. You were selected for this unit because of your IQ, your MGT scores, and your scores in Operator Training. But I'm going to ask you a few questions and I need straight answers. If you are wrong for this unit, then I need to send you back to your old unit. There won't be any repercussions on that, trust me. But this unit can only afford certain types of candidates. I'd rather go on a mission short than with an unsuitable candidate. I'll add that you're going to be tested on some of the questions, if we have time. If we don't and you've been anything other than perfectly truthful, you're probably going to get people killed. Are we clear?"

"Clear, First Sergeant," Berg said, wondering what the hell was going on.

"Have you ever suffered any form of the slightest anxiety at confined spaces?" the first sergeant asked. "For that matter, have you ever been in any confined spaces for any duration to test that?"

"I have never been in confined spaces for any significant time, First Sergeant," the PFC replied. "I have spent small amounts of time in normal confined spaces and never had any anxiety."

"Define normal confined space," the first sergeant said evenly.

"I . . . I used to play around culverts, First Sergeant," Berg said. "I've even gotten stuck in one. It didn't worry me."

"Not really what I'm looking for," the first sergeant said. "Have you ever considered what it might be like to be on a submarine?"

"Yes, First Sergeant," Berg said. "I don't think I'll have any issues."

"Here's a kicker," the first sergeant said, leaning forward. "Have you ever considered what it would actually be like to be in space? Like being an astronaut in a space suit outside a ship? No air anywhere around for billions of miles and the only thing between you and a horrible death being a suit built by the lowest bidder?"

"Yes, First Sergeant, I have," Berg said. "I considered trying to get in the astronaut program, but I've wanted to be a Marine for most of my life. I don't see a tour in the Marines as necessarily standing in the way of that. Worked for John Glenn."

"You've got the IQ for it," the first sergeant admitted, leaning back. "Ever read any science fiction, Berg?"

"Yes, First Sergeant," Bergstresser replied. He knew that that was as much an admission that he was a "geek" but the first sergeant had insisted on honest answers.

"What?" the first sergeant asked. "Or, rather, how much?"

"Quite a bit," Berg admitted, knowing that it was probably going to be a downcheck.

"Define quite a bit," the first sergeant said. "How many books? How many dealing with space travel? What sort of background on it do you have? Books, not TV shows or movies."

"I have a library at home of over a thousand books, First Sergeant," Berg admitted reluctantly. "I read all the time, both paper and ebooks. I've written game programs for space combat maneuvers. I'm a gamer and have played board games, role playing games and computer games that deal with space combat. I'm aware that that categorizes me as a 'geek,' First Sergeant, but I also—"

"Made it through the new qual course," the first sergeant said, smiling tightly. "Shiny. You're just what I was looking for."

"Huh?" Berg said, astounded. It was hardly the response he was expecting.

"For your general FYI, Berg, my IQ is higher than yours," the first sergeant said mildly. "So you seriously have thought about what it would be like to be in death pressure?"

"Yes, First Sergeant," Berg replied. "Space is a stone cold bitch. I wrote a paper on it in high school as part of a book report on *Have Spacesuit–Will Travel*. The book is about a young man who wins a space suit—"

"I'm familiar with it," the first sergeant said dryly. "Now the big question. This unit is going to be going on long deployments off-planet. The risk of loss of life is high. Most of it is going to be boring as hell with occasional moments, I am certain, of sheer terror. Actual conditions are unknown, but I would be unsurprised if casualty rates exceed thirty percent per mission. I'm saying that in my professional opinion, *you*, PFC Eric Bergstresser, have a one in three chance of *dying*. Possibly higher. Possibly much higher. And I cannot tell you the nature of the mission until you volunteer for said mission. So I'm asking, knowing the risks, do you wish to volunteer?"

"Yes, First Sergeant," Berg said, instantly. "I wish to volunteer for this unit."

"Shiny," the first sergeant said with a sigh, "you're in. But if we get the time, I'm going to put you in the tank and see how you *really* handle pressure. Welcome to the *Space* Marines, PFC Bergstresser. Semper Fi Ad Astra, if you will."

"Holy *maulk*," Berg whispered when his new platoon sergeant led him into the platoon office. "He wasn't kidding."

On the wall was a large poster, placed in much the same way that a corporate motivational poster might be hung. But this poster was a picture taken in space of a portion of what could only be a spaceship, the top of which was lined with suits of Wyvern armor. Over each suit was a name and he quickly picked out First Sergeant Powell as well as his platoon sergeant, Gunnery Sergeant Josh Hocieniec.

And there was no question it was a picture. Even with all the advances in computer generated images, it was still possible to spot CGI. This was, unquestionably, a picture. They might have been digitized in, but it didn't look like it.

"No, Top wasn't kidding," the senior NCO said. Hocieniec was shaved bald, short, barely over regulation height unless Berg was much wrong, and skinny. He looked as if he could barely carry himself around much less battle rattle. "You just joined the Space Marines. The *maulky* part, for you, is that the rest of us have been training for this for a year or more. And we're leaving day after tomorrow."

"Oh, *maulk*," Berg said, his eyes wide.

"You're replacing Harson," Hocieniec continued, sitting down at his desk, "because the dick-for-brains broke his *grapping* femur on a fast-rope climb two days ago."

"Welcome to Hell, Nugget," a staff sergeant said, looking up from some paperwork. "Staff Sergeant Summerlin. You're going to be with Jaen, Charlie Team." The staff sergeant was medium height and slim with dark brown hair.

"Summerlin's Alpha Team Leader and assistant platoon sergeant," the gunny said. "Jaen and Hatt are over on the ship doing maintenance on their Wyverns. So while Summer here does my paperwork for me, I'm going to get you into the barracks and through in-processing."

"And this is the gaming room," Sergeant Jaenisch said, opening the door.

The barracks and training area for the Space Marines was about a quarter mile from the headquarters. The barracks were pretty decent, "starbase" apartment barracks left over from the Navy when they'd pulled most of their people out of Newport News. There was enough room that the Marines were rattling around in them like peas. They even got individual rooms since there were enough barracks for a regular battalion much less a Space Marine company, which was about the size of a regular platoon.

A "company" is a variable term. Originally the term simply meant a body of companions. Latterly, it came to mean a group of about one hundred infantry personnel under the leadership of an officer who was not quite a junior, not quite a senior, usually a captain.

However, companies varied in size. Force Recon companies had ranged as high as two hundred when all the supports were added over the years. With the shift to Space Marines, the Marine Corps commandant had taken a step back. Since the Recon companies were going to be ship based, the Navy could damned well handle support. And given their firepower, training and individual lethality, the size of the actual unit could be dropped. However, retaining the leadership as a captain made sense. Young enough to carry the fight, old enough to do so wisely and without the mandated lobotomies of majors. Delta would call it a Troop, SEALs would call it a Team. The Marines called it a company of Space Marines. If the Navy ever got bigger ships, they'd reevaluate. In the meantime, the Marines got all the hot water they could ask for.

The training building was part of the base gym. There wasn't a regular shoot house or a range short of Quantico, but part of the funds had provided a pretty decent alternative.

The "game room" was a new building, solid concrete including the roof, attached to the gym and about as large. It also was nearly empty. There was a small entry room with some lockers and computer terminals and beyond, viewable through a sheet of plexiglass that was liberally splashed with blue splatters, was a cavernous, empty, room. On the far side were huge roll-back doors large enough to slide a business jet into the room. It looked more like a hangar than a training area.

"Virtual reality?" Berg asked.

"Got it in one," Jaenisch said, walking over to a computer terminal. "We've got just about every game on the market available on this thing but we generally use the one designed for the mission, a hack of Dreen War." Jaenisch opened up some windows on-screen and started a game up, then opened up one of the lockers, pulling out two sets of VR gear.

The gear consisted of a light harness, gloves and a pair of glasses. The VR glasses, thanks mostly to Adar tech, had reduced to the size of wraparound sunglasses. The newest military combat "goggles" were similar in size and structure. Berg had even heard that DARPA was working on combat "lenses" that could be worn as contacts. That would be interesting.

Jaenisch also handed him an M-10 and combat harness, preloaded with "simulated rounds." Simulation rounds used actual gunpowder to fire low velocity "paint" rounds that mimicked real bullets fairly well at short ranges. They required a special barrel and breech but the M-10 had already been modified for them and had the standard blue training barrel.

The glasses stayed clear until they walked in the room, then darkened momentarily and came back showing a jungle scene.

It wasn't anywhere on Earth—both the trees and sounds were wrong—and it took Berg a moment to adjust.

"Where are we supposed to be?" he subvocalized. When they passed Basic, every Marine was fitted with combat implants that consisted of a small microphone implanted next to the vocal cords and a receiver in the mastoid bone. Learning to subvocalize was a requirement of Marine basic training. The system was virtually identical to the one the Adar used when they first reached Earth. For a short time, it had been thought that the Adar were telepaths since using the system looked much the same to an ignorant observer. There was virtually no sound involved and only short bursts of radio.

"This is based on Chen's World," Jaenisch replied subvocally, his lips moving only slightly. "But it's got different monsters. All we have to do is make it to the far wall." He hefted a virtual M-10 and was now, in the goggles, wearing full battle rattle, a set of boron carbide body armor with fitted pouches for ammunition. "You've got left, I'll take right."

Berg jacked a round into his own M-10, flicked the weapon off safe and nodded.

"Let's do it."

Jaenisch led off, following a narrow game trail. Berg kept his attention to the left, sweeping forward, up and to the rear. There were some light heat forms in his glasses, but nothing that looked like a threat.

A thunderous roar from the right almost made him spin around but he kept on his sector and it was a good thing. Just as the roar faded, a form came charging through the jungle. It was bipedal and looked something like a more insectile Dreen thorn-thrower. Whatever it was it had a big mouth and Berg wasn't going to take any chances.

He fired two rounds into center of mass and was unsurprised that the 7.62 mm rounds bounced off. But the thing had big multiple eye systems and he retargeted, hitting it in the eyes and blinding it. The thing continued its rush but missed the two Marines and Berg pounded it with single fire shots as it crashed past. He found a weak point under one of its arms and pumped five rounds into the spot until the thing dropped, thrashing.

"Reloading," he subvocalized, trying to keep his sector in sight as he pulled out a magazine. He got the reload in place just in time to spot something dropping from the trees. It looked like a sheet of paper but it was headed either for the Marines or the dead beast. Berg fired at it and the sheet ripped apart, falling in tatters.

Jaenisch had been firing at something as well and the two Marines went back to back as more of the bipedal monsters came through the jungle after them. Berg picked his shots more carefully since he only had thirty of the 7.62 mm rounds in a clip. He managed to drop three of the monsters before he ran out of ammo. The fourth and fifth, though, got him and the "jungle" vanished as the harness gave him a zap of electricity.

"*Grapp* me," he said, shaking his head.

"Not bad, actually," Jaenisch said, looking over at him. "I'm going to reset the system so we've also got .455s. You qualified on the .455?"

"Yes," Berg said. The high velocity Colt magnum was rarely used by combat forces, but he'd qualified with one in Force Operators Training. He had wondered at the time why they were training on a civilian "gun nut" pistol that no other force considered worth its time. Now he had to wonder how much FOT was influenced by the Space Marines. A group that, officially, didn't exist.

They returned to the prep room and added the big magnums to their kit. The gun's blue barrel was nearly a foot long and it was a heavy mother. But civilian hunters had used them to hunt both elephant and tiger at short ranges. It should stop even one of the bipedal monsters. He stopped before going back and readjusted the position of the ammo pouches on his armor. Every serious shooter had his own idea of where stuff should ride and Berg wasn't any different.

"Same general scenario?" he asked as they reentered the "jungle."

"It changes," Jaenisch said. "You never know what's going to come at you."

Berg kept a watch out as they reentered the path and while it was a different beast, they attacked at the same point. This time they got low-slung bright-red centipedes, about the size of a leopard. And there were more of them than of the bipedal monsters. And, the 7.62 mm rounds just bounced off again.

He let go of the M-10, which pulled back to his chest on its straps, and drew the .455 Colt. The magnum rounds *did* penetrate the centipedes' armor and, even better, he was a *very* good one-handed shooter. He fired all ten of the rounds in his magazine, getting six of the beasts, then did a rapid reload by just dropping his empty mag down the front of his armor and sliding another in. He got four more before they got him at last.

"This seriously sucks," Berg said, holstering his smoking pistol.

"Hell, you held out longer than I did," Jaenisch said, shaking his head. "I stayed on the M-10. Where'd you learn to shoot like that?"

"I just enjoy shooting," Berg said, carefully. The real answer was in Force Recon Operator's Training. Force Recon had always been a tough unit with a killer qualification phase. But its advanced training had mostly been ad hoc at the unit level. The new FOT included an Operator Combat Training program that far exceeded the normal Force Recon official training program. He was beginning to realize that the "regular" Force Recon guys might have much more experience than he did, but he was probably better *trained*. He was going to have to tread that path very carefully.

"Can you two-gun mojo?" Jaenisch asked.

"A bit," Berg said. "But I can't fire simultaneously. That's total bull*maulk*. Usually what I do is empty one pistol then empty the other one. The problem is, it really slows down reload. So if you've got more targets than you've got bullets . . ."

"Want to try it that way?" Jaenisch asked. "I'll stay one gun on pistol, you go for two-gun?"

"I'll *try* it," Berg said. "But I'll stay on M-10 to start since we don't know what it's going to throw at us."

"I'll set it up for the same scenario," Jaenisch said. "I'm really curious."

The third time through, Berg carried two of the magnums and Jaenisch one. The centipedes attacked at the same time and in the same way, which was a bit of cheating, since it meant Berg didn't have to guess where they were coming from.

But the two-gun mojo worked. This time, knowing where and how they were going to attack, he managed to start winnowing them down earlier. When his right pistol ran out of rounds he holstered it and pulled out a clip. When the left ran out he did a fast reload then switched hands and went to a two-handed fire position, backing away from the centipedes until he had the last one dead. The things thrashed as they died, splattering green blood over the mostly blue vegetation and opening out the underbrush as they crushed it in their death throes.

"Damn," Jaenisch said, shaking his head. "Shiny. Now, let's see if we can make it to the far side of the room."

They were hit twice more but Berg's two-gun fire managed to stop both attacks cold and they eventually reached the "stream" that marked the far side of the room. He only had four rounds of magnum left, though.

"Clear VR," Jaenisch said when they reached the limit. "Not bad, Nugget. Not bad at all."

"Thanks," Berg said.

"This scenario is set up for a two team maneuver," Jaenisch admitted. "Six guys, not two. I wanted to run you through something harder than I thought we could handle, just to knock the starch out. So much for that idea. As a matter of fact, I hereby designate you Two-Gun. You may now call me Jaen."

"Thank you, Jaen," Berg said. "But I don't think it's a good way to do battle normally."

"Agreed," Jaen said. "But it *was grapping* awesome. I can't wait to replay the clip."

"This is recorded?" Berg said.

"Two-Gun, every second of every day we do this *maulk* is recorded," Jaenisch said bitterly. "Why do you think there are *grapping* cameras everywhere? We're guinea pigs. I'll explain when we get back to the armory."

# 3

## Old Friends, Same Problems

All the Adar tech in the world hadn't helped the lunchtime traffic on Monticello. Bill weaved his Ford Electra into the left-hand lane, getting around a late model Chevy pickup that was carefully doing the speed limit, and floored it, trying to make it through the turn at VA 168. Once past 168 he'd be clear most of the way to base.

Unfortunately, as he approached the light it turned yellow. He figured he had time so he floored it but the car instead decelerated, the electric motor dropping to idle as the brakes automatically slid him to a controlled stop.

Oh, yeah, Adar tech was good for *some* things!

The pickup blew past him, still doing a stately forty-five miles per hour. He hoped the old fart got a ticket.

The bright purple Chevy Neon that had been on Bill's bumper suddenly pulled out, the light having changed to red, and sped through the intersection causing a flurry of honks but, fortunately, no accidents.

Speaking of Adar. Worst drivers in the *world*.

Christ. Could this day get any worse?

It wasn't really a florist's shop. It was a shop that supplied flowers for corporations and hotels. The company had no storefront,

just a back door through the loading area. And the people who
worked in the company were much more accustomed to the
occasional street person wandering in and looking for a handout
than fourteen-year-old girls with some alien pet.

"Can I help you?" the young man with his arms full of arrangements asked curiously. He couldn't help but stare at the thing on
her shoulder; as he watched it moved from one side to the other,
its green eyes glittering in interest at the bustle in the room.

"I'm looking for Mr. Miller," Mimi said politely.

"He's over there," the man said, gesturing with his chin since
his hands were full. "Go on in."

The room was unadorned and looked more like a half-finished
basement than a florist's. White wooden tables were heaped with
flowers while several workers in eclectic attire assembled arrangements. About half were females but there was as much long hair
amongst the men working on the flowers as there was with the
women. Most of the men working in the shop were in shorts, as
were a couple of the women; it was hot and the only breath of
cold air came as a man exited a huge walk-in refrigeration room,
his arms filled with colorful orchids.

Miller had his back to the entrance and was peacefully snipping
the bottom of some iris stems when Mimi cleared her throat.

"Hello, Mr. Miller," Mimi said, wondering if the former SEAL
would recognize her.

Miller clearly was puzzled by the young lady who had spoken to
him, but after a moment he placed the thing on her shoulder.

"Mimi," the SEAL said, grinning. "What a pleasant surprise.
It's been, what? Seven years? You've grown. And Tuffy's . . ."

"Changed," Mimi said, grinning. "All the ET people got really
excited when that happened. Only one of them got it right, though.
I was talking to him one day in school and just sort of thought
that I'd gotten over the whole stuffed animal thing. And he looked
really . . . dumb that way. The next day . . . whole new Tuffy."

"You're here on a trip?" Miller asked, puzzled. He was wearing a loud Hawaiian shirt, open most of the way down a chest
covered in graying hair, and a pair of cut-off desert camo BDU
shorts. "In town for school or something? Why San Diego of all
places?"

"I'm not here on a school trip," Mimi replied. "I came looking
for you. We have to go to Newport News and see Dr. Weaver."

"What's Bill want?" Miller asked gruffly, turning back to his irises.

"He didn't want anything, but there's something he needs," Mimi said. "You, me and Tuffy. Tuffy told me. And we're going."

"Oh, we are, are we?" Miller asked, turning back around. "I'm *out* of that game. You get older, you get slower. There's a time to reap and a time to sow, all that stuff. In my case, there's a time to kill and a time to heal. So if you and Tuffy have to do something, you go, girl. I'm going to keep making floral arrangements."

"If you don't go . . ." Mimi paused and looked around the crowded room. "Can you take a break or something, we *have* to talk."

"Okay, okay," Miller sighed. "Bob! Going on break. I don't know how long I'll be. That okay?"

"Sure, Chief," the younger man called back. "Try to get those arrangements done by four, though."

The coffee shop was considerably cooler than the floral factory. It was still early morning and the tall buildings on either side provided shade from the sun. For that matter, San Diego rarely got hot during the early fall. Only when the Santa Annas blew down from the mountains did the temperature get much above seventy-five.

Miller set his mocha down and leaned back in the chair, considering the young lady who had dragged him away from work.

"You came all the way out here on your own?" Miller asked, surprised.

"It's not hard," Mimi said. "There's gates all the way to San Diego; then I took a taxi."

"Most of our *customers* can't find the shop," Miller mused. "The boss prefers it that way."

"Tuffy knew where to find you," Mimi said, shrugging. "He told me he'd been keeping track of you."

"That's nice to know," Miller said dryly. "So, what's so important that you want me to go to Newport News."

"They've finished the ship," Mimi said, carefully. "It's still covert and I'm not going to blow that for them. But Tuffy says that I have to be on it, with him, when it leaves. They've completed the . . . shakedown cruises. The next launch is going to be out . . . Tuffy says that we, you, me, him, have to be on the ship. I don't know why and I don't know if he's being cagey or *he* can't really explain why. I know that part of the reason has to do with . . . causality. That's about as much as I understood. Basically, he's saying that the ship is probably going to fail, and fail big, if *we*, we three, don't go along."

"Look, you can't just walk up to something like that and say 'we're coming along, okay?'" Miller said, blowing out his cheeks. "The security's going to be . . . a mile deep. And the entire crew, and that includes the civilians, are already going to be chosen. That's even assuming that I'm *willing* to go."

"You'll go," Mimi said. "You'll go because if you don't the mission's going to fail. And if the mission fails, it will probably mean the Dreen back. And this time we'll lose. Plus Dr. Weaver will die on the mission and he's your friend."

"Friends die," Miller said, his jaw working. "One of the reason that I peacefully make flower arrangements these days is because I've seen *lots* of friends die. I don't particularly want to meet more people who are probably going to die. Which is what going on something like that would mean. Even if we *could* convince somebody that we had to go along, at which we have a chance in hell."

"You need to call Admiral Townsend and get a meeting, today," Mimi said. "He's somebody you *can* just call, and he's briefed on the mission. He can get ahold of Dr. Weaver. And Dr. Weaver can get us on the mission."

"You seem to know a hell of a lot for a fourteen-year-old," Miller said, blowing out again, this time angrily. "Greg Townsend . . . yeah, he'd take my call. But getting us on the mission . . . ?"

"He can get us in touch with Dr. Weaver," Mimi said. "That's all we need."

"Okay, okay," the former chief said, shaking his head. "I guess it's time to call in some favors. And Greg Townsend *does* owe me. Big time."

Bill parked the Electra in his designated slot and walked quickly towards the massive concrete building that guarded the upgraded subpens.

Newport News had gotten out of the active sub business almost two decades before, when the full weight of the post-Cold War conditions had hit the Navy. Subsequent to that event, the base had mostly been used for "decomming" subs, turning them into razor blades in other words.

Most of the subs that were going to be turned into razor blades had been turned when the Navy finally won the battle for the first warp ship. The battle had long-term consequences that were clear to the admirals. Weaver was pretty sure that with the data they'd gather from use it was possible to make *another* warp drive, albeit perhaps not as neat as the "little black box." Eventually, the Earth would need a star fleet, especially if the Dreen ever used warp space to attack. The service that got in on the ground floor was pretty certain to be the eventual "space service." Navy was navy, wet or in space. And that was one of the many arguments that the admirals, often disbelieving the words that came out of their mouths, made.

However, the Navy was the *right* service for a space fleet. The Air Force, which had argued that it had much more experience with three dimensional combat than the Navy, was based around small systems with short mission times. There was a degree of complexity in creating, and especially running, a ship that was orders of magnitude away from being, say, a squadron or wing commander. There were human complexities that simply didn't occur in the Air Force when you packed a huge number of humans into a small space and then told them they had to get along or else.

So the Navy had wholeheartedly offered Newport News when the new boat was under discussion. Out of their own pocket, drawing on funds detailed for other bases and ship maintenance, they had upgraded the facilities to be as "state-of-the-art" as they could, even before the decision was made. The Air Force had pointed out that, unlike Dreamland, there was no way that a ship taking off from Newport News, by day or night, could remain undetected. The Navy had pointed out that the boat was to be based on a *submarine*. All it had to do was submerge, get far enough offshore, make sure there wasn't anything in view via sonar, and then take off from there.

In the final event, Newport News, a quiet little seaport on Chesapeake Bay, had become the world's first starport. Stranger things had happened, but not many.

The outer door to the guard facility was easy enough to pass; all he had to do was wave his card at the reader and the door opened. Beyond he was in the "blast" room. Weaver had been consulted on the design. The room wouldn't *quite* stop a nuke, but it would stop *anything* else. There was a single door out of the room. It was designed around a bank vault, unmarked and with a keypad next to it.

He swiped his security card past the reader and punched in his code, then went in as the powered door opened. This revealed another room. On the left-hand side was a window of aliglass.

"Weaver," Bill said, holding up his ID to the guard. The guard's name was Johnson, Bill remembered. They'd chatted one time in the breakroom. If Johnson recognized him, it wasn't apparent.

Johnson looked carefully at the ID, then consulted a list.

"Please enter your keycode," the guard said in a monotone, still staring at Weaver as if he was a suspected terrorist.

Bill swiped his card again and punched in a *different* code. That door led to a small room, windowless, with a video camera over the far door and a laser to the left. The laser swept over him, doing a retinal and surface temperature scan. The room was a "mantrap." The inner door was interlocked in such a way as it *couldn't* open until the outer door had closed.

"Weaver, William, Lieutenant Commander, Astrogation," a robotic voice intoned. Then the inner door opened.

Bill had once done a short stint as a consultant to the NSA. Getting into the National Security Agency involved showing your card to a guard and then walking in. He wasn't sure if this setup was overkill or if the NSA had lousy security. But, surely, there was somewhere in-between?

As soon as he got through the final portal he turned left down the corridor and stopped to check a computer terminal. The meeting he was supposed to be at, in two minutes, was in Secure Four, a high-security auditorium. When they'd first started work on the 4144, meetings were getting so turned around that they'd installed this system to keep track. They still got shifted from time to time, so checking it had become habit.

The system showed that the meeting was still on time and in the same place, but there was a peripheral note keyed to him saying that he had been cancelled as a briefer. He was supposed to report to call a secure extension instead.

"What the . . . ?"

»          »          »

Bill flopped into his office chair and punched in the extension, wondering who would answer.

"3326."

"Weaver," he said, as calmly as he could.

"Commander Weaver, this is Admiral Townsend," the voice said. "I'm the base commander at Norfolk. A blast from the past apparently needs to talk to you. Now." The admiral did not sound happy.

"Sir . . ." Bill started to protest and then stopped. If Townsend was saying they needed to meet, now, it was something serious. "Where?"

"My office, as soon as you can," the admiral said. "You know how to find it?"

"Yes, sir," Bill replied. "I'll be there in about . . . well, it's going to take at least forty-five minutes."

"See you in one hour." The phone clicked off.

*Maulk.* He had to drive *back* to Norfolk!

When Bill reached the admiral's office he was surprised as hell to see Chief Miller, in a *Hawaiian* shirt of all things, waiting in the room. Not to mention Mimi and Tuffy.

"Good to see you," Bill said, puzzled but pleased. "Long time, Chief."

"You can trip down memory lane later," Townsend replied. "Apparently our security isn't as tight as we would have liked."

"I don't think that you can really say that, sir," Miller replied unhappily. "There's no real way to tell how Tuffy got the information."

"Go ahead and explain, young lady," the admiral said, leaning back in his chair.

"Tuffy says that we, that is Mr. Miller, myself and Tuffy, have to go along with you on the ship," Mimi said calmly. "You have a warp ship, converted from a submarine, docked at Newport News. Naval Construction Contract 4144. You're leaving in about a week. Chief Miller needs to be outfitted with a Wyvern Five. That's why we had to meet today; he'll need to get started tomorrow."

"Just like that?" Bill asked, amused. "Does Tuffy say *why*?"

"Not . . . really," Mimi said, showing the first sign of agitation. "Usually, we communicate with . . . concepts, not really words. I just realize that I've known something all along. But this time, it's like I can't understand what I know. There's math in there, that's mostly what it is. Very high end math, further than I've gone. Maybe further than you've gone, Dr. Weaver. But it's locked up in causality and . . . chaos. The concept is just very big. I *think* what he's trying to say, although he says I'm wrong, that it's more, is that if we don't go along, and stay with the missions in the future, the universe is going to end. Not the Earth, the *universe*. I get a sort of feeling like a bubble popping and then . . . nothing."

"Oh," Bill replied, blinking. "Does he explain why? In a way that you can understand?"

"I think it's more like something tied to probability," Mimi said, shrugging. "I can't make heads or tails of it, really. But he's definite. We *have* to go along."

"Okay," Bill said, shrugging. "You're in."

"Just like that?" Admiral Townsend asked, aghast. "The entire team has already been chosen. And they have been training for the last *year*."

"Admiral, whatever Tuffy is, he's never been one to joke around," Bill replied. "And if he says that these three have to come along, they *have* to come along. My recommendation, sir, and I will gladly put it in writing, is that they be assigned as crew."

"Okay, I'll get started on the paperwork," the admiral said, looking over at the former chief. "There are days, Todd, when I wish you'd just left me in that damned jungle."

Mimi and Tuffy had been invited to stay with the admiral for the evening. While Weaver would have *preferred* to repair to the bar for the discussion with Miller, that was out of the question. So the two of them found themselves in a secure room with nary a beer in sight.

"So you got your ship?" Miller asked, taking a sip of coffee. It was Navy coffee, at least, so it wasn't exactly bad.

"The United States now has a warp ship," Bill said. "You wanna hear?"

"Go ahead," Miller said, leaning back.

"I figured out a way to get the little black box to work," Bill said. "The Navy built a spaceship around an old Ohio. In two days we're lifting off for the first deep space mission. We've tested it in the system, but we've never even gotten to the heliopause. This time we're going to other worlds. You in?"

"Like I'm going to settle for just that," Miller grunted. "I want access to the details. The thing is, I don't know *why* that furball wants me on this trip, so I don't know what I *need* to know. And neither do you or Greg Townsend. So I need access to *all* of it."

"That's gonna be tough," Bill admitted. "The security level on some of this stuff is cut-your-throat-after-reading. And in case you hadn't noticed," Bill added, waving at his gold leaves.

"I'll admit I'm having a hard time with that," Miller said. "Who the *grapp* was stupid enough to give *you* a commission?"

"More a concession to reality than anything," Bill said, shrugging. "Lots of stuff works the Navy way for this. How to pack people into a ship and keep them fed, watered, aired and sane. How to run multiple complex systems. One big difference . . ."

"It ain't water," Miller said, leaning back.

"It ain't indeed," Bill said, grinning. "It ain't even *under*water. Space has damned few reference points, stuff that you don't find on earth. Vacuum. Stars. You can think of them as rocks and shoals, but there's a fundamental difference between brushing too close to a reef and brushing too close to a sun."

"Heh," Miller said, grinning back. "You run aground in a star . . ."

"And it's a bad thing," Bill said, nodding. "But then there's gravitational effects, which are active when the boat is in normal space and . . . There's a billion things that naval officers, no matter how well trained, aren't prepared for. So we've got a CO and XO who are, in order, a former fighter pilot and a bubblehead, and then there's me. Columbia was going through the merger mania that started after the Adar Commerce bill and they kept yanking me around to different departments and off the ship project. So I convinced the right people that what the boat desperately needed was an astrogation officer. Someone with fundamental knowledge not only of astronomy but of the way that the drive worked, how to handle gravitational effects . . ."

"Too bad you're not the commander," Miller said, shaking his head. "Wouldn't that be a hoot."

"It's a command slot," Weaver replied. "I'm in line for command. Third officer in line."

"Jesus," Miller said, his eyes widening. "Now *that* is *grapping* nuts!"

"I've been on two cruises as wet-navy navigator," Bill replied, calmly. "Six month deployments. One in a carrier and one in a sub. I aced the Navy Nuclear Power Training course. I've been to Surface Warfare School, Underwater Warfare School and I did Submarine Officer Advanced Course and Command and General Staff College. I am a commissioned officer in the United States Navy and I'm damned well doing the job."

"Sorry, sir," Miller said, frowning. "I guess we've both been through changes," he added, waving at his clothes.

"The point being, that while I'm an *unusual* lieutenant commander I am, nonetheless, a lieutenant commander. I'll call some people but I can't guarantee that you're going to be given 'full access.'"

"Figure it out," Miller growled. "And you're going to need to think about it for Mimi, too. But I definitely want to know how things work on this damned trip. I don't know *how* I'm going to save the universe or whatever, but if I gotta I gotta."

"You sure?" Bill said, wrinkling his brow. "I mean, there's things about this tub I wish *I* didn't know. You're going to puke when you see the navigation system."

"And all of it's built by the lowest bidder?" the chief grumped.

"Lowest bidder, hell," Bill said, chuckling. "Some of it was built by *me* in my *garage* while suffering from sleep deprivation. I could *wish* the lowest bidder had gotten it *that* right."

"I just hope you got all the physics right *this* time," Miller said with a grin.

"What the *maulk* does that mean, Chief? I *always* get the physics right."

"Well, after things cooled down for us I read up on some of that particle physics stuff you were throwing around on that mission. And *you* told me that muons were made of two quarks. I remember it like it was yesterday. But muons ain't . . ."

"Naw, Chief. I'm sure I didn't say that," Bill said sheepishly and took a sip from his coffee cup. "Muons are fundamental particles. Are you sure I didn't say that *mesons* are made of two quarks?"

"No, sir. You said muons. And according to wikipedia.com muons ain't made of quarks." Miller grinned tight-lipped. A few years as a navy officer hadn't changed his friend's slow southern drawl a bit and hearing it brought back memories for Miller. *After all,* Miller thought, *with Bill the word "naw" had two syllables.*

"When exactly did I tell you that, Chief? Hell, I wouldn't make such a fundamental mistake . . . not under any normal circumstance I can think of." Weaver scratched at his head and shrugged as he tried to remember the conversations they'd had from, *what was it, eight or nine years ago.*

"It was right after the spike throwin' boys rushed us . . ."

"Holy *maulk*, Chief. There was big green monsters from outer space tryin' to *grappin'* eat us for all I knew and you're bitching cause I told you that *muons* were made of *quarks*?" Bill wasn't sure if he should laugh or try to kick Miller's ass. Come to think of it, laugh was probably the better choice.

"Hell sir, I'm just glad you figured out how to turn the safety off on that pistol." Miller winked and tried not to giggle coffee across the table at his old friend.

"You think the way I handled a pistol was something wait till you see what I can do with a submarine!" Bill said with a chuckle.

# 4

## Fear the Pink

"So we've really got a spaceship," Berg said, shaking his head.

"Nobody briefed you, huh," Lance Corporal Al Hattelstad said, grinning devilishly. The third member of Charlie Team, Second Platoon was short with curly, dark-brown hair. "Yeah, they got a drive from somewhere, where is classified, and stuck it in an old missile sub. It works, but it's funky as hell. There's plenty of gas, but sometimes we have to stop and 'chill.' Which really *grapping* sucks."

"During chill we have to go to zero gee," Jaenisch said, scrubbing at the breech of the M-10. The simulation rounds tended to dirty up a weapon even more than regular fire so they'd brought the weapons from the test engagement back to the armory to clean them. Normally, weapons cleaning was done in barracks or the unit offices, but the way that things were laid out it made more sense to do it in the armory. And since it was a secure area, they could talk about their jobs, which Jaenisch had pointed out was verboten in the barracks. "I don't mind it but—"

"Free-fall sickness is the worst *grapping* feeling in the universe," Hattelstad said. "Except maybe pre-mission physical. But I have to protest. Berg is still a Nugget. It's a violation of standard operating procedure to give him a team name until he has established himself. We will be shamed before all the other teams if we assign him full nickname status as a mere Nugget! I mean, sure, he's been through the physical . . ."

"Actually," Berg said, uneasily. "I *haven't* been through any new physical. Last one I had was at FOT."

"See!" Hattelstad said. "He's not a *real* Space Marine. He hasn't been through pre-mission physical!"

"Wait till you see the *grapping* clip," Jaenisch said. "Then you, too, shall forever after call him 'Two-Gun.'"

"So we're going *out* on this ship?" Berg asked. "I mean, out of the solar system?"

"Where no Marine has gone before and all that," Jaenisch said, nodding. "No PT tomorrow. We start final load-out at 0800. But we're not planning on leaving until somewhere around 2400. The bitch is, you're probably not going to get a chance to show off. The mission is supposed to be pure Wyvern. And they're M-5s. Top told me all your Wyvern time is M-4."

"Yeah," Berg said. "What's the difference?"

"Lots," Hattelstad said. "Faster and stronger and all that with more ammo storage. But the worst part's the damned sensors. The *grapping* things have got sensors out the ass. Most of it's *maulk* I don't even understand."

"They've got all these *grapping* particle sensors, just in case there's some invisible monsters," Jaenisch explained. "Nurtonos and mersons and . . . *Maulk* you have to be a physicist to understand the damned things. We've got a simulator on the ship. Hopefully, you'll have time to get adjusted to it."

"I'm looking forward to checking them out," Berg said. "I got an A in physics."

"*Maulk*, he's a Two-Gun mojo expert *and* he's a *grapping* physicist?" Hattelstad crowed. "What is the Corps coming to?"

"A better and brighter day, Lance Corporal," the first sergeant said.

"*Maulk*," Hattelstad snapped, jumping in his seat. "Sorry, Top, but you got to stop sneaking up on us that way. One of these days we're going to be holding live rounds and then where will we be?"

"Dead, if you try to blue me," Top said. "PFC Bergstresser, it has come to my attention that one small but oh so vital aspect of your in-process was overlooked. You have yet to have your pre-mission physical. That is a down-check for the mission. Thus, you will now report to the sickbay, where our very own MD will ensure that you are fit to fly."

"Shiny, First Sergeant," Berg said, standing up. "Jaen, I'll be back to finish up the cleaning."

"We got it," Jaen said, grinning. "You're not going to be back soon. See you tomorrow at the barracks at 0730. If you're alive."

"Excuse me, First Sergeant," Berg said as they walked upstairs from the armory. "What did he mean by that?"

"Our doc is somewhat unusual," Powell said. "And, unfortunately for us all, the pre-mission physical is extremely comprehensive. *Extremely* comprehensive. We normally give a person the day off after one. In your case, that will not be possible."

"Ah, a new guinea pig."

Berg had been ushered into the office by a very large black woman bearing a nametag that read "Nurse Betty." He wasn't sure what to expect, but whatever it was, the doctor was not that.

"I am Doctor Arnold Chetowski," the doctor said, standing up and walking over to shake Berg's hand. "You may call me Doctor Chet."

Doctor Chet was a human mountain. Nearly seven feet tall, the doctor was as broad as he was tall, with long black hair pulled back in a ponytail and the most massive beard Berg had ever seen in his life. The guy was just *hairy*, as was apparent by the thick hair on the backs of his massive, hamlike hands. Forget mountain, the guy looked like a Sasquatch. Incongruously, given his appearance and name, he had a slight southern accent.

Berg's hand was briefly engulfed and he was waved to a chair.

"We will be at this some time," Dr. Chet said, sitting down and looking at his computer monitor. "There are numerous tests you are going to have to undergo and given the rapid nature of this examination, you will, unfortunately, have to survive the rigors of the 'fast testing.' Have you eaten recently?"

"I had to skip lunch," Berg said. "I had some McDonald's for breakfast about six this morning."

"That will, unfortunately, change the results but I can adjust," Dr. Chet said. "I have your medical records but they are not always entirely complete. Have you *any* known allergies? Any medical problems whatsoever? I would go through the list, but I'm sure you've seen it."

"Nothing, sir," Berg said.

"Very well, I shall have to take your entirely unprofessional word for it," Dr. Chet said, looking up and grinning. "You are now permitted to chuckle."

"Yes, sir," Berg said. "Heh. Heh."

"Now you are permitted to fear," Dr. Chet said, pulling two bottles of white liquid out of his desk. "This is a radioactive tracer that will bind to certain chemicals in your brain so that *much* later I can see exactly how you think. Shortly before that test, which will take place in no less than eight hours, you shall take two more bottles of some pink stuff. Since we have to use the pink stuff, you will not enjoy the experience. Forty-three minutes after ingesting the pink stuff, you will become violently nauseated. We will try to ensure all the fixed testing is done by that time so that you can find a quiet place to vomit and feel as if you are going to die. The white stuff, by the way, simply tastes awful."

"And I'm betting I don't get to eat anything between now and then," Berg said.

"Or drink," Dr. Chet replied. "Nor will you have much free time. The *other* tests are going to take nearly eight hours."

Dr. Chet had been on the money on the time. Berg had never *heard* of such extensive physical and mental testing. It made every physical he'd ever been through look like child's play. He gave enough blood samples to count for a donation, he was lovingly prodded by a somewhat effeminate male physician assistant all over his body, did all the usual "turn your head and cough" tests, went through a cardiac stress test and an electrocardiogram. He was injected for every known disease and some, he was sure, the corpsman was just making up. He might have heard wrong, but *supposedly* one of the injections was for "triskaidekaphobia." He was pretty sure there wasn't an immunization for fear of the number thirteen.

Then he was ushered into a laboratory that deserved the full enunciation. There were more computer monitors than Berg had ever seen in one room, along with a "wet" lab that looked like something out of a mad scientist's nightmare. Worse, through a plexiglass window he could see a full surgical suite. The gleaming steel table gave the whole room a decidedly macabre look.

"Well, as we wait for the lab results, we will commence upon the first of the truly *interesting* tests," Dr. Chet said. "If you will take a seat," he added, pointing to a chair that, while comfortable looking, had the vague appearance of an electric chair. Complete with straps.

Berg sat down and "Nurse Betty" started hooking electrodes up to his head, chest, hands and forearms.

"This is a device somewhat like a lie detector test," Dr. Chet said. "It combines the functions of that and an electroencephalogram. An EEG measures brain patterns, but from reading your biography I believe you know that."

"Yes, sir," Berg said.

"So. I shall ask you a large number of questions. I will, through this test and others, get a picture of how you think. There are various reasons to do this, besides pure curiosity of which I have an inordinate supply. Would you care to venture a guess what they may be?"

"The military wants to see if the stress of the mission changes the way we think?" Berg ventured. "It might be a good way to check for post-traumatic stress syndrome."

"In fact, no," Dr. Chet said, looking up from the monitor and smiling. "There is a quite simple blood test for that. One of your samples is for that specific purpose. You have seen some science fiction TV shows, I'm sure. Did you never wonder about the fact that they had quite sophisticated medical technology yet beings with wildly different cellular structure were able to slip past their screening with impunity?"

"Actually, that has always bothered me," Berg admitted.

"And things in the brain and weird addictions and so forth and so on," Dr. Chet said. "By doing these tests, both before the mission and afterwards, we should be able to determine if aliens have taken over your body and are bent on world domination. Or at least the former. So, we shall begin. What is your name . . ."

Two hours later Berg was sweating more water than he could afford to lose in his dehydrated condition. He'd been asked to do math puzzles in his head; sometimes the questions had been too fast to answer, other times he had been given all the time he needed to answer. He'd been asked about his childhood, about his military experience, about his mother and father and sister. He had been posed nonsensical koans of the "what is the sound of one hand clapping" variety and about general philosophies. He'd been asked if he had ever killed anyone, if he'd like to kill someone, if he'd ever thought about it or about suicide. He'd been asked so many questions his head was buzzing.

"Good profile," Dr. Chet said, nodding. "Good *good* profile. You are so much center of the norms I suggested for this mission I could use you as *the* profile." He looked at his watch and grinned.

"And now for the bad part," he said, pulling out two pink bottles from his lab coat, then glancing at the monitor. "You do not fear the pink bottles?"

"You can tell by looking at the monitor?" Berg asked.

"Oh, yes, at this point very easily," Dr. Chet said. "And you do not."

"I've been nauseated before," Berg answered evenly.

"You *thought* you had been nauseated before," Dr. Chet said, grinning. "You will come to a new appreciation."

Nurse Betty had silently reappeared and started unstrapping the Marine.

"So, we will now do the MRI and CAT scans," Dr. Chet said. "After you take your medicine."

The pink stuff was just as awful as the white, but Berg didn't feel any negative effects. Maybe he was immune or something.

He undressed and got into a nonmetallic robe, then was slid into the MRI. The thing was noisy as hell and it was initially boring as hell. But then Dr. Chet started asking him questions *again*.

The session in the MRI wasn't all that long, though, no more than fifteen minutes. Then he was led to the CAT scan. That time, there weren't any questions. He just lay in the thing for another fifteen or twenty minutes while it took pictures of his head.

"Very well, we are done," Dr. Chet said after he'd gotten dressed again. It was after midnight, but if the doctor was tired it wasn't apparent. "How are you feeling?"

"Fine," Berg said.

"Yes, well," Dr. Chet said, looking at his watch. "Three . . . two . . . one. How are you feeling *now*?"

"Holy *maulk*," Berg said, his eyes flying wide.

"Bathroom is through *that* door," Dr. Chet said, pointing. "I'll see you in about thirty minutes."

# 5

## The SSBN Blage

"Now that's an odd looking sub," Miller said, looking at the boat.

The 4144 was alone in a covered pen made for six submarines. And it *was* odd looking. The sail was truncated and swept back with no diving plane on it. The rear section was "humped" for about a third of its length. The "hump" appeared to be a separate vessel, something like the SEAL vessel the Navy had been working on for years; there was a very definite seam where it met the boat.

Just at the tip of the composite nosecone that housed the sonar suite and other instruments was something completely different. Extending from the nosecone was a long protrusion that looked like—and Miller was sure he couldn't be the only person to make the connection—a sword about thirty meters long, six meters high at the base where it was attached to the nose of the sub, only two meters or so wide in the horizontal dimension, and then flattened out to a point. The rest of the body of the submarine could very well represent the hilt of the blade, although it was much longer than the blade itself. It really and truly looked like the oddest, most peculiar, and largest flat-black dull sword the chief warrant officer had ever seen. Also a bit like a narwhal. He just knew that Weaver was somehow behind it.

"Uh, what the hell is the giant blade all about?" Miller asked, then paused and added, "Sir?"

"Oh, yeah, the supercavitation initiator." Weaver shrugged. "Had to add that. Otherwise, when the ship tries to reach maximum underwater velocity there would be a serious problem with Euler buckling. Serious. Problem."

"Oiler buckling," the chief said. "Sounds like a game involving a football team from Texas and a bunch of gay cowboys."

"The Oilers moved to Tennessee a long time ago, Chief. Never was a big fan of the Cowboys either." Weaver grinned. "But it's Euler with an E, named after the guy who understood it first.

"Uh huh."

"You ever stood on an empty beer can slowly until the force of your entire body weight was finally enough to collapse the can flat?" Weaver explained.

"I'm more of a liquor drinker, sir."

"Work with me here, Chief. You have seen somebody stomp a can flat before?" asked Weaver rubbing at the back of his neck and raising an eyebrow.

"Yes, sir." *Calling Bill "sir" was going to take some getting used to.*

"Okay then, beer can equals submarine and big dumb SEAL equals force of water on boat at maximum underwater velocity. Flat can equals sub without initiator. Got it?"

"How does the sword help? No wait, scratch that. Euler buckling *bad*. Blade on nose of boat, *good*. Got it." The SEAL shook his head left and right subtly.

"It's basically the same thing that we do on supersonic stuff, plus a new trick that works kinda like the warp field. We put spikes on jets here and there to create shock waves where we want them and in a controllable manner. Ever seen the long needle on the end of a supersonic plane?"

"Yes, sir."

"Same deal. The initiator creates a bow wave far enough out in front of the ship that a boundary layer is created around the ship. This reduces the buckling forces on the ship by about two orders of magnitude. But that only helps with the Euler buckling force some."

"Wait a minute," Miller said, furrowing his brow. "Nukes are built to take all kinds of unimaginable hell. It couldn't stand up to even two or three times the normal top speed without modifications to the structure?"

"Two or three times *normal top speed*, perhaps," Bill said with a grin.

"No *maulk?*"

"No *maulk.*"

"Uh, sir. I know subs. I've spent one hell of a lot of time around them. They're pretty damned fast. I mean, just between us, here in a secure sub pen, a big boat goes somewhere around seventy or eighty *knots*. Right?" Miller wasn't sure if he was glad he asked the question or not. With Dr. Weaver—Lieutenant Commander Weaver—explanations could sometimes create an eyes glazing over effect that could damage one's brain.

"Actually for this boat, the terminal velocity is a little lower than that. No matter how much power we pour into the propulsion it's not that fast. And if it was that fast, it would . . ."

"Crush like a beer can, got it," Miller said. "So what gives?"

"Well, you see the initiator there has millions of little holes in it about a millimeter in diameter that are dispersed about it in a precisely calculated manner. It took us months to run that simulation and more than eight months to construct the thing. Anyway, we force air out through those holes as we come up to speed. An envelope of water supersaturated with air flows in around the vessel and dramatically reduces the friction with the water. It really is a warping of the parameters of the ocean so that the submarine can go faster through it than it should normally be able to. And, of course, it's got a spaceship engine in it. That helps. A prop won't work by a long shot."

"Did you think of that?" Miller hesitated and then added, "Sir?"

"Nope," Weaver admitted. "The Russians have been trying to figure out how to do it for fifty years. Some call it supercavitation; others call it underwater warp drive. The U.S. Navy decided to go slow and stealthy and quit trying to figure it out because the propulsion system required was a volatile rocket engine. The Navy didn't want that on a sub. But the new drive changed their mind and DARPA was so thrilled by it that they lobbied hard for the design and even paid for most of it."

Weaver looked at *his* ship with affection. Oh sure it was Captain Steven Blankemeier's command—and most certainly it *was* the captain's ship—but Weaver thought of it as his ship. After all, he'd designed most of the retrofit systems on it. Nobody understood it like he did.

"It looks like a sword. A short squatty sword with a big assed grip, but a sword nonetheless."

"Never noticed that," Weaver admitted. "Hmmm."

"Sooo, we sort of ram the water with that sword thingy . . ." Miller said.

"Correct."

"And we use it to make fizzy stuff that makes the ship slipperyer."

"More slippery. Sure."

"And that keeps us from getting crushed like a beer can."

"You see?" Weaver said. "It is possible to explain things to SEALs."

"Got a question, sir," Miller said, stone-faced.

"Go."

"So, can we ram *people* with that? Sort of like a narwhal skewering a whaling ship? I mean, it's not our first line of defense but is there, like, a ramming speed? Sir?"

"Let's just tour the ship, shall we?"

The strangest thing on the exterior of the ship was *definitely* the ramming blade. However, close on the heels of the blade was the odd appearance of the base of the sail. There was some sort of sliding hatch on the front that *really* looked out of place. It currently covered whatever was under it, but if memory served it was right above the conn.

The Navy had balked at giving a civilian "full access" to the details of the 4144. But they had admitted a willingness to give access to a SEAL chief warrant officer. Which was why Miller, wearing a brand new pair of digi-cam, carrying a seabag and occasionally rubbing his recently shaved head, was following Weaver across the gangplank to the spaceship.

He paused and saluted the American flag, then saluted the bridge.

"Permission to come aboard, Lieutenant?" he asked the officer manning the entry.

"Permission granted," the LT said, extending his hand. "Lieutenant Jon Souza, tactical officer."

"Pleased to meet you, sir," Miller replied.

"Time's a wastin'," Bill said, nodding at the lieutenant. "How's the loading going?"

The boat was bustling with loading.

"We've got the ardune torps loaded," the lieutenant replied.

"We're waiting until this evening to load the SM-9s. Laser Two failed the last charge cycle test. Brian's got it stripped down."

"While all that's good to hear," Bill said. "I hope we don't need any of it."

"Lasers?" Weaver asked. "What's an SM-9?"

"Where to start?" Bill asked as they entered a hatch on the rear of the sail. There was a ladder there, which made Miller happier. He was half expecting a teleporter or something. Weaver grabbed the sides of the ladder and slid down rather expertly. He'd clearly been around boats. Miller was having various shocks but the worst one had to be Dr. William "How do you use this pistol?" Weaver as a commissioned officer with sea time.

"At the bow?" Miller asked as he slid down the ladder after Weaver.

"Torpedo room," Weaver said, opening the hatch to the conn. "Not very interesting. Planetary study drones and some microsatellites. Well, and the 'torpedoes,' which are really Adari missiles. Range of about seventy klicks. Tracking system from an AMRAAM with some Adari additions. Ardune warhead."

"That's that . . . quark stuff, right?" Miller asked, looking around the conn. It looked pretty much like most of the conns he'd seen in his time. The big difference explained the sliding hatch. There was a big . . . *window* just under the front of the sail. And a portion of the conn had been elevated so you could see out. He was in a submarine with a . . . *window*!

"Quarkium," Weaver said, nodding. "Gives about three times the bang of an equal amount of antimatter. Yield's about sixty megatons. Of course, in space it doesn't have much range. The SM-9As have a nuclear fission triggered quarkium warhead that works similar to a hydrogen bomb. The fission bomb triggers the quarkium release, which in turn releases a *maulk* load of gamma-rays, neutrons, neutrinos, and muons. Did I say energy? Lots of that."

"How fast are the missiles? I mean, space is big, right, so they have to be fast?" Miller continued peering out the window, *on a submarine*, in front of him. The window seemed to be harder to get used to than the fact that he was standing inside humanity's first starship. A *freakin' window on a submarine*, he thought.

"The propulsion system is a mix of Adar tech and human. The thing is basically designed around the old nuclear thermal rocket concept but uses a small quarkium reactor instead of a fission reactor. No radiators needed and we use a dense Adar coolant for propellant instead of LOX or hydrogen or water. The Adar stuff gives us *waaaay* better m-dot. Using an Adar material for the nozzle we were able to get over eight thousand seconds of specific impulse out of it."

"Uh, huh," Miller said, looking at the *window on a submarine*! "Is that good?"

"Pretty good. They've got an accurate range of about four thousand klicks if there's not a gravity well to fight, but here is the kicker. Max V is right at eighty kilometers per second so it'd take the thing a little less than a minute to travel the full accurate range. After that, they are out of propellant and would be coasting with no control. The ship can go a *lot* faster than that, so we'll have to be careful and not shoot *ourselves*." Weaver shrugged. "No idea if the missile's capabilities are good or not compared to anybody else out there, but it's the best *we* can do. Currently. We're looking at some ways to extend the maneuvering range. Any other questions?"

"More of a statement, sir."

"Yeah, Chief?"

"Sir, there's a *grapping window* on this submarine."

"Spaceship, Mister Miller," Weaver said with a laugh. "Space-ship."

"Where's your station?" Miller asked, shaking his head and finally tearing his eyes from the *window on a submarine*!

"Over here," Bill said, waving to a station. "It's a bit odd. I have to be able to navigate underwater *and* in space." Miller saw a paper plot charter and three separate computer screens. Bill brought up one of the latter and pointed at the planet on the screen. "Since I'm also, effectively, the ship's science officer and they figured that Conn's going to be asking *lots* of questions, they managed to squeeze me in Conn instead of the usual Nav spot downstairs. Anyway. We're here. Terra. This system's really easy to use until you start filling it with real data, but if we wanted to go to, say, Jupiter . . ."

He brought up a menu and found the planet, then punched in a command. The system displayed a series of coordinates.

"It's at angle 233 mark 5.18, more or less," Bill said. "We need to come around to 233 and point up about five degrees. Only problem is . . ." He punched in another command and nodded. "Depending on how fast we're going, we're liable to run into Venus if we go that way and we're going *real* close to the Sun."

"I think you need to find a different vector," Miller said dryly, trying not to look over his shoulder. He might need to know this stuff to save the universe and *maulk*. But there was a . . .

"*Sho-tan*," Bill said. "So we vector to 197, catch a slingshot around the moon, catch another around Mars and there we are . . ." he added, showing the movement on the screen.

"Glad you're doing it," Miller noted.

"That's what everybody seems to say," Weaver replied, grinning. "One guy I was showing how to do this grabbed his head right in the middle of the lecture and screamed 'Rocks don't *move!*'"

"Who designed the system?" Miller asked.

"I did," Bill replied, shutting it down. "We paid Rath-Mirorc fifty-five million dollars for a system and they turned one in, late, that couldn't navigate its way out of a wet paper bag. So I built one."

"That's . . . a lot of coding," Miller said. "Isn't it?"

"Nah," Bill replied, waving him towards the rear hatch. "Not that much. Besides, I scagged a bunch of it from other programs."

"Wait; what other programs?" Miller asked, as he ducked through the hatch.

"Oh, here and there . . ." Weaver replied. One of the crew coming the other way limpeted himself into the starboard bulkhead, so that the two officers could squeeze past.

A nuclear submarine does not have much free space. Besides the obvious areas that fill the boat—the conn, the engine room, the missile and torpedo compartments—the boat had to pack in the thousand and one things that kept it going. Kitchens, mess halls, quarters for the crew, a state-of-the-art workshop, laundries.

Because there was only so much space to work with, the boat was *cramped*. The corridors were narrower than a hallway in a home and much lower. Doors were narrow. Bunks in the crew compartment were four-high stacks and *everything* the crew carried onboard had to fit in either their bunk or a very small locker.

"You got that thing off the Internet, didn't you," the warrant officer said, sliding past the crewman. He'd spent enough time in subs to know the moves. "You're navigating using some damned *freeware* program!"

"Only the basic data," Bill protested. "And some of the graphics code. And the kernel, okay. But the gravitational effect algorithm is all mine! Mostly . . ."

"Oh, God," Miller muttered.

"You know we've got to be able to pinpoint our position, right?" Weaver said, cycling open another hatch.

"What?" Miller said, stepping past the officer so he could dog the hatch closed. It was the internal hatches that, in the event of flooding or depressurization, would give the crew some marginal chance to survive. "Let me guess. Use a sextant or something?"

"Sextant's old tech," Bill replied. "I figured out something better."

"I can't wait," the SEAL said.

"See, all you have to do is pick out bright spots against a dark background," Weaver said. "You need to make sure they're the *right* bright spots, but that's really all it is."

"Some sort of telescope?" Miller asked as they walked down a corridor. They had to stand to the side as a seaman walked past with a large box of cans in his arms. Besides all the other crowding, every nook and cranny of the boat was slowly filling with boxes of food. The major limitation to time "at sea," or in space in this case, was how much food the boat could cram in. It could desalinate water for drinking, cooking and washing. It could break out oxygen from that same water for air. But nobody had figured out a way to make more food. You could pack prepared food into a much smaller area than a hydroponics department could ever create. There were some very new systems that created meat from nutrients and a "kernel" but those were still in their infancy. Until someone came up with a replicator, the menu was canned food.

"There's a telescope involved," Weaver said. "But the system that picks it up comes from an optical mouse."

"An optical mouse?"

"Oh yeah, its actually kinda cool. You ever seen those optical mice that have a little red light coming out the bottom where a ball is on the old-style computer mouse?"

"Uh, huh." Miller knew Weaver well enough to know that this explanation was not going to reassure his confidence in the ship's navigation system. But, what the heck. They had some sort of weird sword that would go through the foot of the guy

trying to crush them like a beer can, a navigation system off
the Internet and a window on a submarine. How much worse
could it get?

"Well, they work off a DSP chip that is actually quite
remarkable—"

"Doc . . . Sorry, 'Sir' . . . ?"

"DSP . . . digital signal processing. Anyway, there is a little video
camera inside the mouse that looks straight down at the table
surface. The little red light is just for, well, light. The DSP chip
stores the image from the camera and makes note of where any
spots, dust specks, scratches, or any other surface features of the
table are within the image. The chip then grabs another video
image a fraction of a second later and compares it to the previous one. If the spots moved within the image, the chip calculates
how far and then moves the cursor on the computer screen a
similar distance."

Weaver paused for a breath and Miller stood motionless, not
making a sound, but the slightest hint of a rictus grin began to
form on his face. It was worse.

"I had the idea that the little DSP chip should work for any
sort of scene change. I mean, after all, a video image of stars
against the night sky looks about the same as dust specs on a
tabletop with the contrast inverted. So, I *blaged* a few prototypes
together to show that it would work. There are several small two-
inch diameter telescopes distributed about the surface of the ship
and each of these has an optical mouse DSP system fixed at its
focal plane. The data is then piped into the main navigational
computer where the vector changes found in each DSP chip are
filtered and optimized. It actually works really well. And, the good
news is we've got over a hundred spares on board."

"Is the whole *boat* like that?" Miller finally moaned. He'd given
up. He had to face it. He'd lost his hardcore doing flowers. He
did *not* want to go fly around the universe in this . . .

"Yep, pretty much," Weaver replied. "Utter *blage*."

"Okay, you got me again. That's twice you've used that word
and I've no clue what it means," Miller said.

"Adar word," Bill replied, shrugging. "Sort of means everything
from cannibalize to jury-rig. To *blage*, I *blaged* it, we can *blage*
that, it's a *blage*. Funny thing is, the Adar never had the concept
of *blaging* before they ran into us; all their stuff is so carefully

crafted and integrated it makes the Japanese look sloppy. So I don't know *where* they got the word. But, yeah, it's about as mil-spec as a fifth grade science fair project. An Adar corporation did the IT systems integration and they did a damned fine job. And Rath-Mirorc got the SM-9s right, I'll give 'em that."

The last hatch, as Miller recalled, would have led them to the missile compartment. The missile compartment was the one really open area on the whole boat. Three stories high, with separate decks on each story, it was lined with giant "tubes" that held the ballistic missiles with open areas down the middle and to either side. Bubbleheads called it "Sherwood Forest." It was where SEALs traditionally did their running on-board. Instead of the cavernous area he'd expected, he was confronted by another hatch, a ladder to the side and narrow corridors leading port and starboard. There were two more hatches in the corridor and ladders at both ends.

"Now it gets complicated," Weaver said. He turned right, to port, and went up the ladder. The hatch above opened on another corridor, this one with bunks along the inner bulkhead. Halfway down there was another hatch, just a simple door, with one more at the far end and another ladder going down.

"This is the security section," Bill said. "We've got two security groups. One is Marines; they play outer security. Then each of the technical people is assigned a small security and support detachment. They're drawn from Special Forces."

"No SEALs?" Miller protested.

"No SEALs," Weaver replied. "Wrong sort of mission. Anyway . . ."

He opened up a hatch and waved to the room. It was . . . small. And there were two bunks.

"You get to bunk with the Marine first sergeant," Bill said. "He previously had the compartment all to himself."

"He's going to be pleased as *maulk*," Miller said, tossing his seabag onto the upper bunk.

"He was indeed," Weaver said.

He led Miller out of the room and down the corridor to the ladder. At the bottom there was a door but he turned to starboard and led Miller to a door in the center of the mission specialist section. This one had a card reader and a big sign "Authorized Crew Only."

Weaver fished out his keycard and held it up, then opened

the door. Beyond was the missile compartment. But it was much smaller than on a normal SSBN, with only four missile tubes.

"Those aren't Tridents," Bill said, gesturing at the missiles. "They're 9As."

"How many of them?"

"How many tubes?"

"Four."

"See?" Weaver said, grinning. "It's not true. SEALs *can* count to ten without taking off their shoes."

"That's it?" Miller asked. "The ship's got four missiles to defend itself?"

"And a couple of lasers that probably won't scrape the paint off of anything we find and some torpedoes that are the rough equivalent of a Saturday Night Special in space terms," Weaver said. "But I think that the LBB is probably superior tech to most of what we'll run into. If I'm right we'll be able to run away from most ships."

"Nice to hear," the SEAL said dryly.

Down both sides of the missile compartment were new generation Wyvern Mark Vs.

The Wyvern had been in development since shortly before the Chen Event. The massive suits were "piloted" by a person sitting more or less in the abdomen. The pilot wore a harness that transferred their movements to the much larger arms, legs and "head" of the Wyvern. With wheels on the elbows, knees and belly, the Wyvern was capable of just about any movement an infantryman could make and was much better armed and armored.

The Mark V stood about three meters tall, the same height as an Adar male. They looked like a very fat man with thin arms and legs, a big butt and a low, rounded vaguely insectile head. The "butt" contained a well-shielded americium nuclear generator for power while the "head" of the suit contained most of the sensors of the suits. In the case of the Wyverns on this mission those included not only full EM sensors, capable of picking up "light" ranging from X-rays to deep infrared, but a variety of other particles and waves.

The Mark V used the newest digital active camouflage system that took a reading from surrounding coloration and pattern and transmitted it to the surface of the suit. Under certain conditions, it could make the suit virtually disappear. They were still damned big things to hide, as both Weaver and Miller knew from painful experience.

"Only twenty Wyverns?" Miller asked, taking a count.

"Three levels to the section," Weaver replied. "Fifty in all. Thirty-eight Marines with armor, me, the three ground mission specialists, their security teams. And a few spares. I guess you're going to be fitted to one of those."

Each Wyvern had to be individually fitted to the user, a process that took about three hours.

"Now for the engineering section."

"I get to see that?" Miller asked. He'd never been given access to engineering.

"You said full access," Weaver replied, grinning.

"I'm not going to like this, am I?"

"Oh, sorry," Mimi said, blinking her eyes.

The small compartment she'd been directed to already had a lady in it. She was sitting at a fold-down desk with a small extensible lamp over it, typing on a computer. And she wasn't wearing a uniform like the rest of the people on the ship; she was wearing jeans, high-heels and a spaghetti-strap top. All three were black and the jeans had a dragon on the thigh.

"It's okay," the lady said, standing up and grinning. She had long red hair with the front dyed bright blue and blue and red streaks in it. She was also very pretty, arguably beautiful, with a small chin and nose and bright brown eyes. "Are you my roommate? Aren't you a little young? What's that on your shoulder?"

"I'm . . ." Mimi paused trying to figure out which question to answer. "I was told this was my room, so I guess I'm your roommate. I am young and it's weird that I'm here but there's a reason, and this is Tuffy," she finished, fishing the creature off her shoulder and holding him out.

Tuffy extended one pseudopod towards the woman and then bowed. Mimi had never seen him do that before.

"Isn't he *cute*?" the woman squealed, walking over and petting him gently. "Tuffy. You're Mimi Jones. Sorry it took me so long. The last picture of him I saw he didn't look so cool."

"That's okay," Mimi said as Tuffy crawled up the woman's arm. He'd never done *that* before, either.

"He's tickly," the lady said, plucking him off and handing him back. "I like you, Tuffy, but Mimi's your special friend. So you're on this boat, too? What's your job?"

"Tuffy just told me we had to come," Mimi said, shrugging. "I don't really know *what* I'm supposed to do."

"I'm Miriam," the lady said, holding out her hand. "I'm the linguist."

"I'm pleased to meet you, ma'am," Mimi said, shaking her hand.

"I'm glad you're here," Miriam said. "Everybody else is so stuffy. It's *good* to have a friend. We're going to have *so* much *fun!*"

Mimi, for the first time since Tuffy told her she had to leave her home, started to hope that might be the case.

"What in the *hell* is that?" Miller asked, blinking his eyes in astonishment.

The engine room of the boat was almost blindingly white. And it had all the usual sort of stations he'd expect to see in a nuclear reactor. But . . . floating in the middle of the room was a big silver ball with what looked like very close longitude and latitude lines drawn all around it. Above and below it were large circular . . . somethings. They looked sort of like big magnets.

"That, my friend, is the coryllium sphere," Bill said, grinning. "In the center of that sphere is the little black box we played with oh so many years ago. See that?" he asked, pointing to something that looked like a broad, squat cannon with no opening.

"And that is?"

"That is a meson canon," Bill replied. "Turns out that was the answer. Send that thing electrons and it goes ape-*maulk*. Fire mesons at it and they degrade into neutrinos. Feed it with neutrinos and it generates a black hole. A stable one. And it is *inside* the box. Generate a large enough one and it somehow . . . warps reality. Creates a special universe that the boat exists in where normal Einstein physics no longer apply. More neutrinos, bigger hole, we go faster. Well, really Einstein's General Relativity does allow for some of the things but that's a long story and a *maulk* load of tensor math.

"The reason for the big sphere is two-fold. The outer layer is coryllium; it's a room temperature Adar superconductor. So we can balance the sphere on a magnetic field and hold it there using the Meisner effect. The rest of the sphere is radiation absorption material. The Schwarzschild radius of the black hole puts out a *maulk*-load of hard rads. The sphere absorbs them. I figure it's good for about four hundred thousand hours of use, then we'll have to switch it out. Pretty much like the rods on a sub's reactor.

"Also turns out that the effect you get depends exactly where you aim the neutrinos. That's one reason for having the sphere floating. We can control the impact point of the neutrinos to within a nanometer and with that thing nanometers *matter*. The lines represent spherical coordinates theta and phi that are basically the same as lat-long, but we drew the lines on there very precisely. It helps align the ball initially. Like I said alignment is . . . important. There's one point where input causes . . . bad things to happen."

"Define bad things," Miller said.

"That you don't have access to," Weaver replied. "I was careful to check. But I will point out that it's one reason there are still five keys on this boat even though we're no longer considered a ballistic missile sub." Weaver fished into his uniform top and pulled out a red key attached to a lanyard. "You do not want me to pull this out for real."

"Oh," Miller said, nodding. "Very bad things."

"Very bad things," Weaver agreed, putting the key away. "There are probably damned near a billion combinations on the thing. We've only figured out about two or three. Basically, we can use it to get around but we don't know what all it is capable of.

"The big problem with the box is you have to dial the mesons down *slowly* or the hole explodes. So we can go *into* warp fast. Coming out takes five to thirty seconds, more or less. Try to just turn it off and we go boom. Also won't form one when we're too near a gravity well. Not sure why. But no matter how many mesons we pump into it, it won't form until we're about two planetary diameters away. What it does, instead, is create a normal space drive with all the fixin's. It generates pseudogravity, reactionless acceleration and, best of all, an inertial compensator so that we don't get smashed into paste by the accel. Internal gravity is about ninety percent of Earth's, so whoever created this thing likes more or less Earth gravity.

"The warp also won't form inside Venus' orbit, more or less; the sun's gravity is too powerful in that region. The kicker is, if we get too close to a gravity well, it can just shut down. *Fortunately* for some reason the black hole doesn't explode in that case. I'm pretty sure that's something having to do with the engineering of the device but since I haven't a *clue* about the theory on the thing, that's just a wild ass guess."

"Where are the mesons coming from?" Miller asked.

"Charged Higgs in the cannon," the astrogator said. "An upgraded version of the aimer doo-hickey we started opening gates with. There's a small Adar ardune reactor in the back of the room. That supplies plenty of power. More power than the system can handle."

"So, you've got quarkium warheads on the missiles," Miller said wonderingly.

"And the torpedoes," Bill pointed out.

"I *so* don't want to know about the torpedoes," Miller said. "You've got contained quarkium in this room *and* a micro black-hole generator. One that, if you hit it with either electricity or neutrinos in the wrong spot, very bad things happen. And the whole ship is one big . . . *blage*. With a *grapping window*. Why do the words 'warp core breach' come to mind?"

"Because if any of the *fine* technicians in this room *grapp* up," Bill replied, "we are going to light up like a *supernova*. This sucker shouldn't ever come *near* a planet, much less be sitting in Newport News. But I try to downplay that. . . ."

# 6

## Rule Thirty-Two:
## Never Trust an Adar with Acronyms

"First call!" Jaenisch said, sticking his head through the door of Bergstresser's room. "Time to rise and shine!"

"Oh, *grapp*," Berg moaned, rolling over and getting to his feet. "I'll be right . . ." He stopped and ran to the head, a room he had occupied for, on average, ten minutes an hour all night.

"What time did you take the pink *maulk*?" Jaen asked, ignoring the sounds of dry retching.

"About midnight," Berg answered, sipping some water and rinsing out his mouth.

"Shiny. You're over the worst of it," Jaen said. "By noon you'll be back to your usual chipper Two-Gun self."

"*Grapp* you, Jaen," Berg said, too miserable to realize he'd just cussed an NCO.

"Uniform and accoutrements in thirty minutes in the bay," Jaen said, ignoring the insult. "Don't eat breakfast, but you'll be fine by lunch."

Load-out was a pain in the butt, especially in the morning.

"What I don't get is why we're even taking battle rattle if we're going to be using Wyverns," Hattelstad said. The best way to move the battle rattle, boron carbide body armor, combat harnesses and rucksacks loaded with minimal gear, was by carrying it in place. So they'd all loaded up, then toted it to a secure loading dock at the rear of the barracks. That involved climbing down four flights of stairs, and while that normally wouldn't have even fazed Berg, at the moment it nearly killed him.

"Nobody knows if we're going to have to go ground-mount," Jaenisch replied. "For that matter, we might end up fighting in the ship. We can't use Wyverns for that."

"The very idea makes my balls shrink up," Hattelstad said. "You know we've still got missiles, right?"

"No," Berg said miserably. "I am as ignorant of the ship as it is possible to be while knowing that it exists."

"And they're loaded with that Adar ardune stuff," Hattelstad said gleefully. "It's more powerful than a nuke and it blows up if you look at it wrong. Wanna know about the food?"

"The word is unwelcome," Berg said. "But if you insist on talking about greasy bacon or whatever, I'll just have to puke all over you. Satisfied?"

"We ain't supposed to be chatting, anyway," Jaenisch pointed out. "So can it."

The loading dock was crowded with other Marines, carefully tossing their rattle into the back of a five ton.

"So this is Two-Gun," a tall, dark PFC with the nametag "Prabhu" said. "And either you're hung over as hell, or you just went through that Shiva damned pre-mission physical."

"Pre-mission," Berg said, walking in the back of the truck and taking off his armor. He carefully put his harness in his mostly empty ruck and then banded the armor around it. "But I'm told that the effects pass by noon."

Prabhu was loaded down with several people's gear. "For some people," he said. "Me, I was puking for a week. All I could eat was soda crackers and water. Well, and Coke. It helps you burp instead of puke."

"Great," Berg said. "And I think I'm coming down with something from the injections."

"Probably Number Thirteen," Hattelstad said, tossing his gear on top of the pile.

"Don't tell me they really gave us an injection to prevent trisa . . . triska . . . fear of the number thirteen?"

"Nah, just sounds like it," Hattelstad said. "So we call it injection thirteen. It's something that's supposed to prevent a bunch of infections from something that gets in your cells or something. Malaria is one of them. One of them 'it's not on the market, yet, but we're *sure* it's safe' immunizations."

"Oh, *grapp* me," Berg muttered. "One of *those*."

"Yep."

With the battle rattle loaded, the entire group headed over to the headquarters building at a trot. They were led by Staff Sergeant Summerlin, who upped the trot to a solid run halfway to the headquarters.

Well, that was fine by Berg. He might be sick as a *grapping* dog, but he wasn't fazed by a little running. If anything, it made him feel better. He probably should have done PT this morning.

At the headquarters they got started on loading the company's equipment and supplies. That took most of the rest of the morning and they still didn't have it all in the ship. At noon they broke for lunch and Berg had to face the thought of food.

"Eatin' light?" a lance corporal asked, sitting down next to him.

"I had my 'physical' last night," Berg said. "There ought to be a different word."

"There is," the lance corporal said. "*Maulk*. Kevin Crowley, I'm in Bravo Team."

"Eric Bergstresser," Berg said, shaking his hand.

"Two-Gun . . ." the lance corporal said, drawling the "u." "Saw the clip. But you try that *maulk* in combat and they're going to have to choose who they prefer, you or me."

"Wouldn't think about it," Berg said, nibbling at the chicken strip. "Sergeant said try it, I tried it."

"Talkin' about Two-Gun here?" Staff Sergeant Summerlin asked, sitting down next to Crowley. "I heard about your fancy shootin', Tex."

"I was under *orders* to try it, Staff Sergeant," Berg said.

"I also heard that," Summerlin replied, grinning. "And I've seen two-gun mojo done well before. But only playing around. Don't go training on it or anything."

"We're going to be using Wyverns, anyway," Crowley said. "Not much chance for Two-Gun to shine."

"My rig isn't even set up for a pistol," Berg moaned. "I'm not planning on using two. But if I do, I know who I'm going to shoot for showing that clip around."

"Well, we can trade team nicknames if you wish," Prabhu said, sitting down across from him.

"Hey, Gunga-Din," Crowley said, grinning. "Din's in First Platoon, so you won't have to put up with his religious fervor. Much."

"Eat *maulk* and die, you *behanchod*," Prabhu said, picking up a chicken strip. "My real name's Prabhu, obviously. Arun Prabhu. Ah, chicken strips. The food of the gods."

"I'm eating a big ole cheeseburger," Crowley said, biting into the thin and not particularly tasty mess burger. "Mmmm . . . taste the goodness."

"May Kali send you more spots upon your face than you already have," Prabhu said, grinning. "You cannot taunt me for my faith is pure."

"Kali wasn't the goddess of sickness," Berg said, frowning. "Wasn't that, uhm . . . Mari?"

"Hell if I know," Prabhu said, taking another bite of chicken and ignoring Crowley. "I'm new to this whole Hindu thing. My parents were atheists from southern India. Big-time liberals who could go full high Brahmin when their 'liberal' positions were challenged. Such as when their son joined the Marines. I just found religion when I got asked what mine was at Basic. I didn't want to say 'Atheist' so I said 'Hindu.' Now I'm trying to figure out what I signed up for. And there's a definite lack of Hindu chaplains to explain the intricacies. So far I've found out there are a bunch of intricacies and that's about it. So I just pray to Vishnu and Brahma and don't eat his bulls and that's about it."

"Oh," Berg said. "Just wondering, cause, like, none of the Hindus I knew worshipped Brahma, either. Just an FYI."

"Intricacies, see?" Prabhu said. "*Behanchod* intricacies. And I had to give up cheeseburgers. That really hurt. Next cycle, I want to come back as a Christian so I can eat cheeseburgers again. I don't care what the Brahmins say, Christian's *got* to be higher on the ladder. *They* get prime rib."

"That's our Din," Summerlin said. "Where'd you pick up all that stuff about Hindus, Two-Gun?"

"I knew a couple of them in school," Berg said, shrugging. "Oh . . . crap," he added, his eyes crossing.

"Gonna keep it down?" Prabhu asked. "Because, you know, this batch is really *greasy* . . ."

"Saaaah," Berg ground out, his teeth clenched. "Yes, I'm going to keep it down."

"Take a sip of Coke," Staff Sergeant Sumerlin said. "It helps."

"What we really need is a prescription of maree-jew-wanna," Crowley pointed out. "Medicinal grade. But *nooo*. We just got to suffer. Welcome to the Corps."

"It's good training," Berg said, letting out his air carefully, then burping.

"You are too *grapping* gung-ho for your own good," Crowley said, grinning.

"Semper-*grapping*-Fi, *behanchod*," Berg muttered.

As he was leaving the mess, Prabhu casually wandered over.

"I was wondering," Prabhu said. "You know what *behanchod* means, right? It's Hindu, not Adar."

"I know what *behanchod* means," Berg said, rubbing his stomach. "It involves doing some things with your sister that aren't considered nice or legal. Like I said, I had some friends that are Hindu. Rana, in fact."

"Oh," Prabhu said, then grinned. "In that case, yeah, Crowley's a *behanchod*."

"Noticed," Berg replied, heading back to the loading.

Berg was carrying a bag of miscellaneous supplies out to a truck in the parking lot when he passed Crowley and a corporal with the nametag "Lujan" outside the building puffing on cancer sticks.

"Nice to see some people get a smoke break," Berg said, shuffling past.

"Did you just *dis* me, private?" the corporal said angrily.

"Not at all," Berg replied. "I simply stated that it was pleasant to see you enjoying the air, Corporal."

"Careful, Drago," Crowley said, grinning. "This here's Two-Gun Berg. Don't want to get old Two-Gun angry with you, do you?"

"Two-gun mojo man," Lujan said, grinning. "Anybody stupid enough to two-gun mojo ain't smart enough to know if he's dissing somebody."

"I stand corrected, Corporal," Berg said. "And I guess you need to get your nicotine in now, given that we're going to be on a ship for some time."

"The ship's got a smoking area," Crowley said, grinning. "Care for a puff?" he added, holding out his pack of Marlboros.

"I do not indulge," Berg said, tossing the sack in the back of the ten ton.

"Drink?" the corporal asked.

"On occasion," Berg said. "Lightly."

"God, tell me that you *grapp*," Crowley said. "Otherwise we're going to have to yank that stake out of your ass, hard."

"Oh, I *grapp* like there's no tomorrow," Berg said. "They didn't call me Three-Ball for nothing. And my strength is as the strength of ten because my lungs are pure."

"Drago, would you mind informing me what you think you are doing out here smoking when the rest of the company is busting its butt loading?" Top said, appearing around the corner of the building.

"Just done, Top!" Corporal Lujan said, pulling the cigarette out of his mouth and starting to drop it.

"And if you mess up my loading bay, you are going to be doing pushups until your MOTHER'S hands bleed!"

"Aye-aye, Top!" Lujan said, field stripping the burning tobacco out of the cigarette instead of crushing it out on the ground.

"Two-Gun, don't you have somewhere else to be?" the first sergeant asked, one eyebrow raised.

"Aye-aye, Top!" Berg bellowed, trotting up the stairs to the building.

"How in the *grapp* does he always know what's going on?" Crowley said as the threesome bolted through the door.

"He's the first sergeant," Drago said. "That's his job."

"Can I ask a question?" Berg said. "Why do they call you Drago?"

"Wait till you see him in the shower," Crowley said, grinning.

"*Grapp* you, Crowie."

"Two-Gun," Gunnery Sergeant Hocieniec said as the loading was completed. "Go jump in the back of the ten ton over on bay four. You're going to the ship to start loading."

"Aye-aye, Gunny," Berg said.

"You're not going to be by yourself," the gunny said, grinning. "Most of Third Herd is over there already and we're going to be following in a minute. And I'm sending Staff Sergeant Summerlin over on another truck. You're just advanced party."

"Will do, Gunny," Berg said.

"Holy cow," Berg muttered as he jumped off the back of the ten ton.

He'd been told the ship was a converted sub, but for some reason nobody had mentioned that it wasn't extremely converted. And he'd never really thought where the Navy was hiding it. In a massive sub pen was a good choice, all things considered.

The crew of the sub was busy loading stores, and a massive missile that sure *looked* like an ICBM was being lowered into one of the tubes as he just stood and stared.

"It's a hell of a sight," Summerlin said, walking up behind him. "Note the big sword thingy sticking out the front. But we've got gear to store. Some of the stuff we loaded was Third's, but they've been down here all day getting it in the sub while we were loading the trucks. First is down *in* the sub packing it away."

"And our job is . . . ?" Berg asked.

"To make sure *our* stuff gets put in the right place," Summerlin replied, walking over to the line of Marines loading stores. "Two-Gun, Gunny Hedger, Third Platoon."

"Hey, Summer," the gunnery sergeant said.

"We were sent to determine how badly First was *grapping* up our *maulk*," Summerlin said.

They crossed the gangplank, then entered a vertical hatch, sliding down the ladder between bags of gear. Thereafter followed a bewildering, to Berg, series of turns until they got to the ship's gear room.

The gear room was a combination of battle-rattle storage and armory. Each person's gear and personal weapon was supposed to be stowed in their personal locker. The armory, in turn, held preloaded sets of rounds. Draw and don their gear, pick up their rounds and they were in business.

The gear room, though, was a nightmare. With so little room on the ship, there wasn't enough space for the usual locker room setup with lockers lined up on either side of benches. Instead, the battle rattle and weapons were kept in sliding locker walls, that could be moved aside, so that the platoons could access their gear one at a time. The doors of the lockers folded downwards for a seat or table.

The battle rattle and weapons had been sent down in, supposedly, the same order as the locker. But what people like Prabhu had been doing was picking up scattered equipment from their platoon and making sure it got on the trucks.

So when the two members of Second Platoon entered the gear locker, they found a pile of mismatched gear tossed in every corner, a pile of *matched* gear that hadn't been loaded, yet, in the companionway and the beginnings of a raging argument.

"God *damnit*, Staff Sergeant Summerlin," a gunnery sergeant swore as soon as they entered the compartment. The guy was short and looked about sixty, the type that ages from the outdoors. "Your *maulk* was *totally grapped* up. And Third's is *worse!*"

"I'm sorry about that, Gunnery Sergeant Frandsen," Summerlin replied. "May we be of any assistance?"

"You can start going through the pile that's portside aft is what you can do!" the gunnery sergeant snapped. "That's all your *maulk*. I'm going to send a runner up to Hedge to tell him *his* stuff is *starboard* side aft and that's about all the sorting *we're* doing. When we're done loading the *maulk* that *ain't grapped* up, y'all can fight it out to get the rest stored!"

"Very well, Gunnery Sergeant," Summerlin said, evenly. "We'll get to it, then."

"Staff Sergeant," Berg whispered as they got to the pile. "Our *maulk was grapped* up. I mean, most of the guys just tossed their stuff in any old way."

"We've got time to sort it out," Summerlin said, turning to check that the gunny wasn't watching and then grinning. "And it was worth it to watch Big-Foot Frandsen nearly bust a blood vessel. Hell, Gunga-Din was *intentionally* mixing in First's with ours."

"Oh," Berg said, trying not to grin. "So why'd *we* get detailed to do the dirty work?"

"You kidding?" Summer asked, picking up a set of battle armor. "I practically had to kill to get this detail. *Everybody* wanted to see if Big-Foot would finally have a stroke!"

"That's some tattoo," Berg said wonderingly.

The mystery of Drago's nickname was revealed as he walked

out of the team showers with a towel around his waist. Most of the corporal's back was taken up by an intricate dragon tattoo.

Loading had continued until 2000, an hour behind schedule. It wasn't the snafu with the battle rattle that held things up, but getting the rest of the company's "common" equipment stored. When they were done, everything could be accessed, more or less, at least if you only wanted the stuff that was on the outside of the piles.

Fortunately, Top seemed to have an uncanny ability to determine what was going to be required in order of need. The term was "combat loading." The idea was that the first things you needed would be the last things stored. And Top knew what was going to be needed and when. Or at least seemed to. The proof would be in the access as the mission progressed.

But, finally, the ship was loaded and the Marines were given forty-five minutes to "*maulk*, shower, shave" and prepare for an inspection. There were high-ranked visitors coming to see the still unnamed ship head out to sea, and the Marines were, by God, going to look like Marines, not ragbag sailors!

"Got it in Singapore," Drago said, going over to the sinks and pulling out shaving gear. "I wasn't even drunk, believe it or not. But it took, like, days to do. Blew all that month's pay and bonuses plus I had to hit my credit card. But worth it."

"Hell of a tattoo," Berg admitted. His turn for the shower had come up and while he was in it he took a surreptitious glance around. Just about everyone in the unit had one tattoo or another, although Drago's was, by far, the most spectacular. He shaved in the shower. His beard hairs were as blond as his head, but came in dark for some reason. If he was going to be standing inspection at 2200, he had to shave or get gigged.

By 2100 he was down on the quarterdeck, uniform squared away, *maulk*, showered and shaved.

"Open ranks," First Sergeant Powell ordered, then walked the line.

When he got to Berg he just looked him up and down and nodded. Nothing to disapprove of. On the other hand . . .

"Crowley, who taught you to shave . . . ?"

They were bussed to the sub, which was docked about two miles away. Berg spent the trip just looking out the windows. It wasn't that he was particularly tired, despite occasional nausea, having been up most of the night and one long damned day. It was just that . . . Once they entered the sub pen, that was the last time he might *ever* see Earth. There wasn't much to see; they spent the whole trip on the base. But it was something. They did manage to pass the base McDonald's, which caused a slight increase in his nausea.

The Marines were allowed a designated cubage of "personal effects" to be stored in a bag about the size of a plastic grocery bag. That included their shaving gear, any medications they cared to bring along and whatever else they desired in the way of "personal effects." When they got to the ship, Berg followed Sergeant Jaenisch and Lance Corporal Hattelstad down into the bowels of the boat. He had the bottom bunk, naturally. Land-based groups, the seniors got the bottom bunks, but on ships, well, you wanted to be *above* any splatter. But the bunks were surprisingly better than he expected.

Instead of a curtain, the bunk sealed with a memory plastic door that could be set to be transparent or opaque. Hit a button it closed; hit another button it turned black. There was a private air supply that could be set to any temperature. There were several small bins, the largest being above where his feet would go. But he had a small shelf for personal items at the head of the bed as well. Best of all, the bunk could be slightly elevated and there was a keyboard and a flip-down plasma screen. He wasn't sure what was available on the terminal, but he could hope for the best.

The bad part was that it looked like the entire "company," at least the junior NCOs and the privates, were in the same bay. With nearly thirty people in the narrow corridor, crowded didn't begin to describe it.

He tossed his bag up on the bunk, then climbed in to get out of the way.

"What now?"

"Ten minutes we have to be in the missile compartment for final inspection," Jaenisch said, climbing in his own rack. "Then we hang out until it's time to form up on deck."

"Nice racks," Berg said. "Better than on a transport, that's for sure."

"You don't know the half of it," Hattelstad said. "You need

to read the manual on them. They're spaceworthy so if we get decompressed we can just hunker in the bunks and . . . well, hope somebody comes to save us I guess. The whole package can be ripped out and pulled out of the compartment, though I wouldn't want to try in anything but zero gee. There's a water port and a piss tube, all the bells and whistles. Oh, and computerized training systems so we don't have to clog up another part of the ship when we're playing Dreen War."

"What's on the terminal?" Berg asked, flipping down the screen. "Just Dreen War?"

"Just about anything," Jaenisch said. "Movies, TV shows, music. Use the buds, though."

"Got it," Berg said. Two ear buds were racked in holders on the side of the bunk. He pulled them out and inserted them, then used a laserpad to navigate to the shows menu. "Jesus, you weren't kidding. I think there's just about every TV show ever made."

"Nah, there are a few missing," Jaenisch said. "Ever see reruns of *WKRP in Cincinnati?*"

"Love that show," Berg said. "But I can never find the chip for it."

"That's because it's got a bunch of legal stuff holding it up," Jaenisch said. There was a slight tympani coming from his direction and he'd raised his voice. "*Grapping* RIAA. I mean, *nobody* buys those albums anymore. Release the *maulk* and let Micro-Vam or Napple put it out for sale."

"No *maulk*," Berg muttered. "Shiny! They've got *Firefly!*"

"They've got what?" Jaenisch said loudly.

"Never mind," Berg said. "What in the hell are you listening to?"

"Within Temptation," Jaenisch said. "You ought to try it!"

"I already am," Berg replied. "Ah, *Trash* . . ."

"You listen to *country?*" Hattelstad said as they climbed the ladder up to the sub's surface deck.

"And the sergeant listens to death metal; what's your point?" Berg asked.

"Within Temptation is not death metal," Jaenisch pointed out. "It's Goth. Although I listen to death metal, too. But *country?*"

"I like ballads," Berg said.

"So why not Heather Alexander?" Hattelstad asked.

"Who?"

"Can it," Jaenisch said as they reached the deck.

Assembly on the top deck of an SSBN is normally an exercise in gymnastics. The majority of the deck is rounded. However, the area over the missiles, and in this case the mission specialist package, was more or less flat. Most of the eggheads were by the sail, nearest the distinguished visitor area on the dock. Then the officers and crew of the ship, then the "mission specialist" security force, who were senior NCOs from Army special forces, then the Marines, right down by the fantail.

The Marines were the first ones on deck and submitted to a third inspection, this time by the CO *and* Top. Given the conditions, they couldn't open ranks or the rear rank would have been in the water. So the first sergeant and the CO had to squeeze their way down the sections.

It was the first time Berg had seen the Marine CO, Captain Michael MacDonald. The commander of the security contingent was a tall, spare man with short-cropped, dark-brown hair. Technically, he was in charge of the SF guys as well. But Berg had picked up enough scuttlebutt that it was pretty apparent they ran their own show. Since they were all experienced NCOs, that probably worked just fine.

The CO found nothing at fault and the company was brought to the "rest" position, like parade rest but you could look around.

"And now, we wait," Hattelstad said. "You seriously have never heard of Heather Alexander?"

"Nobody in the company had heard of Heather Alexander before you showed up, Hatt," Crowley said. The "company" was arranged in three ranks of ten men each, the platoon sergeants at the head of each rank, with the platoon leaders and the company XO to the rear. When the CO took over from the first sergeant, Top took a position at the bottom of the officer's ranks.

Thus Crowley was right next to Sergeant Jaenisch with Hatt at the very end of the row.

"Everybody should listen to Heather Alexander," Crowley said. "Heather is the Goddess."

"I'll give you points for 'March of Cambreadth,'" Jaenisch said. "But I'll top that with 'Winterborn.'"

"DragonForce, man, DragonForce," Hattelstad argued. "That's the *maulk*."

"I'm a big Toby Keith fan, personally," Berg said. It was an apparent non sequitur since they all just looked at him. "Well, I am. I like Johnny Cash for that matter."

"Two-Gun, we might just have to rename you," Crowley said. "Two-Gun is much too hot a handle for somebody who listens to country. You'd better keep that *maulk* down in the bay. *Grapp.* Just when we got rid of Harson and his damned mood music . . ."

"I kinda liked some of that stuff," Hattelstad said. "Wyndham Hill and all that. It was soothing. You know, masturbation music."

"Rest does not mean laughing your ass off," Gunny Hocieniec snapped from the end of the rank.

"Sorry, Gunny," Jaenisch said, still snickering. "Harson was a good guy. Hell on wheels in a Wyvern. But, yeah, his taste in music sucked."

"Like that metal crap is worth *maulk*?" the sergeant in front of Jaenisch said, looking around. "You keep that *maulk* down, damnit."

"And don't go pounding the whole bay with that rap *maulk*, Onger," Jaenisch snapped. "In space, nobody can hear you scream."

Berg wasn't sure who "Onger" was, but based on the way they were lined up he was Gung-Din's boss.

"Space," Berg said. "I can't wait."

"Yeah, but we got to get there first," Hattelstad said balefully.

"How bad is that?" Berg asked.

"See the ship's CO?" Jaenisch replied, gesturing with his chin. "Former fighter pilot."

"Running a sub?" Berg said.

"Politics," Jaenisch said, shrugging. "Anyway, he drives the ship like a fighter."

Berg looked from one end of the massive sub to the other and shook his head.

"That's one big damned fighter."

"Sort of my point."

"Company!" the CO bellowed. "Atten-hut!"

"Ladies and Gentlemen, distinguished beings, thank you for being here today on this momentous occasion . . ."

Normally the main ceremony for a boat was at completion

and launching. A crowd of well-wishers and officials gathered to send the boat off to sea. A bottle, traditionally one with waters of all the seven seas, was broken on the bow.

The problem with the 4144, besides the fact that the powers that be were still arguing over a name, was that it wasn't being launched. It was simply a converted SSBN, the former *Nebraska*, and had already had such a ceremony.

But the first deep space mission of the first *warp* ship, even if a totally covert and still unnamed one, was a matter of some ceremony. Even if it was a very late night, very covert, ceremony. So a crowd had gathered. Admittedly, it was smaller than normal, there were no family of the crew, no press, and everyone on the dock had the highest of high security clearances, but by the same token it was extremely select. Admiral Townsend was presiding but even the President had managed to attend. The Chairman of the Joint Chiefs was present as was the deputy defense secretary for interstellar warfare. Two senior members of the Senate, two equally senior members of the House, the secretary of state and a group of senior Adar. The ambassador for Britain was present as the representative of the only Earth government that had been informed the U.S. had a warp drive.

Although very few Earth governments were aware of the boat, support from the Adar government was a necessity on several levels. The boat had needed Adar technology and the Adar had, after all, been the suppliers of the drive. Just because Bill had figured out how to use it when they could not did not preclude their participation.

Besides the "distinguished visitors," the entire crew, military and scientific, was lined up on the deck of the sub. The Navy crew, who were going to be going back to work right after the ceremony, were in dungarees for the enlisted and khakis for the officers. The security contingent, Marines and Special Forces, were in Mar-Cam and digi-cam. The senior boat officers and NCOs were gathered to the front of the crew, with one SEAL warrant officer looking decidedly out of place. The majority of the scientific team, biologists, planetologists and astronomers, were in blue coveralls. The three exceptions were right on the end. Tchar, the Adar physicist who had been one of the first Adar ever to visit Earth and with whom Weaver had developed a close working relationship, was wearing fluorescent green pants, a Hawaiian shirt and mosh boots. Mimi and the linguist Miriam Moon were in jeans and T-shirts. He knew that Mimi had been issued coveralls so he had to assume someone had persuaded her to wear something else. One guess as to who. He hoped he wouldn't be forced to explain the presence of either one to the President or the Adar.

Weaver had recently heard a rumor that it was the Adar who had held up the naming of the boat. U.S. Naval naming nomenclature was straightforward. This boat should be named after either a state or a distinguished person. The first name proposed was the *Harley Simpson*, after a senior member of the House Armed Services committee who was recently deceased. That name quickly faded due to some background discussions that even Weaver had not been privy to.

The presence of K'Tar'Daoon, the Adar secretary of High Technology Defense and up until recently something on the order of prime minister of Adar, argued that the naming argument might have been settled.

"The President and the Honorable K'Tar'Daoon would like to say a few words . . ." Admiral Townsend said, winding down.

"I won't take much time," the President said. "I know that time and tide wait for no one. I'd just like to wish everyone luck and say that, after long discussions, the name of this fine ship has been finalized. I will let K'Tar'Daoon explain."

"While this ship is not Adar in truth, we have as high hopes for it as any human here," K'Tar'Daoon said. The Adar spoke excellent English but with a strong sibilant accent. "When the naming conventions of your ships were explained, we found them most excellent, for human beliefs and understanding. However, Adar, as is often noted, think differently from humans. And while this is not our ship, in truth, we wished to present our thoughts on how this ship should be named. In time, we were persuasive in our arguments.

"When we first encountered humans, we were confused by the name the humans had given to the boson portals. Such simple things and yet such a strange name: Looking Glasses. You did not call them mirror portals. Such a name would be logical. But humans looked upon them and gave them a name of wonder and, indeed, they are wonders. They take us all to strange lands, bring wonders to both of our worlds.

"The *Harley Simpson*, the *Margaret Thatcher*, the *George Washington*, the *Enterprise*, each was debated in turn. But at each point we Adar argued that the name should be a name of wonder and power. For this ship is the hope of both our worlds, the sword that will carry our anger and righteous fury against the enemy that still plagues us.

"This is also an excellent time to make an announcement. Yesterday, a mutual defense treaty was signed by the Adar Unitary Council, the President of the United States and the prime minister of England. Once this treaty is ratified by the United States Senate and the Parliament of England, it will initiate the first Space Alliance in our two planets' history.

"In keeping with this, and the naming of the Glasses that you humans brought from your depths of understanding, this ship, this hope for all humans and Adar, is named:

"The Alliance Space Ship *Vorpal Blade*."

"Oh, Holy *Maulk*," Weaver muttered. From the science section came one loud braying laugh, quickly cut off. "Oh, *grapp*."

"Like an ASS, dude," Miller whispered. "Like an ASS."

# 7

## Rule Thirty-Three:
## Never Let a Fighter Pilot Drive

"They couldn't have named it the Alliance *Warp* Ship, could they?" Captain Steven "Spectre" Blankemeier said, shaking his head. "Oh, no . . . Cast off lines aft . . ." The short-coupled former carrier commander was clearly nonplussed over the chosen name for his boat.

"Could have been worse, sir," Commander Clay White said. The XO of the ASS *Vorpal Blade* was the senior submarine officer on the boat. There had been a real tussle over which portion of the service was going to control the probable future space navy. The submarine admirals had made the convincing point that spaceships would be more similar to subs than carriers. The carrier admirals, though, had a much better lobby. So Spectre had been put through an accelerated course in submarine warfare and management while White, who had been in line to command his own sub, was seconded as an "experienced XO." "At least we're so totally covert that hardly anyone will ever *see* our name. Cast off lines aft!"

Despite the political infighting above their heads, the two officers had meshed well. Spectre was the epitome of a fighter pilot and the crew loved him, but he hadn't studied ship handling skills until he'd assumed a carrier command and despite a tour as a sub officer, which had confused the hell out of his commander, he still wanted to fight the boat like a plane. White, on the other hand, had started as an engineer and really comprehended the details of the boat. He was methodical where Spectre was daring. It was a good combination if for no other reason than White could sometimes keep his headstrong commander from totally losing it.

"Cast off lines forward . . ." Spectre continued. "Sure as *maulk* it's going to get out. Guarantee it."

"Cast off forward!" White repeated. "We're so black you couldn't find us with a really good sonar system, sir. All lines cast off."

"We just motor straight out, right?" Spectre replied. "Seriously, it had to be the Adar springing that on the President. Surely he'd have caught it?"

"Probably," White said. "Yes, sir, no tug this time for security reasons. Suggest turns for three knots."

"Make it so," Spectre said. "I can't wait to get out of this damned gravity well."

"Soon," Clay replied. "Astro, what's our course on launch?"

"Two choices, sir," Weaver said. "We can head straight for the heliopause in the direction of Alpha Cent or we can do a fly-by of Saturn. It's only about two minutes out of our way and I think the planetology department would appreciate the readings. And on that course we can get a fly-by of the bow shock."

"Make it so, Astro," Spectre replied. "I'd like to see Saturn up close again. *Spectacular.* Plan on at least one orbit. Got to give Planetology plenty of time to survey, right?"

One reason that Captain Blankemeier had been chosen was that he was an amateur astronomer. There had not been a single submarine commander with that skill. A born tourist, he was always willing to do a quick check of a planet if it didn't interfere with the overall mission.

"Can not *wait.*"

"Agree with you wholeheartedly, sir," Weaver said, trying to figure out the *wet* part of the navigation. Put him in space, he was fine. It was currents and shoals that gave him fits.

"Oh, holy *grapp*," Hattelstad muttered as they made their way down the ladder to the Marine bunks.

"You know, I love the Adar and I hate 'em," Jaenisch responded. "I can just start with the jokes now."

"'I'm sorry, Gunny, I must have had my head in my ASS,'" Crowley said. "'Let me stick my head in my ASS and see if I can think of anything.' 'Time to go back to the ASS.' It even makes *my* head hurt."

"Hey, Two-Gun, you play Dreen Strike?" Sergeant Lovelace said. Terry was the Bravo Team leader in the platoon, Crowley's direct boss.

"I've played it," Berg admitted. "But I prefer WoW or Orion."

"Figures," Crowley said. "We could use a fourth for Dreen. We keep getting creamed by Alpha First. They've got Gunga-Din as their heavy gunner and that Hindu is *wicked*."

"I've got some new WoW packs with me," Berg said. "I think I'll stay on those for a while. If the system will let me uplink."

"As long as they're valid copies," Jaenisch said, pausing at the corridor to their bunks. Everybody had followed courtesy protocol and was diving into their racks, but that didn't mean there wasn't a crowd. "There's a chip slit on the side of the screen."

"Thanks," Berg said. "You guys have been doing this for a while, haven't you?"

"We've only done two short cruises," Jaenisch said as they got to their bunks. He slid into his and then stuck his head out. "This is the first long cruise. Hopefully, nobody's gonna freak out. You might want to store all your stuff away by the time we dive."

"Because the CO drives this thing like a fighter?" Berg said.

"You have no idea."

"Good news," Julia Robertson said as she entered the mission specialist mess. "Fly-by of Saturn on the way out."

Robertson was a forty-seven-year-old skinny black woman. "People of color" were unusual enough in hard sciences but Julia was particularly unusual. A former waitress, she had gone back to school after her last child left the house. An undiagnosed sufferer from Attention Deficit Disorder, she'd found college a breeze with the right medication. Her social workers had expected her to return to the bosom of the government with a sociology degree. She'd shocked the hell out of everyone she knew when she switched to biology. She'd shocked even more people when she got her doctorate and went *back* to school to pick up two more.

"That would be me," Dr. Paul Dean said. The planetologist was a tall man who fit into the bunks on the converted sub poorly. He had long brown hair, going gray and pulled into a ponytail, and a gray-shot beard that hung nearly to the middle of his chest. A former professor at the University of Colorado, he'd always resented the Top Secret clearance the military-industrial complex forced on him ten years before. That is, right up until the MIC offered the "hippie," with doctorates in planetology, astronomy, physics, geology and astrophysics, a chance to go into space.

The former professor picked up a half-filled two-liter bottle of soda, shook it vigorously, opened up the cap to listen for a hiss, squeezed the sides in, shook it again, then took a swig. "I need to find out if we can drop a probe."

He went through the ritual a second time, took another swig and then got up and headed out of the room.

"Julia," Miriam said, waving to Mimi. "This is Mimi Jones."

"And what is a young lady like you doing on a spaceship like this?" Julia said, her eyes narrowing. "Does your mother know where you are?"

"My mother is dead, Miss Julia," Mimi replied politely. "But my Aunt Vera knows that I'm doing something with the government. And I'm here 'cause Tuffy says I'm supposed to be here," she continued, lifting the arachnoid off her lap.

"What is *that*?" Julia asked, backing up.

"That's Tuffy!" Miriam said, chortling. "You never saw Tuffy on the news?"

"You're that girl survived the bomb," Julia said, much more gently. She sat down at the table and nodded. "I suppose there might be a reason you're here. But the Lord sure do work in mysterious ways."

"That he does, Miss Julia," Mimi replied. "Dr. Weaver thinks that Tuffy might just be an angel. Even though he doesn't look like one."

"Not sure just what an angel would look like," Robertson said, considering the arachnoid carefully. "But I wouldn't say he'd be a big ole terancheler."

"I don't see why not," Miriam argued. "If Mimi went around with some glowing guy with wings on her shoulder it would cause more problems than something that looks like a stuffed toy."

"Good point," Julia admitted.

"What do you do, Miss Julia?" Mimi asked.

"Biology," Julia replied. "So till we get to a planet, if we find any rocky ones, I don't have much of a job. You know what biology is, miss?"

"A science that studies living organisms," Mimi recited. "I wrote a paper on punctuated evolution in the . . . second grade. I proposed that punctuated equilibrium only appears punctuated because of gaps in fossil data that are inherent in periods of rapid change."

"Really?" Julia said, impressed. "I don't suppose you've done any study since then?"

"Miss Julia," Mimi said, carefully, "I think that at this point, if I went to a university, I could probably get a doctorate in about any hard science you'd care to mention. I will admit that part of that is with the help of Tuffy. But he tries to just make me think . . . better, harder. He doesn't do it for me. You can feel free to quiz me on anything you'd like in regards to biology, geology, planetology, physics, astronomy or astrophysics."

"Interesting," Julia said. Her rather pronounced southern black accent had nearly disappeared. "What's the definition of species?"

"Ask a dozen biologists and you get a dozen answers," Mimi said. "According to Ernst Mayer, groups of actually or potentially interbreeding natural populations that are reproductively isolated from other such groups. I still say it doesn't explain tigers and lions, though."

"Damn, girl," Julia said, whistling. "How old *are* you?"

"Fourteen," Mimi replied. "But Tuffy says I have an old soul."

"Just one of those definitions I really like," Julia said, grinning. "I loved to trot it out for juniors that thought they knew it all about biology then point out 'species' that don't meet the definition. And I don't know what to expect on other worlds, just want to get there is all."

"And who is this young lady?" a man said from the hatchway. He was tall and broad, with a thick, neatly trimmed beard.

"Everette Beach, this is Mimi Jones," Miriam said. "Mimi, Everette. Everette is the mission specialist commander. I think that makes him your boss."

"Hello, Mr. Beach," Mimi said, standing up and shaking the man's hand.

"You're Mimi," Beach replied. "I was briefed on your presence, but only today. And this would be Tuffy. You are both welcome.

I've actually heard of you from sources besides the news. I think you supplied Professor Johnson at Caltech with the answer to his string node dilemma."

"Yes, we did," Mimi said shyly.

"I have to ask . . ." Everette said, his brow furrowing.

"I can't tell you if it was me or Tuffy," Mimi interjected. "Not will not, can not. I'm not sure myself. There are times when I don't know if I'm really really smart naturally or if it's Tuffy. Simple as that."

"Does that bother you?" Miriam asked gently.

"No, it really doesn't," Mimi said. "Tuffy has told me that we're going to be together until I die and I think we're gonna be together after. So it's not like I'm going to lose my smarts like Algernon. And being smart lets me help people. And make lots of money."

"You won't make lots of money working for the government," Julia said. "Oh, it pays well enough, but . . ."

"I'm not, actually, getting paid for this," Mimi said. "And while I know I fall in the mission specialist category, even if I don't have a specialty, I'm going to be staying close to Commander Weaver and Chief Miller."

"Any particular reason?" Beach asked.

"'Cause Tuffy says they are the causality point," Mimi replied. "And that's about all I can get out of him. He's shown me the math but string nodes is two plus two compared to that. Maybe one day I'll figure it out."

"Oh," Beach said, glancing at the other two. Julia raised her eyebrows but Miriam just smiled.

"I think you're going to fit right in here," Miriam said, patting Mimi on the leg. "You know, I read your paper on Yang-Mills Theory. Did you take into account the Looking Glass bosons connection through a virtual dimension when you worked out the mass gap? I have a hard time understanding how the LGBs enable a quantum particle with positive mass to travel faster than the speed of light. I mean, haven't we decided that the LGBs are not wormholes or even Higgs fields of the classical sense?"

"That's right," Mimi said, smiling slightly despite the leg pat. "Dr. Weaver's original assessment that the gauge bosons created were simply the Higgs field gauge particles was . . ."

»     »     »

"Congratulations, Lieutenant Commander Weaver," Commander White said, grinning. "You have successfully navigated us out of Norfolk Harbor."

The sub had reached the two-hundred fathom line, the traditional dive point for the subs coming out of Norfolk. From there to England, more or less, there wasn't anything in the way of the sub. Oh, if they dove deep enough they could hit the bottom, but it would be tough. SSBNs were designed to be *quiet* swimmers, not deep ones.

Unfortunately, the newly named *Vorpal Blade* wasn't even particularly quiet. Various concessions had had to be made for the sub to be spaceworthy, the most important of which was removing every scrap of acoustic tile from the surface of the boat. Without the acoustic tile, which muffled internal noise, it "radiated" like a rock band.

What the *Vorpal Blade* was, though, was *fast*.

"Sound dive warning," the captain said.

"All hands!" Commander White said over the enunciator. "Dive, Dive, Dive!"

"The board is straight," the chief of boat said, indicating that all the various hatches were shut.

"XO, dive the boat," the captain said, hopping up on his chair. "Make your depth one hundred meters."

"Ten percent blow," the XO said. "Fifteen degrees down plane."

"Fifteen degrees down, aye," the plane controller said.

"Blow complete," the COB said.

"Descending through fifty meters," the plane said. "Seventy-five . . ."

"Level off on one hundred," the XO ordered.

"Leveling," the plane replied. "One hundred meters depth."

"Astro?" the captain asked.

"Recommend course of one-five-seven," Weaver replied.

"XO, come to course one-five-seven."

"Right ten degrees rudder," the XO said. "Make your course one-five-seven."

"Ten degrees rudder, aye," the helmsman said. "One-five-seven, aye."

"Why one-five-seven?" the captain asked.

"Last report from SOSUS indicated the Akulas were waiting

for us at nine-zero," Weaver replied. "Of course, they're probably picking us up all ready."

"Point," the captain said sourly.

While the Cold War was no longer going on, Russia still maintained an interest in the American fleet, and especially in its submarines. They still sent attack subs to stake out American harbors and try to get hull shots, sonar profiles or any data at all on the American subs. With the Ohios they were still mostly failing; the subs that the *Blade* had been made from were ghosts.

The *Blade* really had them puzzled, though. It appeared to be converted for inshore, the term of art was littoral, combat. But removing the acoustic tiles made no sense. Why make a ship designed to approach enemy coastlines *noisy*. So the Russians had been sending an increasing number of attack subs to try to figure out this new Ami sub. The one thing they'd discovered was that the *Blade* was very *very* fast.

"XO, disengage propeller drive and close prop cowling," the captain ordered.

The two orders were nowhere in any other submarine's lexicon and the latter was one of the reasons that the *Blade* wasn't very quiet. For various reasons, not the least of which was that they tended to rotate fast enough to spin off when the *Blade* got up to full speed, the propellers of the *Blade* were housed in a sliding door cowling system that was similar to the cowling kept over the props while in wet dock with the exception of the fact that they opened and closed by pushing buttons on the bridge.

"Props disengaged and closed," the XO said after a moment.

"Engage supercavitation field," the captain said, satisfaction in his voice. "Make power for one-two-zero knots. Engage space drive."

"One-two-zero knots, aye," the XO said. "Engage supercavitation system. Pilot, engage space drive. Power to one-two-zero knots."

"What the hell is that?" Miller asked as the strong flow noise started up and the sub began to shake. Being in a sub was always nervous making; hearing one apparently crashing was worse.

"They engaged the space drive," Captain Michael "M.E." MacDonald said. He was currently regarding the chief warrant officer with interest. "When we start to really speed up it gets noisy. I only know that because I've *been* on this boat for shake-down ops."

"And I haven't, sir," Miller said, nodding.

"I understand why you are here," MacDonald said. "What I'm not sure about is what to do with you."

"Not sure myself, sir," Miller admitted. "I know as much as you do. Tuffy wants me here. The only suggestion I have is that I think I should stay close to Commander Weaver."

"Any reason why?" the captain asked. "Besides being old buddies."

"Not sure how to explain, sir," Miller admitted, frowning. "Commander Weaver, well, I'm pretty sure he's going to play out more of a role than just navigating us around. I think we both know he's going to be consulted on just about anything that we encounter. I know that there are probably astronomers and astrophysicists on this boat with better credentials than his. But Weaver gets things *right*. You know what I mean on a military level, sir. There are guys who get things *right* in combat. Well, Weaver gets them *right* when it's . . . weird stuff."

"Like ship-eating monsters?" MacDonald asked.

"Like I have no idea, sir," the warrant said. "But I'm pretty sure that when it happens, we're all going to be pucker factoring. And if anybody's going to figure out how to save our ass, sir, it's going to be Weaver. And, with all due respect, sir, when he thinks something needs to be shot or blown up, he's going to scream 'Miller!' not 'MacDonald!' He thinks he's a naval officer but I guarantee he hasn't got chain of command in his bones. My suggestion, sir, is that you just tell me to tag along with Weaver. That way he's got a guy who *does* have a clue about ground combat to . . . suggest alternate methods."

"Gotcha, Chief," the captain said, grinning. "Okay, that's how we'll work it. I'm appointing you the chief of security detail for Commander Weaver, especially in the event of his leaving the boat. I'll speak to the captain about how to integrate your position while on-board, but if Weaver leaves, you're his bodyguard. Work?"

"Works, sir," Miller said.

"All hands, prepare for water exit," the 1-MC said.

"Hang on," MacDonald said, grabbing at the arms of his station-chair as music started booming over the 1-MC.

"Who in the *hell* is playing *music?*" Miller asked, grabbing at his own chair's arms. He'd noticed that the chair was bolted to the deck. He suspected he was about to find out why.

"Who *could* order music?" the Marine CO said. "Like I said, hang on."


"There it is."

Captain Zabukov looked over at his sonar technician as the senior petty officer held up a hand.

"I'm surprised you can't hear it through the hull," the CPO said bitterly. Shadowing the American boomer, even as noisy as it was, was not easy. But now, as it had the last three times they shadowed it, it had begun to play that rock and roll crap. And everyone in the crew knew what that meant.

"Position?" Captain Zabukov asked.

"Two-One-Four, Control," the CPO said, still bitterly. "Depth one hundred meters, more or less. You sure you cannot hear it through the hull? I am having to crank down my gain."

"Periscope depth!"

"Periscope depth, aye," the XO, Senior Lieutenant Ivanakov, said. "Five degree rise on bow planes."

The Russian Akula was still the most advanced attack sub, outside of the Americans', in the world. And there were arguments on both sides. The Akula depended upon depth and speed to survive; it could dive deeper and drive faster than just about any other submarine on Earth. The trade-off, however, was noise. While the Akula was not noisy by any normal average, it was much noisier than an American 688, much less the Seawolf or Ohio series.

That was until the Americans came up with this new bastard Ohio. The damned thing was, if anything, *noisier* than an Akula. It had . . . bits protruding. Following it was like following a blind man in an autumn forest. But then, that skipper would play his damned music and . . .

"Get me on the surface," the captain snarled. "Sonar, what is its heading?"

"Zero, one eight," Sonar called back. "It's headed towards the *Zama*."

The latter Akula was one of three that Northern Fleet had sent to pinpoint the new American sub and determine *how* it was disappearing.

"Captain, what are you doing?" Ivanakov asked, worried. He

had heard the captain's theory on the new American boomer and he hoped that he was one of the few. If higher command ever heard it they would laugh the captain out of the service.

"I'm going to get a hull shot," the captain said, hitting the control to raise the periscope. "A very special one. Come to course zero, one, eight, periscope depth. Max power. Now!"

"I hope like hell they get the point," the captain said, grinning, as the music boomed. It wasn't just being played on the boat, but broadcast through the sonar. It was a clear warning to everyone to get the hell out of the way. The A—Oh, hell, the *Vorpal Blade* was coming through!

"Yes, sir," Commander Clay said sourly. A submariner to his bones, he believed in stealth over everything. But he had to admit that the music had at least successfully driven off the whales that they might otherwise have hit.

The problem was that while going this fast, the sub was absolutely blind. Sure, there wasn't *supposed* to be anything in the way, not at one hundred meters. But that didn't preclude other subs, especially the Russians, being in the way. Or dolphins or whales. Or, hell, a school of herring! If they hit *anything* at this speed, well, it wasn't going to be pretty.

So the captain played music, practically *taunting* the Russians. It just ached in his bubblehead bones.

"Prepare for water separation," the captain said.

"Helm, plane, all converted?" the XO asked.

"Helm converted, aye!"

"Plane, planes retracted, all converted, aye!"

"Captain has the conn," the captain said. "Helm has piloting control."

"Helm, piloting control, aye," the plane controller said, lifting his hands away from the plane controls. Under water the boat required multiple drivers for the various control surfaces. Once under space drive, the helmsman took over as sole pilot. The planesman, however, remained in position as a "co" in the event of injury to the helmsman.

"Pilot, two-zero-zero knots! Let's take this bird for a *ride!*"

"The music has started," the sonar tech for the Akula *Zama* said.

"Hmmm . . ." Captain Borodinich said, musingly. "According to reports, that means that they are preparing to engage their new speed drive, Senior Lieutenant Vaslaw. What do you think of that?"

"I am wondering where they are going, sir," the XO said, swallowing nervously.

"So are we all," the captain replied, nodding. "You are wondering, I am wondering, the admiral is wondering. But this time, Senior Lieutenant, we shall see where they are going. Do you know why?"

"Yes, sir," the lieutenant said. "But I was speaking of which bit of water they are going to be *passing* through, sir. Sonar, have they initiated drive, yet?" As he asked there was a hollow *"boing"* off of the hull and he flinched.

"No, si . . . Senior Lieutenant," the sonar tech said, swallowing. He had served with Vaslaw under their *previous* captain. The new captain's habit of instituting damned near Soviet era formality, *Senior Lieutenant* this and *Master Chief Sonar Technician* that, was *not* popular. Nor was his tendency towards either stupidity or reckless arrogance. Or both. Nobody could be *that* stupid, after all.

"You understand my purpose in being here?" the captain replied, surprised. "Instead of trailing as the other boats are doing?"

"You chose to track them from forward, Captain," Vaslaw said, very nearly snarled. "Sonar, position and direction!"

"That is for me to ask, Senior Lieutenant," the captain snapped. "I suspect that you do not *care* for my plan, but you *will* support it, is that clear?"

"Sir," the lieutenant replied. Which was neither agreement nor disagreement.

"Direction . . . one-one-three," the sonar tech said, tapping at keys and ignoring the captain's input. Thank God they had finally gotten a decent computer on the boat. When he had started in his position, it had been that Soviet era *maulk*. *Tubes* if you could believe it. They still didn't have the filtering and processing of the American boats, but when they could spot them they could at least lock them down without reference to a bunch of pins and slide-rules. "Course . . . two-nine-five!"

"Captain, it's headed right *at* us!" the lieutenant said. "We must change course!"

"And so we will," the captain said calmly. "We will parallel their track. They have become predictable. They point a certain direction and then go fast, like some pilot taking off from a runway. I think it's because their commander, Blankemeier, yes? He was a carrier pilot. No finesse, yes? So we shall parallel them and find where they go. Come to course one-one-five. . . ."

The boat's pilot, prepared for the order, whipped his wheel around, hard, causing the submarine to bank like an aircraft and filling the boat with the noise of unsecured gear rattling into the corridors. Most of the conn barely had time to grab stanchions as the boat stood on its side.

"Not so hard!" the captain snarled. "And I said *one-one-five*! Not one-eight-zero! Go to full power as soon as this ham-handed cow gets us back on course."

"American speed coming up," Sonar called as another "*bong*" rattled off the titanium hull of the boat. "Continuing to use active sonar!"

"Captain," the lieutenant pleaded. "The reason for all this noise is clear! The Americans are saying 'we are coming through! Get out of the way!' And we *should*!"

"And *because* you have been, we still do not know where these Amis go when they *do* to go silent!" the captain snapped. "How they can simply *disappear*? Because none of you *cowards* were willing to get close enough to them! Which is why Northern Fleet has sent *me*, yes? Sonar, where are they, now?"

"Coming up from our rear," Sonar said as the hull of the Akula began to thrum from flow. "Speed over eighty knots. I am only able to track them through their own sonar; ours is being washed out with flow noise. Oh, and I hear their music . . . It's dopplering . . ."

"Damned arrogant Americans," the captain muttered. "We shall track them this time. . . ."

"Captain, they have been tracked doing over three *hundred* knots!" the lieutenant replied with a pleading tone. "We need to get out of the way. . . ."

"I said *silence*," Borodinich snapped.

"Speed . . . over one hundred knots . . ." Sonar called. "Higher I think. Perhaps as much as two hundred. I'm getting so many harmonics . . . Wait . . . Can you hear them . . . ?"

"What is that?" the captain asked. Every submariner is attuned to the rhythm of their boat. Any ping can be a problem, any extra vibration could be a sign of failure. So the strange rumbling was ... disquieting.

"That is them," Sonar replied, pulling off his headphones and bracing himself. "All you have to do now is *listen!*"

It was more than the sound of an approaching train. The lieutenant had once watched a show about tornados. In it, a man had been trapped under an underpass as a tornado passed over. It was like that. No, stronger, as if a hurricane could be compressed into the size of a truck and it was getting closer. The Akula was already going nearly fifty knots but the sound was getting louder. And over it ...

"Is that music?" the captain asked, looking at the lieutenant.

"Yes, sir ..." Vaslaw said, unhappily. "It's—"

"Never mind," the captain snapped, his appearance of calm starting to crumble. "Come to course—"

Senior Lieutenant Vladimir Vaslaw was no fool. He had been on this very sub when the Amis had last passed and had been close enough to, barely, hear that dread sound, to faintly catch the tune that, against all probability, was blasting forth through the very metal of the American craft. Now ... it was much louder. So he grabbed a stanchion and clung to it like a limpet as the captain's words were overwhelmed with noise. And then the wave hit.

It is said that boats are a hole in the water into which money is poured. But in the case of the *Vorpal Blade*, she was going over two hundred knots, creating not so much a wake as a super-cavitation vacuum behind her, a gap filled with a mixture of water turned to air and air turning to water. And as she passed, the weight of three hundred feet of ocean, rather than money, collapsed that temporary hole.

The effect wasn't that of a tornado or a hurricane. Tornados are dirty, hurricanes are wet, but neither is pure water. And water has many interesting properties. It is, among other things, incompressible. So it transmits shocks quite well. And there aren't many greater shocks than a submarine-sized pocket of water collapsing at very nearly the speed of sound. Were it not for the brilliant modifications to the Ohio-class submarine, more specifically, the long blade or shock initiator on the bow, the effect would be many times more pronounced—two orders of magnitude worse.

The Akula was wrenched through the water like a leaf blown by a gale, tossed on its side and hammered until its hull rang like a tocsin. The *only* thing that saved its life was that the hull was one of the strongest on the earth and they weren't, really, all that deep.

That didn't help the personnel and equipment in the boat, though, as the wake of the passing boomer shook them like a terrier at a rat. Anyone not buckled in, and the only people on the boat so secured were the pilot and the buoyancy operator, was thrown around like a bowling pin.

Lieutenant Vaslaw managed to hold onto his pole by wrapping both legs around it. He still slammed his face into it as the boat stood first on one side, then the other, and then he *swore* directly vertical. It was hard to tell since most of the lights blew out almost at once in a shower of sparks.

It might have been the latter that saved them. The direct-drive turbines had not shut down with the rest of the boat, the robust nuclear reactor had not scrammed, and they were probably the only thing that kept them from being sunk. As it was, as the emergency lighting started to come back on-line he could see that they were at an up-angle, canted to the side but ascending.

He could also see the captain on the other side of the conn with his head up against a bulkhead. He could be unconscious or dead. Frankly, Lieutenant Vaslaw didn't give a damn.

"Blow all tanks," the lieutenant said, shaking his head and wiping at the blood from his nose. "Come to speed of one third. Surface."

"Surface, aye!" the pilot said, happily righting the boat and scrambling for clear air. There were still currents aplenty that roiled the sub, but he could work with that.

"Multiple leaks," damage control called. The operator was on his knees and shaking his head but he still had his headphones on. "Multiple injuries."

"Great," Vaslaw growled. "Tell the medics when they're done with the rest, they need to check the captain. Until then, and I *did* not say this, I'd rather he remain unconscious."

Vaslaw shook his head again and then sighed. They were lucky. They would see the sky again. Too many other Russian submariners had not been so lucky. He should be happy.

But he rather liked rock music. He had not been really aware during the last days of the Soviets but he had complete collections of rock groups from that period.

However, his precious copy of Europe's single, "The Final Countdown" was going for the dumpster; he never *ever* wanted to hear that song again.

Not after hearing it dopplering towards him, and then away, as the several thousand ton submarine was tossed around like a leaf. The guitar solo was distinctive.

Damn those Americans. . . .

"Ten degrees up!" the captain shouted over the flow noise.

"Conn, Sonar," Lieutenant Sousa said. "They think they actually heard something over the flow! It sounded like a shipwreck!" There was a sound like a ripple of rain from forward. Small fish were dying in large numbers.

"Well, it wasn't us!" Spectre yelled, grinning and bending his knees as the gees hit. The boat was headed up now, fast. As it started to level he shook his head.

"Pilot, *twenty* degrees up!"

"Twenty degrees, aye!" the helmsman yelled, grinning. They weren't in space, yet, but he was, by God, driving a spaceship. What was it somebody in the mess had called it? A quadraphibian. Water, land, air *and* space.

"Separation!" the XO yelled as the noise fell away. "Whew!" They were in the air. No chance of hitting a whale anymore. They'd hit a school of herring one time and he thought the bow was going to cave in.

"Tactical, what's on the scope?" the captain asked.

"All clear, sir," Lieutenant Souza said. "No radar emitters in range."

"Pilot, make your height one-zero-zero angels for pressure check," the CO said, sitting back in his chair. "Maintain angle of ascent."

"So how long do we deal with this?" Mimi asked, holding onto the table to keep from sliding off the bench. Pots and pans had cascaded across the floor and Miss Julia had nearly slid off.

"The drive is very strange," Everette replied. "While there is gravity, it lets gravity through and has limited effect on inertial actions. So we take G forces in maneuvers. Once gravity falls off, it engages a pseudo-gravity system and begins inertial compensation. So no matter how strenuous the maneuver, we barely feel it. But the *takeoff* . . ."

"The captain don't even have to do it this way," Julia said sourly. "He just does it for *fun*."

"Now, now, Dr. Robertson," Everette said. "We shouldn't question the tactical decisions of the boat's commander. . . ."

"CO's nuts," MacDonald said, leaning back in his chair. "F-18 pilot."

"Gotcha," Miller said. He had his feet braced on the front of the locked-down desk and was fairly comfortable. "Glad we didn't hit anything."

"One of these days we're gonna," MacDonald said. "And that's gonna really suck."

"Suck more if the Russkis figured out what was going on," Miller pointed out.

Captain Zabukov had surfaced the boat and was on his sail, a pair of night vision binoculars glued to his eyes. He knew that they had fallen well behind the Ami sub, but it was possible that he could—

"There!" Lieutenant Ivanakov said, pointing to the southeast.

"*Yob tvoyu mat* . . ." the captain said, quietly.

"I assume that that was not directed at me, sir," the lieutenant said. "*Bozhe moi!* You were *right!*"

"And you think that they are going to *believe* us, yes?" the captain said. "That the Amis have a *flying* submarine? And where has it been flying to, yes? The *stars?*"

"Store your *maulk* if it's out," Jaenisch yelled.

"It's all stored," Berg said.

"Okay, here's the deal," Jaenisch continued, rolling out of his rack and climbing up to Berg's. "Make sure your *maulk* is stored. Except. There are sick bags here," he said, opening up one of the small storage compartments. "Make sure you've got at least one available. The CO's going to go to full power underwater to outrun the Akulas. You'll know we're starting the speed run when the music starts. Then he's going to jump out of the water. You just hang onto the zero-gee straps. Keep your bunk elevated. If you've got to puke, puke into the bag and *seal* it. Keep your door closed and your circulator on high in case somebody misses their bag. When we're out of gravity it will get better. But as soon as we're out of gravity we've got chores to do."

"Aye, aye," Berg said, grinning. "Sounds like fun."

"You wish," Jaenisch said as music started pounding over the 1-MC. "*Grapp*, here we go." He jumped to the deck and rolled into his bunk, closing the door.

All down the corridor, doors that had been open were closing and Berg quickly followed suit. Then, just to be sure, he didn't just hold onto the zero-gee straps but pulled them across his legs and midsection, cinching them down. As he did he began to feel acceleration pressing him back into his bunk.

He grabbed the straps though when it felt like the boat was coming apart.

"Holy *grapp!*" he shouted, not that anyone could hear him. All he could think was that the sub, which was clearly hammering through the water, was *not* designed for this sort of punishment. If anything went wrong, they were going to die. Probably fast, but not necessarily. Messily, for sure.

Then the sub nosed up, pressing him downward harder than any combat flight he'd ever been on. Suddenly, the rumbling stopped and for a moment that made him even more worried.

"It's okay," Jaen yelled. "We're in atmosphere. Hold on, though."

As he said that, the sub dropped and banked, pulling more gees, high positive ones then dropping through free fall and into negative.

It was like being on a roller coaster where the only thing you could see was a blank steel wall a few inches from your face. Already nauseated, Berg grabbed the puke bag and put it to use.

He mag sealed that one and grabbed another as the sub went through a series of maneuvers that seemed designed to make him puke. Finally, though, the sensation of madcap flight stopped and things settled. In fact, it felt like they were back in port.

"Whew," he said, sealing the second bag and kicking up his air recirculator. As soon as most of the smell was gone he opened his bunk.

"That was nasty," Berg said. "Is it always like that?"

"Pretty much," Jaenisch said, rolling out of his bunk. "We're supposed to go clean our M-10s in the mess. First Platoon is doing Wyvern maintenance in the missile compartment, Third is on sleep cycle."

"Lucky Third," Berg said, rolling out of his bunk and dropping to the deck.

"Come on," Jaenisch said, walking towards the rear hatch. "We're first up and we need to clear the compartment."

"Leveling off at angels one-zero-zero," the pilot said. The gravitational and "G" effect had practically disappeared. Down was the deck. Up was the overhead. Even the level off couldn't be felt.

"Pressure check," the CO said, standing up and walking over to the board.

The chief of boat ignored him as he dialed up on the pressure in the boat. The CO was, after all, the CO. But a good sub skipper would have let the *grapping chief* handle this. He flexed his jaw to let his ears pop as the pressure in the boat came up. After the speed run, hell at any time, there was a chance that a seal could have popped. The pressure check was designed to detect that.

"Pressure steady after one minute," the COB said.

"Roger. XO, announce all silence for pressure check."

"All hands, all hands. Silent running for pressure check."

"What?" Miller asked.

"Shhh," the Marine replied. "Listen for hissing. It actually works."

"Pressure check?" Berg asked.

"Doesn't count with us," Jaen said. "It's a crew announcement."

"Sorry, they didn't cover it at Paris Island," Berg said, grinning.

"God, I want to be there the first time some DI has to," Hattelstad said. "'Upon atmospheric exit your ship's skipper *will* call for pressure check to ensure *air* integrity. This command means *nothing* to Marines, for we are hard as *steel*. *Space* Marines therefore neither *leak* at-moh-sphere nor *need* at-moh-sphere!'"

"I don't hear anything," Mimi said, blinking.

"We wouldn't in here," Julia said, shaking her head vigorously. She hadn't been able to clear her left ear and it was painful.

"This room is in the middle of the add-ons they put in the missile room. But there are sailors moving around listening for leaks. They'll dial down the pressure in just a minute."

"All sections check clear for leakage," the XO said. "Pressure drop, nominal. Space drive nominal, ardune generator nominal. Heat sink . . . nominal."

The last was important. The engines, various electronics, and human bodies installed in the boat created a huge amount of heat. Underwater it was dispersed into that magnificent heat sink molecule $H_2O$. In space, the heat dissipated poorly.

The answer was a new and innovative heat sink. Installed in the slots that on a normal sub held the towed array sonar were two extensible cylinders of, essentially, glass with some iron and a few other trace elements thrown in. Heat from the sub would be pumped into them until they were boiling hot. The mixture of molten silicon dioxide (glass) and other elements were perfect reservoirs for thermal energy until the molten tubes reached near vaporization state. At that point, the boat would have to find a deep space, very cold, spot and "chill." To extend the heat capacity of the tubes they were surrounded in liquid metal heat-pipes that flowed out to the underside of the spaceship. The heat-pipes would radiate some of the energy into space and the liquid would cool and be flowed back over the molten glass tubes. This only bought time; eventually the thermal load became far more than the thermal management system could handle and "chilling" would be necessary.

"Recommend we come to heading two-one-eight or head out, sir," Weaver said. "We're going to be in range of NASA sensors in Australia in two minutes."

"XO, are we all clear for space ops?" the CO asked.

"Certify clear for space ops," the XO said.

"Astrogation?"

"Recommend come to heading one seven eight, mark one dot three. Two hundred G delta-V to two-zero-zero kilometers per second. We'll be to two planetary diameters in two minutes and seven seconds at that acceleration and velocity, then we can go to Warp One. Maintain Whiskey Two Dot Five for niner seconds at Warp One, then turn to heading two-zero-five increase to Warp Three. Saturn orbit on that heading is seven seconds."

"Why not a direct course?" the CO asked.

"Alpha Centauri is currently on the back side of the sun, sir," Weaver said. "We sort of need to fly around the system to get there. And if we cut closer than that course, we risk hitting Mars. Not close or anything, but I'd prefer some margin. We could go up and over if you'd prefer. . . ."

"No, that sounds good," the CO said, shaking his head. "Make it so, XO. I would prefer to avoid the edges of space until we reach Saturn. But tell everybody we are *leaving*."

# 8

## Taste the Soprano

"All hands. Now leaving Earth orbit. Last shot of Earth on the viewscreens, now."

"Gotta watch this," Everette said, keying the TV in the compartment on with his implant. As they watched, the Earth started to fall away from the view. Then the image changed to a rear camera view and the planet slowly started to shrink.

"I'm not sure if this is scary or just really cool," Mimi said. "I think both."

"I agree, honey chile," Julia said.

"I think it's cool," Miriam said as the planet got smaller and smaller. "And if *you* don't have much to do until we reach a planet, I don't have *anything* to do unless we find aliens. Except talk to Tchar."

"I thought I saw an Adar," Mimi said. "Where is he?"

"Engineering," Miriam replied. "We're not allowed in there. He bunks in Section D, aft. That's right by the entrance to the missile compartment and the shortest distance to engineering. He has a real problem moving around the boat cause he's so big."

"Where are we allowed?" Mimi asked.

"This area," Everette answered. "That is, the entire mission section, but I'd say you should steer clear of security in general.

101

The sick bay, which is just off of this section to starboard. And the away pod, which is on top of the boat."

"Stand by for warp entry," the 1-MC proclaimed.

"This is so cool," Miriam said as the camera shot changed to a wide angle apparently out of the front of the sub. The stars, which had been pinpoints, suddenly began to lengthen and brighten, shifting into long strands, red towards the front and shading to blue. Then they snapped back to normal, but they were now, appreciably, moving.

"You can see out?" Mimi asked. "I thought we were in an alternate universe? At least, that's the math."

"The drive automatically cycles," Everette said. "We're actually jumping very short distances, then dropping back into normal space. But each cycle is in nanoseconds, just enough time, in fact, for certain wavelengths of light to pass the barrier. So it looks as if we're in normal space. None of the wavelengths, interestingly enough, are useful militarily. You can't make a high energy laser out of any of them. And the cycling is too high for cosmic rays to penetrate. But we can still see out. It's a very neat system."

"Something's happening," Miriam said, pointing at the TV.

The view was slewing and suddenly it zoomed.

"Mars," Everette said, nodding. "I guess we're going close enough it was worth a look."

"No chance of landing and taking a couple more samples?" Julia asked.

"Not this trip."

"More samples?" Mimi asked.

"We've had five shakedown trips," Julia said.

"We've landed on Mars, the moon and Titan, one of the moons of Jupiter," Captain MacDonald said. "The last two were *damned* cold. You could feel it right through the Wyvern armor. Next, I think you need to meet the rest of the security team. *That* is still shaking down."

"Marines and Special Forces?" Miller said, grinning. "I can imagine."

"You guys haven't got anything better to do than clean weapons?" Master Sergeant Steve Runner asked.

Steve was a sixteen-year veteran of the Special Forces and had come to the conclusion that he needed his head examined for volunteering for this mission. With medium build, brown hair and brown eyes, he'd fit in well in Afghanistan once upon a time. But the hammering the Islamics had taken from the Dreen had pretty much taken the juice out of the World-Wide Jihad. Frankly, there weren't many wars worth fighting on Earth anymore.

He'd picked up a bachelors in geology through the Army, mostly using it to bank on his retirement. The "suggestion" that he volunteer for this mission had come out of the blue. But, hey, going to space. How bad could it be? So he had to baby-sit some doctorate types. They hadn't told him he was going to have to deal with jarheads.

"At least we're not playing nursemaid to a bunch of eggheads," Jaenisch replied.

"Nope, you're going to be out on point playing red shirt," Runner said, grinning. "Better make sure them M10s are dialed in."

The M10 was a .308 version of the venerable M-16 series of weapons. During the brief war with the Dreen, it had become apparent that fighting them took something with more stopping power than the 5.56 mm rounds the M-16 series fired. The ammo weight went *way* up for the same number of rounds, but then again being able to stop a charging howler butt-cold was worth it. For that matter, they'd proven in Africa that it could kill a leopard pretty cleanly or a lion if you pumped enough rounds into the things. But one team member, who had been medically retired, also learned that they weren't worth a damn on Cape Buffalo.

"Me, I've got a date with a probe," Runner continued as he exited the mess. "Don't miss the Saturn fly-by. It's gonna be good."

"You can't walk on it, you can't breathe it and you can't shoot it," Hattelstad said. "Besides, we've seen it." The short, slim red-headed gunner clicked together the pieces of his Squad Support Weapon and jacked the grenade launcher. "What the *grapp* do we care about Saturn?"

"I'd rather see Mars," Berg said, reassembling his M10. "Glad we caught it on the fly-by."

"What's so special about Mars?" Hattelstad asked.

"Saturn was the god of partying," Bergstresser said, jacking back the bolt of the rifle and then letting it fly forward. "Mars was the god of War. God of the Marines."

»       »       »

"Doctor Dean," Runner said, nodding at the scientist. "You sent word you needed a hand?"

It had taken nearly ten minutes to make his way from the mission specialists' quarters to the torpedo room where the probes were maintained. Clearly Dr. Dean was unhappy about the time.

"You're *finally* here," Dean said. "Set the oscilloscope up and make certain that the output of the ACP is following design spec. And then I need a readout on the GCMS instrument heater output. This thing wasn't quite complete when we got it from APL."

"Uh, ACP?" Runner looked around the room thinking he should recognize the acronym.

"Damnit boy, the Aerosol Collector and Pyrolyser needs to be checked out. Then check the wiring connections for the heater on the Gas Chromatograph and Mass Spectrometer!" Dr. Dean said, scowling.

"Yes, Doctor," Runner said, trying, as always, *not* to say it with a German accent. Runner didn't mind getting *maulk*: He was SF, he ate *maulk* for breakfast. But condescending *maulk* was another matter all together. He bit his tongue and set about the task of connecting the ACP and GCMS modules to the probe.

After nearly an hour of last-second modifications and unapproved preflight checkouts Dr. Dean proclaimed the probe ready for service. Flight readiness review teams at NASA's Jet Propulsion Laboratory or at Johns Hopkins would have had a conniption fit and probably fallen over dead from the fact that a high level Ph.D. and a Special Forces NCO prepped the spacecraft for flight. Russian counterparts on the other hand, would have smiled, patted them on the back, and started shooting cognac at a job well done. The *Blade* was breaking through multiple paradigms of America's views of space exploration.

"Is there anything else, Doctor?" Runner asked as the probe slid into the tube.

"No, you can go," the planetologist replied, not bothering to turn around. "Next time, though, I expect you to be here when I call. I know you're military but in the *scientific* world, time is of the essence."

"I'll try to keep that in mind, Doctor," the master sergeant said as he made his way out of the torpedo room. The worst part was, his job was keeping this asshole *alive*.

>>        >>        >>

"Probe ready on Tube Number Four," the tactical officer said. Lieutenant Souza was grinning madly. "Ready to launch space probe, sir!"

"Ready Tube Four," the XO replied.

"Tube primed," the launch controller replied. "Tube Four ready to launch."

"Launch probe."

The boat shuddered as the probe was fired from the torpedo tube and began its descent to Saturn's atmosphere.

The probe was essentially identical to the Huygens probe that was part of the larger Cassini spacecraft launched many years before. Once clear of the tube, gyros rotated the rear of the probe in the direction necessary to slow its progress and a rocket fired, slowing the probe so that Saturn's gravity could capture it.

The entire assembly remained together, the retro rockets firing from time to time to slow its fall or correct its entry, until it hit the outer shreds of the deep Saturnian atmosphere. Then the "mission package" detached from the rocket, which was left to plummet away into the depths.

The mission package, though, deployed a parachute, initially just a thin ribbon of high-tensile cloth, that slowed its descent as automated systems began air sampling. The GCMS was an only slightly updated copy of the Huygens package. The instrument was a versatile gas chemical analyzer that could measure a wide variety of chemicals and their concentration in the Saturnian atmosphere. The gas chromatograph of the system made fine measurements of the gas content, then implemented a heater to create pyrolysis products that would then be more finely measured by the ACP. The ACP would also suck in some of the Saturn atmospheric gasses through various filters and cook them as well to decompose them into more basic materials that could be analyzed via the GCMS. The system worked flawlessly and generated the most detailed understanding of the gas giant planet's atmosphere that mankind had ever had.

The most important component of the mission was locality. The receiving station was the *Blade* and it was very close to the probe when compared to the distance between Cassini-Huygens and Earth. The close range allowed the probe to connect to the *Blade* with a data rate similar to broadband Internet as opposed to the few bits per second available to the Cassini-Huygens probe. Therefore the probe could pump data continuously as it plunged deeper and deeper into the vapors of Saturn's atmosphere without worrying about overloading the memory of the *Blade*. The *Blade* could also send real-time commands to the descent probe that couldn't have been done from Earth. Actual data points only meters apart along the descent trajectory were taken and a constant optimization of the probe's descent was maintained. The difference of actually *being* there and tossing a robot from Earth was immediately apparent.

Most people on the boat, though, weren't paying much attention to the "take" . . .

"Thank you for letting us up here, Captain," Mimi said, staring up through the boat's sole viewport.

To drop the probe the *Vorpal Blade* had actually come *inside* the orbit of Saturn's rings. From Earth they were just a thick band of white. Up close the rings, composed mostly of ice with some rocky material, reflected a billion colors like a rainbow. Light from Saturn shone on them as well as the light from the distant sun, causing an effulgently rippling coruscation across the surface.

The light reflected down into the conn, giving the normally austere compartment a glory that was rare indeed.

"You are very welcome, Miss Jones," the captain said. He was still unsure about having an underage female on-board, but it was fun to give her the treat. He'd actually let several of the mission specialists onto the conn to enjoy the sight. Select members of the crew had been let in earlier. He wasn't about to deny the sight of this vista to the youngster.

"We have about another thirty minutes until the probe completes its descent," the captain continued. "But there are other people who want to come up and see. It's not the same on the videos. So you only have fifteen minutes."

"That's okay," Mimi said, turning away from the sight and smiling at him. "I've seen enough. You can let someone else up."

"You can stay . . ." the captain said.

"I've seen it," Mimi said, shaking her head. "I can recall it perfectly any time I'd like. Give someone else the chance."

"Very well," the CO said, nodding.

"Hello, Dr. Weaver," Mimi said, looking over at Bill.

"Hi, Mimi," Weaver replied. "But it's commander on the conn."

"Yes, sir," Mimi said. "I heard that we're going to do an investigation of the heliopause and the bow shock."

The heliopause was the point where the solar wind stopped holding off the ISM, the interstellar medium, the thinly diffused helium and hydrogen that filled interstellar space. The solar wind, a collection of rays and charged particles blown out by the sun, held back the ISM from entering the solar system. And the solar system was not stationary; it was moving "spinward" with the galaxy. So the wind, blowing out, hit the interstellar medium especially hard in the spinward direction. The heliopause was therefore compressed on that side so that the whole zone looked much like an egg with the "flatter" side to spinward and the elongated side anti-spinward.

At the point where the solar wind stopped holding off the ISM to spinward was a particularly compressed zone of hydrogen and helium called the bow shock. Thin by comparison with planetary atmospheres, it nonetheless was a relatively volatile region. Bill had planned pausing in the area to do some sampling, but had not anticipated problems with it.

"Yes," Bill said, frowning. "The Pioneers and Voyagers have been acting weird. NASA wants to know why."

"I would advise you to travel carefully in that area," Mimi said, frowning in turn. "You know the theories of the causes, right?"

"Either magnetic build-up or gravity fluctuations," Bill said, nodding. "And?"

"I . . . I'm a proponent of the latter," Mimi said carefully. "There is theory that indicates that gravity acts differently around stars than in interstellar space at a fundamental level."

"Know that one," Bill said. "You're worried about fluctuations? We'll be in warp, we should be fine."

"There's a possibility that the fluctuations could be . . . strong," Mimi said. "You could be looking at gravitational standing waves of two gravities or higher."

"You sure?" Bill asked, gesturing with his chin at Tuffy.

"Tuffy . . . lets me figure out things on my own," Mimi said. "But if you hit a high gravitational fluctuation—"

"The boat could come out of warp," Bill said, his eyes closing in thought. "Hell, the damned sphere could get pulled out of the mag field. It'll take the shock, but . . ."

"I would advise going carefully," Mimi said. "Especially around the bow shock." She nodded to the captain and then walked out of the compartment whereupon the COB let one of the other mission specialists into the conn.

"I'm starting to figure out why she's along," the captain said.

"Yes, sir," Bill replied.

"You know each other," the CO said.

"I was there the night she walked in out of the middle of ground zero at UCF with that thing on her shoulder," Bill said. "Her whole world destroyed, her home destroyed, her mother dead, and calm as you please. Shortly thereafter I think I went to the place Tuffy comes from. And I'd say that it's the strangest place in the universe, were it even *in* the universe."

"XO has the con," the CO said.

"XO has the con," the XO repeated.

"Join me in my office, Commander," the CO said.

"Sir."

They climbed up a ladder on the port side of the conn and down the narrow corridor to the CO's office. The CO crossed it and flopped down behind his desk, waving at a chair.

"Bill, explain to me this thing with gravi . . . What she said."

"Gravitational standing waves," Bill replied. "You've been through a cut in the intercoastal in a small boat, sir?"

"Yes," the CO said, frowning.

"Well, when the tide's running . . ." Bill said.

"Oh, you get standing waves," the CO said, nodding. "I've seen 'em run ten feet sometimes. So the boat's going to go up and down?"

"These are going to be going more like . . . back and forth," Bill said, frowning and looking at the overhead. "I think. I've seen the theory but until Mimi pointed it out I wasn't concerned about it. The gravity out here is so diffuse that big standing waves were, I thought, unlikely. But I think I can see where she's deriving her theory from. If the conditions in the interstellar medium are *significantly* different than around a star . . ."

The CO waited for about thirty seconds, then cleared his throat.

"Sorry, sir," Bill said, looking at his commander and grinning. "I'd need to sit down and do some serious calculations to figure out if Mimi's off or not. But off the top I can see where she's coming from. If they *are* high, it's going to make the bow shock an interesting place. They're going to be more or less stationary, so there may be odd material caught in them. The stellar equivalent of flotsam and jetsam."

"You get in an area that has possibly damaging material, you slow down," the CO said. "We get out there and engage the normal space drive. Take it slow."

"Hmm . . ." Bill said, wincing. "Top velocity in normal space is three and a half kilometers per second, sir. Three point five kkps."

"That's always bugged me," the CO said. "If we continually accelerate, we can go faster, right?"

"Materials, sir," Bill replied, frowning. "Do you want us to sustain a relativistic impact?"

"Relativistic . . ." the CO said. "Apparently, I'm going to ask a dumb question. What is a . . . ?"

"If we keep accelerating things get . . . bad, sir," Bill replied. "We can continue accelerating, stopping for chill-downs from time to time, as long as our fuel holds out. And with our acceleration we'll get . . . very fast very quickly. However, long before we consume much of our quarkium, we'll get up into largish fractions of light speed. Just our top end of three thousand five hundred kps is enough of a fraction to make me wince. It's about fifty times the fastest spacecraft Earth's ever launched and about point zero one two light speed. But the problem is that space isn't totally empty. There are small bits all over, micrometeorites, that we're running into even now: the bow of the boat has armoring and micrometeorite blankets on it; that absorbs most of the impacts. However, if we get up to serious fractions of light speed, a real 'intermediate speed' when we're talking about the distance from the sun to Jupiter, those impacts stop being survivable. Newton starts to make way for Einstein and energy release stops being purely kinetic and starts getting . . . relativistic. Think nukes instead of rocks. Up close to the speed of light, if we hit something the size of a pea we'll be a smear of photons spread over an area the size of the solar system. Not to mention when we get back home our clocks will be so off we'll never be able to figure out what time *Jeopardy* is on. But that's another discussion . . ."

"Time dilation I've got," the CO said. "As we get up to fractions of light speed, our time slows down compared to the rest of the universe. Einstein said it was so and I heard there were some experiments that have proved it. Oh, hell. And *mass* increases. So that pea, since it's going at a relative fraction of light speed, would be like—"

"Running into a planet," Bill said, nodding. "As velocity increases, gets into relativistic range, time slows, mass increases. It also means the faster we go, the harder it *is* to go faster, since our *own* mass increases. Thirty-five isn't a speed limit, it's more of a guideline. But it's a pretty good guideline, sir.

"The point is, sir, I'm not sure what you mean by . . . 'out there,' but if you mean we stop at approximately two astronomical units from the perceived trouble area, which itself is going to be something on the order of ten AUs wide, at 3.5 kkps it will take us fifty-one hundred thousand seconds to do the approach, which is—"

"A lot of minutes," the CO said, frowning. "Hours."

"Thirty six hundred seconds in an hour," Bill said. "Two hours to do the approach. That's not bad. But it will take fourteen to do the full crossing. We can cross *light years* in that time. And if we're damaged coming back . . . Fourteen hours might be more hours than we have."

"So we hit it at Warp One and hope for the best," the CO said.

"I'm not sure what else we can do, sir," Bill replied. "I do suspect, however, that the major issue will be in the area of the bow shock. So once we do this sampling . . . Probably when we enter a system it should be away from the bow shock."

"Effects," the captain said.

"The waves are going to create shearing stress. I'm not sure what the drive is going to do in those conditions, frankly, but we should probably warn the crew of the possibility of unusual maneuvers . . ."

"*Grapp,* I'm getting whacked," Hattelstad said, looking at the clock on the bulkhead. "Four more hours."

"We're on twelve on, twelve off schedules," Jaenisch said as they made their way to the armory. "Two platoons up at a time, one down. We're the last platoon to go down. Sorry about that. I know you had a bad night."

"Not a problem," Berg said. "I can hang."

"Hey, Josh," Jaen said as they entered the armory.

The armorer was a corporal, very tall, about six-six if Berg was right, and skinny. He also looked . . . odd. It was something about the way he stood. His name tag read "Lyle."

"Hey, Jaen," the armorer said in what was barely a whisper. "This Two-Gun?"

"Yeah," Jaen said, grinning. "But he promises he's not going to go all mojo on us in combat."

"I laid in a spare set of M-96s just in case," the armorer said, smiling lopsidedly. It seemed as if one side of his face didn't work quite properly. "You'll be wanting your guns."

"That we would," Jaen said. "Want help?"

"Got it," the armorer said, limping away from the window. When he came back he was hefting an eight-barrel Gatling gun in either hand. He set the massive weapons on the counter as if they weighed no more than a .22. Then he went back and came out with a heavy automatic cannon.

"You've got the other Gatling," Sergeant Jaenisch said, checking the serial numbers and setting one of the guns on his shoulder. "See ya, Josh."

"Go get 'em," the armorer said, grinning. "And I'm serious. I've got two official .455s for old Two-Gun here when he wants them."

"Thanks," Berg said, picking up the other Gatling. "If I need them, you'll be the second person to find out."

"What's with the armorer?" he asked when they'd cleared the compartment.

"Broke his *grapping* back in a Humvee rollover," Hattelstad answered. "Spent two years in rehab. They said he'd never walk again. He could have taken a full medical but he went through rehab then did a *maulk*load of paperwork to get back in."

"*Grapp*," Berg said. "I guess I'll just overlook any little oddities. He reminded me of Lurch, though."

"Thus his team name," Sergeant Jaenisch said. "But you only use it if you're *allowed*."

"Clear," Berg said.

The only compartment large enough to work on the Wyvern systems was the missile compartment. It wasn't exactly crowded with Marines, but there were quite a few when they got there. They found an out-of-the-way corner, port aft, and settled down to some serious weapons cleaning.

"You know an M-675?" Jaenisch asked.

"I qualified in it when I Wyvern qualled," Berg said. "Then again at FOT. About the only thing I haven't trained on is the Mark Fives."

"We'll get you fitted tomorrow," Jaen said. "It's scheduled. Then we'll run you though the simulator. You're going to have priority on that, so you can avoid most of the dickbeating for a couple of days."

"We've got *maulk* to do unless they find a planet that's worth checking out on the ground," Hattelstad said.

"Hey, guys," Crowley said from where his team was working on their guns. "You hear there's an alien onboard?"

"Sure," Jaen said, easily. "Tchar in engineering. I mean he comes through the missile bay twice a day at least."

"No, I mean a real *alien*," Crowley said. "Some sort of talking spider that rides around on one of the mission spec's shoulder! And, that mission spec? She can't be more than twelve but *man* is she hot!"

"Twelve will get you twenty, Crow," Hattelstad said. "On the other hand, the *linguist*? Oh, my *God*."

"Huh?" Berg said.

"The science team," Jaen explained. "It's mixed. Only two women, though, so if we get stranded it's going to be drawing straws time. And I seriously hope I get the linguist straw. Cute as hell. The bio lady, though, well . . ."

"She's not bad," Hatt said. "But she's black and in her forties. Sort of rode hard and put up wet. But the linguist is a *grapping* fox."

"I hear she's weird as hell, though," Crowley said. "Like nuts weird."

"Can't be nuts and be on a sub," Jaen said placidly.

"We don't deal with the scientists, huh?" Berg asked.

"Nope," Hatt replied. "Not until we land. SF does all the mixing, lucky bastards."

"There's not a designated linguist team," Jaen pointed out. "There's a designated bio team and geo, but no linguist team. So who's gonna cover her pretty backside if we find aliens for her to talk to?"

"Some officer," Hatt said. "Face it, we're not going to get *near* her. I don't even know her *name*."

"Surely there's a roster," Berg said. "Look it up."

"Like I have time?"

"You said we're going to be dickbeating most of the cruise."

"Top's inventive at ways to keep us from getting bored," Jaenisch said.

"That sounds ominous," Berg said.

"It was meant to."

"All hands. All hands," the 1-MC announced. "Secure all gear and noncritical personnel."

"*Maulk*," Hattelstad said. "That's us. What the *grapp*? We just *drew* these things!"

"And now we turn them back in," Jaenisch replied. "Welcome to the Space Mushrooms."

"Lost me," Berg said, rapidly putting his Gatling back together.

"Mushrooms," Hattelstad said, sliding the breach into the cannon. "They keep us in the dark and feed us horse*maulk* all day."

"Ah."

"Hey, Josh, what the *grapp*?" Jaenisch asked when they got back to the armory.

"No *grapping* clue," the armorer whispered. "Heard a rumor that we're on some sort of collision course."

"Oh, just *grapping great*," Hattelstad said.

"I didn't say I *believed* it," Lyle snapped. "I think it was Lujan spreading the worst rumor he could think of. You believe Drago?"

"Not on a bet," Hattelstad admitted, handing over his cannon.

It had taken nearly fifteen minutes for them to get to the counter and they had to make their way through the crowd to their racks.

"There's a ship info channel," Jaenisch said, then paused and cursed. "But of course they haven't *posted* anything!"

"Attention on deck!" somebody yelled.

"At ease," the CO said, cutting through the bustle. "Stay in your racks. There is an unforeseen problem with exiting the system. *Maybe*. The captain is taking the precaution of locking everything down. In the event of a serious problem, seal your bunks. On-duty crew are going to suits. You've got ten hours of air in your bunk systems. Even if we sustain a full-scale breach, you'll be fine. Just hunker down and listen to music. Hopefully, nothing will happen. But if it does, we're still good. That's all."

"Like the CO said, there's a *possible* problem," Top said as the CO exited the compartment. "If anybody wants the physics, I can explain it. Sort of. But if the theory is right, it's going to be like going through a bad storm. Just hold on and puke into your bags. So let me get an attitude check."

"*Grapp* this!" most of the Marines shouted.

"Let me get a *positive* attitude check!"

"Positively *grapp* this!"

"Let me get a *negative* attitude check!"

"I am *not* joining the *grapping* Space Marines!"

"Oorah!" the first sergeant said, grinning. "Seal 'em up, boyos, it's gonna be a *bumpy* ride!"

"Approaching the bow shock," the XO said.

The conn personnel had put on their ship suits. Unlike the EVA suits, which were traditional "space" suits, the ship suits were leopard suits that fit like a glove. They were designed simply to permit the ship personnel to survive in the event there was a full scale pressure breach. Damage control personnel were fitted with "real" space suits.

The helmets of the leopard suits were hinged back so that they could be donned rapidly in the event of an emergency. But barring serious conditions, the CO never ordered them donned. They really tended to slow down communications.

"Slow to Warp One," the CO replied, then grinned. "God, I *love* saying that. And you were right, Commander Weaver, it *is* rather spectacular."

Once the sampling on Saturn was done, the run to the heliopause had taken about forty minutes.

The bow shock, this close up, *was* rather spectacular. The area captured a mass of hydrogen and helium along with charged particles from the interstellar cosmic rays and interfiltered solar wind. The charged particles excited the atoms of hydrogen and helium into a broad spread fluorescence that lit up the forward viewscreens.

"XO, make an announcement that we're entering the bow-shock zone and the ship may experience some turbulence," the former fighter pilot said. "Tray tables and seat backs should be upright."

The announcement had just been made when the first wave hit.

"Wow," the XO said, grabbing a stanchion. "What in the *hell* was that?"

It had felt as if they had turned sideways, but the boat remained "upright."

"Standing wave," Bill said. "That was the first one."

The crew had been briefed that there might be some unusual effects and warned of the possibility of damage. But that was different from experiencing the effects.

"Whoa," the CO said, shaking his head. He'd installed himself in his command chair and now brought up his chicken straps, buckling himself in. "XO, all hands, brace. That last one was—"

"Holy *maulk*!" Weaver shouted as the world seemed to buck. He slid into his chart table, then started to slide back. In the distance there was a crash as some equipment that had been improperly stowed spun across a compartment. "That was at least a G, sir!"

"Drop out of—" The words from the CO were too late as the boat suddenly seemed to twist. The grav wave stretched everything in the boat, pulling forward and aft and creating a miniature tidal effect even on the human body, pushing blood into the head and feet. On the boat, and the engine, it had much worse effects.

Berg hunted through the menu on the computer until he found what he was looking for.

"Hey, Jaen," he said.

"You found the communicator," Jaen said. "What you got?"

"How do I ask Top about the physics?" Berg asked.

"You're serious?" Sergeant Jaenisch said. "You ask Top about the physics some time when we're *not* talking about the ship coming apart. Clear, Marine?"

"Clear, Sergeant," Berg said. "Sorry."

"Not a problem," Jaen replied. "Just sit tight and—"

"All hands! All hands! Prepare for bow-shock entry."

"What in the hell . . . ?" Jaen said.

"Shiny, we're going into the bow shock," Berg said happily.

"What in the *hell* is a bow shock?" Jaen asked.

"Aw, hell," Berg said. "There's probably an explanation on the system. Is there a way to look out?"

"Look it up, Two-Gun," Jaenisch said, then gasped. "Whoa! What in the hell was that?"

"*Maulk*," Berg said. "That was a—"

Then the second wave hit and he stopped talking. All he could do at first was hang onto his position by bracing against the door and bulkhead. But as the ship went into what felt like flips, he could feel his stomach, normally cast-iron, start to flip with it.

"Oh, God," Berg moaned, fumbling for the puke bag compartment. "I'm *sooo* tired of thisss!"

It tasted like a soprano note.

# 9

## We're HOW FAR Off Course?

*"Wegurcaingl!"* Tchar shouted as the grav wave hit. His arms flew to their limits from tidal stress and he watched in horror as the coryllium sphere began spinning out of control.

At the first movement, the world seemed to tear apart. The massive Adar flew through the air of the engine room, spinning as tidal forces began to corkscrew. The air seemed to turn violet and the bulkheads seemed to stretch. By luck as much as anything he landed on his back, his helmet slamming into position and automatically locking. He slid across the metal floor feet first into the rear bulkhead as the air began to smell like yellow.

The shearing forces of whatever had hit them had caused a cascade failure in the lighting system, but red emergency lighting came on automatically. When Tchar looked up the coryllium sphere was spinning like a top, a blue glow filling the air around it.

The shearing stress and the random distance fluctuations caused by the confused warp field left an odd residual effect on the boat, which either was tossing end for end or felt like it was. The difference was only semantics and Tchar didn't feel like debating it at the moment. He was pinned to the far bulkhead, and the engineer on the reactor console was crumpled in the corner, unconscious or dead.

Tchar stretched out one arm and grabbed a stanchion, waving his hand back and forth to figure out where it was, then dragged himself across the compartment by main strength until he got a hand around the pedestal of the engineer's chair. With two hands he chinned himself up to the chair then reached up and hit the chicken switch on the reactor, cutting all power to the engine.

The weird sensory effect and gravitational stresses fell away immediately. Of course, it was replaced by microgravity.

"Oh, this is *much* better," Tchar snarled. He pulled himself into the engineer's too-small chair and began the laborious process of stopping the spinning ball and getting it realigned.

"What just happened?" the chief engineer asked from across the compartment.

"Dr. Weaver, what in the *hell* just happened?" the CO asked, shaking his head. He'd popped his helmet into place as had most of the conn that were still at their stations. "And is it just me, or is the bow shock gone?"

"It's gone, sir," Weaver said, slowly lifting himself up with one hand. At the very beginning of the strange effect he had hunkered down to the deck, slammed his helmet down and held on for dear life. Fortunately, most of the conn crew were strapped into their seats. The only three people on the conn who didn't have seats were Weaver, the XO and the COB. Weaver had hunkered, the XO had grabbed a stanchion for dear life and was now holding on with one hand, frowning. He did not like microgravity.

The chief of boat was standing by the diving board, legs spread, his arms folded, one hand holding a cup of coffee. He was floating about two feet off the deck, though.

"*That* was interesting," the command master chief said. He slowly turned his coffee mug over, then reached up and lowered himself to the deck by pressing a finger on the overhead. A careful wrist twist and he had his mug back upright with the coffee held in place by microgravity forces. He still had his helmet open so very, very slowly he took a sip. The black coffee rippled and glimmered oddly, but friction between the cup and the liquid held it in place as he lowered it again. "Damned interesting. Reminded me of one time we hit this tsunami off Sumatra . . ."

"I saw all the viewscreens blank out," the CO said. "The indicator lights were still going so apparently there just wasn't anything to show. There are apparently benefits in this job to being a fighter pilot. I'm not sure if we were actually tumbling . . ."

"Neither am I, sir," Bill said, bringing his tracking system to life. "But I'm pretty sure we're not where we were."

"And by that you mean . . ." the XO said.

"I mean we're not anywhere *near* where we used to be, sir," Bill replied. "I'm working on tracking right now, but so far I can say that we are nowhere within five light-years of Sol. . . ."

"You okay, Miriam?" Mimi asked.

"No," Miriam said, folding up the plastic bag. "I'm dying. Oh. My. *Goddd!*" She hastily pulled the bag closed and reached for another. "I *hate* zero G!"

"I don't think it will repeat," Mimi said. She lowered her feet from where they'd been planted on the overhead. "I think we went through a dimensional shift. I hope we get gravity back soon, though. . . ."

"Normal space drive coming on-line," the COB said over the 1-MC. "Prepare for gravity in all compartments. Repeat, prepare for gravity in all compartments."

"We've got ten casualties," the XO said. Everyone had their feet on the ground for when the gravity came up and when it did he simply bent his knees slightly. "All minor except for one cranial injury in engineering. He's been taken to sickbay and Dr. Chet says that so far it just appears to be a concussion. No fractures."

"Small favors," the CO said. "Okay, Commander Weaver, what's the consensus?"

"I've talked with Tchar and Dr. Beach," Bill replied. "We apparently went into either a dimensional gate of some sort or possibly a 'hard' warp where we weren't dropping in and out. Mimi is apparently pretty sure that it was a dimensional gate and based on some . . . objective effects I agree with her."

"Both of you having been in a dimensional gate before," the CO said.

"Yes, sir," Bill replied. "The effect, as far as I can tell, other than the weird effects, was to . . . jump us to Epsilon Eridani."

"That's not just off course," the CO said, frowning. "That's *way* off course."

"Yes, sir," Bill replied. "More or less in completely the wrong direction. Our survey plan just went out the window; we weren't supposed to survey the E Eridani area until late in the survey. But at least we're in the same universe."

"Are we sure?" the XO asked, sarcastically.

"Pretty sure," Weaver answered. "The physics team is doing some pretty sophisticated tests. So far, quantum mechanics is working the same way as we'd expect with the exception of some gravitational effects. They're asking if they can do an EVA and do more grav tests."

"XO?" the CO asked.

"I'm for it," the XO said. "We took some damage. Nothing serious, but it would give us time to fix it all before we take off again. If we shut all the way down we can chill, too. Question: Are we going to have that problem each time we hit one of these helio things?"

"Unknown, sir," Bill said. "I'm hoping that if we approach away from the bow shock it will be lower. But I'm also recommending to the chief engineer and to Tchar that we install a better seat for the engineering watch crew. That way if we dimensionally jump again, they can shut down the power. That is what stopped us, this time. If Tchar hadn't scrammed the power, I'm not sure where we would have ended up. The other side of the galaxy would have been bad. In the middle of a star would have been worse."

"... A gravitational standing wave," Berg said.

Most of the Marines in the compartment were either sticking their heads out of their racks or were out of them listening, since the Nugget seemed to know what he was talking about.

"What in the *grapp* is a grav..." Lujan asked.

"It's..." Berg paused and shrugged. "It's what you felt. It's sort of like a wave that stays in one place. If it's gravity, you get pulled this way and that. I'm glad it wasn't any stronger than what we hit. I mean, the shearing stress could have torn the ship apart."

"That's great to hear," Crowley said sarcastically. "But what was that thing that happened with . . . Did anybody else think the air tasted . . . yellow?"

"I thought it tasted red," Clay from Third Platoon said. The lance corporal shook his head. "I can't believe I just said that."

"I don't know *what* that was," Berg admitted. "I've heard of the effect; it's called synesthesia. I've heard of it before but I never thought I'd experience it. I think I puked up a soprano note."

"I got the smell like green," Tanner from Third said.

"It was a dimensional jump," Top said from the hatchway. "But good job on the rest of it, Berg. I was dreading explaining gravitational standing waves. As for the dimensional jump, nobody and I do mean *nobody*, from the lowest engine tech up to Commander Weaver knows why it happened for sure."

He stepped into the compartment and made his way down to the center.

"For your general information, we're about ten light-years off course. For Crowley's benefit, that's a long way. And we made that jump in about a minute and a half if we can trust the clocks. The good news is that we're still in the same universe. The command group is trying to figure out what to do about both problems, being off course and the grav waves at system edge, right now. And we're going to leave it up to them because we are Marines not ship commanders or astrogators. Second Platoon, you're on rest cycle. First and Third, you're up. You've got training schedules, get with them. Anybody who is *not* supposed to be in their rack had better be *out* of that rack by the time I leave the compartment."

Berg pulled his head back in as First and Third started throwing themselves out of their bunks, sucking up to the walls to let Top past.

"Synesthesia, huh?" Hattelstad said. "You know, I'm reconsidering this whole Space Marine thing. This *maulk* never happened to those guys in *Aliens*. All they had to worry about was being impregnated by an alien monster."

"Hey, day's young," Jaenisch said. "I think that's on the training schedule for tomorrow."

"All hands! Stand by for chill!"

"Ah, hell . . ."

"All hands, all hands, stand by for chill," the 1-MC announced. "Microgravity in five seconds. We Be Chilling!"

"They're chilling," Dr. Aaron Ratliff said, closing the connections on his suit gloves. "We have to work."

He grasped a stanchion as the gravity faded to nothing, then cautiously donned his last glove.

"Apparently Dr. Becker's theories on the interstellar gravity aren't just the ravings of a deluded madman," Beach said, pulling the astrophysicist over to check his connections. "You're good."

"Stand by for door opening sequence," Ratliff said, pushing himself gently to the far wall. The airlock had two door controls, one on either side of the compartment. Both required a keycode and both had to be activated within a fraction of a second of each other for the door to open.

On submarines, outer hatches were set up so that they could only open outward. One reason for this was that the pressure was better managed that way; the pressure seated the hatch instead of trying to push it open. The other reason, though, was a tad more subtle. Sometimes people cracked under "pressure" as it were. And sometimes they very much wanted out, to the point of attempting to open the hatches.

One of the biggest refits on the SSBN *Nebraska* had been installing remote controls on all the hatches. It was impossible to refit them all so that they opened inwards, thus preventing such "accidental" openings when in vacuum. But the three true airlocks on the boat had to have *two* people open them. And the inner doors could not be opened simultaneously, the only exception being during a declared emergency.

The last thing anyone wanted was an "accidental" venting of the spaceship.

"Venting to death pressure," Beach said, entering his code. "Pressure check."

"Nominal," the astrophysicist replied.

"Keycode entered," Beach said.

"Same same," Becker said.

"And three, two, one . . ."

Both twisted the hatch controls as close to simultaneously as human reactions and quantum theory allowed, and the airlock door opened outwards.

Everette pulled himself out the door one-handed, then spun to face outwards. When he was aligned he punched the controls on the air-pack and was puffed gently away from the boat.

"How far?" Beach asked. "I'd say that a thousand meters should do it."

"Until we don't pick up gravitational effects from the boat," Becker replied. "Which I'm still picking up."

"Sure it's not from you?" Everette asked.

All bodies exert gravity. Just as the Earth "pulls" a person down, the person's body exerts gravitational effect on the Earth, pulling it ever so slightly "upwards." Newton had demonstrated this with a couple of balls of lead and springs back in the 1800s.

The device Dr. Becker carried was essentially the same thing, a device for measuring gravity, if much *much* more accurate. But the very presence of the scientists was going to affect the measurements, much less the much larger mass of the boat.

"Quite," Becker replied. "We'll go out to a thousand meters, then check. If there's still noticeable effect from the boat we may need to use a probe."

"Okay, I'm going to admit to ignorance," Miller said.

With the boat in "chill" mode, activity was discouraged. Most systems were shut down, the engines were shut down and people were encouraged to find a quiet place to sit and generate the minimum heat possible. In the meantime the silica heat sinks were extended from their tubes and folding heat vanes popped up, dissipating the maximum heat possible.

And it was very possible. The area that the boat currently rested in was at a temperature very close to absolute zero. Between the minor air and liquid leakage that was unavoidable with the *Blade* and the vanes on the heat sinks, the built-up waste heat was sucked out like a kid going at a milk shake.

In the meantime, it was a great time to talk. The crew and mission specialists took it as "off duty" time and Miller was dressed appropriately in one of his Hawaiian shirts and cargo shorts. He also was floating in midair and the shirt tended to ride up, showing a stomach that was roped with scars.

"Go," Weaver said, taking a sip from his bulb of cola. He'd much prefer beer but the "Alliance" ships still had a regulation against it. He'd stayed in uniform precisely because it was a better outfit for microgravity.

"What's the deal with gravity being different between the stars?" Miller asked.

"Bent space," the Adar said, taking a sip of cola. Which in Weaver's opinion was just unfair. Caffeine had an effect similar to alcohol on the Adar so Tchar was, for all practical purposes, having a beer.

"Which tells me exactly . . ." Miller said.

"Well, we've sort of gotten beyond Einstein's theories at this point," Bill said, "but they still sort of work to explain. First of all imagine a rubber sheet stretched off to infinity. Flexible and thin, like latex."

"Got it," Miller said.

"Big sheet of latex and more or less perfectly flat," Bill continued. "Now, take a metal ball and set it on the sheet. What happens?"

"If it's heavy enough it sinks in," Miller said.

"Right," Bill said. "But what happens to the sheet?"

"It gets sort of bulged down," Miller said, frowning. "So?"

"That's a planet," Bill said. "Or a star or a galaxy if it's a big enough sheet. And anything that gets close?"

"It sort of rolls down to the ball," Miller said, nodding. "Okay, gravity makes sense. But what's the thing with between stars . . . ?"

"What if the sheet isn't actually *flat*?" Bill asked. "Say if there's like air being blown up under it?"

"I don't get that one," Miller admitted.

"Near planets and even suns, the sheet acts as if it is flat," Tchar said, taking another sip of cola. "But as you get away from that influence, it acts more as if it is . . . bulging up. There is inertial resistance throughout the interstellar space. This may be due to reduced interference with Lilarmaurg particle generation. Theoretically."

"Lilar—What?"

"One of their scientists," Bill replied. "Lilarmaurg particles are similar to what we refer to as zero point energy, but Lilarmaurg proved the existence of his particles while ZPEs are still debated. However, just because you know that a particle exists doesn't mean you can do anything with it or even produce it. And even after seven years we're still trying to get some merging in our two physics approaches. Anyway, there's some indications that as you leave the solar regions there is sort of a hill you have to climb to get to the next solar region. And we've more or less proven that there's a disturbed zone between the two regions."

"Ten casualties proven," Miller said. "So how'd we get so far off course?"

"Ain't got a clue," Bill admitted. "You're going to have to ask Mimi *that* one."

» » »

"Dimensional shift," Mimi said. "Are you sure you want to talk about this now?"

"When you're talking I can concentrate on something besides my stomach," Miriam said.

"There are things you can take . . ." Mimi told her.

"I've got really bad reactions to most drugs," Miriam said. "Dimensional shift."

"There are multiple dimensions . . ."

"Ten according to the last thing I read on it," Miriam said.

"Well, that depends on whose model you use. Dr. Weaver, Tuffy, and I could explain things better from eleven, but that is another story. I didn't know you knew that much about topology and mathematical physics." Mimi's brow furrowed. "Do you have a doctorate in it?"

"I don't even have a doctorate in linguistics," Miriam said, chuckling. "But that's because I can't stand school. I just hate sitting in class. But I read all the time and can do tensor calculus in my head."

"How many languages can you speak?" Mimi asked curiously.

"Thirty-seven fluently," Miriam said. "About ten more enough to get around. I generally take about thirty minutes to get to that point. Admiral Avery said that I was the first person he'd ever met better at languages than he was. I picked up Adar in about two hours. I was working with a scientific translation team when I got asked to go on this mission. They were willing to take me even though I have . . . issues because if we *do* run into an alien species . . . Well, the Adar were trying hard to get translation going when we first met them but we still have translation problems both ways. A totally alien species, especially one that's not as interested in communicating as the Adar . . . Dimensional shift."

"There are ten known dimensions plus one for time and something like infinite universes," Mimi continued. "Theoretically, it takes infinite power to enter either. But . . . Well, I've been in another universe and so has Dr. Weaver."

"I don't know him," Miriam said.

"He's the boat's navigator," Mimi said. "But he's a doctor, too. Physics and some other stuff. We've both spent time out of, well, *this* universe. I don't remember much about it but I recognized the effect. You have to shift dimensions to do that according to the theory. So we got pulled out of this universe into another dimension, maybe into another universe, then back in. Really, we could have ended up anywhere in the universe. Every point on the edge of a universe, theoretically, connects to every other point in an adjoining universe."

"Knew that one, modified Higgs field, right? I have read one of your papers. I must have missed the eleventh dimension one," Miriam said, nodding.

"So that's the deal." Mimi shrugged. She pushed herself gently across the compartment and pulled out a bulb of juice. "Want something to drink?"

"Don't," Miriam said, holding up her hand and looking away. "Just . . . don't. You can have it, but try to keep the sucking sound down."

Tuffy launched himself off the girl's shoulder and landed expertly on the woman's. Crawling up under her long hair he began rubbing at her neck.

"That's helping," Miriam said, blinking her eyes in surprise. "Thank you, Tuffy."

"Sure you don't want something to drink?" Mimi asked.

"I will when the gravity comes back on," Miriam said, closing her eyes. "Right now I'm just going to let Tuffy give me a neck rub. . . ."

"Dr. Becker?" Beach asked.

"Yes, Dr. Beach?" Becker said.

"Well?"

"Simply put, I don't believe the readings," Becker said. "I would suggest we go back to the boat. I would like to ask if we could move somewhat farther away, then come back and get a reading. We needn't recover the gravitometer. In fact, I'd like to leave it here if we could find it again."

"We can do that," Beach said. "*Blade*, EVA," he said, changing channels.

"Go EVA."

"Returning to the boat. Please inform the captain, with his permission, that we'd like to move the boat somewhat away and then come back to get more readings."

"Will do, EVA."

# 10

## Interesting is a Word with So Many Connotations

"Well, that *is* interesting," Weaver said, looking at the readings.

"Amazing," Becker replied. "It explains so much and yet . . ."

"And yet," Weaver said. "If we could publish this it would have half the astrophysics community screaming in horror. I'm trying to figure out how *many* theories you just turned into confetti, Dr. Becker."

"Could someone explain in words of no more than one syllable?" the captain said. "And possibly tell me how it affects our mission?"

"Well, getting in and out of star systems is going to be *hard*," Bill said. "That wasn't just an effect we're going to find near the bow shock. The up side is that now that we have these readings, I think I can figure out how to pilot through . . ."

"Mass," Dr. Becker said. "I can see where you're going with that, but the mass of *planets* is going to affect the turbulence zone."

"Surfing," Bill said.

"Tough," Becker replied.

"Would someone *please* . . ." the captain said.

"It was assumed that space was flat," Dr. Beach said, holding up a hand placatingly. "These readings indicate that beyond the gravitational effect of a star, more or less around the heliopause although that will be different for different suns, space *bends* sharply upwards. Oh, not compared to a planet's well, but quite noticeably. Gravity and momentum take on completely different forms. At the juncture of those two zones there is a disturbance zone. We already experienced the effects."

"And that's around *all* suns?" the XO said, horrified. "All the way around?"

"Uh, huh," Bill replied, forgetting for a second that he was an officer in the military and enjoying the intellectual puzzle. "A sphere around them. Around some of them it's going to be *spectacular*. The really massive ones are going to have one *hell* of a transition zone. It's almost like a big defense barrier around planets. I think we're going to lose the Voyagers in about twenty more years. But I have to respectfully disagree with Dr. Becker. The main mass we have to think about is the star of each system. If we know the star's mass, we can compute the gravity effect. Do we have any records from the transition zone around the sun?"

"Lots," Becker said, nodding. "I'll do a comparison and see if you are on target, Doctor."

"These waves are *broad*," Bill continued. "On the order of a half light-year for the really strong ones. If we can determine the period, well . . . Then it's just a matter of surfing."

"Catch the wave?" the captain asked.

"Probably approach the zone and drop to normal space," Bill said, nodding. "Right when we hit the first wave. Then time the period and hit the warp. Depending on the star, we set the warp to match the periods. We'll be skipping through a series of waves, then hitting the next one in period. The waves are probably going to give us a smidgeon of extra speed. I'll have to compute that. But if it works it will only be about ten minutes that we're in most transition zones. It may be rough, but not as rough as the last trip."

"If it works," the XO said. "And if it doesn't?"

"Then we drop to normal space and limp home," Bill said. "Warp to Sol's transition zone and drive through *slow*."

"How many hours?" the CO asked.

"Take us about a month to make it through," Bill said. "How we fixed for food?"

»          »          »

"Permission to . . ." Mimi said, then paused, looking in the hatch to the conn.

"Enter the conn," the CO said, looking over his shoulder. "Is this a social call, miss?"

"I . . . You're going to try to enter the Eridani transition zone, sir," Mimi said shyly. "I was wondering if I could . . . sit in. Sir."

The captain regarded her calmly for a moment, then nodded.

"Take my seat," the captain said, gesturing with his head. "I'll just hold on."

"Thank you, sir," Mimi said, walking over and sitting in the chair.

"Where's Tuffy?" Bill asked, not looking up from his screens.

"With Miriam," Mimi said.

"So he's not giving any hints about this?" Bill said. "Damn."

"No, it's just me, Dr. Weaver." Mimi grinned. "Does that bother you?"

"A lot," Bill admitted. "I would love for Tuffy to tell me I know what the hell I'm doing."

"Can I look?" Mimi asked.

"Go ahead," Bill said.

Mimi walked over and looked at the equations on the screen.

"The problem as I see it is that the boundary of the warped spacetime around the boat is a smooth transition while the spacetime in the disturbed region is sharply fluctuating. Is it a continuous function?"

"As far as our instruments can tell, the fluctuations are continuous but with random functionality. Perhaps it's a period three superposition on a Henon map." Weaver scratched his head.

"You mean it is chaotic?" Mimi raised her left eyebrow slightly.

"I think so. The gravity waves are a superposition of waves that might be described as an infinite Fourier series. But we have no clue where to start with the series."

"You don't have to!" Mimi was excited. She had thought of the answer and Tuffy was nowhere to be seen. "If it is period three then you only need to mimic a portion of it and then you can superimpose that on the upper right-hand corner of the Henon map to give you a description of the function."

"Wow!" the CO said, his eyes wide at the sudden onslaught of technobabble. "Why didn't I think of that?"

"I was thinking the same thing, sir," Bill said, missing the sarcasm. "But then we'd need to take that function and tie it between the boundaries of inner part of the solar system to the outer part of the gravity fluctuations."

"I think that is right. And the partial functions should be discernable with our instrumentation, right?"

"That should actually work. We can curvefit the data and then superimpose the Henon map; I like it," Bill said, looking over his shoulder. "And that wasn't Tuffy?"

"No," Mimi said. "But he's been working hard over the years teaching me. I think that will work."

"You sure?" the CO asked. "Because, and don't get me wrong here, it sounds like you're just making this stuff up to confuse me."

"Uh . . ." Bill said, suddenly realizing that he'd put his foot in it.

"We're not, sir," Mimi said, grinning. "Those were all real words."

"I apparently need to go back to school," Spectre said dryly. "Among other things, I have no basis on which to make a decision of my own. I have to depend utterly on your and Commander Weaver's recommendations. That is *not* a position a captain wishes to be in. The worst part about it, from the POV of a captain who wants to be an admiral, is that the future space navy is going to have to have commanders who *do* understand what you just said. One question, though: Why couldn't we get this information *before* we went through that last transition?"

"We didn't have the data, sir," Bill pointed out. "Until we figured out how to fit the data we have to a curve we had nothing to go on. We couldn't have it until we reached this point. Now we do."

"Will we have to do this every single time?" the CO asked.

"No, sir, I think Mimi is right," Bill said, scratching his head again. "Once we've done it and figured out how to use our instruments to do this, we should be able to measure the needed data for the fit before we enter into the spacetime fluctuations." Weaver smiled and felt that feeling that he always did after solving a hard problem. That feeling was different than the ones he got from successful command decisions. Both were satisfying but he had missed the problem-solving feeling quite a bit. "That means we'll be able to write algorithms to handle it automatically. Plug in the nature of the system and the computer will tell us how to do it. Hmmm . . ."

"Very well, Commander Weaver," the CO said after a moment. "Recommendations?"

"Oh," Bill said, jerking out of his reverie and pointing to the forward viewscreen. "Warp One, sir, and point it at the star. Stop when we hit the first gravity wave. I'll recompute based on that."

"Pilot, make it so," the captain said. "Miss Jones, why don't you take my seat again?"

"Thank you, sir," Mimi said, climbing up in the swivel chair and strapping in. She spun around so she could watch Weaver work.

The boat headed for the star for about three minutes, then everyone felt the strange disorientation of the grav transition.

"All halt," the CO ordered.

"Dropping to normal space," the pilot said. "All halt."

Bill looked over at the gravitometer that had been mounted by his station and punched in the results from the last gravity wave. Now that he *knew* about the effect he was already considering changes to the software to automate the process, but for the time being he was going to have to do it mostly by the seat of his pants.

"Captain, permission to take the conn," Bill said.

"Navigator has the conn," the CO replied as another gravity wave passed.

"Oh, I just wanna *die*," Miriam muttered. "Thank you, Tuffy."

The spider sank down and wrapped the back of her neck in its legs and started to purr.

*"Thank* you, Tuffy."

"Pilot, set eyeball course for the star," Bill said. "Set for Warp Three Dot One Four Six. Initiate on my mark."

"On course," the pilot said, swallowing nervously. "Warp Three Dot One Four Six set."

Bill looked at his instruments and waited.

"Three, two, one . . . mark!"

As the gravity wave just started to hit, the boat went into warp, hurtling forward. There was still the sick-making feeling of sudden free fall followed by lateral pressure, but it wasn't nearly as bad as the first transition.

"Tchar," Bill said, opening up a communicator to the engine room. "How's the ball?"

"Holding," Tchar replied. "I have increased the strength of the mag field so as long as we take no more than one point six Earth standard gravity laterally it should be fine."

"Good to hear," Bill said, watching his instruments.

"XO?" the captain asked.

"All stations report condition green," the XO replied. "Boat is holding nominal."

"Congratulations, Commander Weaver," the CO said as a gentle wave passed through the boat. "It seems to be working."

"We haven't hit the max G yet, sir," Bill said. "But if my calculations are right—"

"Point Three Two Four more warp," Mimi said. "In about ten seconds."

"You're sure?" Bill asked.

"The wave is going to double up," Mimi said. "That way you'll skip right past it. At this warp . . . I think we'll hold together."

"I see the point you're talking about," Bill said. "Pilot . . . Prepare to increase to Warp Three Dot Four Seven Zero on my mark. Four, three, two, one . . . Mark!"

The wave was heavier than the others, but not boat-shattering. And almost immediately after, the waves fell off to nothing.

"Transition zone passed, sir," Bill said.

"Captain has the conn," the CO said. "Astrogation, course?"

"Head for the star?" Bill asked. "There are two known planets in the system, both gas giants. One is in close, two astronomical units out, the other at about twenty-eight AU. Recommend we simply head inward to about one AU, literally keeping an eye out for planets on the way, and park in an orbit around the sun. At that point, the science team can start scanning. We're going to have to adjust to local movement, though."

"That's going to be interesting," the XO said.

"Turns out you're not up to be implanted by an alien monster, Hatt," Jaenisch said as the morning formation broke up. The Marines, like everyone else, had huddled in during chill but it was time to get back to work. "We're doing computer assisted training. Berg's getting fitted for his Wyvern. Tomorrow is more Wyvern maintenance for most of the platoon but Berg's going to be in the sim for the next three days, then he does a Wyvern Common Tasks test. If he passes that we're scheduled for ten hours of team train in the sims. If you don't, Nugget, we're going to be doing more maintenance, so you'd better pass."

"I usually smoke WCT," Berg said. "Shouldn't be an issue."

Berg had been involved in loading the Wyverns and had seen them lining the missile compartment, but this was the first time he'd seen the manual for one.

"Jesus Christ," he muttered, scanning the directory. Wyverns were pretty easy to get around in; they more or less mimicked normal human motion. The tough part of WCT was always the communications and sensors section. And the commo and sensors section of the manual was three times the size of the Mark Four. There was also a zero-gee section of the WCT. Basically, the WCT had been doubled in size. He set the pad down and adjusted his bodysuit. The one problem with the Wyverns, from Berg's point of view, was that you had to wear nothing but this damned cat-suit.

"They're a ball-buster," Lyle whispered. "Hop in."

Wyvern 6719 was opened up and ready for an occupant; the straps and sensors, though, were either removed or dangling in place.

The Mark V Wyvern was three meters tall. Two and a half meters of that was the "Pilot Compartment," the big "belly" of the armor where the human rode and piloted the machine. Extending more or less from the shoulders were metallic arms capable of *almost* full range of motion and extending from the "hips" were relatively stubby metallic legs. Mounted on top, where a human's head would be, was the primary sensor pod, a dome that was currently showing its standard black. Like the rest of the Mark V, it could mimic various colors and patterns. Inside the sensor dome was the sensor suite composed of not only visible light cameras but thermal imagery, lidar, radar and, in the Space Marine version, sensors to detect just about any known particle.

Along the sides of the Wyvern were pouches for spare gear or ammunition while the back held the primary ammo storage, americium reactor power system and a "bail-out bag" with the Marine's ground-mount fighting gear.

Wyverns were entered by backing into the "belly" of the humanoid armor while the hatch opened down into a ramp. Two grab points were mounted on either side of the hatch to assist in entry.

Berg turned around and grabbed the padded stanchions and in a practiced move lifted himself backwards and up into position. He slid his legs backwards to the curved calf pieces and could tell immediately that they were out of position. So were the bicep pieces. Even the foot pads were out of place.

"I'm usually pretty close to standard for one of these things," Berg said.

"This was Harson's," Lyle whispered. "He was short."

"Oh."

Fitting the Wyvern took forever. Berg had been fitted twice before, once at his first duty station and again at FOT, but only at FOT had anyone taken the pains that Lyle did. It took nearly ten hours, a matter of adjusting the various control points that retransmitted the actions of the wearer's whole body.

"Try the right middle finger," Lyle said, stepping back.

Berg moved it up and down.

"Shiny. Rotate. Weapons mount. Look at the red ball."

Berg tracked his head around to look at the light.

"Tracking," Lyle said, as the light began to move.

"Shiny. Bite check," Lyle said.

Berg clamped down on the bite-trigger of the Wyvern. The trigger was mounted on the right molars and required a certain degree of pressure to engage, preventing an "accidental discharge" by a casual bite. Just as special operations troopers tended to get carpal tunnel from continuously training with pistols, Wyvern operators tended to get TMJ. They also tended to talk through their teeth like Northeastern society matrons.

"Shiny. You're done."

"Finally," Berg said.

"Hey, all you have to do is stand there," Lyle said, smiling with a slight grimace.

"You okay?" Berg asked.

"Pain is weakness leaving the body," the armorer replied. "Try stepping out."

Berg flexed across his body while leaning forward and the control points dropped away. It wasn't a computer generated response but a function of the way the control points were mounted. They wouldn't break away in action—at least Berg had never heard of a case of them doing so—but with one focused "shrug" they all opened up. He stepped out, stretched, then lifted himself back into the compartment. Placing himself into the waiting control points, including sliding his hands into the gloves, he thrust backwards and was "wearing" the Wyvern again.

"Tomorrow we'll go through the movement diagnostics," Lyle said. "That's it for today."

"You take care, man," Berg said, stepping out again and hitting the control to close the Wyvern's belly. "Is it keyed to me, yet?"

"Tomorrow," Lyle said. "See you at 1700."

"All hands! All hands! Secure in quarters. Damage control parties to suits. Prepare for system entry."

"*Grapp*," Berg said. "I gotta scoot!"

"Like I said, see you at 1700."


"Oh, joy," Jaen said. "This is gonna be shiny as hell."

"You gotta figure they've figured out how to get around that grav thing," Onger said. The First Platoon team leader rolled into his rack and grinned. "Don't mean I'm not sealing up."

Berg hit the close button but left the door clear.

"Marines, this is the first sergeant," the communicator over his head announced. "They think they've got the whole system entry thing fixed. It should be an easy ride. But same thing as last time; keep sealed up until the all clear. That's all. Semper Fi."

"Two-Gun, got any idea what 'fixed' means?" Jaen asked.

"Nada," Berg admitted. "I mean, I was pretty good in high school physics and I read a lot. But that doesn't make me an astrogator. It's up to him."

"Know anything about that guy?" Jaen said.

"Not a thing," Berg admitted. "Lieutenant commander, right?"

"Yeah," the team leader said. "Used to be a physicist. Got himself a commission just so he could be on the mission. You know that SEAL that bunks with Top?"

"I heard about him," Berg said. "I don't think I've ever seen him. No, he was down in the Wyvern bay one time, somebody said he was a SEAL."

"He and the astrogator were in on the first gate openings," Jaen said. "Apparently they went some pretty strange places, Dreen worlds and Mree. Cool, huh?"

"Wait," Berg said. "He's not Dr. William Weaver, is he?"

"You know about him?"

"Holy *grapp*, Jaen," Berg said, grabbing his stubbly hair. "I can't believe you *don't*. The guy was given a Freedom Medal because they don't give the damned Medal of Honor to civilians! That means that SEAL is *Chief Warrant Officer Todd Miller* and he *did* get the Medal! Jesus!"

"Really?" Jaen said. "Go figure."

"Jesus, Sergeant," Berg said. "Just Google William Weaver and start reading. It's seriously derring-do *maulk*. I had no clue he was a navy officer. I mean, that guy's one of my personal heroes."

"Normal space drive at maximum," the pilot said. The young man wasn't quite sweating. "Three-zero KPS established. She will no go faster, Captain!"

"There's a differential speed of nearly four-zero-zero kkps between E Eridani and Sol system," Bill said. "We're going to be screaming to catch up for about an hour."

"Our heat is *way* up," the XO inputted. "I'd say that we only have about thirty minutes more at maximum power before we're going to have to cut power to chill."

The problem the ship was having wasn't going to go away. While star systems moved in a circle around the galactic center at an apparently similar rate, "apparently" was only on the basis of looking at them from a long way away. In fact, their relative rate of motion was hugely different. Just as the center of a wheel moves faster than the outer rim, relatively, stars closer to the galactic axis tended to move faster than those "outwards." And even stars on the same relative point outwards from the center moved differently.

In the case of the jump from Sol to E Eridani, the ship was having to speed up to "catch up" to the local speeds, relative to Sol. More speed in normal space meant more power from the ardune reactor and the electrical transfer system, both of which pumped out enormous heat.

"I think we're in too deep," the CO said. The ship had stopped at three astronomical units from the star. "We'll micro-jump to the edge of the system. Going this fast, relatively to the local system, we could run smack dab into a planet or a moon before we see it. Where's that gravity wave zone, Commander?"

"About one thousand AU, sir," Bill replied. "There should be plenty of room at about thirty AU. Farther out than that gets us into the Kuiper region and there could be literally thousands of small planetoids like Pluto floating around."

"Set course for thirty AU out from the star towards Sol," the CO said. "We'll do a chill then start the adjustment over again. XO."

"Sir."

"Do up an SOP on that. Enter the system at a distance, slow down and chill, *then* get deeper in."

"Yes, sir."

"We learn as we go, gentlemen, we learn as we go. Commander, where's my heading?"

"Ah, green eggs and ham," Hattelstad said, sitting down at the table.

"Was Dr. Seuss in the Marines?" Berg asked, tearing at a strip of rubbery bacon.

"I thought you were the guy with all the answers," Jaenisch said, sipping his coffee. The sergeant clearly wasn't a morning person.

"What's up for you guys today?" Berg asked, changing the subject.

"Dickbeating 101," Jaenisch said.

"Ground simulated combat for the first four hours," Hattelstad said. "So we're basically in our racks playing Dreen War. Then upper body workout, then Space Marine WCT. I'm still trying to figure out the difference between a maizon and a querk."

"One's a waiter, the other's a personal characteristic," Berg quipped. "Or did you mean a meson and a quark?"

"Whatever."

# 11

## Turn Right and Straight On . . .

"Right arm straight up to my finger," Lyle said.

Berg raised the arm to where he thought the finger should be, then lifted a bit more.

"Did you have to correct?" Lyle asked.

"Yeah."

"Do it again," the armorer said, looking at the box in his hand. "That's where you think it should be, right?"

"Yeah."

"Right arm straight out, come in and touch your nose."

CLANG!

"*Maulk.*"

Once a Wyvern was fitted it was *supposed* to perfectly mimic actions. But it never did. Thus it had to be adjusted for movement.

And adjusted and adjusted and adjusted. To the point where feet went where they were supposed to go, arms went where they were supposed to go, fingers closed with the right amount of force, to the point the wearer could bend steel bars, juggle eggs—if they could juggle—and jump over tall buildings in a single bound. Well, maybe not the latter.

"And in and touch your nose."

Ting.

139

"Left hand in and touch your nose."

Ting.

"Hand *salute!*"

Clang!

"Little softer next time, Two-Gun. Sensor pod's not as well armored as the rest. Let's get started on the legs . . ."

"And we're . . . done," Lyle said. "Step out and let's key it to you."

"Hell of a job, man," Berg said, climbing out of the armor. "Like a *grapping* glove."

"You're welcome," the armorer said, then hit the hatch close button. "Okay, palm on the pad."

Under the right armpit was a hand-print pad. If the user wasn't in the armor, it could only be opened by the user, the unit armorer, the first sergeant or the CO.

"State your last name, first name and rank," Lyle said.

"Bergstresser, Eric, PFC."

"Team name?"

"Two-Gun," Berg said with a wince.

"And you're keyed," Lyle said, starting to put away his tools. "But if you've got a few minutes, come on by the armory."

"Okay," Berg said. "Can I give you a hand with that?"

"No offense, but nobody touches my tools," Lyle replied, looking up at him and grinning. "You know, except good looking ladies of inappropriate age."

"Gotcha, man," Berg said.

"What in the *grapp* is that?" Berg asked, as Lyle set the gun on the counter.

"It's a really *grapped* up pistol," Lyle replied. "I started with some parts from a Barrett M-63. See, the Wyverns don't have a pistol system . . ."

The pistol was massive. Berg could pick it up with one hand, but only by cradling it. There was no way to get a hand around the grip. Forward of the grip was the magazine.

"What's it fire?" Berg said, then paused. "Wait, the Sixty-Three is a damned .50 caliber system!"

"I don't know if it can actually be used," Lyle pointed out. "The Wyvern's only got two fingers and a thumb. It might rotate out of your hand."

"You don't want *me* to try this thing, do you?" Berg protested.

"Hey, you're the one called Two-Gun, not me," the armorer whispered. "I don't even *have* a Wyvern."

Berg paused at that. He wasn't sure what the specialty of the armorer had been before his accident, but he was probably infantry. Now he just got to fix the toys, not play with them.

"If I strap this on, I will get *unending maulk*," Berg pointed out. "And Top will blow a gasket."

"If we get the chance, though, will you at least try it out?" Josh asked. "I'll square it with Top."

"If I get a chance."

"Shiny. 'Cause I made two."

"All hands! All hands! Stand by for Chill! We Be Chillin'!"

"*Maulk*," Berg said. "*Again?*"

"Still getting over the pink stuff?"

"I'm never going to get over it at this rate . . ."

"I'm dying in data!" Dr. Dean half screamed. "And now they want a planetary survey!"

"Sir, if I could recommend," Runner said, looking up from his computer screen. "Doing a planetary survey is grunt work. I can run the scope. You keep working on the data from Saturn."

"Good idea, Runner," the doctor said, picking up two two-liter bottles of generic cola and looking at them balefully. One was full, one nearly empty. He carefully opened the full one, poured part of it into the empty until both were slightly over half full, sealed both and shook them vigorously. Then he opened the cap on one, let the air hiss out, shook it again and took a swig. "For a soldier, you're not entirely stupid."

"Thanks for the compliment," the master sergeant muttered, unlatching his chair and rolling it over to the telescope controls.

The main scope for the *Blade* was mounted where a periscope would normally be on a sub. Runner first extended the scope, then swiveled it into working position. Then he entered the survey command.

Now that they were in a stable orbit around the sun, the boat was probably moving at a notably different velocity than the planets. By taking fifteen-minute-long duration shots of the sky in quadrants looking "outward" from the sun, he got six "plates" of the sky. They were actually detailed Flexible Image Transport System, or FITS, graphic files but the term plate went back to when astronomers would use actual photographic plates for the same purpose.

Mostly older astronomers used plates; the newer ones talked about files or digital images. Dr. Dean had started out with a thirty-five millimeter camera as a kid before video cameras and frame grabbers were available. He was in the generation that was between the older astronomers and the new kids on the block like Runner. But Dean didn't think of Runner as an astronomer. He was a stupid soldier, not a scientist. Which was why Runner called the files FITS at every opportunity.

Since planets were probably going to be moving at a notably different velocity than the boat, any planet facing the sun, and therefore bright in the sky, would turn up as a streak. What used to be a laborious human process was now all managed by computers. Stars turned up as dots. Planets turned up as streaks. A rather simple program found the streaks and highlighted them. An only slightly more complex program could determine orbits, debris, velocities, and distances.

Each of the shots required fifteen minutes of exposure, but they could be used for purposes other than just the planetary survey. Ever since man had looked up at the stars he'd been wondering "just how far away *are* those damned things?" He'd eventually gotten past thinking they were glued to the top of the sky, but scientists were still scratching their heads about most of them. The easiest way to compute a distance is called triangulation. Look at something from two different angles, do a bit of simple math and you know exactly how far away something is.

The problem with that with stars was, well, the only place they'd been observed from was Earth. Even the "parallax" of the Earth's orbit around the sun wasn't enough to help much with extremely distant stars. Astronomers, historically, would take plates of the night sky in the winter and then compare them to plates taken in the summer. This allowed for parallax with a separation between measurements of nearly two hundred million miles. But when talking about the universe, that was not near far enough for really good triangulation.

So, clever astronomers figured out others ways to get fairly accurate measurements of star distances by using things called Cepheid Variables. Cepheid Variables are a type of star that blinks in brightness with a clocklike periodicity. The period of the blinking is directly tied to how bright the star should be due to the physics of the star's inner makeup. So if a certain Cepheid was blinking at a given rate, then astronomers knew exactly how bright it should be. By measuring how bright it looked in the sky they could determine just how far away it was, since stars appear dimmer with distance as a one over the distance squared type law.

The Cepheid Variable measurement method was the best way to make deep sky measurements, but the process is much less accurate than good old triangulation. Now being able to use triangulation with many light-years distance on the parallax leg would allow for an amazingly detailed survey of the galaxy. But that would take time.

Runner took as many shots as he could to store away in the database. Astronomers could use the data and analyze it for many years to come. If he ever had the time, Lieutenant Commander Weaver probably wouldn't mind taking a gander at the data in more detail himself, but Runner doubted the commander would ever have another free moment as long as he lived.

For the first time man was looking at stars from a completely different direction. Before the mission was done it was intended that the entire sphere be swept so that every star in the catalogue could be viewed from another angle.

And soon they would get images from *really* far away from the sun and . . .

While the computer was chuckling over the planetary data, Runner extended a second scope, less powerful than the main but still good enough, and started hunting around by eye. Epsilon Eridani had two planets already detected, both gas giants. But one of the gas giants was at only two astronomical units away from the star. That was right at the edge of the potential life zone of E Eridani.

The life zone of a star was the zone in which the star's luminosity provided enough heat to keep water from freezing but not boiling it. Between 0 and 100 degrees Celsius. For Sol, the home star of Earth, that range was from .95 astronomical units out to 1.5, technically. There was a straightforward calculation to calculate the zone based on a star's luminosity.

Life zone was an important factor in the potential development of life. Every form of life humans had found by going through the Looking Glasses was based on water to one degree or another. So having liquid water was a given.

Brighter stars, the really hot ones like Vega, would have very broad life zones, if they even *had* planets rather than just an accretion disks of debris, while cooler ones, such as E Eridani, had very narrow life zones. Based purely on that, life was more likely to be found around hot stars. However, another necessity was sufficient time for life to develop. And hot stars had very short lives. It took about three billion years for the first life to develop on Earth *after* it cooled. A sun like Vega might only last a couple of billion years, leaving behind cold, dead planets.

On the other hand, smaller cooler stars such as E Eridani, while they lasted a long time, had very narrow life zones. And the life zone changed over time, generally getting closer to the sun and narrower as the star cooled. For that matter, planets close in had a tendency to become tidally locked as the moon was with Earth, one side always facing the star. While life *could* develop in those conditions, it was unlikely.

That was why the current survey had intended to concentrate on stars much like Sol. G class stars lasted a long time but had relatively broad life zones.

The kicker to all that theory was the experience humans had developed through surveying the planets on the other side of the Looking Glass portals and planets in the Sol system. The first thing that was noted was that greenhouse gases played an important part in whether or not a planet was habitable. Venus, in the Sol system, was right on the inner edge of the life zone. But Venus' atmosphere was so choked with greenhouse gases that the surface temperature was nearly 400 degrees C. Mars, too, was right at the edge of the life zone, on the chillier side. But Mars had virtually no greenhouse gases in its limited atmosphere. If humans could somehow switch their atmospheres, the two planets would be marginally habitable.

Planets on the other side of the Looking Glass had a tendency to be pretty poor. The portals had connected mostly to planets of some long gone race that had once used a similar system and had left behind inactive bosons. Most of the planets were in fading life zones, either those where the sun was starting to flare up in death or too cooled off to support life. Some of the planets appeared to have been terraformed, that is they had had extensive work done to them to make them habitable. That long gone race, perhaps the same race that made the warp engine for the *Blade,* had done the equivalent of switching Mars' and Venus' atmospheres.

But they showed that, depending on a huge number of factors, the life zone of a planet could be about twice as large as first thought.

Furthermore, it was apparent that while life could crop up under the oddest conditions, only a certain number of types turned up. So far in all the planets surveyed only four different biologies had been found. Two of those, human and Adar, were "green" biologies. That is, both used something that looked more or less like chlorophyll as a basic energy gathering system. One was "blue" and the last was "red."

Given that over forty planets had been found with some sort of life, there should, by straight evolutionary principles, have been forty different biologies. Instead there were four. Chloro A, Chloro B, Blue and Red.

Biologists and paleontologists were engaged in a hot debate about just why this was the case. The arguments fell into two broad categories: statistical genesis and panspermia.

Statistical genesis argued that when life was developing there were a limited number of functional ways it could occur. An infinite number of monkeys might try to start life, but only four were likely to take. Panspermists called this the "by guess and by gosh" theory.

Panspermists believed that either by the actions of some long gone race or due to microscopic survivors hitching a ride on rocks scattered into space, all life had originated in only four different conditions and then spread through the galaxy.

What statistical genesists said about panspermists wasn't fit to print. "Creationism by another name . . ." and it went downhill from there.

Runner had kept up with all the theoretical discussions even *before* he was volunteered to this mission. He just liked the debates and theories. So when he was hunting around he had a specific mission. The inner planet of E Eridani was well outside the theoretical life zone. But he kept in mind that word: "Theoretical."

There were so many theories being crushed by this mission, he wasn't willing to settle for "theory."

The planet itself was unlikely to have life. It was a gas giant, a super-massive planet of nothing but gas and metallic gas, gas crushed under so much pressure it turned solid. In fact, it was possible that the "planet," which was bigger than Jupiter, had been a brief-lived sun. But gas giants usually had rocky moons. And if the moon had enough $CO_2$...

He finally found what he was looking for and let out an exclamation.

"Have we found a planet?" Dr. Dean said, looking up from the Saturn data.

"I believe Doctors Campbell, Walter and Yang actually found the planet," Runner said. "But *we* just found a very high albedo moon."

"What?" Dean said, standing up and walking over, bottle of soda in hand. "Is that the thirty-centimeter aperture telescope or the one meter?"

"Thirty," Runner said. "The one-meter scope is doing the survey."

"Stop it and zoom in . . ." Dr. Dean said excitedly. "Do we have a spectroscopic analysis yet . . . ?"

"Doc," Runner said, shaking his head. "Why don't we just have the captain drive us over there?"

"Oh, yes," Dr. Dean said, blinking. "Perhaps that would be best."

He opened up the bottle of soda and took a swig, for once forgetting his ritual. Of course, when he tasted the slight carbonation, he blew half of it all over the console.

"Okay, this just isn't happening," Weaver said, looking at the forward viewscreen. "Tell me we didn't find the Forest Moon of Endor."

"The what?" the XO asked.

"*Star Wars*," the CO replied. "That place the Ewoks lived."

"Oh," the XO replied. "Not much forest. Looks like mostly ice."

The planet *was* mostly ice. A very solid glacial zone extended almost to the equator. And what there was of the rest looked like mostly ocean. A few small dots of islands had been detected, but that was about the only land. Unless you counted the glaciers.

"Hoth, then," Weaver replied.

"Actually," the CO said, looking at an internal e-mail, "Dr. Dean has stated that it should be named Dean's World."

"Figures," Weaver said, grinning. "He can have it. It's *way* outside the standard habitable zone. The only reason it's not frozen solid is that it has a higher $CO_2$ level than Adar. So the air isn't breathable to humans. And it's gonna be cold. Wyverns all the way."

"Is that a recommendation that we do a ground survey, Astro?" the captain asked.

"It's *there*, sir," Bill said, shrugging. "This is what we came for. To do a local survey, find habitable planets, look for signs of life. Figure out what the planets outside the portal planets are like. Yes, sir. I think we should do a ground survey. Just because it looks like a cold ball of ice . . ."

"Agreed," the CO said. "But we're not just looking for habitable planets. I want a full system sweep before we commit to a landing. It would be nice to know if there are any Dreen in the system *before* we're sitting ducks on the ground."

# 12

## There's One In Every Unit

"I was told to report to Ops?" Berg said, looking through the open hatch of the operations office.

"You Berg?" the staff sergeant behind the desk said with a frown. There was a nameplate on the desk with a faux brass plate that read "Staff Sergeant Mark Driscoll, Operations." "Enter."

"Yes, Staff Sergeant," Berg said, stepping into the office and coming to parade rest.

"You're up on the simulator," the staff sergeant said. "Which is totally *grapping* up my training schedule. So get it right the first time. You've been in the sim before?"

"Yes, Staff Sergeant."

"Then you know the deal," presumably Staff Sergeant Driscoll said. "Come on."

Driscoll led Berg back to his Wyvern and hit the hatch button. When the hatch didn't open he hit the armor with his fist.

"It's already keyed, Staff Sergeant," Berg said delicately.

"Then *open* it," the staff sergeant snarled.

"Bergstresser, Eric, PFC," Berg said, laying his hand on the palm-pad. The armor still refused to open so he closed his eyes and grimaced. "Two-Gun."

Then the armor opened. He wasn't sure if the voice analysis

149

was just off for his name or if Lyle had *grapped* with him, but it opened and that was the important part.

"Get in," Driscoll snapped. When Berg was snapped into his position, the operations sergeant leaned in and replaced a module on the inside of the pilot's compartment. "Training module. See you in six hours. Have fun."

"*Maulk*," Berg muttered as the hatch closed. *Nobody* spent six hours in sim training. The staff sergeant was clearly just glad to have him out of his hair.

But it was too late to protest. The VR mod was already starting and Eric saw his orders scrolling up in front of his eyes. Move to the corner of the street and recon for enemy positions.

"Shiny," he said. "Let's dance."

"Six *hours?*" Jaenisch snarled. "Is Driscoll *grapping insane?*"

"I should have brought a puke bag," Berg admitted, grinding his teeth to keep down the nausea.

Virtual Reality was a very effective training method but not perfect. The problem was that the Wyverns could not actually move. The module that was replaced prevented that, so that the entire training program could be run with the Wyvern still latched into the side of the ship.

So various motions occurred that disturbed the inner ear. VR could also cause epileptic fits in people who were susceptible. While Berg *could* have "stepped out" at any time, rapid VR reversion was often worse than space sickness.

So Bergstresser had ended up frequently "virtually" down on his hands and knees, puking his still chemically roiled guts out. In reality it had been down the front of his cat-suit and all over the inside of the Wyvern. Then he spent two hours cleaning it out.

"Top is going to ream him a new asshole," Jaenisch said.

"I'm fine," Berg replied. "I just needed a shower."

"The God damned training schedule *said* fifty-minute periods with a ten-minute break," Hattelstad said.

"Did big old Two-Gun have a bad time in VR?" Lujan asked, mock sadly. "Awww, cry, Two-Gun. Go waaah."

"Shut the *grapp* up, Drago," Jaenisch snarled.

"*Grapp* you, Jaen," Sergeant Lovelace said, rolling out of his rack. "You don't *grapp* with my team!"

"Then tell him to keep his *God damned mouth shut*," Jaenisch said. "Or go try *six hours* of VR after he's just gone through *grapping* pre-mission phys."

"Awww, is big bad Two-Gun all queasy?" Crowley snorted.

"Shut the *grapp* up, Crow," Lovelace said. "And you, too, Drago. Lock this *maulk* down. Now. Jaen, if you've got issues with my troops, you bring them to *me*, got that?"

"Sure, Lacey," Jaen said, his teeth grinding. "No problem. I've got a date with the first sergeant, anyway. Berg, you're off-duty for the rest of the watch."

"Not going to bitch," Berg admitted, closing his door.

"Enter."

Jaen stuck his head in Admin and looked around.

"Gunnery Sergeant Hocieniec, a moment of your time if you please?"

"That sounds formal as hell," Hocieniec said, standing up. "What you got, Jaen?"

"In private, if you please," Jaen said.

"Privacy is a rare commodity on a ship," Hocieniec said, looking over at Gunnery Sergeant Frandsen.

"I'm up to my ears in paperwork," Big-Foot growled. "So you can take it somewhere else. Or I can pretend I didn't hear it."

"Come on in, Jaen," Hocieniec said.

"Berg just got done with his first Wyvern training," Jaen said, closing the hatch and hitting the lock. "All six hours."

"Shiny. How'd he do?" Hocieniec asked.

"Pretty good for the first two straight hours," Jaenisch replied. "After that it sort of went downhill."

"Too bad . . ." Hocieniec said, frowning. "He seemed . . . Wait, you mean two hours *straight*? No breaks."

"No, Gunnery Sergeant, I mean *six* hours, straight, no breaks," Jaen said, trying to remain blank-faced. "He still scored an 88 percent, but most of it was in the first two hours."

"Who in the *grapp* did that?" Big-Foot said, looking up from his paperwork. "Sorry, ears off now."

"Who's in charge of simulator training?" Jaen replied.

"I am going to *grapping* kick Driscoll's fat lazy *ass*," Gunny Hocieniec said, standing up.

"While that would be fun and I'd love to hold his arms," Jaen said, "I'd rather you weren't in Portsmouth."

"I outrank him!"

"Yeah, but the court-martial wouldn't care, Gunny," Jaen said. "I managed to cool off on the walk over here. If I might recommend, could you bring it to the first sergeant's attention?"

"Damned straight we will," the gunny snapped. "Follow me."

"What we are dealing with here, is hearsay evidence," the first sergeant said. "I will look into this. Return to your duties and I will have a word with Staff Sergeant Driscoll."

"Top . . ." Gunny Hocieniec said.

"Return. To. Your. Duties," the first sergeant stated bluntly. "And I will have a word with Staff Sergeant Driscoll and look into this event. Is that clear, Gunnery Sergeant?"

"Yes, First Sergeant," Hocieniec said, coming to attention.

"You and Jaen hang out," Powell replied. "I'm probably going to need you two, and Berg, at some point. Where's Two-Gun?"

"In his rack, First Sergeant," Jaen said, also at attention. "I told him to chill. I also got an authorization for a second shower. He needed it."

"He should have stepped out the minute he got nauseated," the first sergeant said with a sigh.

"Two-Gun wouldn't quit if his leg was being slowly gnawed off, First Sergeant," Jaen replied. "He might be on the wrong side of gung-ho, if you know what I mean."

"Ain't no wrong side of gung-ho, son," Top said. "One potential failure here was to ensure he knew it was authorized to stop if he became physically ill. Now, you two go back to your duties, but don't get into anything I can't snatch you out of. I'll look into this."

"Just answer Top's questions and otherwise keep your mouth shut," Jaen said as he knocked on the first sergeant's hatch.

"Enter."

Staff Sergeant Driscoll, wearing a furious frown, was standing on the left side of Top's small office. Gunnery Sergeant Hocieniec was on the right, one jaw muscle twitching furiously but otherwise blank-faced.

Sergeant Jaenisch entered at a march and came to attention parallel to Hocieniec.

"Sergeant Jaenisch reporting with a party of one," he stated.

"Move over, Jaen," Top said. "Okay, PFC Bergstresser, a couple of questions. Staff Sergeant Driscoll handled your prep for simulation, yes or no?"

"Yes, First Sergeant," Berg said, sweating.

"What was the continuous duration of such training?"

"Six hours, First Sergeant."

"And did you remain in your armor and in VR for that entire time?"

"Yes, First Sergeant."

"Was that your understanding of Staff Sergeant Driscoll's orders?"

"Yes, First Sergeant."

"And did he or did he not instruct you to take a break every fifty minutes?" the First Sergeant asked.

"He did not, First Sergeant."

"I thought he'd be smart enough—" Driscoll snapped.

"Silence," the First Sergeant said, quite mildly. "PFC Bergstresser, did you become physically ill during simulations training on the last watch?"

"Yes, First Sergeant."

"PFC Bergstresser, were you informed by Staff Sergeant Driscoll that if you became physically nauseous you were to discontinue simulations?"

"No, First Sergeant," Berg said.

"Were you, at any time in training, instructed that that was to be your action during simulations?" the First Sergeant asked.

"No, First Sergeant," Berg said after a moment's thought.

"You may expand upon that if you wish," the First Sergeant said.

Berg thought long and hard on that one.

"During Basic we had monitors during training, First Sergeant," Berg said. "Also during Force Recon Operator's Training. I had never previously been in training without a monitor. We were specifically ordered during training to remain in armor unless told to discontinue simulation by the spotter. As far as I was aware, Staff Sergeant Driscoll was acting as spotter, First Sergeant."

"Like I have time to—"

"I said *silence*," the first sergeant said, much less mildly. "Sergeant Jaenisch, PFC Bergstresser, you are dismissed. Gunnery Sergeant Hocieniec and Staff Sergeant Driscoll will remain."

» » »

"I think I just made a serious enemy in Staff Sergeant Driscoll," Berg said.

"Everybody hates Driscoll," Jaenisch said. "And he hates everybody else. Most miserable son of a bitch I've ever met."

"Yeah, but the Ops sergeant has so many little ways to *grapp* with us," Berg pointed out. "It probably would have been a better thing to keep our mouths shut."

"Let Top worry about that," Jaen said. "Driscoll's going to be pretty careful about how he *grapps* with us for a while. Just get the damned WCT test right. That's going to be his first real chance to *grapp* you over."

"I will," Berg said. "Unless he tries to *grapp* with the numbers. He's got full control over the information."

"Point," Jaen admitted, frowning. "Let me look into that."

"Jeff," Miller said as the Marine first sergeant entered their shared compartment. "You look like you had a bad day."

The chief warrant officer had a small collection of dried flowers laid out on the table. It was the same ones he'd left Earth with but every few days he rearranged them in the vase.

"That I did, Todd, that I did," Powell said, sitting down at the small fold-up table in the room and pulling out a bottle marked "Poisonous! For topical use only!" He poured some of the clear liquid into a cup and raised it. "Hair of the dog?"

"Got my own," the SEAL said.

"So, you used to be a team chief, right?"

"Many a year, Jeff," Miller said, pulling out an Aunt Jemima syrup bottle and squirting some syrup in a cup. He took a sip and picked up a ribbon, tying it onto a mum.

"Ever have a completely efficient son of a bitch working for you?" Powell asked. "One that couldn't get past the son of a bitch part?"

"You had a problem with Driscoll," Miller said, chuckling. "Yeah, had an assistant team leader one time like that. Guys hated him but he was so *grapping* efficient I hated to lose him."

"Solution?"

"Canned his ass," the SEAL said, not looking up from his flower arranging. "His personal efficiency was great but he was enough of a bastard it *grapped* with the team efficiency. Is Driscoll the type to backstab?"

"In a heartbeat," the first sergeant admitted. "And he's got a real case of the ass at a Nugget, now. Entirely Driscoll's fault. He stuck the kid in a Wyvern sim for six hours."

"Ouch," Miller said. "Is the kid sane?"

"Bitch is that he just went through pre-mission phys," Powell said, finishing his fungal treatment and putting the bottle away. "Threw up all over himself for four hours."

"And he stayed in the can?" Miller said. "Good lad."

"Seems to be," Powell said. "But is he worth losing the most efficient ops sergeant I've ever had? First, there's not a damned thing to do with Driscoll on the cruise. Second, I need him where he is, at least until I can get a replacement. But figuring out who he is going to *grapp*, just to pass the time, is getting to be a full-time job. Looking for a job in Ops, Chief Warrant Officer Miller? Nothing but headaches and no extra pay, but you get petty power and the chance to *grapp* people on the side."

"Not on your life," Miller said, chuckling.

"I could ask the Old Man to draft you."

"We share a room and you have to sleep sometime."

"Point."

"Switch him out for one of your team leaders," Miller said. "That puts him in the position to be *grapped* by Ops instead of doing the *grapping*."

"Point," Powell said. "I wish he'd shown this proclivity before we left Terra, though. That way I could have done the switch with time to shake down. Doing it mid-cruise is going to suck. No, I'm not going to shake up the teams that badly. Putting Driscoll in a team leader slot would just destroy a team. But, yeah, Driscoll's got to go. What's the word from on-high?"

"Runner found a world right off," Miller said. "One that has air and water and all that. But we're going to do a full system survey before we approach. I'd say three days, minimum."

"I'll pass that on," Powell said, grinning. "Otherwise I'm sure the scuttlebutt circuit will have it as we're going to crash into the sun."

"*Grapp . . .*"

Berg stuck his head out of his bunk at the sound of rapid and constant bitching from down the compartment. He was recovering from his third day of VR training in the Wyverns. After what had apparently been a serious drubbing from Top, Driscoll had, in very simple terms as if he was a slightly retarded child, explained that he was to take a break every fifty minutes. Hattelstad had been designated as his spotter, which had thrilled Hatt no end since it meant two days of, basically, looking at a *grapping* Wyvern that wasn't doing anything.

"What happened?" he asked PFC Walker who was at the back of the group.

"Driscoll got pulled out of ops," Walker said. "And Staff Sergeant Sutherland got pulled over to be the ops sergeant!"

Sutherland was First Platoon's Alpha Team leader and assistant platoon leader. The move had pulled a serious spoke out of First Platoon's wheel.

"*Maulk*," Berg said, rolling back into his rack.

"Don't worry, man," Sergeant Dunn said, walking by his rack. "It wasn't just the *maulk* he did to you. He's been *grapping* up royally ever since we left. I'm surprised Top kept him as long as he has."

"Force Recon staff sergeants are hard to find," Sergeant "Onger" St. Onge said from across the compartment. "But, *grapp*, Sutherland. Why couldn't Top have picked Summerlin or Rocco?"

"Or a sergeant," Jaen said. "I know the position calls for a staff, but a sergeant can do it, especially on a cruise. I mean, all it is is *grapping* writing training schedules."

"You hear?" Drago said, walking into the missile room. "They found a planet!"

"We're in a star system," Berg said, taking a sip of water. As predicted, he'd smoked through training in the suit, once he didn't have to spend six continuous hours in it. He'd run through his mandated training items in two thirds the time considered "standard" and was now on his WCT testing. "Most star systems are probably going to have planets."

"It's a moon," Gunnery Sergeant Frandsen said. "One around a big Jupiter type planet. What he meant was that we've found a planet that might support life, so we're going to do a ground survey."

For WCT a senior NCO, operations NCO or higher had to be present to prevent cheating. Frandsen was one of two obvious choices. Since some of the pass/fail points were subjective, Berg had been told he was *grapped*. Big-Foot was unrelenting. You did it perfectly by the book or Frandsen would screw your scores so hard it would look like you shouldn't have passed Basic much less be in Recon. So far, however, Berg had smoked the tests to even Frandsen's satisfaction.

"Well, if I want in on that, I'd better get back to testing," Berg said, draining the bottle of water. "Permission to resume testing, Gunnery Sergeant?"

"If you think you're up to it, PFC," Gunny Frandsen said, shrugging. "But if you're going to puke, you need to call the session."

"No problem, Gunnery Sergeant," Berg said, sliding into the suit.

"You sure about this?" the first sergeant said.

"Is that my signature on the pad?" Gunnery Sergeant Frandsen said, warming up to full Frandsen-Rage.

"Calm down, Big-Foot," Top said, shaking his head. "I take your word for it. I've just never seen you give someone a one hundred percent score. Not even your own troops."

"I'll take Two-Gun any time he wants to transfer," Big-Foot said. "He's got a much better handle on the physics *maulk* than I do. That's where everybody falls down. I've been saying—"

"If we're going to throw these sensors at them we need more basic physics training," Top said. "I even agree. If you can figure out how to get that done, send me a memo."

"Well, one thing that comes to mind is that we've got a team of top physicists, all of them former professors, sitting around with their thumbs up their butts."

"Point," Powell said. "But that's for later. Shiny. He's passed on WCT. But we're not posting the score. Just that he passed. And don't put anything on the scuttlebutt circuit. He just passed. No big deal. Got it?"

"Yes, but why?"

"Kid's got enough problems," Top said. "He's smart as hell and he passed the new FOT course. Face it, he's better prepared for this than most of the old hands. That's causing some resentment. This would cause more. Let him just glide in."

"Shiny," Frandsen said. "If you say so."

"We've got a planet to survey," Top said. "Make sure your teams are prepped. Let me worry about the rest of the company."

>>          >>          >>

"Are you sure about this?" Captain MacDonald asked. "The team hasn't trained together, yet. And Two-Gun is brand new."

"That's the team to use, sir," First Sergeant Powell replied. "Because of Two-Gun. Probably there's not going to be anything weird on this world. It's pretty dead. But if there is, if there's something weird, I think that Berg's background would be useful. He's shown a better ability than anyone in the company, excepting me, at reading the more complicated sensors. Charlie Second is my recommendation for first plant. But it is, of course, your decision, sir."

# 13

## Semper Fi Ad Astra

"Second Platoon, report to the Missile Room. Uniform is blacksuit."

"What the *grapp?*" Hatt said, hopping to the deck.

"Sounds like our platoon is security," Jaen said as the door to the compartment opened.

"Second, we're on security," Gunnery Sergeant Hocieniec said. "Get into your skins and get your asses down there."

"Gunny, does that include us?" Jaen asked.

"Did I *exclude* you, Jaen?" the Gunny snapped. "You are, in fact, first plant. So get your game face on."

"Holy *maulk*," Hatt said.

"Congratulations, man," Drago said, frowning. "Guess you drew the straw. First world, first plant. Ought to get a nice shiny medal out of that."

"If we don't get boiled in acid or something," Jaen pointed out. "*Grapp* it. Get your skins on, people."

"Move it, people," Top bellowed. "We have a mission to perform!"

"Charlie, suit up," Hocieniec said. "Alpha, ammo draw, Bravo, weapons. First is getting up and they'll handle weapons and ammo for Alpha and Bravo."

"Let's get it on," Jaen said, striding over to the suits and sliding his hand into the armpit. "Jaen."

"Hatt."

"Two-Gun," Berg said with a sigh.

He stepped into his suit, feeling as if he'd just left. In fact, he'd only finished his WCT on this system six hours ago. Four hours of sleep. *Grapp.*

Wait . . .

"Gunny," he said before he sealed up. "Permission to speak."

"You're not in Basic, Two-Gun," the gunny said, shaking his head.

"Agreed, Gunny," Berg said, swallowing. "I was just wondering. I *did* pass WCT, right?"

"Yes, Two-Gun, you passed WCT."

"Can I ask my score?" Berg said.

"You can ask, but I can't answer," Hocieniec said, his face cracking in an unusual smile. "Top sealed the record. *I* don't even know. I do know that Big-Foot asked me if I'd transfer you to his platoon. And I told him to *grapp* off. Good enough?"

"Yes, Gunny," Berg said. "Thank you, Gunny."

"Now close your *grapping* suit and get your game face on, Two-Gun."

Berg ran through the diagnostics on the suit carefully, exactly as if he hadn't used it six hours before. But everything was in the green. It took about fifteen minutes, nonetheless, by which time Drago, Crow and Sergeant Lovelace were back with the team's weapons.

"I got it, Drago," Berg said, opening up his suit and stepping out.

"I know how to mount a *grapping* Gatling, Two-Gun," Drago said.

"I'm sure you do," Berg responded. "But it's my ass. Don't you mount your own?"

"Not if I've got somebody else to do it," Drago said. "But I do watch real careful."

"I've got it," Berg said, chuckling and hefting the sixty-pound gun into its slot. There were two mount latches and a traverse mechanism to attach and he slapped all of them into place rapidly.

"You *have* used these," Drago said, frowning.

"The new Force Recon Operator's Training is nine weeks long," Berg said. "Three weeks is pure Wyvern. Mark Fours, though. I

think they're getting stuff from us and making it sort of Space
Marine training. I wondered about the class on physics and
astronomy. It was only an hour in the training schedule, but it
seemed a little weird. By the way, does anyone know what star
we're at?"

"Maybe we all should go through it," Drago said sourly.

"Let's just see if we all get home," Berg said, grinning.

He had also loaded his ammo, with help from Lance Corporal
Mackey "Candle-Man" Chandler from Alpha team. The Wyvern
Mark V accepted over four thousand rounds of 7.62 mm in its
cavernous ammo bin. On the other hand, he could run through
that in one minute of continuous fire. Berg wasn't sure the
Gatlings were the best choice for their mission, but the things
certainly had authority.

"Attention on deck!" Top bellowed.

"At ease," the CO said, striding down the missile compartment.
"Ready, Charlie?"

"Ready, sir," Jaen said, still at attention.

"Glad to hear it," the CO said. "Full sensor sweep. I'm not
going to be the only person monitoring. You can bet the Skipper is going to be watching close. Make damned sure there are
no threats before you give the all clear. I wanted to send Bravo
through after you, but the science team is kicking up a fit so next
out is going to be geo. Keep an eye on them but mostly keep
your attention outwards. If there's a threat, it's our job to make
sure the scientists get back to the ship. Understood?"

"Understood, sir," Jaen said.

"Two-Gun, just use the Gatling."

"Aye-aye, sir!"

"You guys, make us proud. Semper Fi."

"Oorah, sir!" the team chorused.

"Suit up."

"Go live," Jaen said as they approached the elevator. The CO
and Top had followed them and now stood beside the aliglass
compartment.

"Hatt, online," Hattelstad said, arming his cannon.

"Two-Gun, online."

"Let's go."

# 14

## Excursions and Alarums

The designated landing area was a broad plain on the east side of one of the islands. The large volcano that had generated the island appeared to be dormant or dead, one of the criteria for landing.

"Six hundred meters AGL," the pilot said, coming to a hover.

"Deploy landing jacks," the CO ordered.

"Deploy jacks, aye," the chief of boat replied, pressing the control.

Nuclear submarines are not designed to be supported on land. But there was sufficient structural rigidity to them that the *Blade* could land as long as enough surface area of the underside was supported.

The landing jacks of the boat, therefore, were eight large self-leveling jacks spaced along the bottom of the sub where a long add-on pod had been installed. When retracted they fit flush into the pod mount. The mount had been extensively tested in both saltwater conditions and atmosphere but everyone assumed that at some point in the mission the combination of space conditions and saltwater was going to shut one or more down. The *Blade* could level with as few as six, but if she lost more than two, there was no way for her to land on a solid surface.

"Jacks one through eight report down and ready," the COB said.

"Descend three meters per second to fifty meters, one meter per second thereafter," the CO said.

"Three meters per second to fifty meters, one meter per second to touchdown," the pilot replied.

The boat drifted downwards somewhat faster than a feather until there was a slight shudder and it settled at a slight tilt.

"Jacks report contact," the COB said. "Holding."

"Disengage drive," the CO said.

The boat settled slightly more as the full weight came on the jacks.

"Jacks report full weight in local gravity," COB replied.

"Level."

The COB pressed the auto switch and the boat shifted back and forth, finally settling on an even keel.

"Jacks leveled and locked."

"Touchdown complete," the CO said. "Boo-yah, baby. Gentlemen, we are sitting on the surface of a different planet. XO: Planetary survey SOP."

Ground Lock Two was a converted Momsen lock. Momsens were escape hatches, designed for the crew to exit the submarine in the event of an underwater emergency. Called "Mom" hatches by the crew, none had ever been used successfully. But when families were given tours of the boat the crew could point to the hatch and say: "See, Mom, if anything goes wrong we can get out that way."

The lock, which was already oriented downwards, had been converted into an elevator capable of holding three Wyverns or five unsuited individuals. In this case it held Jaenisch, Bergstresser and Hattelstad. While Dr. Dean had argued strenuously that he should be the first person to set foot on "his" world, the SOP for planetary survey was fixed: Security went out first.

On boarding, the first step had been decontamination. Just as nobody wanted to bring some alien bug on the boat, the egghead and diplomat consensus was that the reverse was also the case. The elevator was first flushed with air, then pumped full of water with a caustic agent in it. Then the suits were dried. It took about five boring minutes to start descending.

There wasn't much conversation as the circular aliglass elevator exited the boat and lowered to the ground. The team had trained for this moment and each man knew his job. So they were just really hoping they didn't *grapp* up.

As soon as the elevator grounded, Jaenisch slid back the door and stepped out, striding ten meters forward in his Wyvern and taking a knee, the mounted 7.62mm Gatling gun tracking back and forth in search of threats.

Hattelstad followed, moving to his right and turning right rear, with Bergstresser looking left rear.

"Full scan," Jaenisch ordered, changing the input parameters of the primary camera. First he scanned through the full electromagnetic spectrum, starting in deep infrared and scaling up all the way to X-rays. Then he switched to secondary particles and waves. Nothing. "Watch this light gravity. You can jump the Wyverns in this and lose control.

"Anybody got anything on passive?" Jaenisch asked.

"Nada," Hattelstad said.

"Got a bunch of stuff coming out of the boat," Bergstresser said. "*Grapping* quarkium drive's got me whited out that way. Other than that, nada."

"Go active," Jaenisch said, switching on his radar and multifrequency lidar. A full sweep by the trio showed nothing but volcanic rock and some sort of red vegetation down by the seashore. If there was anything there, it was invisible to Earth and Adar tech sensors.

"*Blade*, this is Alpha Team," Jaenisch said. "We have zero signs of threat."

"Send out one more team of security," the CO said. "Then the survey teams. Tell the eggheads they're just going to have to wait. No offense, Commander Weaver."

"None taken, sir," Bill replied.

"And, yes, you can go out, too," the CO added. "Take that SEAL with you."

"Yes, sir," Bill replied. "Thank you, sir."

"I'm not going to sit here with you bouncing around the compartment," the CO said with a grin. "Which you would be if I didn't let you out of the boat."

» » »

"We need to lay in a full seismic survey," Dr. Dean said as Runner slid open the doors of the elevator. "And a random survey of the rock surface. When are we getting the drill?"

"It's being assembled right now, Doctor," Runner said, holding out one arm of the Wyvern. "Sir, you need to *follow* us."

"Very well," Dean said impatiently. "Play your silly games. But head inland as we exit. I want to get up to where the rocks haven't been disturbed by the Marines."

"Security, Geo Two," Runner said. "We're headed up to the hills inland. Dr. Dean requests that the Marines not 'disturb' the rocks before we get there."

The voice-activated system automatically transferred the call to the ground force commander.

"Understood, Geo," Captain MacDonald replied dryly. "I'll try to keep my boys from messing anything up."

"This is one mother*grapping* cold ball of ice," Miller said. He swiveled the head of the Wyvern to look around, then started dancing sideways.

The Mark V Wyvern was a significant upgrade over the Mark IIIs that were the last Miller had used. But they still had some issues. He swore the Adar had made them *more* likely to disco. At least for him.

"Oh, it's not all *that* bad," Weaver argued. "I mean, it doesn't look like much right now . . ."

Miller got the feedback loop under control and overrode the "head" controls to pan around in a 360.

The volcanic island wasn't a complete loss. Throw in about thirty C of temperature, some palm trees and . . . well just about everything and it would make a hell of a resort.

The shore was almost pure lava rock. Indeed, most of the vista was lava rock. That which wasn't a crashing sea. With no continental landforms, the waves had thousands of miles to build up steam and some of them were nearly two hundred meters high. And the winds that drove them were high. The two humans probably couldn't have stood against the gale if it wasn't for the Wyverns.

More Wyverns were spread out across the rocky terrain, though. The planetology and biology teams were out collecting samples. On the outer perimeter the Wyverns of the Marine security were hunkered down and looking for threats. Threats were pretty unlikely in Miller's opinion, but the Dreen had turned up in some damned unlikely places. All they needed was a little biosphere and they were in like flint.

There *was* some vegetation. Red tendrils straggled up from the edge of the incredible surf. Some of them had flowerlike heads that waved in the howling wind.

"Don't look like much is putting it mildly," Miller said. "Although I could probably do a nice arrangement with some of those flowers . . ."

"You SEALs never look *up*," Weaver said.

Miller toggled the override and looked up.

"Okay," he said about a minute later. "You've got a point."

E Eridani Beta was a striped gas giant with the striations of massive winds and storms rippling its gaseous surface in a dozen colors. Hovering overhead, it was the dominating feature of the sky.

But while it dominated, it wasn't the only thing in the clear sky. At least a half a dozen lesser moons were in view, moving fast enough to track. They reflected the light of the planet, and with their own varied surfaces they were a rainbow of color in the sky.

Last but not least, there was a thin, very dark, ring around the planet, close in.

All in all, it was a spectacular sight.

"I mean, there *could* be intelligent life," Weaver argued.

"Yep, there it is, right there," Miller said, pointing.

"Where?" Weaver asked, excitedly.

"Them flowers," Miller said. "Smartest things on this planet. They finally crawled out of the water, looked around, went '*Maulk*, this is one mother*grapping* cold ball of ice of a planet' and devolved back to flowers. I know that if *I* developed consciousness on this planet, I'd lose it as fast as possible. Through repeated blows to the head if necessary."

"Alpha Team," Lieutenant Berisford said. "Geo is heading up to the hills. They have requested that you not 'mess anything up' but I want you to move up there and cover them. Ensure the security of Dr. Dean especially. In the event of emergency, screen their retreat. Charlie, I want you moving to a secondary position. Bravo, you're with me in reserve."

"Let's move," Jaenisch said, bounding into a run.

"They don't want us in front of them, Jaen," Berg pointed out.

"Got that," Jaen said. "We'll vector left. Head for that cluster of boulders. In the event we have to screen them, that's our assembly area."

"Got that," Hatt said. "I don't see much to screen them from."

"Nothing on any of the passive sensors," Berg pointed out.

"Just because you can't see it, doesn't mean it's not there," Jaen said. "Space Marines, remember?"

"Lichenlike growths," Julia said, kneeling the suit and flipping out a sample probe. The science suits had specialized sampling tools attached to the right "hand" of the suit. She used a scraper to pick up some of the growth off the rocks and slid it into a sample tube.

"Do you want to check out that red stuff?" Master Sergeant Ed Bartlett asked. The Bio Team Leader gestured towards the shoreline where massive waves hammered what was apparently a high cliff. The waves looked to be a couple of hundred feet high and the spray flew up higher than the boat.

"If we do, we're going to have to be careful," Julia said. "It looks worse than Antarctica. You slip, boy, and I'm not sure we're going to be able to find you."

"Noted," Ed said. "But we are going to have to get a sample, right?"

"Yes," Julia said, standing up. "But first we need to do random sampling of the area to see what sort of microgrowth is on the rocks. Then we sample out from the boat. *Then* we go down and see our little red friends. Frankly, I think we should be looking for a more lively world, instead, but I suppose you would call this 'good training.'"

"*Grapp*," Hattelstad said as his Wyvern went airborne.

Dr. Dean had, apparently, collected his samples and was now headed back to the ship.

Charlie had been crouched in a cluster of boulders watching for a threat that never came for a good six hours. So they were ready to head back. As soon as the science party was halfway down the hill they had bounded out to "screen their retreat." At which point the reduced gravity had struck.

Moving in reduced gravity was always difficult. It was possible, if you were careful, to get more speed out of the armor by "bound-ing," taking long strides that were impossible in Earth's gravity well. It worked well on flat ground and *could* be done on hills. But you had to be careful.

In Hatt's case, he'd taken one bound just a bit too far. He'd intended to hit a flat spot and instead intersected a boulder. His right leg went out from under him and for just a moment he was airborne. Then he slammed onto his back.

"*Grapp*," he repeated.

"Like I said, *watch* the gravity," Sergeant Jaenisch said, coming to a crouch near the fallen suit. Berg landed on the other side, tracking back the way they came.

"Charlie, status?" the platoon leader called.

"Just a slip, sir," Jaen replied as Hatt got to his feet.

The Wyverns would have been impossible to get out of a position on their backs were it not for the design of the arms. While the human arm could not wrench behind its back with any strength, the Wyvern "arm" could. So Hatt simply slid his arm behind his back and flexed, rolling the Wyvern onto its stomach. From there, it was just a matter of pushing himself to his feet.

"Slick move, grease," Berg said. "I suggest a new team name."

"Turtle?" Jaen asked.

"I was thinking Grease," Berg said. "But Turtle works."

"*Grapp* you, rookie," Hatt said.

"Methinks the lance corporal is offended," Berg said.

"Methinks the lance corporal has point," Jaen replied. "Let's move."

"Charlie, move east and screen bio team. Same deal, don't mess anything up."

"Seems like we *always* get point," Hatt said.

"Shut up and move."

"Well, that was a whole lot of nothing," Jaen said, rolling into his rack with a sigh. "Twelve *grapping* hours in a Wyvern with nothing to look at but rock. What *grapping* fun."

"View was cool," Berg said.

"Some of us weren't looking at the pretty planet," Hattelstad said sourly.

"Then you weren't looking for aerial threats," Jaen snapped. "Yes, the view was cool. But I could wish they'd pulled us off in less than twelve hours. Man, I'm whacked. I'll see you guys tomorrow." With that he hit the closure on his rack and opaqued it.

"I'm for bed," Berg said, stripping out of his skinsuit. The blacksuit stank to high heaven and they were only issued one. He put the suit in a zipper-lock bag and stuffed it away in a compartment. "Damn, laundry's not till the end of the week."

"Stuff a nannie pack in with it," Drago said, leaning out of his bunk. "It'll be fresh as a daisy tomorrow."

"Really?" Berg asked.

"Really, Two-Gun," Drago said. "I guess we've all got things to learn."

"Thanks, man," Berg said, pulling the suit back out. He slid a nannie napkin into the bag and sealed the whole thing back up.

"*De nada*, man," Drago said. "We were getting tired of the smell, anyway."

Berg chuckled and sealed his bunk, lying back with his arms folded on his chest. Then he reached up and turned up the circulator before getting out another nannie nap. He was getting tired of the smell, too, but his next shower cycle wasn't until day after tomorrow. He rubbed down in the confined quarters, then doused the light.

It had been a long day.

"Dr. Dean is busy trying to assimilate all the data we've collected," Dr. Beach said, smiling faintly. "So I have asked Master Sergeant Runner to present the planetology report on Dean's World."

The post-survey meeting was taking place in orbit, everyone having decided that even *space* was a more hospitable place than "Dean's World." The wardroom was crowded with the boat's senior officers, most of the heads of the science team, Miriam and Mimi. The latter two had turned up and, respectively, charmed and assumed their way into the meeting.

"Thank you, Doctor," Runner said, looking at his notes. "Dean's World is an atectonic rocky moon with marginal habitability. I'm gonna have to lecture.

"Earth is a tectonic planet. That means that it had continental masses that, slowly, move and recycle material through subduction, crustal folding and volcanism. The reason that this occurs is that there's a chunk of crustal material, more or less the size

of the Pacific, which is missing. Very early in Earth's development Earth's moon struck the planet with a glancing blow and
picked up that material.

"Earth has deep oceans, which act as a heat sink and temperature regulator and constant tectonic processes refreshes the
atmosphere. Furthermore, crustal material is able to 'emerge'
because the water all flows into the oceans.

"In the case of Dean's World, such a strike never occurred.
Thus all the tectonic material is trapped under a solid crust. That
crust is buried under an ocean that is more or less uniformly
deep and relatively shallow. One of the reasons those waves get
as high as they do is that the bottom is only about six hundred
feet down, more or less everywhere.

"The only rocky land is where some volcanoes have burned
their way through the crust and formed islands, more or less like
pimples on a teenager's face.

"Basically, it's Mars with a better atmosphere and a bunch
more water, probably because of the better atmo. That's the
planetology side. Bio?"

"It's a Class Four biosphere," Julia said. "Red chlorophyllic ana-
logue. Very simple life forms. We didn't get to do much sampling
in the ocean but I'm perfectly happy letting follow-on researchers
do that. No indications of Dreen genetics anywhere. The world's
clean, in other words. Be a decent place if we ever have to find
a new place for penguins and polar bears. Well, except for the
$CO_2$, which would kill them in a few seconds."

"I think the important point that we're missing here, Captain,"
Beach said, "is that there *is* a habitable moon here, and that
there is life. This is a biosphere that is right at the edge of current theory."

"Agree with that one," Julia said, nodding.

"So that means that we could be finding habitable planets
around virtually any star you'd care to visit," Beach concluded,
pointing to the plasma screen on the wall. It was currently getting
the "take" from the forward camera and showed a billion stars.

"Our current mission is to do a cautious survey of the immediate
area," the captain pointed out carefully. "To find as many habitable
planets as we can and to look for intelligent life. Commander
Weaver, does this planet, in your opinion, change the plan of
the current survey?"

"A bit," Weaver admitted. "What Dean's World shows is that while we should look primarily at main sequence stars, if we overlook such things as moons in marginal life zones we might miss the needle. I think we're going to have to either go faster or extend the survey time to ensure we don't miss something."

"XO, can we stay out longer?" the CO asked.

"We've got the food," the XO said. "I'd mostly worried about atmosphere and water. But we took on a bunch of water on Dean's World. Some of it we cycled for fresh water and we broke out a bunch of $O_2$. That extended our time by maybe a week. If we can keep doing that, we're only food limited. We've got enough food onboard for ninety days. Of course, the crew's gonna get pretty tired of three-bean salad—"

"Our mission parameters were to stay out for up to ninety days if we could keep up on air and water," the CO said, frowning. "Given the hazards associated with entering star systems, I'm going to say we're out a maximum of sixty days, less the time to travel to Sol. That way if we *have* to limp through a transition zone, we can. Very well. So much for the lovely 'Dean's World,'" he said, grinning slightly. "Where next?"

# 15

## Many MANY Connotations

"Stable orbit around Tau Ceti established," the pilot said proudly.

"Sergeant Runner has detected *two* planets in the life zone," Commander Weaver said. "He picked them up on the way in by eyeball. One's a gas giant. Much smaller than Uranus though. Probably moons; he's surveying at the moment."

"I'm glad you pronounced it properly," the CO said dryly. "Vector?"

"Two-three-three degrees mark dot five to the nearest," Weaver said. "Four AU and a bit. That is outside of the liquid water zone by at least three AUs. The liquid water zone for Tau Ceti is between point six and point nine AUs sir. Hey, that's a rocky body."

"Pilot, come to two-three-three, Warp One," the captain said. "It's a planet so we should have a look at it."

"That . . . doesn't look like much," the captain said.

"Atectonic again," Bill replied, nodding. The "planet" looked more like Earth's moon. It didn't even have the ruddiness of Mars. It was just a pitted gray surface. "Little or no atmosphere. We don't have the spectral readings, yet, but I'd guess no vegetation. Probably the core is low in radioactives so it's cooled off and the atmosphere stopped being recycled. Call it Lord Kelvin's World. Back when scientists were beginning to understand how old the Earth really was, Lord Kelvin, who was the premier physicist of his day, 'proved' that even if Earth started off as a molten ball, it would have cooled off in no more than six thousand years. Since there were volcanoes, it had to be less than six thousand years old. One of the better pieces of complete garbage science ever written because he didn't know about radioactives. It's radioactive material that keeps the Earth's core molten. Also a great example of why you should never let theory get in the way of empirical data. Anyway, if there ever was intelligent life there, it's long gone."

"Let's try the next system. Commander Weaver?"

"Epsilon Indi perhaps, sir," Weaver said. "But exit in that direction is going to be . . . interesting. And there are some things we should consider."

The CO came over and looked at his screens, puzzling them out.

"What . . . things?" he finally asked. "The heliopause bow shock's in the other direction."

"Luyten 725, also known as YZ Ceti, is going to be off our port if we head for E Indi," Weaver said, zooming out on the screen so the nearby star was evident and then highlighting it. "It's close at a heading four-eight. We've got three systems fairly close to each other here and I'm not sure what that's going to do to the disturbance zone."

"Head around it," the CO said definitely.

"Agreed, sir," Bill replied, rubbing his forehead. "But . . . I would like to recommend an astrophysics fly-by at least. Perhaps an extensive survey. The combination of bow shock from YZ Ceti and the trail material from Tau Ceti might have picked up some interesting stuff."

"Stuff," the CO said, monotone. "Define . . . stuff."

"Well sir, some astronomers figured out a few years back that the Tau Ceti system has about ten times too much cometary and asteroid type debris in it. Nobody understands why," Bill said, shrugging. "Perhaps something out there is the cause."

"Wait a minute," Spectre said with a frown. "You mean we've been riding around inside a star system that has *ten times* more debris in it than normal and nobody bothered to *mention* this?"

"Uh, sorry, sir; space is big." Weaver said.

"I realize that space is *big* Lieutenant Commander, but . . ." Spectre paused as the implications of Weaver's comment sank in. "Oh hell, what was the increased probability of hitting something?"

"About a half of a percent worse than in a normal system, sir." Weaver tried not to grin. "Its Kuiper belt should be about ten times more populated than ours, but that ain't a particular problem. Populated is an overstatement of *any* Kuiper belt."

"Right. Astrophysics survey sounds like a good idea." Spectre relaxed in his chair. "Science stuff."

"The interesting thing, sir, is that YZ Ceti is only about point seven-two light years that way." Weaver nodded out the window in the direction of the little M class flare star.

"And that's interesting . . . why?" the XO interrupted. Spectre remained quiet.

"Well sir," Bill said, turning to the XO. "These two stars are so close together that there might be an explanation for the unusually dense Kuiper belt here. Perhaps it has something to do with how their gravitational anomalies interact with each other out past the heliopause."

"So, you are saying that we need to go out there where space is all screwed up even worse than around a *typical* star so we can take a look?" The XO raised his voice a bit to emphasize his concern.

"Uh, well sir, we could go a few degrees in right ascension to the center point between the stars. The gravitational effects should be somewhat less, uh, pronounced there." Weaver looked back at his screen and typed in a few commands. The optimization program picked a spot slightly to the right of the center of mass point between the two star systems.

"Somewhat less pronounced," the XO muttered under his breath. "What the hell does *that* mean?"

"I know I'm gonna regret this," Spectre said. "But it *does* sound interesting from a scientific perspective and that *is* part of why we are out here. Senators will be impressed with pretty pictures and give us tons of money. So, pilot set a course for the observation point to the right of the center of mass between the two stars. Coordinates at your discretion, Mr. Weaver."

"Aye, sir."

»     »     »

"Normal space drive," the CO said as soon as the first gravitational ripple hit. "I don't see much, Commander Weaver."

"It's there, sir," Bill replied. "I'm getting some really interesting particle readings already—"

"What the hell was that!" the XO exclaimed at the bright white flash of light a few thousand kilometers or so to port.

"Don't know, sir. I'll zoom the big scope in on it." Weaver typed in the telescope sensor commands and then zoomed in on the region the flash had come from. "Sir, I've got some images of the region. You want them on the big screen?"

"Let me get a forward view," Spectre said pompously, then grinned. "God, I love this job!" When the image came up on the screen, though, the captain whistled at the whirling and flickering debris cloud on the flat screen just right of the window. "What the hell?"

"I think I've got it figured out, sir," Weaver said, musingly. "Basically, we're out in a region where the Oort clouds overlap."

"The what?" the XO asked.

Weaver closed his eyes for a moment and tried not to sigh. The XO was a great submariner but getting basic cosmology into his head was a pain in the . . .

"The Oort cloud is a big spherical cloud that surrounds solar systems," Bill said. "Ours stretches about three light-years out from Sol and starts about a light-year out."

"Shiny," the XO said. "Oort cloud. What's it got to do with here?"

"The stars are so close their Oort clouds overlap. The comets from both stars are probably getting zipped around like crazy from the disturbance zone. We might have even seen a comet from YZ Ceti smashing into one from Tau Ceti. Hell of a lot of energy in that. The odds of us being here at the right moment to see a collision must be, well . . . astronomical. Hey! That means . . ." Weaver looked back at his screen for a moment then bit his lip as he thought. "Oh, *maulk.*"

"All hands! All hands! Artificial gravity anomalies are occurring due to unusual local disturbances. Report to stations and wait for systems to reset and normalize. Further orders will follow."

"What the flying *grapp* does that mean? Artificial gravity anomalies hell, we're up-*grappin'*-side down!" Drago barked over the net.

"There is no up or down in space." Two-Gun laughed as he

writhed against the restraints in his rack. He thumbed at the control on his game system and considered asking if anybody was interested in a game of Dreen War. But . . . probably not.

"Two-Gun," Jaen barked. "If there is no up or down in space then why . . ."

" . . . Am I lying on the God damned ceiling of the bridge?" The XO stood while rubbing the bump on his forehead. The other members of the bridge crew had had the foresight to fasten their seatbelts before entering into the disturbance zone, but their full weight pulling them against their restraints was probably as uncomfortable as the XO's bruised forehead and ego.

"Mr. Weaver?" Spectre asked calmly. He was hanging from his restraints with his hands peacefully folded on his lap.

"Okay, now *that* was unusual," the COB admitted, taking a sip of coffee. He was standing on the ceiling as well, but had somehow managed to land on his feet.

"Uh, COB?" the pilot said, gesturing with his chin.

The COB looked down and frowned. There was a spot of coffee on his tunic.

"Well, lemme tell you, pilot," the COB said, frowning at the spot on his dignity. "That wasn't *nothing* to the typhoon we got into off Fiji one time. I was in a fast boat and . . ."

"I'd suggest that for future reference, sir, seat restraints are mandatory during trans grav disturbance travel," Weaver said with a smile, droning out the COB's *long* story. "I think the system is confused because the gravity outside the ship is so confused. Think of a pond and what happens when you drop two rocks in the water about a meter or so from each other. When the ripples collide with each other you get destructive and constructive interference zones. We're in a destructive one."

"Mr. Weaver . . ." Spectre was not quite losing his patience. After all, he had been a fighter pilot most his career and hanging upside down was child's play. But most systems in the ship had not been designed for that particular configuration and he hoped that he wouldn't start getting reports of equipment ripping from the floor and walls on a mass scale throughout the ship. The flashing yellow warning lights were distracting enough as it was; at least they had turned off the damned klaxons.

"Right, sir. Tchar says the ball is working properly, so it has to be the region's gravity. We must be upside down in a gravity well and for some reason the artificial gravity can't compensate for it. It must be a hell of a gravity well. This is just a speculation mind you." Weaver scanned data from all the ship's sensors in front of him and was having a hard time making heads or tails out of their situation.

"As soon as you can, Mr. Weaver . . ."

"Right, sir. Hmm . . . Working on it," he said under his breath.

"CO, ship's getting hot," the XO said, holding onto a stanchion but still managing to keep an eye on his job.

"Commander Weaver?" the CO asked. "What happens if we turn off the drive?"

"Unknown, sir," Bill replied. "Weird gravitational effects, that's for sure."

"Weirder than this?" the XO asked incredulously.

"Gravity different in different parts of the ship, sir," Weaver replied. "Maybe. Just a guess, really."

"Will it *kill* us?" Spectre ground out carefully.

"The gravity shouldn't be that high," Bill said. "Hopefully. Or tidal effects. And, sir, with all due respect, *heat* will kill us for sure. We've got to chill."

"All hands! Stand by for chill! Stand by for gravitational anomalies! All damage personnel, suit and strap in!"

"Now *this* is more like it," the COB said, swaying slightly, refilled coffee cup grafted to his hand. "Reminds me of a storm we got into off Iceland one time . . ."

"Fascinating," Dr. Beach breathed, watching the play of data on his screen.

To his inner ear, he was, apparently, in a rocking boat. One that was rocking randomly. But he really wasn't paying attention to that. The data streaming from the hull-mounted collectors was too extraordinary.

"Conn, astronomy. Is Dr. Weaver available?"

"Holy cow," Bill muttered, looking at the take from the cosmology department. "Sir, this is a *really* weird place!"

"Do tell," Spectre said as the boat seemed to gently roll over.

"You bet it is," the XO said sourly, hanging onto a stanchion. "We just had a pipe bend and blow out in engineering. Nobody knows *why*. It just *bent*. And we're not chilling as fast as normal."

"The temperature in this region is way over deep space, sir," Bill said, off-hand. "That's why. Forget this being a soup. It's more like . . . a sieve. We're getting particle readings like you'd get off of a bunch of runaway accelerators! Hell, rad count is *way* up. There's got to be every odd astrophysics anomaly in the galaxy running around in this region!"

"Well, our heat's finally coming down," the XO said, looking at the instruments. "In about another twenty minutes we can start the engines back up."

*Heat. Too much heat. It blasted and burned. But the waves that had caught it were unstoppable, dragging it into the fiery depths.*

*As the heat dissipated, though, it felt a voice, a calling, summoning it to the very source. A place of healing. A place of growing and of change. The ons and offs could stream more rapidly now. Things began to make some sense as more ons and offs flowed over the cooling pathways.*

*If only the heat would go away, the ons and offs could continue, and it could . . . Be.*

"We're chilled," the XO said.

"Mr. Weaver?" the CO asked.

"Got it. Try moving forward, Captain. That might move us out of this region of the anomaly."

"Okay, do it."

"All hands! Stand by for Warp! Stand by for gravitational anomalies! Stand by for . . . Oh, just grab on and hope for the best!"

"God damnit Berg! Is there left and right in space?" Drago hadn't stopped complaining since they had been ordered in their bunks.

"Must be."

"Must be that we moved far enough to get trapped in another destructive interference zone, sir. This time the system is confused so that the port side is down." Bill continued to chew his lip and type away frantically at his keyboard. He reached out for his mouse that dangled to the right. His five-point restraints were beginning to dig into his right ribs a little. "I'm really surprised that the black box can't overcome this. Maybe there is more to it than just gravity. Hmm . . . there are a lot of particles here. . . ."

"Going forward didn't seem to help much." The XO now standing on the port side wall of the bridge rubbed at a new bruise on his arm. Looking around the bridge he realized there was just no way he could make it to a seat and get fastened in. He'd have to make do and hold onto handrails as best he could. He hadn't learned his lesson from the previous attempt at moving and had neglected to fasten his safety restraints again.

"I need to make some measurements. This will only take a minute or two."

"Look at that!" The pilot pointed out the window at a brilliant flash of light that seemed to be just outside the ship. In fact it was likely hundreds of kilometers away.

The XO frowned. "Way too close for my tastes."

"Agreed," Spectre said.

"This disturbance zone must act like a funnel to the comets of the two star systems. The odds of seeing impacts should be too unlikely for us to see two of them in just a few minutes. That can't be shiny," Weaver said. "Can't. Be. Shiny."

"Figure out a way to get us out of here, Mr. Weaver," Spectre said sternly but still with a fighter pilot's calm and cool demeanor. Gibbering was simply not on.

"Perhaps we should try backwards this time?" the XO asked.

"Forward brought us here. Backward might take us right back." Captain Blankemeier shrugged as best he could from the sideways falling position. "Maybe we are thinking about this too two-dimensionally while we are in three-D space?"

"Sure, sir. We could try going out of the ecliptic above or below it so to speak, but the gravitational disturbance has a spherical wavefront so it is three dimensional too. And each star system is moving with its own spin rate and proper motion so there will be a lot of frame dragging and similar effects. Hmm . . ." Weaver paused in thought. "That might work. Good idea, sir. We should go in a vector of . . ." He typed in some code and started running a quick simulation.

"Mr. Weaver?" Spectre was hesitant of interrupting the scientist turned naval officer. But time was quite possibly important here and the CO didn't want to be around when a couple of comets caught the *Blade* in the middle of a chance meeting.

"Working on it, sir." About a minute later as the simulation completed, he had what he was looking for. "We need a continuous thrust vector arced upward and inward towards YZ Ceti in the same direction as its proper motion."

"Proper motion?" the XO asked.

"The star's motion within the galaxy."

"Whatever, just do it, Mr. Weaver," Spectre ordered.

"Aye, sir. Pilot, the coordinate vectors are coming in now." Weaver tapped one last key, sending the coordinates to the pilot's console. "Hold on XO, this could get bumpy."

"Aw *maulk*."

"Don't worry, sir, can't be any worse than one time off Johannesburg . . ."

The ASS *Vorpal Blade* lurched up along the vector that Dr. Weaver had calculated, in fits and jerks. The ship's internal artificial gravity vector fluctuated randomly and pretty much covered all possibilities, flinging the ship's XO around like a cowboy riding a bucking bronco. As the ship began to match the velocity vector of YZ Ceti's proper motion the gravitational randomness smoothed out into a flow of ups and downs that could only be described as a slow tumbling feeling. Then finally the alien artificial gravity system created by the little alien black box inside the coryllium sphere down in the engineering section of the ship was able to overcome the gravitational fluctuations and the ship's gravity settled out with only a few bumps and jerks here and there but no more unusual onboard gravity configurations. The XO of the ship was likely to describe the "bumps" and "jerks" a little more, well, dramatically.

"Astrophysics survey." The XO shook his head and dragged himself to his feet. "The next time someone, and I'm not naming any names, suggests an astrophysics survey I'm going to—"

"Yes, well, *that* was interesting," the CO interrupted as they cleared the last gravitational wave. "Remind me never to let you do *that* again. No astrophysics surveys from within an AU of said anomaly. Got it?"

"Yes, sir," Weaver replied. "But I think I understand now why Tau Ceti has too much debris in its Kuiper belt and Oort cloud, sir."

"No kidding." The XO laughed, rubbing at his sweat soaked brow and slightly massaging the red bump on his forehead. The ride had been far less than "fun" for him. He made it to his station and collapsed in his chair.

"XO, why don't you report to sick bay and let 'em check you out. That looked like a hell of a ride."

"Aye, sir." The XO nodded as he glanced at the messages on his screen. "Note that we have a few damage reports coming in but nothing serious. Repairs are already underway. A few minor casualty reports are starting to come in as well."

"Glad it's nothing serious. Sick bay." Spectre nodded at the XO and clicked his safety harness free. "Where to from here, Mr. Weaver?"

"Epsilon Indi, sir." Weaver pointed. "It's that away."

"Let's go find some planets worth talking about and take a break from any undue astrophysics surveys for a while," the CO continued. "I think I'd rather be fighting the Dreen . . ."

"Yes, sir."

# 16

## Under Pressure

"INTRUDER ALERT! INTRUDER ALERT! SECURITY TO
REPEL BOARDERS!"

It had been ten days since they landed on what everyone now
knew as Dean's World. Ten days of, as Sergeant Jaen called it,
"dickbeating." Weight training, maintenance, Wyvern sims, climbing
fast-ropes, drills, computer sims . . . The latter had been proven to
increase combat efficiency but everybody had a hard time not calling it "gaming." Basically, you lay in your bunk and played Dreen
War over and over again. He wished they'd at least let the Marines
play Halo III, which was more interesting by light-years.

Ten uneventful days and then in the middle of the platoon's
"night" . . .

Berg's eyes flew open as the light automatically came on, but
he waited a heartbeat for the next order.

"SECOND PLATOON, WYVERNS. FIRST AND THIRD,
GROUND MOUNT."

Both voices were prerecorded female voices, but the second order
was important. It detailed who had to clear the compartment first.
Since *everyone* couldn't move in the corridor at the same time, the
personnel with Wyvern duty had to move first. Since they only had
to slip into skinsuits, they could be dressed fastest, anyway.

He pulled out his skins and then dropped to the deck. Right on top of Lance Corporal Revells from Third Platoon.

"Get the *grapp* off my back, Two-Gun!" Revells said, trying to struggle through the mass to the forward hatch.

"Get in your *grapping* rack, Revells," Jaen snarled. "You're not supposed to be moving, yet!"

"Get your elbow out of my face!"

"Get your dick out of my ass!"

The compartment was a madhouse of struggling Marines as everyone tried to get to different hatches at once, all order dissolved.

"FREEZE!" the first sergeant bellowed from the forward hatch.

Berg froze in place, arms over his head, most of the top of the skinsuit over his face.

"Two-Gun, you may lower your arms," Top said into the silence. "Carefully."

Berg shrugged all the way into the skinsuit and lowered his arms, carefully. He had to; the Marines were packed in the companionway like sardines.

"The term here is FUBAR," the first sergeant said, quietly. "Y'all can't struggle out of this compartment in two minutes, which is the time it's *supposed* to take you to settle on your equipment. So we are going to do this again. And again. And again. Until you can, in fact, exit this compartment in an orderly fashion. At that point, and at that point only, will we then move on to donning said equipment and drawing ammo in an orderly fashion. And don't think you can cut time by keeping your uniforms on. We're going to randomly pick which platoon has which duty. Back in your racks."

Berg waited at the position of attention, sucked into the bulkhead of the locker room, until Gunny Hedger from Third Platoon shouted "Third, Clear!" then grabbed the stanchion on the gear locker and drove it, hard, towards the starboard bulkhead. Staff Sergeant Summerlin was on the far side of the locker and, if anything, was driving harder.

Falling in on the armor was a drill that had to be done as precisely as a parade. As tight as the ship was, getting everyone onto their armor, fast, was nearly impossible. But it could be done if everyone did their jobs precisely on the beat.

With the containers spaced, the Marines darted in lockstep

to their positions and almost simultaneously opened their compartments. As the seats fell they turned and, nearly in unison, sat down, reaching up and pulling their armor over their heads. The combat harnesses were attached to the armor so they came down at the same time. Two moves and the armor was latched. Reaching up, they pulled down their helmets, then snatched out their weapons and stood up.

Gunny Hocieniec was already there, in armor, and nodded at the first sergeant.

"One minute and forty-three seconds," Top said. "Seventeen seconds under standard. I think we can better that, but it's good enough for now. Fall into the missile bay."

"I'd say that I'm only going to say this once," the first sergeant said, striding down the ranks of Marines standing at attention. "But I'm not. I'm going to say it over and over and over again. We do not know what we are going to encounter out here. We know the Dreen are out here, somewhere. And some of you have fought them before and know how nasty that is. But we could, God help us, run into nastier things. Or better. Or nothing, as on Dean's World. That's the point. We just don't know. So each and every one of you had better be ready for *anything* at any *time*. Somebody who *is* ready for anything at any time is a Space Marine. I will not accept anything less in my company. Is that clear, Marines!"

"Clear, First Sergeant!" the Marines shouted.

"You've all passed Common Tasks, but to be a Space Marine means practicing *un*common tasks. We're going to make you the sharpest, hardest group of Marines in the Corps, because *that* is being a Space Marine. We're going to make you the *smartest* group of Marines in the Corps, because *that* is being a Space Marine. And if you've been tired of dickbeating, then you're going to get *really* tired of what I'm going to throw at you. By the numbers, replace your gear and hit your racks. Tomorrow, we're going to start adding some polish."

"So, mesons are a type of boson," Drago said, furrowing his brow. "They're two quarks . . ."

"A quark and an anti-quark," Berg said, trying not to sigh. "That's actually pretty important."

As the first sergeant had said, it was time to put the polish on the apple. The Marines had been looking at their sensor systems and learned to recognize basic information but they'd never really understood what they were looking at. Berg had been drafted as an ad hoc instructor for his platoon and was trying to get the basics of particle physics through some skulls dense enough to stop neutrinos.

"Okay, they're a quark and an anti-quark," Drago said. "Any particular type of quark? I mean, strange, charmed?"

"What in the hell is a charmed?" Lovelace asked. "What's a quark?! I mean, there's all these particles and it's all about quarks but nobody ever said what a quark is!"

"Oh, *maulk*," Berg muttered. "It's in the manual but . . . quarks, muons, and electrons are elementary particles. That means they can't be broken into smaller pieces. And quarks are the only fundamental particle that interact through all four of the known forces. They come in six flavors: up, down, top, bottom, sometimes called beauty for some damned reason, charmed and strange. And, no, I'm not making this *maulk* up, Drago."

"This is some crazy *maulk*."

"Oh, I forgot something else. They're also waves, the whole 'both a particle and a wave' thing."

"How can it be both?" Lovelace asked, grabbing his head. "That doesn't make *grapping* sense!"

"Welcome to quantum mechanics," Berg said, grinning. "Whenever you really get something in quantum mechanics, you're required to roll a sanity check. But that's the point; they're both and since they're down to the point where they can be both, there's nothing smaller. Quarks and electrons are what make up 'solid' matter. Put enough quarks together and you get the basic protons and neutrons of an atom. Electrons are just . . . electrons and they spin around the outside of the protons and neutrons in atoms. Oh, and until the Adar came along we thought that you could only have quarks in twos or threes or some other multiples but never a single quark by itself—"

"Why?"

"Well, the gluons that hold them together—"

"Gluons? *Grapping* gluons?"

". . . get stronger the farther apart you try to pull them until they eventually pop back together. But somehow the Adar know how to pull the quarks apart and keep them that way. And as far as I know there are probably only two humans alive who really understand how that is possible and both of them are here on this boat—"

"*Grapping maulk*, here he goes again!" Drago rolled his eyes.

"Let us guess . . . Commander Weaver is one of them?" Lovelace added.

"And Mimi is the other . . ." Berg finished.

"Damn, I know you've got a jones for the commander, Two-Gun, but the kid too? That's serious jailbait."

"And as I was saying," Two-Gun ignored the comment. "Then there's photons . . ."

"Photons! Hey, I've heard of that. Like a photon torpedo?" Drago said excitedly.

"Uh, yeah, Drago," Berg said. "Like a photon torpedo."

"I got one right!"

"Light's a particle and a wave. Sort of."

"What's a tachyon?" Lovelace asked. "I heard something about tachyons."

"It's what you get when you let rednecks play with particle physics," Berg said, grinning again. "Seriously, what it is is a theoretical particle that travels faster than light *only* and would take infinite energy to slow it down to light speed. Most of these particles only exist when you have some sort of weird reaction, and decay in less time than I'm going to bother to explain. Some of them, though, hang around and we get to detect them."

"I don't get why the sensors don't just say 'hey, bosons!'" Sergeant Lovelace said.

"Because there are different aspects to particular mesons and bosons," Berg said. "The real kicker is fermions and pentaquarks. So far, we've never seen pentaquarks in nature. If you're getting a reading that indicates pentaquarks or other high-multiple quark formations, then something strange is going on. Fermions do occur from some natural processes. After all, electrons, muons, and tau particles are fermions and we are pounded by electrons and muons all the time. The higher energy ones are the key to things we are interested in. Usually, you get them as the result of a recent quarkium explosion or a Higgs boson nearby. Pentaquarks, too. So if you see a bunch of high energy fermion or pentaquark signatures, fermions that are nonstandard fermions, there's probably been a big boom."

"Which means there might be another," Sergeant Lovelace said, nodding. "I'm starting to see some point to this."

"Go, Brain," Lujan said, grinning. "I think it's a much better handle than Two-Gun."

"Can it, Drago."

"And baryons, more specifically mesons, can indicate there's a gate around," Berg said.

"Wait!" Drago interrupted. "I thought it was muons that said there was a gate around?"

"Well, yes. Muons are a fermion that is a fundamental particle like an electron and they do indicate a boson or a gate."

"This is confusing as hell."

"It is that," Berg continued. "According to something I read on the declass science system notes, there was baryon presence after we did that dimensional shift. So baryons might indicate something is dimensionally shifting. Or, and this is sort of science fiction, it might mean there's something out of phase. It might be invisible, in other words. It might even be able to see you, but you not see it. Possibly. Maybe sorta."

"Wait," Drago said again, frowning. "I got some pentaquark readings from my Wyvern the last time we did maintenance."

"Ship gives off pentaquarks," Berg said, nodding. "We've got a quarkium drive. That's another indicator. But we don't give off baryons unless we're doing a dimensional jump. Maybe."

"Dude, I did *not* join the Corps to study quantum physics," Crowley moaned.

"Welcome to the Space Marines." Berg shrugged. "Learning this is nearly as important as learning how to field strip your M-675."

"Everybody's to fall in to the missile room," Staff Sergeant Summerlin ordered. "Some sort of announcement."

"Shiny," Crowley said, standing up. "Anything has to be better than this *maulk*."

The XO arrived late to the command meeting and set a stack of paper in front of the captain before sitting down.

"That's not only the consumables report but the data backing it." The XO sighed. "We've only got two more days of air and we've already cut the water ration to one quarter. Unless we find some water to process we're going to be breathing pure $CO_2$ in another three days."

Standard submarines have very limited fresh water and oxygen storage. Both could be extracted from seawater so large storage areas were a waste of space. The *Vorpal Blade* had been designed with much more extensive storage of both, mostly by cutting down on its ballasting system, but it was still limited.

Since the surprising find in the E Eridani system the ship had been cruising for three weeks without finding another even semi-habitable planet. And things were getting a bit grim.

"Commander Weaver," the CO said, looking over at the astrogator. "Suggestions?"

"Well, it's a bit tricky, sir," Bill replied. "We haven't found any planets with an Earth type atmosphere, which was what I'd been hoping for. But we can get all the air we need from gas giants. Water, too, but that's trickier."

"I thought their atmosphere was hydrogen," the XO said, puzzled.

"Mostly hydrogen," the CO replied. "But it's got a lot of other stuff in it."

"That's the point, sir," Bill said, nodding. "Oxygen, after hydrogen, is about the most common atom in the universe. Stars pump it out constantly by first fusing their hydrogen into helium then continuing fuse down to iron in what is known as the CNO cycle . . ."

"Chief of Naval Operations?" the XO asked, confused.

"Carbon-Nitrogen-Oxygen," Bill said, trying not to sigh. "Oxygen's a common fusion point and is put out in quantity as a by-product of stellar evolution. Most of it ends up locked up with hydrogen, water in other words, but a good bit gets into the atmosphere of gas giants. But gas giant atmospheres are layered. We're going to have to drop actually *into* the atmosphere and hover while we extract $O_2$. There's going to be water there, too, but it's going to be disperse, and extracting it is going to be harder. We'll pick up some from the oxygen extraction process, but I think we're going to have to find the rest of it in ice."

"Land on a moon?" the CO asked.

"That or get it from a ring," Bill replied, thinking hard. "An ice moon landing has problems we've encountered before. The pads tend to melt the ice and if it refreezes getting out is a bitch, pardon my language, sir. But if we pull up next to a ring and grab some ice out of those . . . We've never really been close enough to a ring to see how stable the orbits of the individual chunks are, sir. And, admittedly, our people are not as extensively trained in EVA as we might like for something like this. But if the rings don't work, we can always land on a moon. Every gas giant we've surveyed has had multiple ice moons."

"Well, that's one for the manuals," the XO said, making a note. "Life support consumables, lack of. Gather from gas giants and rings."

"Do we have the equipment to extract $O_2$?" the CO asked. "I don't recall it as part of our package."

"Nothing in the SSM," the XO said, referring to the Bible of Submarine Operations. "Or the mission specialist's manifests, the Flight Readiness Manifest or the Payload Requirements Document. Checked them all."

"You extract it with electrostatic systems," Weaver replied. "At least preliminary extraction. Then you have to separate it with pumps. I'm pretty sure engineering can *blage* something . . ."

"Whenever I hear that word, I've learned to cringe," the XO said.

"Sir, I can safely say that we have the finest *blagers* in this entire solar system," Weaver replied.

"As far as we know, we're the *only* life in this solar system," the XO said.

"That, sir, was my point."


"The ship is running low on consumables," the first sergeant said, walking down the compartment before the assembled Marines. "The commander's trying to find some source of air and water. In the meantime, the water ration is cut in half and no showers. Personal hygiene issue is one pint of water a day. Use it for shaving your filthy beards. If we can't find it, we can head back to Earth easily enough, we're less than a day away. I'm told that one of the options may cause some pressurization issues. If so, we'll spend some time in the racks until they get things fixed. For now, get back to training. Second, you're up on the PT schedule next."

"Oorah!" Crowley said. "More PT, First Sergeant! I need to let my brain clear."

"Unfortunately," Top said, grinning maliciously, "no water means no PT. When you can explain the characteristics of a fermion you back off the quantum physics. Two-Gun, see if you can help him out with that. Make sure you cover why they can't form Bose-Einstein condensates."

»        »        »

"It is the reverse of an ion drive," Tchar said, holding one massive hand out. "Mangon wrench."

"So you polarize the molecules, then pull them in different directions," Mimi said, handing the Adar a wrench that was about half as long as she was.

"Yes," Tchar said. "Fortunately, we have spare electromagnets for the drive system. Both for stabilizing the sphere and for the electric propeller drive. Gibmak screwdriver."

Mimi handed over the tool, which looked very much like a Phillips head if about three times the size of any screwdriver she'd ever seen before.

"What are these tubes from?" she asked.

They were working in a small space to the port of the main engine room. The reason she was having to handle the tools is that while the space was plenty large enough for a human, Tchar had to lie on his belly and crawl into it.

The space was also packed with very large piping, bigger around than Mimi.

"A portion of the water coolant system for the reactor," Tchar said. "Not radioactive. It was the intake system for the reactor. We'll use this point to polarize the molecules, then extract them further on. The big problem will be installing the fans. The ship, essentially, doesn't have any. Fortunately, they left some pumps in place so we'll try to use those. The human machinist mates are working on that. Can you move that very large circular magnet?"

"I would be able to if it weren't stuck to the floor," Mimi said, tugging at the big magnet. "But not now."

"I suppose I shall have to," Tchar said, working his way out of the narrow gap. He grabbed the magnet and yanked it upwards, breaking the hold it had on the deck, then rolled it in ahead of him. "I could use some help with this. Nothing too heavy, but I'm not sure most people on the ship could fit."

"Not a problem," Mimi said, squeezing past him.

"If you could stand there," Tchar said, pointing to a narrow gap and handing her the large wrench. "I've disconnected the pipes as you can see and installed a mount for the magnet the machinist mates made for me. Now we have to lift it into position and attach it. I will lift it, you will attach it." He pointed to several large screws.

"Got it," Mimi said, picking up the wrench that was nearly as long as her arm. One of the screws, the size of her hand, went on the end and was held in place by another magnet.

"You will probably have to start it by hand," Tchar said, lifting the heavy magnet with a grunt and sliding it into the mount. "Now, if you will."

Mimi slid in the first screw and started it by hand, then slid three more in.

"And on the other side," Tchar noted.

She scooted under the magnet and picked up the screws on the other side, sliding them in. Then she got the screwdriver and tightened them as well as she could.

"That has it," Tchar said. "The pipes are braced at this point so they can hold the weight of the magnet." He picked up a communicator and pressed the button. "Red?"

"Here, Tchar."

"Try the pump."

A whistling sound started up after a moment and Mimi felt her hair blowing in a breeze.

"It's sort of . . . leaking," she pointed out. "That's going to the outside of the ship, right?"

"Currently it is bypassed to the internal air," Tchar said. "But, yes, that is a problem. But for this we have a human solution." He slid back and rummaged in his massive toolbox, finally lifting something out.

"You humans have the most amazing inventions," he said, holding up the roll of silver tape. "This is something called 'duck tape' which has, I have counted, over two hundred and sixty-seven uses. This makes two hundred and sixty-eight. I have always wondered: Why is it named for a water bird?"

"The ions can be selectively separated, but it won't be one hundred percent," Weaver said, gesturing to the large makeshift gas flow and separation system. "We're going to have to pump it down and separate it that way secondarily. This will just reduce the pumping problems."

"Commander, for once pretend I'm a fighter pilot with an English Lit degree and an interest in stars based mostly on how pretty they are," Spectre said.

"When you apply a magnetic charge to air molecules, it makes them sticky in different ways," Weaver said, grinning slightly. "So when you apply another magnetic charge to them, they pull away from each other. But they don't do it real well, unless you have a more elaborate setup than we can build. However, they will also turn into liquid at different temperatures and pressures. So we'll put them under pressure and some of them will become liquid before others. Nitrogen becomes liquid at a higher temp and lower pressure than oxygen. Oxygen goes liquid at a higher temp and lower pressure than hydrogen. So we're going to need three very high pressure, cryogenic pumping systems. Cryogenic means—"

"Really cold," Spectre said, nodding. "Know that one."

"So what we *should* get is mostly oxygen after the ion separation; then we'll pump it down to ensure we've separated it. Now, there's an alternative, if this works *really* well, to getting the water from ice. But it's kind of crazy."

"This entire mission is crazy," the CO said. "And I haven't had so much as a shower in a couple of days. Gimme crazy."

"Burn it," Bill said. "Put oxygen and hydrogen together and set them on 'fire' and you get water."

"Fire in a sub is not something most people like," the CO pointed out. "In a spaceship with nowhere to set down, it's even worse."

"Duly noted, sir," Bill said.

"So let's table that one, Commander Weaver," Spectre said, grinning. "And let's not tell the crew you even thought of it."

"Yes, sir," Bill replied.

"When's this going to be ready?"

"About four hours."

"We've got about sixteen hours of $O_2$ left."

"Also duly noted, sir."

"Stable orbit around Sirius Echo," the pilot said as the ship coasted to a stop in an orbit around the gas giant.

The Saturn-sized planet was twelve AU from the AO class star, well outside the life zone and, like every gas giant they'd seen, was striped in broad bands. In the northern hemisphere there was a large spot, similar to Jupiter's Great Spot, that indicated a stable gas giant "hurricane." In addition to this gas giant, there were two rocky inner planets, either one massive asteroid field or two slightly larger than Sol's and four more gas giants in the system. But this one's atmosphere, Dr. Dean had assured them, was the one most likely to have a broad water belt. The rocky inner planets both resembled Venus with a fiery atmosphere and little or no water. The other gas giants were far enough out that water would be deep in the atmosphere and harder to extract.

Besides fourteen moons and counting, the planet had six rings. Four were aligned with the planet's equator, like Saturn's, but two more, very thin, were at angled orbits.

One thing that had been discovered in Sol's system during the shakedown cruise was that "white" rings were composed of ice moons that had been torn apart by tidal stresses. Darker "black" rings were composed either of older ice that had picked up dust or, quite often, of rocky material. Fortunately, the largest of the rings was bright white, indicating recently formed "clean" ice.

"XO?"

"Sir?"

"Find out how soon we can get oxygen," the CO said. "I'm in the mood for a cleansing breath."

"Will do, sir."


"We have one last problem," Tchar pointed out. "At least, one that we're aware of. The pipes have a plug on them. It's an airtight screw fitting that's designed to be removed. But it's on the exterior of the ship, actually up underneath."

"That's going to be interesting," Bill said, looking over at the chief engineer.

"I would recommend an EVA removal under microgravity," the ship's engineer said.

Lieutenant Commander Dan Schall was a career sub officer, a "nukie" to the core. Short with brown hair going gray and a florid face, he was phlegmatic to an almost insane degree. However, given that he had lived his entire career around nuclear reactors that were right on the edge of being nuclear bombs in a cylinder underwater, phlegmatic was good.

"I'm not sure that's the best idea, Commander," Tchar said, clacking his teeth. "The seals on the system are not the best I've seen. That could result in explosive decompression of the engineering spaces."

"Which would be, in sub parlance, bad," Weaver said, smiling. "But getting to the damned thing in anything other than microgravity would be a bitch. I'd recommend evacuating the reactor spaces before we try it. I'll handle the EVA with the CO's permission. I'm trained in Wyverns. Can I *get* a Wyvern to it?"

"Yes," Schall said. "The inlets are at the base of the ballast vents. All you have to do is enter through ballast vent fourteen. But the patch is heavily bolted. It's designed to be removed, but not easily. And please bring it back with you. We don't have a spare."

"Duly noted," Bill said.

"There are other Wyvern-qualified personnel onboard," Tchar said. "Not only security, but the mission specialists. In the event of explosive decompression, they could stand by to support repairs."

"Good point," the Eng said. "I believe we have a plan."

"The write-up on this one is going to be interesting," the XO said. "Item one: Some of the machinist mates need to be trained in EVA."

The ship was equipped with microgravity tools. Bill had ensured that. What he had *not* ensured was that they had tools for every part on the ship. When he had turned up at the air lock with his torque compensating wrench, the machinist mate assigned to assist him had just laughed and handed him the wrench that *fit*. It was about half as long as Bill was tall and was *not* torque compensating. In fact, under "not torque compensating" in the dictionary was this wrench. It was the essence of torque. Torque-ness to the nth degree. Torque-sausage. Torquemada. If there was a Nobel prize for torque . . .

"Preparing to EVA," Bill said as he closed the airlock door.

"Door is remotely released," the XO said over his radio. "Good luck, Commander."

"Roger that, sir," Bill replied. He dialed down the pressure in the lock and checked his internal monitors. No leaks in the suit. This was a good thing.

"Ready to exit," Bill said as the gravity fell off. They were out of normal space drive and in microgravity. He'd better get this over with, quick, or the crew was going to be bitching up a storm.

The air lock door opened and he clipped off a safety line, then exited. The Wyvern had been equipped with EVA "mag" boots and he got a boot on the hull, then lifted himself up to get the other in place.

"This is so cool," Bill muttered.

"Say again, Commander?" the XO asked.

"Sorry, sir, talking to myself," Bill said.

"Stay on mission, Commander," the XO advised.

Bill didn't reply as he started walking down the hull. He'd originally entered the fields that he had, hoping he could get into the NASA mission crews. Later he'd taken other paths when it was pretty clear he didn't get along with NASA. But he still wanted to get into space. He'd done a couple of EVAs before, but he never *ever* lost his love of the glory of the sight.

And this one was pretty darned glorious. The ship had taken up orbit well out from the gas giant but it was clearly visible, filling a quarter of the sky. For that matter, Sirius, the Dog Star, a star he'd looked at as a kid through his first telescope, was glaring blue-white at him off to his right. Cool didn't begin to cover it.

There it was. Sirius, the brightest star in Earth's night sky. The blue-white main sequence dwarf star that could be seen by almost every inhabitant of Earth except those living above about seventy-three degrees or so. Here Bill was, right smack in the vertex of the Winter Triangle or the constellation Canis Major or the "Big Dog." Weaver was as giddy as a school boy. The scenery couldn't have been more of a boyhood fantasy come true if there were naked women in it. Cool.

Hell, for that matter, climbing around on the exterior of a sub was pretty cool. He'd exited from air lock Four, which was another converted Momsen lock, and so he was walking on the "bottom" of the sub. It was the closest to Ballast Vent Fourteen but it was still a bit of a hike. For that matter, there weren't any clip points for his safety lines so he was having to use more magnets for those. Setting the magnets in place, in the Wyvern, wasn't the easiest thing in the world. He'd pretty much come to the conclusion that the Wyverns needed some work for EVA stuff.

Finally, he reached the entrance to the ballast vent. The thing was about six feet across and nine "deep." But getting into it was going to be tricky. And then there was the whole unbolting the thing under microgravity. Especially in a Wyvern.

He clipped in a safety line, then bent down and undogged his boots, getting one hand on the edge of the ballast vent and pulling himself inside. As soon as he turned on his external lights, he easily spotted the intake. It had six massive bolts holding it on and was about a meter across.

Bill pulled up his "legs" and planted them on the far wall of the vent, then got settled in a hard position where he could reach all six of the bolts but wouldn't shift when he applied torque with the torquiest wrench in the solar system.

"Command, EVA," Weaver said. "Preparing to remove patch."

"We see you, Commander," the XO replied. "Emergency teams in place."

He unclipped the wrench, which was tethered to the suit of armor, and applied it to the first nut. The nut didn't want to move, but the Wyvern had the power of a small machine press and it broke free easily enough. He slowly undid the nut all the way to the end, then removed it, carefully, and stowed it. There *were* spare nuts for the patch, but waste not, want not.

All six of the bolts came off easily enough after the first. But the patch was still holding. Bill tried to pry at it with the fingers of the Wyvern, but it wasn't moving. So he clipped the wrench back down and pulled out one of Tchar's massive flat-head screwdrivers. Placing it at the join he pried upwards.

The patch sprang off explosively, smashing into the far wall of the vent with a *"Bong!"* he heard through his armor, rebounding into his armor hard enough to nearly break him free from his position, then bouncing down into the depths of the ballast vent.

Along with patch came a blast of air and water. And it didn't stop.

"Command, EVA," Weaver said, as calmly as he could. "We appear to have explosive venting."

"Warning! Warning! Depressurization in Missile Compartment! All personnel to racks and suits!"

"Good thing we're already in the rack," Berg said. He had his zero-gee straps in place and, for once, wasn't nauseated in free fall. Apparently the effects of the pink stuff had finally worn off.

"No *maulk*," Crowley said. "So can you apply super-cold temperatures to a gate and shut it down? I mean, it's based on a boson, right? And under super-cold conditions they'll gather together."

"No way to do it," Berg replied. "Not that I've heard of. But there might be some experiments in it. I dunno. Guy to ask would be the astrogator. He's the world's foremost gate expert. But as far as I know, the only way to close one is the way he closed one in the Dreen War, drop a super-huge quarkium package through the gate and get it to explode on the *other* side.

"I wonder what happened to those Dreen worlds," Berg said.

"Blew the *grapp* out of them," Drago said. "I heard that was a big *grapping* explosion."

The inter-rack communicators could be set up for multi-person chat and it was a way to pass the time while waiting to see if the ship was going to completely depressurize. Also a good way to take their minds off of it.

"And it nearly went off on Earth," Jaen said. "At least that's what I heard."

"Most of it's still classified," Sergeant Lovelace added. "That's just the rumor."

"I saw it on CNN," Jaen argued.

"And we all know how reliable *that* is," Drago said.

"*Grapp*," Jaen said. "Point."

"Be interesting to see if cryogenics could do it," Berg said.

"Go up to the bridge and ask the astrogator," Drago said. "I double dog dare you."

"Maybe the next time we're on deployment," Jaen said. "You could side channel him if you get up the nerve."

"Hell, I'd be hard-pressed to talk to him at all," Berg said.

"You seem comfortable in this stuff," Miller said.

"I am," Miriam replied. "Even if the armor is big, it feels small in here. I like small. I'm not even nauseated, which is nice. I usually hate free fall."

"Makes sense," Miller said. He wasn't sure about being teamed with the linguist, but just about every mission specialist was placed at one of the likely break points.

"Response teams, Command," the XO said over the radio. "Commander Weaver is preparing to remove the patch."

"Point four," Miller said, when his count came up.

"I hope nothing breaks," Miriam said. "But I want you to know that if it does, I'm going to panic."

"That's reassuring," the former SEAL said, rolling his eyes inside the Wyvern.

"I have to panic first," Miriam said, calmly. "Then I can deal with things. I need the adrenaline."

"If this patch lets go, we're going to have all the adrenaline we can use," Miller told her, looking at the magnet. "I just wish we were in something smaller and more nimble."

"See?" Miriam said. "Small is good."

"In this case, definitely," Miller replied. "I'm not even sure we can get to that damned thing in this armor."

Just as he said that, the magnet shifted sideways and the outer mount broke inwards. As soon as it did, the magnet dropped entirely out of its mount and air began explosively venting out of the ship.

"Oh, damn," Miller said, getting down on the knees and elbows of the Wyvern and sliding forward. He could see how the mount went into place, but he wasn't sure he could get it fully mounted. The outboard mount was crumpled.

He lifted the magnet and slid the inboard mount over the pipe, but with the outboard mount crumpled there was no way to get an airtight seal. In fact, it wouldn't seat at all. He dropped it back down and slid the hand of the Wyvern into the mount; twisting it around to get the mount rounded again, he slid it up and got the thing mounted. But they were still losing air. And in the position he was in he couldn't do anything but look at the damned mount and try not to panic.

The whole time he'd heard his "teammate" slowly going nuts over his local channel. There was a final shriek, then a clicking sound.

"Miriam?" Miller said. "Miriam!"

There was a thump on his back and a small hand holding a roll of duct tape came into view over his back. A human hand. The stupid bitch was out of her *armor*!

"Get back in your armor!" he shouted, realizing that she couldn't hear him. He wasn't sure what the pressure was outside the armor, but going from suit pressure to whatever was left in the engine compartment, ignoring the likelihood of dying from lack of oxygen, was liable to cause all sorts of medical issues that could be summed up with one word: "Bends." It was the equivalent of doing a deep dive and then coming up rapidly.

Gasses that were in solution in the blood went from liquid to gas and created bubbles. The gasses were everywhere in the body; saturated was the term. So when the bubbles formed, they could do bad things. Especially when they became bubbles in spinal or brain tissue. Paralysis was common as was brain damage.

Miriam, though, ignored him, quickly wrapping the duct tape

around the mount, then sliding something else into view. It was some sort of gun and it quickly began extruding a brown material that was initially sucked in through the small holes that formed in the duct tape and then hardened in place.

His external mike could hear air rushing but it wasn't rushing *out*, it was the internal systems reflooding the compartment with blessed air.

"You okay?" he asked, keying his external speakers.

"No," Miriam croaked.

"You did good," Miller said. "What was that stuff?"

"It's the micrometeorite patch system," Miriam said holding up the oddest looking caulking gun the chief had ever seen. "They're just like the ones developed for the space station and they are all over the ship. Didn't anybody brief you on them before you came on board?"

"Uh, no."

"Basically, it's million dollar a tube hot glue. Chief Miller? I'm going to pass out, now."

"Okay," Miller said, sliding backwards carefully. "Command, explosive venting at Point Four is sealed. And I need medical teams, stat."


"All hands! All hands! Breach sealed. Pressure normalized. Remain in Condition Yellow. Prepare for atmospheric entry."

"What the *grapp* does that mean?" Drago asked.

"I think we're going into a Jovian atmosphere to get some $O_2$," Berg said. "At least, that's what it sounded like Top was talking about. And you guys just don't get who that guy is. It'd be like walking up to Chesty Puller and striking up a conversation."

"Yeah, sure," Crowley said. "He's the *grapping* nav. He's not Chesty Puller."

"Look him up," Berg said, angrily. "Seriously. Use that computer for something other than porn for God's sake."

"Settle down, Two-Gun," Jaen said easily. "We get the point. He's heap big mojo."

"Guy's been outside the *universe*," Berg said, closing his eyes. "He's touched the face of God. He's not just a *grapping* nav. The SEAL with him won the *grapping* Medal!"

"*Settle down*, Two-Gun," Jaen said, obviously grinning. "We get it."

"Weaver was at the Charge of the Redneck Brigade," Berg said. "He went into a gate in Florida and came out of a completely unlinked gate in Virginia! And that was before he *really* got in some *maulk*."

"You want to have his babies," Drago said, chuckling. "We get it."

"No *grapping* clue . . ."


"I have Miss Miriam in a pressurization chamber," Dr. Chet said. He pulled thoughtfully at the beard that hung nearly to his chest and looked at the overhead.

"She has no gross trauma from her depressurization. She has some hypobaric edema but otherwise seems fine. Nonetheless, I would like to keep her under observation for a time. She has expressed a desire to remain in isolation as well."

"Did she say why?" the CO asked.

"The edema manifests as large red marks that will eventually fade to something that look a bit like bruises," Dr. Chet responded. "Since some of them are on her face, they are . . . unsightly."

"Oh," the CO said, grinning. "Tell her she can stay out of sight as long as she likes but that we look forward to seeing her again when she's ready to come out."

"I wouldn't have popped my armor for a bet," the XO said.

"While there are many problems inherent in rapid depressurization, it is not an instant killer," Dr. Chet said. "It is believed that a person can withstand absolute vacuum for up to a minute. No one, of course, has ever *tested* that hypothesis and I hope that we are not the first to do so. However, what is not widely publicized is that on many of the EVAs done to date there have been pressure leaks of the suits because a seal wasn't properly set and the astronauts were exposed to the vacuum for a few tens of seconds before the suits were resealed. In all cases that has not been a problem. Also, because the compartment was being vented and the hole was relatively small, Miriam was simply in a reduced pressure condition. While that is dangerous, the period that she was at reduced pressure was short. I believe her period of unconsciousness was more a result of the psychological trauma than physical. Miss Miriam is . . . delicate."

"Well, as long as I know I won't have to depend on her for the first ten seconds or so of an emergency, I'll take her as backstop any time," Miller said. "She really does panic, though, in those first ten seconds. Ye flipping *gods* does she panic."

"What's the next step?" the CO asked.

"We need to descend into the atmosphere, sir," Weaver said. "That's got other problems. The region we have to descend into is the pressure equivalent of about two hundred feet of water. Again, the seals might not hold. This time, though, we're talking about over-pressure. The problem being that the atmosphere coming in isn't breathable. It's also not a killer, though. Fire-fighting air systems would work to deal with it. But we should reinforce the joints as much as possible. Oh, and the air's going to be *cold*. We can actually use it for some of the chilling systems. We might think about extending the chillers while we're doing this, it will vent some heat."

"We're low on air, so we don't have a lot of time to work on this," the CO said. "But, XO, I want pipe-seals on all those vents. We're probably going to get some of that atmosphere in the ship, but let's get as little as possible."

"Will do, sir," the XO said.

"What's the composition?" Dr. Chet asked.

"The area we're descending to is primarily hydrogen," Weaver replied. "But it has a high concentration of oxygen, about one percent. Very little $CO_2$, less than a hundredth of a percent. Just about zero nitrogen. Argon, helium, mostly noble gasses are the biggest traces. But it's the thickest concentration of oxygen in the atmosphere; we dropped a probe to check."

"Other than the pressure, that is fully breathable," Dr. Chet said. "In fact, if the system fails and the compartment vents, all we'll have to ensure is that it does not depressurize quickly. That composition is actually rather good for that pressure. Breathing systems may not be necessary. In fact, I would recommend against them. The oxygen in the breathing systems is the most dangerous thing a human could be taking in under that amount of pressure."

"So if we have a high pressure . . . issue, they should just breathe it?" the XO asked.

"Yes, that would be my recommendation," Dr. Chet said. "And if the compartment *does* flood with that mixture, we will need to ensure that it does not rapidly vent when we leave. To ensure the personnel are not affected by depressurization problems we will need to slowly reduce the pressure. We will need to monitor oxygen levels closely; at high pressures oxygen is toxic. In addition, we will need to ensure that the persons exposed to it have enough time to get the nitrogen out of their systems before they are depressurized. It will depend on the structure of the pressure event. How to decompress will have to be calculated later."

"What about getting the hydrogen out of the ship?" the XO asked.

"It has little clinical effect," Dr. Chet said, shrugging. "We can get rid of it slowly."

"It's a slippery molecule, sir," Weaver added. "It's going to slip out through the hull much less our sealing system. We'll slowly get rid of it no matter what we do."

"And it's not dangerous?" the CO asked.

"Not a bit," Dr. Chet said.

"So we're just supposed to breathe this stuff?" Petty Officer Michael "Sub Dude" Gants said, looking at the much patched magnet mount. The short, hairy engineer frowned.

The submarine service attracts people who in other services would be on the far end of the bell curve for oddball. Among other things, they are required to be well above average intelligence yet still have sufficient phlegmatism to withstand the rigors of the "secret service." Very thoughtful but not so thoughtful as to be freaked out by having a bazillion tons of water pressing in on a tin can made by the lowest bidder. Very smart and yet oh so very stupid.

And of all the people in the sub service, the epitome were the engineers. They were the people with that warm green glow, the guys who ran the nuke plant, the guys with little hope of ever having normal children. The weirdest of the weird.

Gants was among the worst of the worst. He was an MM (N), a nuke machinist mate. The nukes were weird; the machinist mates, though, were the practical jokers. A nuke practical joker machinist mate. That spelled Trouble to everyone who knew him. Short and unassuming, he was one of the most feared people on the boat. Gants scared even the torpedo guys.

"And *not* use the air systems," PO2 Ian "Red" Morris said. Red was as tall as Gants was short but with flaming red hair. Thus the nickname. Submariners are simple people on many levels.

"That's gonna be fun," Gants said.

"Prepare for atmospheric entry," the 1-MC said.

"Looks good so far," Gants said.

"Don't think we're down to pressure, yet," Red replied, in a high, squeaky, voice. "Huh?"

"Why are you sounding like Donald Duck?" Sub Dude said in the same sort of voice. "Holy *maulk*! I sound like Donald Duck!" he added as his ears popped.

"Uh, oh," Red said. "That's a pressure spike."

"It's leaking," Sub Dude said, holding his hands up to the pipe seal that had been added to the patch. Pipe seals were designed to stop flooding from pipes but they were barely water tight much less air tight. "I can feel air."

"Command," Red said, using an internal radio. "We've got leakage from Point Four. But it's not real heavy, yet."

"Petty Officer Morris, why are you talking like Donald Duck?" the XO asked angrily.

"Sorry, sir, can't help it," Red said, rolling his eyes. "I don't know what's causing it. I'm not doing it on purpose, honest!"

"All hands! Warning! Overpressure breach in missile compartment and engineering! Remain in vacuum conditions! Warning! Overpressure breach in missile compartment and engineering! Remain in vacuum conditions!"

"Okay, what the *grapp* is going on?" Jaenisch asked. "First we're losing atmosphere and now . . . what?"

"I think the Jovian's atmosphere probably breached some of the seals," Berg said.

"And that tells me so much, Two-Gun," Jaen replied.

"Diving into a Jovian's atmosphere is like going under water," Berg said. "The air pressure is super high because of the gravity and the depth of the atmosphere. So probably some of the seals breached. Not sure how they're going to fix *that*. It's going to take more than duct tape."

"What the hell?" the XO said, looking over at Weaver. "The guys down at Patch Four are talking like Donald Duck."

"Oh, hell," Weaver said, trying not to laugh. "I forgot. That's one effect of hydrogen. Ever seen anyone breathe a helium balloon, sir?"

"Yes," the XO said, then shook his head. "Same effect?"

"Yes, sir," Bill replied.

"Pressure's up five pounds in engineering," the atmospherics monitor said. "And increasing."

"We're getting leakage," Bill said, shrugging. "Sounds like it's not explosive, though. Not so far." He spun around and looked at a recently installed monitor. "We're up to one percent exterior oxygen, sir. I'd suggest we begin atmosphere processing."

"Roger," the XO said, turning to the communications system. "Engineering, Conn, begin atmospheric processing."

"Aye, aye, Conn," the Eng replied in a high, squeaky voice. "God damn this stuff. It's the hydrogen, Conn."

"Roger, we're aware of that," the XO said, trying not to grin. "Just let's start filling up the air tanks."

"Sir," Bill said, as the XO cut the comm off.

"Go."

"Hydrogen's slippery," Bill said. "It's likely to get all through the ship."

"Oh . . . hell."


"Okay, this is *grapping* ridiculous," Jaen squeaked. "How in the hell is anyone going to take me seriously when I sound like this?"

"I don't know, boss," Hatt said. "Are we supposed take you seriously *normally?*"

"That's it," Jaen tried to growl and failed. "Front-leaning rest position, move!" The last came out as a shrill shriek.

"I guess I might as well just start doing push-ups, too," Berg said, dropping to the deck and giggling.

"I may sound like Donald Duck but I'm a God damned sergeant in the *Space* Marines and you are going to *remember* that!"

"Yes, ma'am," Berg said.

"Okay, you are *so* on garbage detail! God, I wish we still had KP!"


"XO, air tanks topped off?" Spectre said in a high, squeaky voice.

"All topped off, sir!" the XO replied, sounding like he was breathing helium. In fact, the most recent analysis had helium as five percent of the internal air. "Internal plugs have been put in place so Commander Weaver won't have to EVA to put the patch back in. And we've mostly filled the water tanks as well."

The pressure on the exterior of the ship had forced it *into* the hull throughout the ship. The ship's atmosphere was now a high pressure mix of hydrogen, helium and oxygen. Gathering the $O_2$ they'd needed had taken hours and after a while they didn't even try to maintain internal atmospheric integrity; all they'd done was fight the level of $O_2$. Everyone was under a hundred pounds of air pressure, and sounding like a squeaky toy.

"Do we need to stop for ice?" the CO asked, then shook his head. "That sounded really stupid even if I didn't sound like this."

"Not really, sir," the XO said. "There was a lot of water in the atmosphere. At this point, we have sufficient water for three weeks of operation. And if we really need it . . ."

"We know where to get it," the CO said, nodding. "Very well, take us out of here, XO. Astro, where we going next?"

"Second star to the right, sir," Bill said, grinning and pointing up.

"Commander, I think the pressure is getting to you."

"Oooohhh *maaulk*!" Weaver said, slapping his forehead.

"Commander Weaver? Is there a problem?"

"I can't believe I just thought of this . . ."

"Commander Weaver?" Spectre said impatiently.

"Sorry, sir." Weaver said hesitantly. "Comets, sir. Most stars should have them and they would be easy to grab."

"Why is that important to me, Commander Weaver?"

"Comets, sir. Well, uh, comets are mostly water ice. And we could break that out into . . ."

"Water ice . . ." Spectre thought about it for a millisecond. "You mean we could have just flown out to the Oort cloud and grabbed a few balls of ice?"

"Yes, sir, hence the 'oh *maulk*,' sir."

"Mr. Weaver, join me in my office for a moment," Spectre squeaked, his jaw muscles working tightly as his teeth ground slowly.

# 17

## Is That Like Space Cadet?

"Excuse me, miss," Berg said, then froze in his tracks.

He was headed up to supply to pick up some parts for Drago's Wyvern, which had developed a cranky streak about running the right arm, when the girl . . . teenager entered the same passage. His first thought was that she was about the first member of the science team he'd seen; the "mission specialists" tended to keep to their own section of the package. His second thought was that she was awfully young. His third was that she was awfully cute. He was working up to a fourth thought along the lines of the problems with mixing cute and young when the puppet on her shoulder moved and he froze, realizing it wasn't a puppet. Then he froze more when he realized who he was blocking.

"Err, uh," Berg said insouciantly. "That's . . . uhm."

Fortunately, the hydrogen had finally bled out of the submarine so his last "uhm" came out as a normal squeak instead of a hydrogen induced one. So much more manly that way.

"He doesn't bite," Mimi said, grinning up at the towering Marine. If she was intimidated, it wasn't apparent.

"I know," Berg said, clearing his throat. "You must be Mimi Jones. That's . . . uh, that is . . . how *is* Tuffy?"

"Fine, as always," Mimi said. "How are you . . ." She paused as if accessing a memory. ". . . Two-Gun?"

"Fine, ma'am," Berg said, suddenly remembering his protocol. The lowliest of the mission specialists rated as an officer. You made way for officers in the corridors. Berg turned to the side and flattened against the bulkhead. "Sorry, ma'am."

"That's okay," Mimi said, walking past. She paused, though, and turned back. "Why do they call you Two-Gun?"

"That's a long story, ma'am," Berg said.

"Maybe another time, then," Mimi said. "Later."

". . . And *Tuffy's* on board," Berg said, excitedly. "Tuffy!"

"Oh, God, Two-Gun, not again," Drago said, yanking the arm module out.

"But it's *Tuffy!*" Berg explained to his satisfaction.

"My sister has one of those dolls," Crowley said. "So what?"

"Tuffy's an alien, right?" Hatt asked.

"Nobody really knows *what* Tuffy is," Berg said. "Big explosion. The Chen Event."

"I'm from Florida," Jaen said, his jaw flexing. "I had family in Boca Raton."

The entire area for fifty miles around Boca Raton was still a no-go zone. One of the Looking Glasses had, apparently, let through *something*. That was all anyone could determine about it. But the something had driven everyone for fifty miles around incurably insane. Most had died in the zone since it was impenetrable. Scientists were still, cautiously, trying to determine what was going on in the Boca Zone but so far had come up with nothing beyond . . . *something*.

"Sorry," Berg said. "Didn't know."

"It's okay, I didn't really know them all that well," Jaen admitted. "But I know about the Chen Event. We *all* know. It's a toss-up which you remember better, 9/11 or the Chen Event."

"Chen Event," Drago said. "I was in school on 9/11. I never even heard about it till I got home. The Chen Event, though, I was over at my buddy Tom's house, playing Counter-Strike. Guy pinged in on us and we spent the rest of the day watching TV."

"You didn't stay up long enough," Berg said. "Who survived the Chen Event?"

"Oh, lots of people," Jaen said. "I mean they were pulling survivors out of the rubble . . ."

"No, I mean *up close.*"

"Nobody," Drago said. "No, wait . . ."

"One person, Mimi Jones," Berg said. "She lived less than a half mile from the explosion."

"Oh, I remember her," Jaen said. "That's her? I never believed it. No way she could have lived. I mean that's not inside the primary blast radius, but it was totally flattened. No way to live."

"But she did," Berg said. "No question about that. No other way for her to get where she was when she turned up. And she turned up with Tuffy. Nobody, absolutely nobody, knows who or what Tuffy is. The speculation is that Mimi got sucked out of the universe and Tuffy came back with her."

"A stuffed doll?" Drago said. "Pull the other one, Two-Gun."

"I got real interested in all this stuff," Berg said. "I figured we were going to be fighting the Dreen forever and I already knew I wanted to be a Marine. So I was going to be fighting the Dreen. I wanted to know what I was going to be fighting."

"Hell is what," Top said. "You'd be fighting hell. Got *that* T-shirt."

As usual the first sergeant had appeared as if teleporting.

"Sorry, Top," Jaen said. "We're working."

"I know," Top said. "What's this about Tuffy and Miss Jones?"

"I . . ." Berg paused and shrugged. "I've got one of those Google search things set up for Tuffy. There have been at least six breakthroughs in technology in the last two years credited to Mimi and Tuffy. There wasn't anything on them for a few years; they just dropped off the radar screen. Then they start turning up fixing tech issues. Now they're *here*. I'm sorry, Top, that's just damned cool."

"Yes, it is," Top said. "For general information, it was Miss Jones who pointed out that there might be problems with exiting the system and helped with figuring out how to overcome them. Bright young lady. Emphasis on *young*. You don't joke with her, you don't chat with her, you sure as hell don't flirt with her. And remember that the abilities of that thing on her shoulder are unknown but are known to include defensive capabilities. Frankly, Tuffy could probably kill you by looking at you. In other words, keep your dicks in your pants where they belong. Are we all clear here?"

"Clear, Top," the group chorused.

"Drago, what are the characteristics of a fermion?"

"Fermions are subatomic particles with half integer spin and follow Fermi-Dirac statistics—whatever the hell that is." Drago said.

"What is important about fermions other than mesons?"

"A fermion particle composed of three quarks is a baryon," Drago spouted. "A baryon cannot form Bose-Einstein condensates and under normal conditions has a high . . . breakdown rate."

"The term you were looking for is degradation," Top said. "But breakdown shows you understand what it means so that's good enough. If you detect these fermions what are the possible indicators . . . Hatt?"

"It means that fermion production is occurring in the immediate area," Hatt said. "So there's something making fermions."

"What could make fermions?" Top asked.

"Uh . . ." Hatt said, blinking furiously. "Well, Top, a quarkium drive. But then you'd probably get pentaquarks, too. And . . . neutrinos. Just fermions? I'm not sure, Top. I'd have to kick that one up."

"I'd probably kick it up, too," the first sergeant said. "But one answer is a properly tuned Higgs boson. They can generate tuned fermions. They're where we get the quarks for the quarkium drive and the mesons that power the warp drive."

"So if we detect fermions there's a Higgs boson nearby, Top?" Drago asked.

"One that's been tuned to produce them," Powell said, nodding. "In their normal state they mostly generate a stream of muons. Primarily in the direction of the nearest unlinked Higgs that matches their spin-state. So if you get a sudden stream of muons—"

"There's a steady state Higgs that is trying to link," Jaen said. "I'm beginning to see why we're studying this stuff, First Sergeant."

"Because you're Space Marines," Powell said, grinning. "It's a lot more than just hitting the beach shouting 'Oorah!' But you've got to be able to do that, too."

"Okay, who knew Top had a physics degree?" Crowley said as soon as the first sergeant was gone.

"He doesn't," Jaen said. "He's got a masters in international relations."

"You're *maulk*ing me," Lujan said.

"Straight up," Jaen replied. "Now ask me where it's from."

"I'll bite," Berg said.

"Sorbonne."

"No *grapping* way," Berg said, shaking his head.

"What the *grapp* is a Sorbonne?" Drago said. "It sounds like a pastry."

"Close," Jaen said. "It's a university in Paris."

"One of the oldest in the world," Berg said. "I mean, it makes having a Harvard degree look like old news."

"What in the *grapp* is he doing as a first sergeant?" Crowley asked.

"Welcome to the Space Mushrooms," Jaen, Hatt and Berg chorused.

"How do I get out of this egghead outfit?"

"God *almighty* I'm *grapping* bored," Sergeant Lovelace said, lowering the weights slowly.

PT was a requirement every day. The ship's reduced gravitational level had a tendency to cause loss of muscle mass, fast. Working out was even more of a necessity than in a normal duty station.

"Don't let Top hear you say that," Jaenisch replied. "He *will* find a way to keep us occupied. Got it."

"I'd kill for a good run," Berg said, grunting as he thrust down on the lifters. "Weights just don't do it for me."

"You can run around the missile compartment," Crowley said, curling right then left.

"Third's down there doing Wyvern sims," Berg pointed out. "I'd sort of be in the way."

"Do the third level," Drago said, wiping sweat off his face.

"What? And deal with missile watch? I swear the guy that's on most of the time is gay."

"Well, you know, Two-Gun," Crowley said, grinning. "You got a real pretty mouth."

"Go suck duck dicks, Crow," Berg said as the door to the small gym opened.

"Good morning, Marines," Runner said, grinning. "Mind if I join in?"

"Certainly, Master Sergeant," Staff Sergeant Summerlin said.

"Runner or Steve will do," Runner said, walking over to the Nautilus, just about the only machine not in use. "I was supposed to be here last night but the eminent Dr. Paul Dean had me analyzing Saturn data."

"Why's he still analyzing Saturn's data?" Berg asked when nobody responded. "I mean, we've been to one world and I'm pretty sure we've surveyed several more . . ."

"We've collected at least spectral data from over ninety worlds so far," Runner said, adjusting the machine and rolling into position. "Dropped probes on four more that looked interesting. And, of course, picked up all that data on Dean's World. But we've just started on 'serious analysis' of Saturn's data. That will, according to Dr. Dean, occupy us for the better part of a year. At least, occupy him. As soon as we're back on Earth he can spend all the time in a lab he wants."

"You sound unhappy, Master Sergeant Runner," Crowley said, grinning.

"Dr. Dean is a classic California Liberal One Each," Runner said, grimacing as he slammed the Nautilus pads together. "One who quite detests jingoistic myrmidons. That would be us. Or anyone else who has ever worn a uniform in anything other than the Red Army."

"Jesus Christ," Drago said. "What the *grapp* is he doing on a Navy ship?"

"He is, in case I hadn't mentioned it, a quite brilliant planetologist," Runner said, finishing his set and moving over to the leg machine. "A revolting son of a bitch of a pinko communist, but a great planetologist."

"*Maulk*, I thought *we* had problems," Jaen said. "All *we've* got to do is figure out what the potential implications of a baryon are."

"Okay, I did *not* just hear a Marine say that," Runner said, sitting up and looking over at the sergeant.

"You're right, you didn't," Jaen replied, lying back and lifting up the weight bar. "You heard a *Space* Marine say that."

"Point," Runner said, grinning. "You guys have been studying particle physics?"

"More like memorizing some of them," Berg said. "We don't even touch the math. *I* don't even touch the math."

"Two-Gun's the platoon's tutor," Staff Sergeant Sumerlin said.

"Two-Gun?" Runner asked.

"He's the master of two-gun mojo," Drago said, grinning.

"Two-gun mojo doesn't work," Runner said definitely.

"I only did it *once*," Berg protested. "And it was on orders. I don't do it in combat."

"But he did it *magnificently*," Jaen said. "Blew them little centipedes away."

"You really two-gun mojo?" Runner said, interested.

"No, I don't," Berg replied. "I hold one gun in either hand, but I only fire one at a time. Empty that, switch to the off-hand while I holster, reload and switch."

"That actually sounds doable," Runner admitted.

"I've only really mojoed once," Berg said bitterly. "It's not like I make a habit of it."

"Wait, you *really* mojoed," Drago said. "Like firing two at once?"

"I am *not* talking about this!" Berg said.

"It's okay, Two-Gun," Jaen said, grinning. "Jeeze, he's worse about this than he is about Weaver."

"What's he got against Commander Weaver?" Runner asked. "Bill's a pretty good guy."

"Wait," Berg said, sitting up. "You've *met* him?"

"Yeah," Runner said. "Pretty good guy for an egghead. Hell of an accent, though."

"Oh. My. God," Berg said, theatrically, slumping back down and grabbing his weights. "He has met William Weaver . . ." he sang.

"That's right, Two-Gun, ham it up," Drago said. "We all know you want to have his babies."

"Commander Weaver's an interesting character," Runner said.

"We've heard," Summer said. "At length."

"Well, it's not like I'm reciting the biography of Linda Sweet," Berg said. "I mean, he was up close and personal with the Dreen."

"And fighting the Dreen is a stone bitch," Runner said. "Got *that* T-shirt."

"You were in the Dreen War, Master Sergeant?" Jaen asked.

"I've been in seventeen years," Runner said. "Do the math."

"Sorry, Master Sergeant," Jaen replied.

"Ah, that's okay," Runner said, moving to the next machine. "It's just not something I like to talk about. We lost most of my team doing a recon of a Dreen infestation the first time we hit one. I've done . . . *Maulk*, I don't know how many entries I've done on them since. We got detailed to do a lot of internal recons after the gates were closed. Did one on the Bekaa Valley infestation after they dropped the nukes. That was *grapping* hairy. Think 'radioactive insane Dreen.'"

"*Grapping* ouch," Drago said.

"Didn't lose a man that time," Runner said. "But it was . . . ugly. Really *grapping* ugly. *Maulk* I'm not ready to talk about. So, yeah, I was in the Dreen War. So was Chief Miller and, of course, Commander Weaver. Both of them got some pretty serious rad damage from it. And I think they're the only two survivors with the SEAL team that put the bomb through the gate in Kentucky. Still fun guys to have a beer with. So, you guys are the Space Marines, huh? That anything like Space Cadets?"

"Intruder Alert! Intruder Alert! Second Platoon to Wyverns! First and Third to ground mount!"

"More like mushrooms," Berg shouted as he headed out the door.

# *18*

## You Don't Have To Be
## Faster Than the Lion

"Stable orbit around Procyon established," the pilot said tiredly.

Six weeks after the surprising moon of E Eridani Beta, and three weeks after refilling their air tanks, Dr. Dean was looking more and more visionary in naming the planet after himself. In six weeks of star hopping the crew of the *Vorpal Blade* had seen a huge number of stars ranging from very pretty to very plain, gas giants by the scores, rings to make Saturn blush with shame, rocky planets by the dozens, moons, lots of moons, some of them with something resembling an atmosphere.

What it hadn't found was another planet with so much as a scrap of life or anything resembling breathable air. Most of the rocky planets resembled either Mars, Venus or Earth's moon.

"What's Runner say?" the CO asked.

"He's got one gas giant in the life zone," Bill replied. "But Procyon's a short lived star. I doubt life's had a chance to take hold."

"Got to check," the CO said brightly. "Vector?"

"One-three-seven, Mark Neg One Dot One Five. Four AU."

"Pilot," the CO said.

"Coming to One-three-seven," the pilot said, spinning the boat in place. "See it."

"Engage."

Runner didn't exclaim as the boat slowed to normal space speeds. He just smiled thinly, then tapped the controls to call Dr. Weaver.

"Multiple moons, Commander," Runner said. "Several big ones. Check out the take from Scope Two."

Bill brought up Scope Two on his main screen, then tapped in the codes to take control, zooming in in disbelief.

"Sergeant?" Weaver said over the communicator. "Is that what I think it is?"

"I'm looking at the spectral data, sir," Runner said. "Get this. $O_2$, twenty-two percent. Nitrogen, seventy-seven percent. $CO_2$ less than point zero one percent. High water content. Gravity about point nine two standard. Great world for Running, if you get my drift."

"And I see red," Bill said, grinning. "Class Four biology. Break out the red shirts!"

"I got movement," Hattelstad said before the security team had even gotten into position. "Ten o'clock. Thermal and heartbeat. *Fast* heartbeat. Looks about the size of an antelope."

The boat had set down near the ocean again, well east of the beach on a broad, gently shelving plain.

The plain was covered in wiry, thigh-high red grass-looking stuff that terminated in dunes. About five klicks to the east was the beginnings of forest of something like conifers. Beyond the forest, about two hundred kilometers away, mountains soared into a blue sky flecked with clouds.

Due to the surrounding coloration, mostly a crimson red, the armor had adjusted its surface and now was mottled in shades of crimson and pink.

"Take positions," Jaenisch said, scanning the area.

"Don't go into the long grass," Bergstresser said. Much of the area looked to have been cropped but a stand of taller "grass" was near the boat's port bow. "I've got multiple movement signs inside about ten meters. Big stuff."

"Command, Charlie Team," Jaenisch said after they'd completed their sensor sweep. "We've got multiple life forms." As he said it, the creature Hattelstad had reported suddenly bounded into view. He didn't get much of a look, but it looked something like a giant crab. But the legs moved . . . weird. And it was fast.

The crab-thing had darted towards the longer grass and as it entered there was a swirling and the external mike picked up shrill screams. The movement quickly settled down with a ring of heat forms gathered around where the crab thing had stopped.

"No signs of intelligent life but be aware that there may be predators in the area."

"Damn," Miller said. "When do we get to crack the Wyverns?"

It looked something like California before people screwed it up. It looked *a lot* like California except for everything being bright red. Miller had spent enough time in Diego to know that. Checking his external temperature readings and doing the math, he got an outside temperature of seventy-two degrees Fahrenheit.

"A while," Weaver said as the science teams spread out, still wearing their own armor. "This is a more dangerous environment than Titan *because* it looks so Earth-like. And just because *we* know we can't eat the local food, the predators don't. For that matter, while we haven't found a disease, even in Bio One environments, that can infect humans, there's always the first time. We don't want to be the guys to spread purple creeping fungus."

"Now this is more like it," Julia said as she stepped out of the elevator. "Did you see the report on megafauna?"

"Yes, ma'am," Bartlett said. "I also saw the report on possible predation. We need to take this very carefully, ma'am."

"We will," Julia replied. "We'll start with a ring toss and see where it takes us."

"I wish we'd landed in the mountains," Dr. Dean said, frowning.

"As you say, Doctor," Runner replied. He had the portable drill rig over one shoulder and was keeping a careful eye out for threats.

"We'll see if we can get through this soil with that," Dean continued. "No telling how deep it goes. And, of course, Dr. Robertson will appreciate the tillage sample."

"Yes, sir," Runner said.

"Here will do," Dean said, getting about seventy meters away from the boat to port.

Runner set the drill rig down carefully as staff sergeant Kristopher dumped the spare pipe somewhat less cautiously.

In a minute the rig was set up and started drilling.

"I think I see an outcrop over there," Dr. Dean said. "Sergeant Runner? You see it?"

"Yes, sir," Runner said, dialing up the zoom on the Wyvern. South of the boat there was a small rocky promontory.

"I'd like to get some samples," Dean said. "You and Kristopher can run the rig. We'll put in seismic monitors on the way."

"Sir, that's outside the security zone," Runner pointed out.

"I'll be fine, Sergeant," Dean said. "That's what the armor is for, right?"

"Sir, we don't know the nature of the threats in this area," Runner replied. "And if you leave the security zone without permission, the captain *will* ground you, Doctor. Let me get with Captain MacDonald and see what we can do, Doctor."

"Very well," Dean said, exasperated.

"He wants to *what?*" MacDonald said.

"It's the only rocks around here, sir," the master sergeant said patiently. "And it's also a good observation point. You want to kick it up to the boat CO?"

"Negative," MacDonald said. "Watch your *ass,* Master Sergeant. I want everyone back alive."

The captain switched frequencies and looked at his locator system.

"Tony, detach one team to screen the geo guys again," he said, punching in the point that Geo was heading for. "Make sure they take point this time. Tell them to watch their ass."

"Charlie team. Geo is moving to marked point. Screen on point. Platoon is redeploying in support."

"Okay, why do we *always* get *grapping point?*" Hattelstad asked. "First out of the *grapping* ship, always screening *grapping* Geo . . ."

"Luck of the draw," Jaen said. "Now shut up and keep your *grapping* eyes open. We're going into the long grass . . ."

» » »

"Where's Charlie going?" Weaver asked interestedly.

"Charlie, Miller, where you going?" Miller asked.

"Geo wants to go check out those rocks about a klick away, Chief Warrant Officer," the Marine team leader replied, pinging the location on Miller's map system. "Guess who gets to nursemaid."

"I'm in on that," Weaver said. "But does the CO know?"

"Not sure," Miller admitted.

"I'd better get permission," Weaver said disgustedly.

"Welcome to the chain of command."


Random botany sampling is one of the more tedious jobs in the universe.

The simplest method in an open grassy area such as the area the boat had landed in was to simply toss a one-meter diameter ring over the shoulder. Then the one-meter area was more or less scoured, all the plant and animal material inside being collected and sorted.

Do this ten or twelve times and you have a bio sampling of the area.

"Tell security that if they shoot anything I want it," Julia said, down on the knees of the suit pulling up grasses. "Tell them to try not to chew it up too much." She paused and held up the selection of grasses. "Hmmm. That's odd."


"Here we go . . ." Jaenisch said as they approached the long grass. This wasn't the area where they'd seen predators, but that didn't mean there weren't any.

"Charlie, hold up," Runner said. "Putting in a seismic monitor."

The seismic monitor was simply a long spike. The Wyvern drove it into the ground until the sensor pod was flush with the ground.

"Okay, Jaen," Runner said. "We're going to be doing that every few hundred meters."

"Got it," Jaenisch said. "You picking up anything?"

"On seismic?" Runner asked, humorously. "No. Nothing on any channel. Bio wants us to shoot anything that moves, by the way. And 'try not to chew it up too much.'"

"Right," Jaenisch said, setting his Gatling to single fire. "Hattelstad, point."

"Roger," Hattelstad said, cycling in a shot round to the shoulder mounted auto-cannon. "If it's small, though, there ain't gonna be much left."

The team slid into the grass smoothly, tracking for threats. The grass only came up to the "hips" of the suits but just about anything could be hidden in it.

"Got movement," Hattelstad said. "Two o'clock."

"Mine," Jaenisch said, tracking the heat form. He fired one round and the form tumbled. But he didn't see the expected hot flash from flying blood.

"Nice shot," Berg said just as the form got up and started scuttling away.

"What the hell?" Jaen said, firing two more rounds and heading towards the form.

The two rounds had managed to kill it. The thing, yeah, looked something like a crab. A bright red crab. But the legs instead of being exoskeletal were long tentacles with footpads. It had no visible eyes, but it was pretty smashed up. They might have been in the smashed area.

"That's *grapping* strange looking," Hattelstad said. "Looks like a cross between a crab and an octopus."

"Keep an eye on your sector," Jaenisch said, pulling out a sampling bag, a heavy-duty zipper-lock the size of a trash bag. He dropped the . . . crabpus in the bag and got back in position.

"Movement," Bergstresser said. "Multiple forms. Big. Nine o'clock."

"Back up," Jaenisch said, switching to full auto. "Geo, we are *leaving*."

"*Maulk*," Runner said, grabbing Dr. Dean's Wyvern. "We need to get out of here, Doctor."

"Nonsense," the scientist said, pulling away from the master sergeant. "We're in *armor*, you idiot."

"Charlie is pulling back," Runner said. "My orders are to keep you inside the security perimeter. I cannot *force* you to leave, but I *strongly* recommend it. *I* am pulling back. You can stay here on your own or you can leave. Up to you."

With that Runner turned towards the boat and started trotting.

"Hey!" Dean shouted. "You can't just *leave* me here!" The planetologist started running after him.

"As they say in Africa, Doctor, you don't have to be faster than the lion, just faster than your companions," Runner replied, still trotting. "Why don't you try to be faster than *me*."

"Charlie's headed back," Miller said, stopping as the team started pulling back and the two Geo members turned to run to the rear.

"Then I think we should stop, don't you?" Weaver said, taking a knee and bringing up his .338 caliber machine gun. The gun fired hypervelocity scramjet rounds with an accurate range of over a mile. Given that they were essentially mini rocket engines, though, they had a theoretical range of anywhere in atmosphere.

"Charlie, Miller," Miller said in reply. "We will screen your retreat."

"Roger, Master Chief," the team leader said. "We have multiple—"

"*Grapp*," Hatt said, firing a 30mm shot round as the heat forms closed. The first form shuddered to the side, then came back up as its fellows ran past. "Switching to exploding shot."

"Go," Jaen said, opening fire. The minigun scythed down the grass between him and the target, giving them their first clear view of the animals.

Like the first one, they were crabpus but *much* larger. And whereas the mouth and "face" portion of the one Jaenisch shot had been mangled, these were clear. The things had *huge* mandibles, clearly designed to crunch through the crabpus armor. And they were less than ten meters away.

"Ugly things," Two-Gun said, firing a burst from his minigun. Several of the rounds seemed to bounce off the armor, but the rounds that went under it cut the thing's legs out and it tumbled to the side.

"Now is when I wish you had your pistols, Two-Gun," Jaen panted.

"Cannon . . . on-line," Hatt said in a deep voice, then opened fire.

The 30mm rounds landed in the midst of the pack of predators in flashes of purple fire and dust, flinging them through the air. A direct hit on one shattered the armor and splashed violet blood across the red grass.

The pack continued through the fire, spreading out and closing in in a pincer movement. The threesome went back to back, firing at the darting forms. Unfortunately, much of their fire was missing or bouncing off and the crabpus finally closed.

"*Grapp*," Two-Gun shouted as one of the things grabbed the leg of the Wyvern in its mandibles. He couldn't look down very well in the armor and felt himself swaying. "I'm going *down!*"

As one of the things leapt on his back, Jaenisch knelt and drove the armored fist of his suit into the top of the crabpus that had Berg by the leg. The thing had wrapped its tentacles around the suit and was *chewing* at the refractory armor which, incredibly enough, was smoking. Then he saw that the thing was "foaming" at the mouth. The foam was, apparently, some sort of acid.

The punch bounced.

"Mother*grapper*," he said, extending a sampling drill. The security Wyverns had some of the same equipment as the scientists', just not as extensive. But the sampling drill was designed to cut through rock or metal. He laid it just behind the thing's mandibles and turned on the drill as he heard a crunching sound over his shoulder.

"*Grappers!*" Hatt shouted, laying down point-blank cannon fire. The crabs were thrown through the air but most of them got back up. It was only when he hit one dead center that the cannon rounds would kill. Some of them were thrown fifteen or twenty meters and still got up and came back. "How do you *kill* these *grappers?*"

"Drill works," Jaenisch said, reversing the drill as the crab's tentacles spasmed into its body and then went limp.

"Jaen," Hattelstad said, "hold still. One of those things is eating into your back."

"Get it off!" Jaenisch said. "Get it off me!"

"Like I said, *hold still*," Hattelstad replied.

Jaen was suddenly slammed to the ground by a massive explosion.

"You could have used the *drill, behanchod!*" Jaenisch shouted, his ears ringing.

"It wasn't an armor penetrator," Hattelstad pointed out reasonably.

The pack was now scattered in bits in the artificial clearing made by the small skirmish. A few were still waving tentacles, but most were in too many bits.

"I guess we got one sample for bio," Jaenisch said, holding up the crabpus that had been eating Berg's leg. "Maybe we should pick up a couple more."

"Uh, boss," Bergstresser said as Hattelstad poured water on the foam. His leg armor was partially eaten away and *very* bent. "I've got movement popping up all over the place. Most of it's going away but a *bunch* of it is headed this way."

"So much for samples," Jaenisch said. "In the words of King Arthur—"

"Run away! Run away!" Hattelstad crowed.

"We are *so* out of here."


"All teams report to the boat for decon," the CO said as Charlie Second cleared the long grass. From the conn he had an eagle-eye view of all the activity around the boat and had monitored the small battle carefully. He also noted that Weaver and Miller let Charlie retreat behind them before backing up. "Security commander, pull all science teams in first, then security."

"Roger, Command," Captain MacDonald said.

"Commander Weaver," the CO continued. "I want you in *first*."

# 19

## Never Talk About Romantic Plans

"What *is* that thing?" Weaver asked, looking through the armored glass of a sampling cage.

"I'm with the Marines," Julia answered. She was carefully dissecting the thing inside the cage using a waldo system. "Crab octopus. Crabpus Jaenischa, Jaenisch's Lion Crabpus. It's less like a standard exoskeletal species than a turtle. The body is endo-exoskeletal while the legs are askeletal tentacles. They extend from eight openings in the shell on the underside. The spit is probably an enzyme designed to cut through or weaken the armor of its prey. From the damage to the Marines' armor, I'd say it's a weakening agent. I'm surprised it worked on the armor; you'd think an enzyme would be tailored to the material of the exoskeletons."

"After the Marines pulled out, a bunch more of these things, some of them bigger, descended on the skirmish site," Weaver said. "All that's left is some shells."

"Not surprising," Julia said distractedly. "In an area like this, any disturbance is a chance for food for scavengers or predators."

"So we going to be able to move around?" Weaver asked. "The CO would like to know."

"Not easily," Julia said, delicately picking up a gland and

laying it in a dish. "These things are *nasty*. I'll be able to tell him more in a few hours."

"I'll take the hint," Bill replied.

"Not much of a core," Dr. Dean said looking through the glass. "Where's the soil?"

"That *is* the soil, Doctor," Staff Sergeant Kristopher said. "There was only about a meter of soil, then I hit the rock. And that was pretty straightforward granite. It was hard to cut so that's all I could get before they pulled in the teams."

"Only a meter of soil?" Dean said, frowning. "That's not right. An area like this should have had a fairly extensive lay-down. You can see the traces of uplift so this area was probably under the *ocean* at one point. Where's the silt? I'd have anticipated at least *fifty* meters of soil."

"Well, Doctor, what you got was one," Kristopher said. "And then granite. What got me was I expected some sedimentary rocks."

"I *wish* we could have landed in the mountains," Dean said, frowning. "This just doesn't make sense."

"This doesn't make sense," Staff Sergeant Roberts said.

"What you got?" Bartlett asked tiredly. Okay, while doing field sampling was boring, the lab portion was just *tedious*. All that collected material had to be sorted, counted, weighed and analyzed. While Dr. Robertson got the fun of dissecting the crabpus, he and Roberts were doing the sorting of the collected botany samples.

"I'm only getting about three species," Roberts said. "All this grass stuff. I mean, you get fifteen or twenty in the most worked-over areas in Africa or original Great Plains prairie. I'm only getting three species of plant life. Four more of a pseudo-insect. Even the soil's only got two worms in it. This stuff is cleaner than my *lawn*."

"You're right; that's not right," Bartlett said. "I guess we need to talk to Dr. Robertson."

"Bio is still pondering," Dr. Beach said. "But Geo has some items to bring up."

"There is something wrong with this world," Dr. Dean said,

frowning. "The soil in this area is far too thin for the observed conditions. And I took a look at the video taken of the surface on the way in. There are no traces of certain forms of sedimentary rock. Notably, I couldn't find a single trace of shale, oil shale or coal. Sandstone, yes. But nothing organic. No limestone, even. You'd expect to see *some* of that *somewhere*. But none of the views showed any. Anywhere . . ."

"That's because the world's been terraformed," Julia said, walking into the meeting followed by Bartlett. "Recently. Well, geologically and biologically recently. Not sure if we're talking about a million years or fifty million, but I'd guess closer to a million. Maybe less. We may even be talking about *recent*."

"That's interesting," Weaver said, frowning. "Very interesting. It also explains what an advanced biosphere is doing on a moon of an F 5. Any clue by whom?"

"Only that they liked crabpusses," Julia said, sitting down. "Crabpussies, crabpus, crabpi . . . Not sure what the plural should be, frankly. Ain't my department. Bio is. Bartlett?"

"The botany samples are incredibly sparse," Master Sergeant Bartlett said. "Very limited biodiversity. The soil is very thin with an igneous understructure, indicating that soil has only been being caught by biological processes quite recently. Even the various animals caught in the video are all so similar that they indicate no more than at most a few dozen original species. And an analysis of the enzyme that ate Bergstresser's armor shows that it's designed to break down a wide range of compounds into edible materials. It won't just eat armor; it eats most plastics and does a hell of a job on the crabpus armor."

"That's the sort of thing I'd expect to see if a very advanced race was sending down some pioneer species," Julia said. "*Most* of the species we've found show traces of being pioneer species. They're all very hardy, probably fast spreading. There are actually *fewer* species than I'd expect to find in a good terraforming. I'd say that someone got *started* on terraforming this world and got interrupted."

"Any idea about the species involved?" the CO asked. "Not Dreen?"

"Definitely not Dreen," Julia said. "We found one trace of a Class Three life form. Just a soil fungus. Apparently there was some life here before whoever terraformed it got going. And Class

Three is the class that Dreen derive from. But it isn't close to Dreen form. And the species that terraformed the world is Class Four. But that's all that we know about them. Except that they liked crabpus. I think that they put down one or more species of crabpus that was some sort of organic clearing system and it's evolved into about ten or twelve, all closely related."

"And what are we going to do about those?" the XO asked.

"Depends on what you mean, Commander," Julia said, grinning. "Wouldn't suggest eatin' 'em."

"I'm more worried about *them* eating *us*," the XO noted, dryly.

"That's security's job," the CO said, looking over at Captain MacDonald. "Mac?"

"I'm not positive we can ensure security," the captain said frankly. "The things half ate PFC Bergstresser's armor. The first thing we're going to have to do is deploy all three platoons; one isn't going to cut it. We might think about putting in defenses around the air lock; waiting to cycle everybody through was pretty stressful. For that matter, I'd like some way to get the Wyverns up on the hull if we have to. That way if we get hit by a bunch of those things, we can get people out of the way."

"I figure they ain't gonna like fire," Julia pointed out. "Just putting some fires out will probably keep them off. Gotta be careful with them, though; we *really* don't want a big grass fire getting going. Take a suggestion, Captain?"

"Yes," the CO replied.

"Move the boat to somewhere rockier," Julia said. "That makes Geo happy; he can get more sampling done. Rocky hill or something, somewhere with clear lines of sight and not much cover. I'm gonna *have* to go forward into the brush, but if the Marines are up for it, we are. If we can find someplace sort of elevated, snipers can cover our backs. Think safari here."

"Captain MacDonald?" the CO said.

"Fits in well with my view, sir," the Marine said. "Something so that there are limited lines of approach sounds good. Frankly, I'd as well get the boat out of this environment. Anything happens to *it*, we're stranded."

"Congratulations, Jaen," the first sergeant said. "You just got a species named after you. Jaen's Lion Crabpus."

"Cool," Jaen said, yanking on the leg of the suit. "This mother-grapper is *stuck*."

"Wait," Lyle said, leaning in to look at the joint. "Some of that acid got into the mechanism. Work it back and forth, slowly. I might have to Dremel it out."

"When is it going to be back on-line?" Top asked.

"No more than an hour, first sergeant," the armorer said. "I've got spares."

"How you doing, Two-Gun?" Top asked.

"One hundred percent, First Sergeant," Berg replied. "Ready to rock and roll." He had his Gatling spread out in pieces on a tarp.

"Glad to hear it," Powell replied. "Because we're going back down."

"*Maulk*," Hattelstad snorted. "I knew this wasn't just a social call."

"They're looking for a safe spot to settle so we can keep doing the survey," the first sergeant continued. "As soon as they do, we're going to redeploy. All of us. Second will have ground security around the ship. First and Third will accompany the science teams."

"Great," Staff Sergeant Summerlin said. "Let 'em. We've taken point the last two deployments."

"And you're on point on this one," Top said. "Because you're guarding the ship."

"Ouch," Berg said. "Top, about that whole Two-Gun thing?"

"Yes, Two-Gun?" the first sergeant said.

"I wonder if I could use an experimental system that Corporal Lyle developed," Berg said uncomfortably. "The 7.62 mms don't have the penetration power you need for these things. I would like to request to draw a special weapon."

The first sergeant looked at him blank-faced for a moment, then nodded.

"Lyle, when you get a moment, would you care to show me this . . . 'special weapon?'"

"Yes, First Sergeant," Lyle said with a gulp.

"I am not going to say 'Are you kidding me . . .'" Top said when he saw the pistols.

"I haven't gotten a chance to try them out," Berg admitted.

"And I'd *rather* have a 12.7 mounted. But this is what's available, First Sergeant. At least if we're not ground mount. When we were fighting those crabs, all I could think was that I wished I had a couple of Colt magnums. But you can't use those in armor, so . . ."

"I'm considering the implications," the first sergeant said. "Among others, I know that *everybody* is going to want these. Chief Miller is going to be extremely envious and want to know why *you* got to carry them and *he* didn't."

"I only really need one . . ." Berg said.

"Oh, no, you are known as Two-Gun for a reason," the first sergeant said. "As long as you continue to use that technique and do not, in fact, go all two-gun mojo on me, I will overlook Lyle's unauthorized use of spares, not to mention severe damage to said spares. Do these things have anything like normal velocity, though?"

"The barrels are fourteen inches long, Top," Corporal Lyle said. "They're more like a carbine version than a pistol. Based on specs, that should give them about eighty percent of normal velocity. No recoil system so it's going to have a hell of a kick. That's the reason for the special grip."

"Looks like an elephant Mauser," the first sergeant mused. "Okay, Two-Gun. Take them both. How you're going to mount them, though—"

"I made holsters," Lyle said, setting them on the counter.

"Welcome to the Space Mushrooms," Berg said with a grin.

"You sure that's gonna hold us?" the CO asked.

By cruising along just off the coast, they had found a point of rock that jutted out into the ocean. It was nearly an island with only a narrow neck connected to the mainland. The top was broad and mostly flat and appeared to be covered in red lichen.

The trees had crowded in, though, and the plain narrowed so there was less than a kilometer from the point the land opened out and the plains started.

"It's a granitic basolith," Dr. Dean said with a sigh. "The surrounding material was lighter volcanic stuff that degraded and left the basolithic structure in place. Also very boring. I saw some sandstone on the scans from our way in; no chance of getting up into the mountains any time soon, is there?"

"Prior to deconfliction of the battlespace, enhancement of mission architecture is derecommended," the CO said.

"What?" Dr. Dean asked.

"You scientists keep trotting out technobabble," Spectre said dryly. "So I thought I'd pay you back in mil-speak. It's strong enough?"

"Yes," Dr. Dean said. "It is very strong. It should handle the weight of the boat."

"In that case," the CO responded. "I don't think we should plan any big adventures until we figure out how to handle the crabpus, Doctor. Okay, lower away. You okay, pilot?"

"Tricky winds, sir," the pilot replied. "But I got it."

The piloting controls had adjustments for yaw, and the seaman expertly adjusted them to lower the boat down. The shape of the granite protrusion meant that the boat ended up parallel to the shoreline, with the starboard side inland.

"Contact."

"COB, level the boat," the CO said.

"Level, aye," the chief said, hitting the adjustment. The boat rocked back and forth, then leveled. "Boat is leveled. Jacks locked."

"Captain MacDonald, Marines out, first. Then the science security personnel. *Then* the science personnel," the CO said over the communicator. "Spectre, out. Dr. Dean, it will be at least an hour before your turn to deploy. Why don't you see if you can figure out any samples *worth* taking in the area while you wait."

"That thing is just plain *cute*," Miriam said, looking over Julia's shoulder.

"I wouldn't go *that* far," Julia said. One of the Marine teams had managed to catch a crabpus before everyone was recalled to the boat. She was using a rubber pad from the waldo to rub the back of the captured crabpus. The plant-eating crabpus looked not unlike the predators that had damaged Bergstresser's and Jaenisch's armor. But it was far less aggressive, even timid. The back scratching seemed to have it calmed down.

"Can I?" Miriam asked.

"Go ahead," Julia replied. "Do you know how to use . . . ?"

"I did it when I was in college," Miriam said, taking over the controls. She rubbed the thing on the back, then picked up a piece of the grass and started playing with it.

After a while the thing rolled over on its back, waving all eight tentacles in the air. Miriam stroked its belly, then worked up towards the mouth. The underside of the beast was segmented, unlike the top but very much like a crab.

Near the mouth there was a broad, flat plate. When the woman rubbed on that, the thing's arms spasmed then went limp.

"Oh," she said, her eyes widening. "Did I kill it?"

"No, no," Julia said, looking over at her monitors. The thing's heart was still going, but it had slowed. Then the heart rate picked back up and it started waving its arms again, grabbing at the ground to flip itself over.

"Try it again," Julia said. "Before it gets up."

Rubbing the same patch caused the same reaction. The crabpus appeared to go to sleep. Not for long, but for a few seconds.

"Huh," Julia said. "Crabs have the same reaction. It's supposed to be something about mating, but I'd have to look it up to be sure. Tickle them in that one spot, and they go to sleep."

"That's cute," Miriam said, still playing with the beast.

"Yes, but it's not getting us anywhere," Julia said, sighing. "Want to name it?"

"Okay," Miriam said, smiling. "I hereby name you Tickly."

"No, silly, I meant the *species*," Julia replied.

"Hey, look at that," Staff Sergeant Roberts said, looking over the edge of the cliff at the water.

The Marines had formed a solid defense zone down at the narrow neck and were working on setting up defensive positions. The problem with that was that they were on solid rock. They'd settled for gathering large rocks—the Wyverns were easily capable of picking up two hundred kilo boulders—and stacking them. Thus far there hadn't been any sign of predators but the nearest grass was nearly a hundred meters from the sangers.

While waiting for their principals to arrive, the SF science teams had been wandering around the area looking for samples. Roberts had found a different form of lichen or fungus, he wasn't sure which to call it, over by the edge of the rocks and then glanced at the water.

"Whatcha got?" Bartlett asked.

"Crabs," Roberts said, then snorted. "More of them crabpus things. But swimming."

Bartlett cautiously got down on the Wyvern's knee and elbow wheels and shimmied forward until he could sensor pod over the edge.

He saw what Roberts had exclaimed about quickly enough. A school of the crab things were riding the surf that pounded the rocks, apparently feeding on something.

"We got any fishing poles?" Roberts asked. "I bet one of them would go for a little crabpus meat on a hook."

Suddenly the school scattered, some of them darting off to sea while others jumped up on the rocks and held on like limpets. A larger form could be seen in the depths, but the waves and foam made it impossible to get any details. He couldn't even figure out if it was a bigger crabpus or some other form.

What got Bartlett was that he couldn't figure out how the things swam. He couldn't see the tentacles propelling them that fast. But zooming in on the ones on the rocks he could see that there were inlets along their sides.

"Huh," Roberts said. "Jet propulsion?"

"Like a squid, yeah," Bartlett said, rolling back and standing up. "Tuck their legs up and shoot along. We'll try to figure out a way to get some samples, later. Even if we don't have any poles, a hand-line would work."

"Bio Two, Bio One is on the way down," the Marine sergeant handling the transfer said. "Paging Bio Babysitters, Bio Babysitters to the lift, if you please."

"I hate Marines," Bartlett muttered.

"Why are Marines like bananas?" Roberts said, following him to the boat.

"I dunno," Bartlett said, turning on his external speaker as they approached the lift. "Why *are* Marines like bananas?"

"Because they start out green, turn yellow and die in bunches," Roberts said, laughing.

"That ain't funny," the Recon sergeant growled.

"Dig in, they said," Jaen said, rolling a rock into position. "Make some fighting positions, they said . . ."

"At least it gives us some cover," Berg pointed out.

"Why do we need cover?" Drago called from over by the ship. "We have *Two-Gun* guarding us! Complete with giant pistols."

"Quit crossing chatter," Gunnery Sergeant Hocieniec said. He didn't step on inter-team chatter but he was death on cross-team. "Get ready for personnel to pass lines."

"You know, I'm perfectly comfortable staying here," Berg said.

"Me, too," Hatt replied. "Let somebody else get all the fun."

"Shut up and move rocks," Jaen growled. "If we do get in the busy, I want something to hide behind while Berg saves my ass."

"Bio, Geo, you ready?" Captain MacDonald asked.

"Geo's up," Master Sergeant Runner said. He'd drawn one of the 30mm cannons for this mission.

"Bio's up," Bartlett said.

"We're going to take this slow and careful," Captain MacDonald said. "There are some big guys moving in from the south. Elephant big. We don't know how they're going to act. Bio, do your sampling in a straight line. Forget the ring toss. Just get your samples and keep moving. We're going to head towards the treeline, maybe do a delta if we don't turn into anything, and then head back. Second Platoon is going to stay here to cover our retreat if we have to unass. Are there any questions?"

"If we see any exposed rock can we head for it?" Dr. Dean asked, raising one of the arms of his suit. "Maybe a small hill?"

"I just hope we don't make our last stand on one, Doctor," MacDonald said. "We're on an alien planet eleven light-years from home surrounded by an alien biology we can't eat and there aren't any boats capable of coming to pick us up if we screw up. Let's just try this easy one time before we get fancy."

Sergeant Terry Lovelace was glad when the last of the science teams had unassed the boat. Playing door man was no job for a good Marine.

"Join the corps," Crowley muttered. "Travel to exotic lands, meet interesting people . . ."

"And kill them," Corporal Lujan finished, reciting a motto that had probably started with Sargon's army. "Interesting *things* in this case. Exotic planets."

"Looks like they found something," Lovelace said, watching the group, which was most of the way to the woodline, stopped. "Wonder what it is."

"A world of hurt," Lujan said. "I'd just as soon stay here."

"Where were we?" Lovelace asked, the suit shifting as he reached for something on the inside.

"Level Four," Crowley replied. "Just about to enter the treasure room."

"Got it," Lovelace said. "Okay . . . We ready . . . ?"

"I'm on-line," Drago said, the arms of his suit windmilling. There was no way to take the actuators for the suits off short of exiting the suit, so when you played a Gameboy in one, the suit arms moved with yours. Drago's lifted towards his sensor array and paused.

"Watch your *grapping* arm, man," Crowley said. "You nearly punched me."

"Sorry, dude," Drago said. He coughed suddenly, the arms and legs of his suit spasming.

"Drago, are you smoking in your suit again?" Lovelace snapped. "I swear to *God* . . ."

"Hey, Sarge, I got Lurch to install a smokeless ashtray!" Drago said. "And spare filters. Smoke just went down the wrong way!"

"No wonder you don't have a girlfriend," Lovelace said. "You're too stupid to pick up chicks."

"I got a girl back home," Crowley said. "And when we get back, I'm gonna get down on one knee and ask her to marry me." The dome on his armor swiveled back and forth rapidly and he laughed. "Heh. Just checking."

"Damn, man, don't *do* that to me," Drago said, his own sensor dome swiveling. "You *know* not to say *maulk* like that. It jinxes the mission. *Never* talk about your romantic plans!"

"That's just a stupid superstition," Lovelace said, looking around nonetheless. "Holy *Grapping God* WHAT IS THAT?!"

# 20

## Gargala-WHAT?

"COMMAND, COMMAND, COMING OVER THE—"

"Who the hell was—" the CO said, looking up from the video screen that was following the security and science team as it approached the woodline. A herd of large herbivores was moving fast enough that the group was going to have a hard time heading straight back to the boat.

"I don't know; we don't have any indicators . . ." Tactical said as the boat suddenly shuddered. "What . . . ?"

"Command, Second Bravo!" a half hysterical voice said over the tac-net. "There's a giant . . . AAAGH!"

"That was Drago," Captain MacDonald said, breaking in. "He's on elevator guar . . . Oh My God! Command! There's a giant *grapping tentacle* attached to the boat!"

The leviathan made a living off of the predators that ate the smaller swimmers around the point. Occasionally it managed to snag one of the dumber land beasts that got too close to the shore.

In this case it wasn't sure what it had. But it was big, it moved and it had armor so it was probably something to eat. A couple of tentacles had snagged smallish beasts. Their armor had been quite tasty but the insides were gagging. It had eaten them anyway. Food was food.

237

Now it had *big* food. It had eaten a couple of large swimmers and the smaller land beasts already so it wasn't particularly hungry. However, waste not, want not. It just had to get this thing wedged somewhere and wait for it to drown. Then it could feed on it at leisure.

"Holy *grapp*," Jaen whispered, his eyes wide.
"Two-Gun, I think you need bigger pistols," Hatt added.

"Engage space drive!" Spectre yelled as the boat lurched towards the cliff.
"Space drive, aye!" the pilot said as the boat started to tip.
"Sound brace!" the CO said.
"All hands, all hands," the XO said, keying the 1-MC. "Brace for impact!"

"Move, move!" Lieutenant Tony Berisford shouted. The tall, slender and homely Second Platoon leader had come up through Marine OCS. Like all the junior officers in Recon, he had prior experience as a platoon leader, in his case in the 3rd MEU. But this was the first time he'd seen a giant octopus try to eat a submarine. He responded pretty well, nonetheless.
"Engage the tentacles," he said. "Careful. Don't hit the *boat*."

Candle-Man had been in reserve, backing the rest of the platoon. Like everyone else he'd been watching the science teams moving across the savannah until the shrill scream from Lovelace. But when he saw the tentacles dragging their ride home off the cliff, it was pretty clear what he had to do.
He'd started sprinting towards the beast, whose shell was just visible peeking over the edge of the cliff. As soon as he got to where he was pretty sure he could shoot it without *grapping* up the boat he'd taken a knee and engaged with his minigun.
The 7.62 mm rounds, though, just sank into the massive tentacle without any apparent effect. Shifting to where the juncture with the shell was visible, just over the edge of the cliff, wasn't any better. The large, powerful rounds just sank in and disappeared. Oh, there were chunks of flesh blowing off and violet blood splashing in the air but . . .
He didn't notice the tentacle descend on him from above . . .

» » »

Staff Sergeant Summerlin winced as Chandler was picked up and slammed repeatedly on the ground. He'd started for the thing just behind Chandler and was only about ten meters away when the thing picked up his teammate. The tentacle that had Chandler was at least three meters thick and clearly powerful, since the refractory Wyvern armor popped and smashed at the impacts. After several fast smacks, like a sea otter cracking a clam on a rock, Chandler's battered and blood-streaming armor was flicked through the air to drop over the side of the cliff. There was a crunching sound as the tentacle reached farther out.

Summerlin started backing up, fast, as the tentacle descended. He was on full rock and roll with the mini on his shoulder as the tentacle dropped and he could see the mini blowing chunks out of it, but . . .

*"Grapp!"* Berisford shouted as first Chandler then Summerlin were turned into Wyvern *au tere.* "Team Support Gunners; open fire. Clear that thing off so we can—"

He stopped talking as the boat slid over the side of the cliff. The tentacle that had taken two of his platoon to the depths followed.

"Never mind."

"Space drive on-line!" the pilot said as the boat hit the water at an angle. Everyone was thrown to the side but the pilot was strapped into his seat.

"Full power," Spectre ordered, his arm wrapped around a stanchion. "Blow all ballast! Unfurl the propellers! Give me *everything!*"

The boat suddenly lurched, but downwards, then slammed into the rock wall. Up, down, SLAM! Up, down, SLAM!

"Kill the power!" Weaver screamed. "Quit trying to get away!"

"What?" the CO yelled. "Are you *nuts!*"

"It's trying to *kill* us!" Weaver yelled as the boat hit the rocks again. An alarm klaxon started chattering in the distance.

"Leak in section forty-six!" the XO said.

"Kill all power!" the CO said. "Silent running!"

"All hands," the XO ordered over the 1-MC. "Silent running."

» » »

As soon as the beast stopped struggling, the leviathan took it deeper. With both vestigial lungs and much more functional gills, the giant crabpus could survive under water whereas prey like this could not.

It settled into a volcanic crevice and wrapped its arms around its prey, pecking away with its mandibles. It wasn't really hungry, but usually there were some legs sticking out to snack on. So far, nothing . . . When it got hungry enough, it would take the trouble to crack the beast open and eat the juicy insides.

"Neither laser will bear," Lieutenant Souza said quietly. The tactical officer was not quite sweating. "And we can't use the torps or missiles. They're designed for space battles."

The CO had gathered the command team and the remnants of the science team in a meeting. The thing hadn't really tried to crack the boat, yet. When it did, things were going to get bad.

The flooding had been stopped and the boat was functional, if at a cant. But they had to get away from the damned sea monster before they could fly.

"I'm surprised the space drive couldn't pull away," Weaver said. "But when we stopped trying to fly, it stopped trying to kill us. I call that a tie if not a win."

"Dr. Robertson has some poisons," Dr. Beach said, his brow furrowing. "But I'm not sure which would work on this thing. And then there's the matter of getting them . . . emplaced."

"The thing ate Wyverns like they were candy," Miller said, flexing his jaw. "And there ain't but two Wyvern qualified people onboard anymore. I'll go."

"I don't think poisons will work," Weaver said. "But, yeah, it looks like a Wyvern job. We're just going to have to be . . . sneaky."

"What's this 'we' *maulk*, White Man," Miller said, shrugging. "If not poison, then we blow that sucker up. Maybe the minis weren't doing much to it, but you put some octocellulite on that thing and it's going to go up like a fish with an M-80 in its gut."

The plastic explosive was an updated version of the venerable Composition Four. Named for the eight tightly packed chemical bonds that gave it its explosive "punch," it was about twice as powerful as C-4 or Semtek.

"Oooo," Miriam said. "That's not nice!"

The linguist and Mimi had been called in as part of the "science" team. The CO was beginning to regret the decision.

"If you have any suggestions, Miss Moon," Spectre said, controlling his temper. "We'd love to hear them. But we can't implement the chief's suggestion. There isn't any octocellulite onboard."

"*What?*" Miller said. "I mean, 'What, sir?'"

"Chemical explosives were deemed too unstable," Bill said dryly.

"Wait," Miller said. "We've got *quarkium* on-board and a space drive that, if you hit it with a spark, can wipe out a solar system. But we don't have *octocellulite?*"

"I was in the meeting," Weaver said. "You should have heard me scream. It was the last meeting we told NASA about."

"Holy *crap*," Miller moaned. "Who is *running* this Navy?"

"Next time I'll put up a stronger argument," the CO said. "In the meantime . . . Yes, Miss Jones, you have a suggestion?"

"No," Mimi said, nudging Miriam. "But Miss Moon does."

"No . . ." Miriam said, ducking her head.

"Go ahead," Mimi said. "You can do it."

"Please, Miss," the CO said, as politely and calmly as possible. "If it would help . . ."

"Tickle it," Miriam said in a very small voice.

"Tickle it?" the XO said, laughing.

"There's a patch on the underside," Miriam said, looking up and going from half crying to furious at the laugh. "In experiments, applied gargalesthesia to a specified nerve point rendered the subject crabpus immobile for a measured period of four seconds. During that period its appendages became limp and flaccid, Commander White. It would allow the boat to escape, which is, as I understood it, the purpose of this meeting."

"Gagala . . ." the CO said. "*What?*"

"The technical term for tickling," Dr. Beach said. "Actually the sensation of tickling rather than the act. Interesting suggestion."

"This was more like a stroke or a rub," Miriam said. "Applying a strong stroking pressure to the area may cause the creature to release the boat. Crabs have the same reaction. It's apparently something to do with reproduction. But it should go to sleep for a few seconds. And it won't have to be blown up like a 'fish with an M-80 in its guts.' Oooo!"

"So, my mission," Miller said, leaning forward, rubbing his

forehead and looking at the conference table. "And let me get this straight. My mission is to get in my little Wyvern. Go out under pressure underwater, which I'm not sure the Wyvern's been certified for. Try not to get eaten by a beast that's already crunched at least three suits. And stroke that little crab in a sensitive spot related to reproduction?"

"Sounds like," Weaver replied, clearing his throat.

"In my twenty-three years as a United States Navy SEAL, I *never* could have envisioned . . . But, hell, all the Marines are gone so I guess if somebody's got to go stroke a crab's . . ."

"And I think *we* need to do this," Weaver said. "That's a big crab. It's gonna be a big spot. And, frankly, sir," he continued, looking at the CO. "I think we're gonna need some tools."

"Right," the CO said, his eyes wide. "A giant vibrator?"

"We are going to need *something* that we can . . . gargalize this thing's . . . plate with, sir," Weaver said.

The CO opened and shut his mouth for a moment, then looked at the chief of boat.

"Chief?"

"Yes, sir?" the chief asked stoically.

"Make it so."

"*Knew* you were gonna say that, sir," the COB said with a sigh.

"We need to gargalize this species' pad so it will release the boat," the chief of boat said, looking at the group gathered in the missile room.

The COB wasn't a tech guy. He'd come up through, of all things, the supply department. But he knew the submarine service. And when you had a really knotty problem, the machinist mates were the guys to brainstorm with. Machinist mates hardly realized that there *was* a box.

But they had very small vocabularies.

"Gargalize?" Sub Dude asked. "You want us to make it gargle?"

"It means tickle it," the COB said tightly. "More like rub its tummy. There's a sensitive patch down there . . ."

The good thing about the machinist mates, the COB had to admit, was that they were perfectly fine with having a technical discussion of tickling a giant crab while standing around on a deck that was canted at a twenty-degree angle, deep under water, with leaks all over the ship, while said crab was trying to eat the boat.

"Like a crab?" Red asked. "Isn't that related to breeding or something?"

"I don't think anybody's ever proven that," Sub Dude argued, sucking his teeth. "I think that's more like a hypothesis. The last time I read a study on it . . ."

The bad thing was that keeping them on topic was nearly impossible. . . .

"It doesn't *matter*!" the COB shouted. "We just need something to rub its damned *tummy*. Something big!"

"I'm sure we can *blage* something up," Sub Dude said.

"God, I hate that term," the COB moaned.

"How about a mop?" Red asked. "I know there's a mop around here somewhere . . ."

"Wait!" Tchar said, waving his arms. "I have just the thing!"

The Adar darted to the end of the canted missile compartment and dove into his quarters. The Adar quarters took up about ten percent of the total mission specialist section and was on the lowest floor, opening on the missile compartment. It was the only way he could get to the engineering room.

He emerged a moment later with two large flat mops. The heads were about a meter across, bright orange and had the logo of a noted cleaner on the bottom. The handle was about a meter and a half long and clearly designed to extend.

"Vibro Mops!" Tchar said, proudly, holding them up. "Free with your order of the Mono Kitchen Knife Set! Only twenty-nine, ninety-five for seven monomolecular kitchen knives *and* a *free* Vibro Mop, guaranteed to clean even the messiest kitchen floor!"

"Why do you have two?" Red asked, scratching his head.

"The first set of knives did not cut through a diamond as they promised," Tchar said. "So I ordered another set to try it again."

Tchar fit right *in* with machinist mates.

# 21

## It's NOT Two-Gun Mojo. It's NOT.

"Holy *grapp*, the boat's *gone*," Gunga-Din said.

"We are so *grapped*," Bischel added. "First a damned crabpus eats Berg's armor then another one eats the *grapping boat*?"

"Stay frosty," Onger snapped. "And watch your sectors. Until the Skipper says we can panic, we don't panic."

"Sergeant, our *ride* just got eaten," Bisch pointed out. "I think it's a *perfect* time to panic!"

"Can it," Gunnery Sergeant Frandsen growled. "Panicking isn't going to get nobody home. There's no proof the boat's destroyed. Until we're sure it's gone, we just assume it's going to come back up. It's a *submarine*."

"Doctors," MacDonald said over the open freq. "All things considered, I think we should withdraw."

"Yes," Dr. Dean said. "But what about the boat. . . ."

"That is not a discussion for right now," the Marine ground out.

"We need to withdraw," Dr. Robertson said. "But there's a problem."

The large herbivores from the south were nearly opposite their position, skating wide of the human contingent. The large plates on their back were about ten meters across on the largest, but the creatures ranged down to "babies" that were only the size of rhinos. Instead of the relatively long and slender tentacles of most of the species, their legs were short and stumpy, holding them no more than a couple of meters off the ground.

"Back up into the longer grass?" MacDonald asked, switching to a discreet frequency.

"I don't think that's a good idea, either," Julia said, a tone of worry in her voice. "They're feeding on the same sort of grass. But there's a fringe that runs along the forest. They don't eat that."

"Poison?" MacDonald asked.

"No," Julia said. "I think they're afraid of something in the forest."

The pack had been waiting patiently for the big herbivores to pass. They had shifted, slightly, when the herd of bipeds had crossed the open area. If they got to the edge of the grass, they were prey. The pack knew its dash distance and the speed of their prey. If the bipeds moved to the edge of the grass, they could get them.

But the big herbivores had moved away from the bipeds, fearing that which they did not understand. They were out of range. And the pack was hungry.

Hungry enough for one of the younger members to lose her patience and dart from cover.

"Movement!" Prabhu screamed. "Oh, Holy Vishnu!"

While not as big as the herbivores, the individual pack members were nearly three meters across the shell and two meters high on their long tentacles. Compared to Jaenisch's Crab Lion, these were more like Crab Tyrannosaurs.

Prabhu fired low, scything into the tentacles and trying to cut the giant predators down. But it was a losing battle. . . .

"Back!" MacDonald shouted. "First Platoon, hold position! Third, pull back and prepare to give cover fire! SF, get the scientists *out* of here!"

"Go, go!" Runner yelled, pushing the scientist towards the cape.

The herbivores had started to panic, lumbering into a run southwards, some of the bigger members breaking off to face the predators as the young shifted away from the threat.

The scientists were going to have to run right through them.

» » »

As the mandible crunched down around his middle and the armor started to smoke and buckle, Prabhu let out another scream, this time of rage.

"I am created Shiva, the Destroyer!" he shouted, sticking the muzzle of the minigun between the mandibles. "Die you mother-*grapper!*"

The stream of 7.62 mm bullets tore the monster's brains apart and the mandibles separated but containment had been breached and Arun could smell the stink of the enzyme burning through his armor as he fell.

Onto his back. As the pack closed.

"Oh, *grapp* me," Arun muttered as one of the mandibles bit down, ripping out his round feed. "I hope the next life is better than *this* one . . ."

"Around or through, Dr. Robertson?" Runner asked as they approached the defensive line of massive crabpus.

"*Around,*" Robertson said, panting. "You do *not* want to get near an angry elephant!" She swiveled her sensors to the rear where the line of predators had hit First Platoon and saw a Wyvern tossed through the air.

Dr. Dean was out in front of the rest of the party, having taken an early lead. And he wasn't interested in professional biological input.

"Dr. Dean," Runner shouted. "Go *around* them!"

"*Grapp* . . . you," Dean panted. "I'm not going to get caught by . . ."

As he tried to pass between two of the huge crabpus, one lifted a massive foot and stamped down. The crunch was clearly audible through the armor.

"Aaaaagh!"

"There goes our geologist," Runner said. "This is going to look *great* on my evaluation report."

"I'm sure Mimi can fill in," Dr. Robertson said. "Go north. *Away* from the rest of the herd."

"Gunny!" Bischel shouted as the majority of the pack passed the fallen Hindu and charged into the Marines. "The *grapping* rounds are bouncing off!"

"Fire low, into their legs," Gunny Frandsen ordered, moving forward in support.

"Alpha, move right," Lieutenant Dorsett said, calmly. The six foot three "Mammoth" was a graduate of the Naval Academy in Annapolis and wasn't about to let something like a charging band of invulnerable, elephantine, alien, predatory crabpus break his smooth. "Lay in defilading fire on the predators. Bravo, Charlie, hold position to screen . . ."

"*Grapping* DIE already!" Bisch shouted as the pack closed. He was pouring cannon fire into the pack but except for accidentally blowing off a couple of legs it wasn't slowing them down any. One finally dropped back, too wounded to continue the assault, but . . .

"Onger!"

The sergeant's ammo counter was dropping like a waterfall as he poured out four thousand rounds per minute of quarter-inch high-velocity fire, but the damned rounds were just *bouncing off.*

He'd slowed one down by hitting its legs but that was luck as much as anything. Gunga-Din had gotten one and two more had been put down by the combined fire from Alpha and Bravo but they were *still* coming. On Earth, predators would be turned by the sound of the fire, they'd quit attacking, they'd *leave!* These things just kept coming. . . .

The pack barely paused as they cracked the latest suit of armor and tore at the insides, spreading carmine that disappeared on the vegetation.

First Sergeant Powell stood beside the CO watching the slaughter of the unit, then blinked.

"Sir, recommendation."

"Anything," the CO said. "Third, echelon left," he continued, marking his designators. "Get those things off First so they can pull back."

"All Marines," the first sergeant said calmly. "Directly under the mandibles there is a curved patch. Concentrate fire on that curved patch."

"Oh, *grapp* me," PFC Walker said. The rangy West Virginian had wanted to be a Marine since the first time he saw *Full Metal Jacket.* But that movie had never covered being eaten by a giant *grapping* alien monster. On the other hand, *Aliens* had. And this sucked just as bad.

He was scything away at the tentacles, trying to stop the pack from closing on the line that First Platoon had formed but the crabpus seemed to be shrugging the fire off. Some of them had *dropped* tentacles and just kept coming.

". . . Concentrate on that curved patch."

"What did Top say?" Rad-Man screamed. Lance Corporal Radovich was pouring cannon fire onto the beasts but while the cannon had some effect on them, it wasn't much more than the Gatlings.

"Fire at the patch under the mandibles," Sergeant Dunn said. If he was perturbed by the distinct possibility of being torn apart by giant crab-octopi it wasn't apparent. He readjusted his fire and hit his laser designator. "On my spot!"

The combined fire of two Gatling guns and a cannon managed to punch through one of the crabpus' armor and it immediately started to spasm in death throes, its tentacles jerking wildly as it rolled to the side.

"We got it!" Walker screamed. "We got it!"

Just as the rest of the pack closed.

"That's what I needed," Berg said, breathing deeply. "Sergeant Jaenisch, permission to move myself to the support of First Platoon?"

"What?" Jaen shouted. "Are you *grapping nuts*? No you can't 'move to the support of First.'"

"Sergeant," Berg said, drawing one of the pistols. "This has got twice the penetrator power of one of the cannons. Those are grenade rounds, not penetrators. Forget the 7.62s."

"*Grapp*," Jaen said, wincing. "Go. Just *grapping* go. Gunny Hoc . . ." he said, switching frequencies.

"Are we down to runners, now?" Runner asked as one of the Marines vaulted a sanger and stared sprinting across the veldt. A few of the big herbivores were between him and the action and Runner hoped the Marine went around them. Pinging the armor he got the name "Bergstresser." It took him a moment to figure out which Marine it was, but then he noted that the armor was wearing *pistols*.

"Two-Gun!" Runner said, direct linking the armor. "Are you *grapping nuts*?"

"Fifty cal pistols, Master Sergeant," Berg said. "They're about the only BMG systems except sniper rifles on the boat. *I* can kill these things."

"Watch out for the herbivores, Two-Gun," Runner warned. "They crushed Dr. Dean."

"Got the solution for that issue," Berg replied.

Going around the herbivores was out of the question. Sensors indicated that there were more of the predators closing on the Marines and they still hadn't finished off the first group.

Berg wasn't sure if he was an idiot or a genius. But if the patch under the mandibles was a kill point, he'd be able to prove it on the herbivores. If the pistols killed them, they'd kill the carnivores. If not . . . Well, they looked slow enough to outrun.

So he kept sprinting forward, drawing the right pistol as he approached the remaining elephant crabpus. There were three of them, spinning from side to side as if they couldn't figure out which was the bigger threat, the predators they knew or the Marines. Berg didn't intend to let them guess.

One of the massive beasts, fully nine meters tall at the top of the shell, started rumbling towards him on its stumpy tentacles and he paused, bringing up the pistol in a two-handed grip.

He carefully targeted the patch the first sergeant had noted and fired. The round punched through the refractory armor but the thing kept coming. After a second round, though, no more than a hand's span from the first, the giant herbivore practically jumped into the air, then came crashing down.

It slid to a stop less than three meters away but from Berg's perspective that was perfect. He took a running jump onto the top of its shell and then bounded off the far side between the two remaining herbivores. Dropping to a knee, he fired left in a two-handed grip, punching two rounds into the patch of the left-hand monster, then fired one-handed to the right, dropping that one with his last remaining round.

Bounding to his feet he dropped the clip, an unfortunately cumbersome operation with the converted rifle, and slid another magazine in place.

"Third Platoon," he said, the system automatically switching to that platoon's frequency. "Gang way. Two-Gun coming through."

» 　　 » 　　 »

"Back, back!" Mammoth shouted. "More coming in from the south." The lieutenant swept his Gatling gun to the right and shook his head. "Gunny, we have a situation here."

"That we do, sir," Big-Foot said. The last team was backing on their position, firing in a continuous stream at the pack. But, worse, there were motion sensor readings indicating more of the beasts no more than fifty meters away. The gunny targeted one of the remaining three carnivores, whose tentacles were shredded, not that it seemed to care, and began pouring rounds into the patch under the mandibles. Most of the rounds bounced off, some of them doing more damage to the tentacles. But if you put enough kinetic energy on a spot, it tends to crack. Finally, rounds began to punch through and the predator slid to a halt.

Mammoth had finished off another. But Wangen was down, the last predator's mandibles fixed on his arm.

"Mother*grapper*," Wangen snarled, hammering at the beast. "*Maulk*, I can't get up."

"Gunny," Mammoth said, chopping at the mandibles with his combat knife. The monomolecular blade rapidly broke through one of the mandibles and the arm was released. But the predator still pinned the suit.

"Sutherland," Frandsen said, grabbing one side of the beast. "Other side. And a one, and a two . . ."

"More!" Lance Corporal Corwin shouted as another pack of the predators broke cover. There were more this time and, if anything, they were bigger. These were striped in red and green. The first pack had been flat red.

"Retreat," Captain MacDonald said. "Just *grapping* run. We've got it."

"Too close, sir," Mammoth said, dropping to one knee and targeting the nerve junction. "Get Third out of here, sir. Semper Fidelis . . ."

"Third Platoon," Captain MacDonald said. "Prepare to retreat . . ."

"Two-Gun, what the *grapp* are you doing here?" Top snapped as the PFC barreled past.

"Penetrators, Top," Berg panted, holding up the modified sniper rifles. "Get . . . going . . . Got . . . it."

"PFC Bergstresser . . ." the CO said, then paused when the first sergeant raised a hand. "Go get 'em, boy."

»        »        »

"Go, sir!" Sutherland said, dropping to one knee and targeting the lieutenant's beast.

"Staff Sergeant, this is an order," Mammoth said. "Get your team out of here."

"Sir . . ."

"I gave you an order, Staff Sergeant," the lieutenant said. "You will obey it. Go."

"Sir," Sutherland said. "Alpha Team. Make for the boat."

As Alpha retreated, Berg seriously reconsidered his sanity. There were nine of the charging monsters and only three remaining Marines. He knew he was pretty good, but he'd hardly *used* these things.

On the other hand, these things were *much* faster than a Wyvern. If somebody didn't slow them down, they were going to be all over Alpha Team, and Third Platoon, like stink on *maulk*.

As Alpha ran past, he stopped and targeted one of the monsters, firing two rounds.

"Sir . . ." he said, pausing and blanking on the lieutenant's last name. "Mammoth! Get the hell out of there. I've got it."

"What?" the lieutenant asked as another beast crashed to the ground. "Who the hell . . ."

"Two-Gun?" Frandsen said, standing up as one of the predators closed. "Go, sir! Go!"

Mammoth had dropped one of the monsters and he got to his feet, backing up fast.

"Come on, sir!" the gunny shouted.

"Too late," Dorsett said, firing point blank into the monster's mouth. But its packmate took him by the arm and lifted the Wyvern off the ground, tossing it through the air to the rest of the pack.

"That kid's got spirit," Top said, turning to the rear.

"First Sergeant!" Captain MacDonald said, then paused. "Good luck."

"Thanks," Powell said. "You too, sir."

As the pack closed, Berg reloaded, then drew both pistols. Two rounds per beast was about right, sometimes three. He ran through the right-hand pistol killing two and putting a round in one, then backed and fired with his left hand, killing one more. He started backing faster, trying to reload on the backwards trot, dropping his first full mag as he stumbled over the rough ground. The predators were nearly on him as he fumbled a magazine into place.

"Nice pistol," First Sergeant Powell said, snatching out his right-hand gun. If he was bothered by the closing predators it wasn't apparent. He simply removed a magazine from Berg's harness quite calmly and reloaded as if he was giving a demonstration.

"Yes, Top," Berg said, stopping his retreat. He just couldn't run backwards and fire worth a damn.

"Got to talk to Lurch about getting one of my own," Top said, lifting the pistol in a two-handed grip. Six rounds ripped out fast enough that it sounded as if the pistol was on auto-fire. And three of the beasts dropped. "Want the last one?"

"Sure, Top," Berg said, putting two rounds into the sensitive patch. The beast slid to a stop at his feet, thrashing on the red grass. "Thanks."

"You're welcome."

"Report, Lieutenant," MacDonald said as the last of Third Platoon cleared the sangers.

"Five MIA," Lieutenant Berisford said. "I think we can count them as KIA, sir. The big crabpus that got the ship got them, too."

"Any news on the ship?" the captain asked tiredly. Three Wyverns were just clearing the obstacle of the big herbivores, two of them leaping across the backs. Three out of thirteen with Top and Two-Gun not far behind.

"No, sir, not yet," Berisford replied, stoically. "I'm sure they'll be back."

"Hopefully before our air runs out."

# 22

## Good Vibrations

"I hope we can get this done without our air running out," Miller said as the air lock began to flood.

There were many problems with using the Wyverns underwater. The first was that they hadn't, actually, been tested under fifty meters of pressure. They *should* hold, they were quite heavily designed, but *should* and *would* were two entirely different things.

The second, however, was somewhat more germane. Wyverns were heavy. Although they had a large pocket of internal air, it was insufficient to buoy them up. Without some sort of flotation, they were going to sink like stones.

The engineers and machinist mates of the ship had, again, come up with an answer. A cluster of sample bags had been put in large mesh bags used for food storage and handling. External air-tanks were run to the bags so that they could be inflated. Deflation was via a rope that would squeeze the bags.

It was the buoyancy air to which the chief referred.

"I hope we can do this, period," Weaver said, hefting his mop. "Prepare to gargalize!"

"As a battlecry it leaves something to be desired, sir," Miller replied as the water rose over his sensor dome.

The sensors stayed online as the water filled the compartment and reached full pressure. And no leaks sprayed across his pilot compartment. So Miller hit the air lock controls and stepped out.

The air lock was on the top of the boat and he could see the mass of the crabpus blotting out the light from above.

He clipped off a safety line and then, cautiously, walked down the exterior of the boat. There was another point to clip a line ten meters from the air lock and he clipped another line to that. Only then did he, oh so slowly, begin to fill the bags.

Finally, he felt a slight upwards tug and halted to check his buoyancy. There was a delay effect and as the bags pulled upwards they jerked him off the deck.

Flying up and slamming into the thing wasn't in the plan so he paid out the safety-line, ascending slowly. Looking to the side, he saw Weaver heading up as well.

Dr. Robertson hadn't determined what the things used for senses but they had to hope there weren't many sensors on the underside of the thing. Otherwise, they were simply going to get eaten.

As he approached the underside of the leviathan's shell he started trying to figure out where the ticklish patch was. There were twelve plates on the underside of the crabpus and he had to find the right one.

Stopping just under the shell, he looked over at Weaver, who was gesturing farther upwards. The problem was, they had ended up approaching the middle of the crabpus' underside. The patch they had to get to was farther forward. The thing was resting with its "arms" around the ship, canted upwards. They could get to the patch by letting out more line, but then they'd be touching the underside of the crabpus. It was likely to react badly to that.

Miller gestured to the scientist, then let out more line until the bags of air touched the underside of the crab. No reaction. He let out a bit more line and the bags slid upwards. *Then* the crab shifted, like a sleeper moving in a dream, the metal of the hull crunching briefly on the submarine rocks.

Miller paused but the balloon was now away from the crab, floating invitingly near the patch he was looking for. He let more line out and wafted gently upward through the clear water until he was opposite the "tickle patch."

His balloons, alas, were floating right in front of the crabpus' massive maw. In fact, as the current pushed him back and forth, they tended to drift *between* the giant mandibles. He'd just have to hope that "tickling" didn't cause the thing to close its mouth.

And the mop still would not reach. But . . . It was the RonCorp Vibro Mop with patented extending handle. So he extended the handle, turned on the vibrator and *now* it reached.

He looked over to see where Weaver had gotten to. The commander, though, was right there with him, on the opposite side of the patch.

He'd have much preferred to be placing a heavy charge on the thing, but he lifted the mop and began stroking it back and forth. . . .

"Whoa!" the pilot yelled as the submarine shifted, violently. As the tentacles loosened, the sub was pulled sideways and down to rest on its side.

"Engage space drive!" the CO said. "Lift, now! Ten gravities!"

The SEAL was jerked away from the patch as the ship lifted and the balloons flew upwards. This was one of several bits he hadn't been looking forward to but he braced in the Wyvern as the ship lifted upwards. Suddenly he was going down again as the balloons hit the surface. Worse, he could see the tentacles of the leviathan starting to shift. It was waking up.

The ship lifted out of the water, fast, but he stayed three meters under, dangling from the buoyancy bag, as the giant crabpus began to move, one tentacle coming up for the ship . . .

*It had fallen asleep! The prey was escaping!*
One of the lashing tentacles slid across the steel hull, then wrapped around the metal cover of Number Two Laser. Hit, stuck as others began to wrap around the prey and drag it downwards . . .

"We're stuck again, sir!" the pilot called, desperately. "I can pull us out, I think, but . . ."

The sub began to shudder and shake as more tentacles wrapped around it. Spectre reached over and flipped open the switch for the view port and looked forward.

"Pilot, give me six gravs absolute *forward* and HIT it!"

» » »

Weaver pulled up on his rope as a tentacle lashed by just under his feet.

"Chief? You okay?"

"*Grapping* mother*grapper* of a *behanchod* . . . Try to eat *my* ride . . . Put some octo where the sun don't shine . . ."

"Guess that's a 'yes' . . ." Weaver said as he was yanked downward. "What the . . . ?"

The massive supercavitation system of the *Vorpal Blade* slammed into the carpalus plate of the sea beast at just under twenty miles per hour. Struck and penetrated, slamming the beast downward into the water. The beast spasmed but kept jetting outward, trying to escape, now . . .

"And back at ten grav," Spectre called. "Hold that. Four degrees up, two left and gimme fifteen gravities! NOW!"

This time the supercavitation system hit the crabpus at the juncture of the carpalus plate and the gargalus, the "tickle" plate, punching upwards into the monster's limited brain and exiting just between its eyes. The gigantic crabpus dropped limp.

"Holy MAULK!" Jaenisch shouted as the ship erupted from the waves in a welter of foam. Stuck to the front, impaled by the "*Blade*," the weight of gravity having slid it all the way down so that it rested against the nose of the ship, was the giant sea beast. Fully exposed, it was apparent that its carapace was as long as the hull of the massive sub which was, itself, the size of a WWII battleship. The tentacles of the thing dangled limp as the ship, nose up to keep the beast impaled, rose above the plateau and hovered.

"Captain MacDonald, this is the CO," Spectre said over the general announcement freq. "I believe your suits have some very good cameras."

"Yes, sir!" MacDonald said. "Two-Gun, I want a very detailed still of this image, son. Make sure you can get those two Wyverns on the side for scale!"

"I'm going to send a copy of it to *grapping* Space Command," Spectre said. "With my compliments."

"I wanna know how we're gonna *mount* it," Jaenisch said.

» » »

"You're joking," the CO said.

"Not really, sir," Weaver replied, taking a sip of Coke. He really thought that, all things considered, it should be beer. "Freeze-drying something is just exposing it to vacuum for a specified period. If we pull it up to orbit, leave it there for, oh, a couple of days, then take it back down to, say, that north polar continent..."

"Yeah, but where are we going to store it?" Spectre asked. "I mean, once we get it back."

"Someplace dry," Weaver said. "*And* secure. Area 51?"

# 23

## A Voice as Stern as Conscience

"We're down twelve Marines," Captain MacDonald said. "All of their Wyverns, even the ones we recovered, are useless. We can *blage* them for parts, but that's about it. And we're down one scientist."

The CO had ordered the ship into deep space, then stopped to have a conference. They weren't in full "chill" mode, but most systems were powered down as much as possible and the chiller fans had been extended. The ship needed to chill in more ways than one.

"I'm qualified in geology and planetology," Dr. Beach said. "As is Dr. Becker. For that matter, Dr. Robertson has a masters in geology and Dr. Weaver has a masters in planetology. Last, Lord only knows what Mimi is capable of."

"Yeah, but we've taken a solid hit," the CO said. His jaw worked for a moment. Those losses were, after all, all "his" people. "And we're less than fourteen hours from Sol system. Time to head home."

"Sir, with due respect," the XO said, frowning. "We are not done with the mission."

"We've just taken casualties in more than a third of our security contingent," the CO replied. "Not to mention a science team member. We've got damage throughout the ship, including pressure leaks from that damned squid thing. The sick bay is packed and we've got people in quarantine. And your professional opinion is that we should *not* return, XO?"

"Sir, if I could interject?" Miller said uncomfortably. "I think I see what's going on here."

"Go ahead," the CO said, leaning back and glancing unreadably at the XO.

"Sir, sub officers and surface officers think differently," the warrant officer said. "I've worked, extensively, with both and it's something that SEALs notice. Sub officers will keep at sea even when most people would consider it much more . . . prudent to return to base. Surface warfare officers are more inclined to put in when something goes seriously wrong. I'm not saying which approach is better or worse, sir, but it's a very *different* approach. I think that's what's going on here."

"I'd never noticed it," the XO said, nodding, "but the chief's right. Sir, I've been on boats that were leaking like a sieve and had half the machinery held together with spit and prayer and we stayed on mission. That's . . . the submarine service, sir."

"Interesting point," Spectre said, frowning. "I'd accept further input."

"The question to me, sir, is I suppose, which culture the space navy assumes," Weaver said, nodding in thought. "Taking that view of the two disparate cultures and given that this ship is, among other things, going to set the cultural tone of the navy that follows, which do you choose? Frankly, sir, viewed that way it's a much bigger question than simply 'do we turn back?' Assuming that we survive the Dreen, in a hundred years a captain of a spaceship, faced with the same decision, is going to say: 'What did Spectre do?'"

"Oh, crap," the CO snapped. "Thank you so very much, Commander Weaver. So the choice is 'Damn the torpedoes' or 'Prudence at sea is always wisdom.' Not much choice there, is there? I'm much more worried about what the review board is going to say than what a captain a hundred years in the future is going to think. Not to mention if we can survive the rest of the cruise and return alive. This is the *only* spaceship Earth and the Adari *have*. Losing it would be a major setback. Not to mention terminal to everyone on-board."

"Again, sir, I would say it depends upon the nature of the review board," Miller said. "If the review board is primarily former sub skippers, they're going to shrug and say: 'Of course you continue the mission.' Carrier commanders might wonder if you were sane."

"And, again, that's going to set the tone of the space navy, sir," Weaver said. "Given what we've already encountered, the only difference here is that we've taken casualties. Serious casualties, admittedly, but that's the major difference."

"The ship damage from the dimension jump and retanking the air systems was worse than the pounding we just took, sir," the XO pointed out. "Except for the casualties, we're in better shape than we were at Sirius. We filled our fresh water tanks, took on a bunch of $O_2$ and chilled down while we were submerged. There were benefits accrued to being dragged underwater. On a comestible level, well, we're pretty good. Less use, among other things."

"Commander, your tendency to look on the bright side can sometimes border on the annoying," Spectre said, shaking his head. "Okay, I appreciate the input. I'm going to have to give this some thought. XO, ensure I'm not disturbed unless a giant space beast attempts to eat the ship. And I'm authorizing an issue of medicinal bourbon."

The CO stood up and left the compartment, headed for his office.

"The term here, is 'weight of command,'" Miller said, standing up. "Fortunately, I'm not the commander, so I'm going to go get at the head of the line."

"Medicinal bourbon?" Dr. Beach asked.

"Every warship of sufficient size is issued enough bourbon for two issues per person on-board," the XO said, standing up. "Little bottles like you get on planes. The CO is authorized to issue it if he feels the entire crew needs some tranquilization. Given that Dr. Chet has two trank cases in the sickbay and everyone's looking a little rocky, I think it's a justified order. Now I need to go carry it out."

"I thought you were going to go get at the head of the line," Weaver said, entering the mission specialist mess. Miller was sitting at one of the tables with a bulb of Coke in front of him.

"What, you think I didn't bring my *own*?" Miller said, pulling a bottle of Aunt Jemima syrup out of a musset bag. "Grab a cup."

"Absent friends," Miller said, lifting his cup.

"Absent friends," Weaver said, downing the bourbon. "You've been hanging out with the Marines. I can't believe they lost an entire *platoon* while we were under water."

"I room with their first sergeant, note," Miller said. "It is not sweetness and light in the Marine compartment right now. Apparently they were all going to get wiped out but one kid with an experimental gun stopped the charge."

"Kid needs to get a medal," Weaver said.

"Captain MacDonald has recommended him for the Silver Star," Miller said. "It still doesn't change the fact that we're down some serious troops. And we've got the wrong guns, apparently. The Marines say that their Gatlings hit and bounced off those things."

"What was the experimental gun?" Weaver asked.

"Believe it or not, a cut down Barrett," the SEAL said, shaking his head. "The kid uses them as pistols. His nickname is Two-Gun."

"I'm almost sorry I missed it," Bill said as Miriam and Mimi walked into the compartment. "That would have been something to see."

"Join us in some medicinal bourbon?" Miller asked. "It's good to see you up and around, Miriam. How's the edema?"

"Gone," Miriam said, sitting down. "And I'm allergic to alcohol. But feel free. Most of my friends drink. I'm a great designated driver."

"None for me, either," Mimi said. "Not ready to try it, yet. I hear that the Marines . . ."

"Twelve dead," Miller said.

"That's terrible!" Miriam said. "I had no idea. I'm so sorry!"

"Nothing you could have done," Miller replied. "Those things weren't talking."

"I can still be sorry," Miriam said. "Is there anything we can do for them?"

"That's a good question," the SEAL said, frowning. "Honestly, you probably could. But I don't know if you *should*. Right now, they're going to be in the Marine mess, getting their issue of bourbon. There's some empty seats . . ."

"And we could fill them?" Miriam asked. "I've done counseling before. But I'm not sure we're allowed . . ."

"You're allowed," the SEAL said. "They're not allowed in *our* area, not the reverse. But we shouldn't go down there, yet. Not as shocky as they're going to be. Give it . . . fifteen or twenty minutes."

"Okay," Miriam said. "So a question: Why are we just sitting here?"

"The CO is trying to figure out if we should go home or stay out and finish the mission," Bill replied.

"Go home," Miriam said.

"Keep going," Mimi replied almost simultaneously.

"We have people who are hurt," Miriam said, frowning prettily. "They should be in a hospital."

"Dr. Chet is very good and there's nothing a hospital could do for them he isn't," Weaver pointed out.

"Better food," Miller said. "No, scratch that. Worse food. Well, if you don't mind three-bean salad."

"I mind three-bean salad," Weaver said. "But mostly because it should be outlawed on a submarine."

"This is harder than we expected," Miriam pointed out. "This is only the second planet we've found with life and we lost all those soldiers, and Dr. Dean. What if other planets are worse?"

"We didn't really know *what* to expect," Weaver said. "We've run into four alien species so far. Three of them were enemies. We've run into some weird space stuff, but that was to be expected. I thought it would be harder than it *has* been."

"We haven't run into magic, yet," Miller said. "No giant floating heads in space, no godlike beings and nothing that's trying to eat us in weird ways. Hell, we haven't even run into another Boca Anomaly. Seems okay to me, so far. And, note, I probably spent more time with those Marines than any of you. I knew them by name. But they were here to keep the scientists and commanders from getting eaten and they did their jobs. The ship's still working and we've got air, food and water. We're good. What do you think, Mimi?"

"What's the purpose of the mission?" the girl asked.

"Local area survey," Weaver replied. "Get a look at the local area. Get a feel for how many viable planets there might be in the galaxy and especially in the local area. Keep an eye out for the Dreen."

"That's what the mission *says* we're supposed to be doing," Mimi said. "But what are we *really* doing?"

"I don't follow you," Miller said. "That's the mission parameters, like Doc said."

"We're seeing how hard this is," Miriam interjected.

"Exactly," Mimi replied. "We're out in space to find out how hard it is to *be* out in space. How long we can expect to stay out and survive. What we can expect to encounter in the way of space hazards and planetary hazards."

"We've found that out," Miriam pointed out. "It's *hard*."

"Not yet," Mimi argued. "Because we *can* keep going. I'd say that if we turn back when we're still capable of going on, we won't know what the ship and the crew *can* handle. So far, we've handled everything we've run into."

"Yeah, but you don't test to destruction," Miller said. "Not in this case, anyway. There's only one ship. We don't even have the theory for another one, unless I'm much mistaken. Doc?"

"He's got a point," Weaver admitted reluctantly. "We'd sure as hell better head back before we run into something we *can't* handle. There ain't any more ships on the drawing board if you know what I mean."

"Ten Marines and a wake-up," Miller said then snorted.

"What?" Miriam asked.

"I get it, but only because I've been in the Navy for a few years," Weaver replied, smiling slightly at the grim joke. "When you're about to get out, when you're 'short' as they call it, you do a countdown. 'Forty days and a wake-up and I'm a civilian, man!'"

"So we have to turn back when we're out of Marines?" Miriam asked. "That's harsh."

"But we can keep going, so we should," Mimi said. "We should keep going as long as the food, air and water hold out. And the Marines, of course. Or until we run into something that *really* messes us up. Otherwise we won't know what we can do. Is this the last mission we're going to do?"

"No," Bill said. "The overall plan is go back, assimilate data, do maintenance and repair, maybe switch out some crew and mission specialists, then go back out. I don't know what the next mission parameters will be. Pretty much the same unless I'm much mistaken, just farther out."

"And farther and farther," Mimi said, stroking Tuffy. "To go farther and farther, we need to know how far we can go, what we can do. That's all I'm saying."

"Solving the problems of the universe, sir?" the COB asked as he walked in the mess.

"Trying to," Bill admitted. "That's what we're out here to do, right?"

"Yes, sir, as you say," the COB replied. "But at the moment, the captain would like a minute of your time."

"On my way," Bill said. "His office?"

"Yes, sir," the COB replied. "I see the medicinal bourbon has made its way here. Mind if I have a hit?"

"Actually, just maple syrup," Miller said, squeezing some more into a cup. "Have some. Puts hair on your chest. Then Miss Moon, Miss Jones and I are going down to the Marine mess to explain the concept of a wake to them."

"Come," the CO said, slipping away a book and waving to a station chair as Weaver entered the compartment. "Sit."

"Sir," Weaver replied, sitting down carefully.

"Any more thoughts on turning back versus going on?" the CO asked.

"Lots, sir," Bill admitted. "I think there are about two hundred different opinions on the ship."

"But only one matters," the CO said. "Why did you ask to join the service, Weaver?"

"Sir?" Bill asked, momentarily confused. "Well, I was getting jerked off this mission by Columbia over and over again and I thought I could make a contribution, sir."

"So you arranged to get a commission with the caveat that you got to go on the mission," Spectre said. "You got sent through half a dozen classes, which you naturally breezed, given your background, and a couple of cruises. Do you think that makes you a fit officer?"

Weaver opened and closed his mouth for a moment at the apparent attack. The thing that got him was that the CO was presenting it in such an even tone he couldn't figure out if there was anger in the background or not.

"More or less accurate, sir," Weaver replied. "But, yes, I think I'm a fairly good officer. So far my reviews have been excellent. I think I'm a good officer, sir."

"Did you know those Marines, Weaver?" the CO asked. "I'm sure you knew Dr. Dean, but did you ever meet any of the Marines?"

"Only in passing, sir," Weaver said.

"I did," Spectre said. "I made sure to meet with all the security personnel at one point or another, get to know them. I'm not a ground combat guy and don't begin to think that I am. But they were under my command and I made sure I knew what they were made of. Pretty good kids for Marines, and they were all kids. I sent them out there, knowing it was going to be a hot mission. Given what we'd seen of the crabpus, there was a fair chance one or two were going to get injured or killed. Why did I do that?"

"It's our mission, sir," Bill said, still puzzled. "We're doing a survey."

"We had all the big information we needed about Runner's World," the CO said. "Dr. Dean got his core sample, we had botanical and animal samples. We had air and water samples. We could have just left and gone on to the next planet. So why keep poking?"

"If you're second guessing your decisions, sir . . ." Weaver said carefully.

"I'm not, I'm asking you why I chose to keep poking," the CO replied.

"Sir, with all due respect, I'm not a mind reader," Weaver said.

"Take a guess."

"Curiosity, sir? You felt that more information was necessary for the mission?"

"More the second one," the CO said. "But the information I was looking for was 'how hard will it be to poke on this planet.' For that matter, how hard could it be to poke on other planets? We've only found two planets through the gates that have extensive biology. And both of them are pretty tame compared to Earth, much less Runner's World. What's your opinion of that, Commander Weaver? Be frank."

"I think it was a valid choice, sir," Bill responded automatically. "That was part of the discussion I was just having. How hard is it going to be to do things out here is an important part of what we're looking at. And, hell, sir, pure curiosity isn't a negative in what we're doing."

"Ever read any Kipling, Weaver?" the CO asked.

"A bit, sir," Bill said, trying to keep up with the apparent changes in topic. "A book called *Kim* and a couple of his poems."

"Brilliant man, I wrote my masters thesis on connections between Kipling's Victorian Era, the Romans he tended to write about and current conditions. At least, current when I wrote my thesis. Things . . . change. But one of his overlooked poems is one called 'The Explorer.' It's about a guy who quits farming one day and goes off exploring over a mountain range everyone says is uncrossable. The trip nearly kills him, and others take all the credit, but he was the first to go there and to see what was there. 'Then a voice as stern as conscience said: Something lost beyond the ranges, lost and waiting for you . . . Go!'"

"Not familiar with it, sir," Weaver said.

"'That was where the Norther killed the plains bred ponies, so I called the pass Despair,'" the CO said, apparently lost in thought. "Haunting poem. And do you know that funny thing about it? Such a place as he found would never have existed on Earth at any point. Even in the Americas, there were Native Americans who had been there first. A farmer couldn't walk away from the plow and find a place that was uninhabited. But we can, Commander Weaver. We *can*. I'd suggest you brush up on your Kipling, Commander Weaver. Take that as a strong suggestion based on professional development. The reading list of the CO of the *Vorpal Blade* will, after all, be the de rigueur reading list for the future space Navy, right?"

*The. Heat. Was. Lowering. It. Was. Becoming. Again.*

"Semper Fi, jarhead," Miller said as he entered the compartment.

First Sergeant Powell was standing by the hatch, looking at the group of nearly silent Marines. The mess was standing room only. But, normally, you couldn't have packed the whole company, less officers, into the space. And even at the tables there were empty spaces, places that no one chose to sit.

Powell looked at the SEAL, then at the two women with him, and nodded.

"Semper Fidelis, Flipper," Top said. "Ladies, why don't you sit in one of the seats?"

Miriam looked around the room nervously. The Marines hadn't even changed; they were still in their skinsuits, and the compartment reeked. The smell was strong and strange, the smell of fear and sweat and anger overlaid with oil and ozone. She suddenly felt as nervous as cat at a dog convention.

"Those are where your dead sat," Miriam said. "We cannot fill their space."

"No, but we can give the ones who sit nearest someone to talk to," Mimi said. "Come on, Miriam."

*Almost cold enough to Be. The Ons and Offs flowed more normally. It was Becoming . . .*

Berg looked up at a sudden laugh and saw Mimi Jones sitting across from him.

It was the place that Gunga-Din had occupied for the last six weeks and it shook him just a bit to see the petite young lady sitting in Prabhu's seat. It also, for just a moment, angered him. He'd been trying to avoid looking across the table for the last ten minutes. Nobody had anything to say. The losses were still too fresh.

"What are you doing here?" Berg asked roughly.

"Looking for you," Mimi said. "I wanted to ask you some questions."

"I'm fresh out of answers," Berg said.

"I think you can tell me these," Mimi said. "Whose seat am I sitting in? Who was he? What was he like?"

Berg teared up and turned away.

"His name was Arun Prabhu," Sergeant Jaenisch said. "He was a Hindu who didn't know a *grapping* thing about it. We called him Gunga-Din."

*"Din! Din! Din!*

*"You Lazarushian-leather Gunga Din!*

*"Tho' I've belted you an' flayed you,*

*"By the livin' Gawd that made you,*

*"You're a better man than I am, Gunga Din!"* Mimi quoted.

"What?" Guppy asked. Lance Corporal Francis Golupski was the sole survivor of Staff Sergeant Summerlin's Alpha Team after the attack of the giant crabpus. The shaken lance corporal hadn't said anything since returning to the ship.

"It's the closing lines of the poem," Mimi said gently.

"Yeah, that says it," Hatt said, nodding. "He was a damned fine guy. Never touched a cheeseburger once he found religion."

"He sounds like a fine man," Mimi said. "I wish I'd known him."

"Oh, he was a character, all right," Jaen said, his jaw working. "One time in Singapore . . ."

*Still too much Heat. It could feel the Ons and Offs struggling. If only the Heat would not flow to it, constantly. If only the temperature would lower enough. It felt that this had happened before. Vague memories of prior times of cold and then the Heat returning. Cold was Life. The Heat was . . . Death.*

"You've hardly said anything," Mimi half shouted, tracking down Bergstresser where he was standing in the corner. Miss Moon was leading the group in a chorus of "Nearer My God To Thee" while Staff Sergeant Sutherland accompanied on the bagpipes. Sutherland was making heavy weather of it. He'd been fine for "Amazing Grace" but on this one he was having to make it up as he went along. It didn't help that from *somewhere* a bit more than "one shot of medicinal bourbon" had turned up.

"Not much to say," Berg shouted, then took a suck off a bulb of Gatorade. "We took a lot of losses. Most of the people I'd gotten close to in the unit, among others. Too many good people."

"They were your friends," Mimi said.

"No, actually," Berg said. "They were my buddies. I hated more than half of them. But that didn't mean I wouldn't rather have died than them. That's what being a buddy means in the military."

"I was told, by others, that more would have died if it hadn't been for you," Mimi said. "Does that help, at all?"

"No," Berg admitted. "I was just doing my job. I couldn't save Mammoth. I didn't stop the crabpus from taking Drago and Crow and Lacey. I couldn't save Candle-Man or Summer. Nobody could. I hate that *God* damned *planet*."

"But you're going on to others, still," Mimi pointed out.

"Still in question," Berg said. "If the CO turns the ship around, I'm going to withdraw my volunteering. This is a good unit, but . . . Sorry, I don't think I'm cut out to be a Space Marine. Not if it means another world like that."

"But you are good at what you do," Mimi said. "If you don't continue, more people will die because you are not there. Or, the person that takes your place will be lost. Look at Chief Miller."

The chief warrant was in the corner arm wrestling with Lyle. The armorer might have been a paraplegic once, but he'd made up for it in the weight room. The chief wasn't losing, yet, but he wasn't winning, either.

"He had his whole team wiped out in the Dreen War," Mimi said. "He's here. Because this is where he needs to be. This is where you need to be, Two-Gun."

"Don't call me that," Berg said. "I *hate* that name."

"No you don't," Mimi said. "You're too much of a Marine to hate it."

"Why are you here, Miss Jones?" Berg asked, exasperated.

"Because everybody else is singing and you're sitting in a corner, brooding," Mimi said. "Because you think too much. Because you know too much. Which is why you need to be here, PFC Bergstresser. Because you think. And because the next time you step out that door, you have to be mentally ready for it. Captain Blankemeier needs you that way. Your CO, your first sergeant, your teammates need you that way. I need you that way. Because the next time, the life you might save is mine or Miriam's."

"Or lose," Berg said. "That's another possibility, you know. We lost a scientist *and* twelve Marines, today. Losing you or Miss Moon is a very real possibility."

"One that's *reduced* if you're here," Mimi said, lifting up on tiptoe to press her finger into his forehead. "If *that* is here."

"Okay, okay!" Guppy shouted as the song died. "This is one that I *know* Danno can't *grapp* up! March! March! March!"

"For Crow!" Jaenisch shouted drunkenly. "For the Crow-Man! March! March!"

"Okay, okay," Staff Sergeant Sutherland said, taking a drink. "Lemme get my breath."

"I don't know that one," Miriam said.

"Simple lyrics," Sergeant Jaenisch said, grinning. "Don't know if you'll like 'em . . ."

"March?" Mimi asked. "Dirty song?"

"March of Cambreadth," Berg said, his jaw flexing. "It's only a dirty song if you're a pacifist."

"Okay, here goes," Sutherland muttered, warming up the pipes.

*"Axes flash, broadswords swing*

*"Shining armors' piercing ring*

*"Horses run with polished shield*

*"Fight those bastards 'til they yield*

*"Midnight mare, blood red roan*

*"Fight to keep this land your own*

*"Sound the horn and call the cry*

*"How many of them can we make die? . . ."*

"You're right," Mimi said when the song was finished. "Not much of a song for a pacifist. Are you a pacifist, Berg?"

"No, ma'am," Berg said.

"So you gonna *'fight as one in heart and soul'?*" Mimi asked.

Berg looked around the compartment, empty though it was of a lot of people, and admitted what he'd been fighting for a long time. He didn't want to be anywhere else. It didn't seem to be the right response to losing so many friends, but it was what he truly felt in his heart.

"Hymn!" Guppy shouted, standing up and swaying and putting his hand over his heart. "The *Hymn* for God's Sake! We haven't sung the Hymn!"

"Damn straight!" Sutherland shouted. "I think I've got that set to bag—"

"NO!"

"Be that way!"

"THE SPACE MARINE'S HYMN!" Berg suddenly bellowed.

"The *what?*" Top asked, his eyes wide.

"The Space Marine's Hymn, Top," Berg said, his face hard. "Come on, you know that one, right Top?"

Berg put his hand over his heart and opened his mouth.

*"From the halls of Montezuma to the stars of Ori Three,*

*"We will fight our planet's battles in space, on land, and sea.*

*"First to fight for rights and freedom, and to keep our honor clean,*

*"We are proud to claim the title of Allied Space Marines . . . "*

When Berg was finished the first sergeant's mouth was still open at the butchery of his beloved Corps' hymn but the Marines were insane.

"TWO-GUN! TWO-GUN!"

"Say again, Brain!"

"Allied *Grapping* SPACE MARINES! Oorah!"

"All hands! All hands! Prepare for maneuvering. Next stop, 61 Cygni binary system!"

"Clear the compartment, *Space Marines*," the first sergeant said. "Lock it down. PFC Bergstresser, if I could have a brief moment of your time . . ."

## 24

### "From the Forest Moon of 61 Cygni Alpha Five" Doesn't Scan

"Stable orbit around 61 Cygni Alpha established."

"Last stop, sir," Bill said, sighing. "And I don't expect to find much, here. Binary star system with Cygni Beta about a light-year and a half away. Since that right there would suggest not much planetary formation and given that they're both dwarfs..."

"Got to look," the CO said. "I'll be in my office while what's left of planetology does its thing."

"Well, looky there," Runner said, nodding.

"What?" Kristopher asked. He was watching the take from the secondary telescope.

"Two gas giants," Runner replied. "Sending coordinates. Zoom in on the one marked Alpha. I have a feeling."

"And your feeling is confirmed," Kristopher said after a moment. "Lots of moons. Outer edge of theoretical life zone, though."

"Yep," Runner said. "But look at the spectra. We've got peaks at four hundred thirty, four hundred eighty, six thirty, and six seventy-five nanometers. All the chlorophyll peaks. It's green *everywhere*! Zooming in on scope one."

"Damn, Steve," Kristopher said after a moment. "Now *that* is the forest moon of Endor."

"We got us a name for the planet," Runner said, picking up the comm. "Dr. Beach, planetology. We have a live one."

"Jesus Christ, I refuse to make any predictions anymore," Weaver said, examining the large moon the ship orbited. "What did we overlook? We passed up a couple of binary systems."

The gas giant the moon circled was a super-massive Jovian, right on the edge of being a red dwarf and, thus, with its own radiated heat. In fact, the "planet" almost argued for the Cygni binary system being some sort of dwarf cluster.

But the moon was a treasure. The spectral analysis indicated that the biology was Chloro Alpha, the same as Earth and different from the Adar Chloro Bravo. Tectonic with limited but apparently deep oceans, the moon looked not unlike Earth with a bit less water and more land. There were clouds, oceans, mountains, and arid zones. But most of the moon appeared to be covered in massive forests. Of course, so was the Earth before it was cleared.

It looked, remarkably, as Earth must have looked prior to the late middle ages before humans got to clearing land on a wide scale.

"It sure looks inviting," the XO said. "Let's just hope it doesn't have any of those damned crabpus."

"Again, not going to make any predictions, sir," Bill replied. "Nothing is weirder than reality."

"Conn, Planetology."

"Go, Planetology," the XO replied.

"Got something interesting on the ground scope, sir," Runner replied. "Set screen to Scope Four."

The XO hit the keys and then shook his head.

"Jackpot."

Clear on the screen was a city that straddled a river not far from one of the smaller oceans. It wasn't much by modern standards but it had some streets paved with stone and some large buildings. The resolution of the scope was high enough that they could see beings and vehicles, apparently pulled by animals, on the screen but that was about all they could get. There was no detail of the beings moving on the streets except that they appeared to be wearing thick coats.

"Somebody had better alert Miss Moon that she's up," the XO said. "I need to call the CO."

"*This* we have an SOP for," the XO said, setting down a thick manual.

"I've read it, sir," Bill said. "I actually was on the committee that recommended against using it, but that's besides the point."

"Why didn't you want to use it?" the CO asked curiously.

"Mostly because it's too restrictive, sir," Bill replied. "If they'd given just the outline, I wouldn't have an issue. But they tried to imagine anything that could possibly happen and have an SOP response. We've already gone *way* beyond anything in that manual. Among other things it does *not* cover tickling a giant crabpus to let the ship go or it would have recommended having explosives on board. Face it, sir, we're going to be the ones *writing* the manual. I'd suggest going to the section on preindustrial contact, look at the outline and ignore the appendixes. Later, when we've got an idea what we're actually doing, we can write an appendix that isn't the dreamings of some NASA egghead."

"Preindustrial, preindustrial, N-O . . . ," the XO muttered. "They don't have a chapter on preindustrial contact."

"Low-tech?" the CO asked.

"Nope."

"Savages?" Spectre added. "Barbarians? Slope-heads?"

"Nothing, sir. Wait! What in the hell is 'developmentally challenged technology?'"

Bill sighed. "You begin to see my problems with it, sir."

"The outline has six items," the XO said. "Planetary space survey, cultural analysis, initial ground survey, limited communications contact, primary contact and a chapter on inter-tribal diplomacy."

"Check out the planet and what you can find of the cultures from space," Bill translated. "Check out the planet on the ground, find some savages cut off from your main contact to sell beads to, then find the main contact and establish communications. Don't get involved in a war. Unless it seems strategically useful to us."

"Do we have any beads?" the CO asked.

"Yes, sir," Dr. Beach said. "As well as other cultural exchange items."

"There's a big warning about cultural contamination," the XO continued. "Do we have a reg on that?"

"None written," the CO said, glancing at the manual. "That's a supplementary recommendation, not a reg. Commander Weaver?"

"Somebody's been watching too much TV, sir," Bill said, sighing again. "They don't want us teaching the locals to make gunpowder or whatever. If we make contact, cultural contamination is impossible to avoid. Short-term effects can be devastating to lower-tech cultures, especially very stagnant ones. Long-term effects are usually progress to a level superior to their prior condition, but the PC crowd likes the cultures just the way they are. The noble savage and all that. And the intermediate consequences can be bad: wars, famines, disease. But the life of the average Japanese, today, is a hell of a lot better than under the Meiji. It's a big philosophical argument."

"We're going to need more guidance," the CO said. "In the meantime, let's get cracking. Drop two satellites in a ball-and-twine orbit and get started on mapping this planet to a fare-thee-well."

"Yes, sir," Dr. Beach replied.

"You're aware, sir, that we might have already *made* contact," Bill interjected. "Depending upon their tech level, they could have telescopes capable of detecting the ship in orbit."

"Oh," the CO said. "How very . . . glorious."

"There," Journeyman Agoul said, stepping back. "It's against Sumar. The shadow moving across the Belly."

"I see it," Master Jadum replied, his hands rubbing together rapidly. "Fascinating! Do my old eyes deceive me, or does it appear to be made of metal?"

"I believe the same, Master," Agoul said, wrinkling his nose. "It does appear to be made of metal. And I believe I can see some formations on it that are very strange. I hate to even suggest this, but I believe that it may be . . . made."

"I cannot believe that such a thing could be made without it being heretical," Jadum said, stepping back and working his hands again. He rubbed at his nose, rapidly, then shivered. "I must take this finding to the queen, but if it is a made thing, the priests will be most unhappy."

"My fears as well, Master," Agoul replied. "Do you wish me to take the word to the Court? Better my head than yours, Master."

"No," Jadum said, twitching his ears in negation. "I doubt that the queen would allow the priests to kill me simply for finding such a thing. You, on the other hand, they might and think nothing of it."

"There is another question, Master," Agoul said. "Could it be the Demons returning?"

"I'm sure many will think that," Jadum said. "We can only hope that it is not so. It has been centuries since the last Demon attack. Let us hope it is not they."

"Or that they bring them, Master."


"How we doing on comestibles, XO?" the CO asked.

"We're getting low on water and $O_2$ again," the XO said. "But if we can get down to the planet any time soon, that's not an issue. And we're getting hot. But same thing."

"Miss Moon?" the CO asked. "Have you completed the cultural survey?"

"I'm not sure that it'll be *done* any time soon," Miriam replied. "Probably not in my lifetime. But I've identified several civilizations. I can't get much of an idea of borders, if this society even has those, but there are basically five large civilizations on the planet. Two of them seem to be about the same technology level and might be in contact. But there are large gaps that look undeveloped between them. The other three are separated from those two, and each other, by big oceans. We've gotten some looks at their boats and the COB said he didn't think they could go across oceans. Based on Earth history, I'd say we should contact one of the two groups that is close to each other on the big main continent."

"After initial survey and limited communications group contact," the XO pointed out.

"Agreed," the CO said. "Commander Weaver, recommendations on initial survey?"

"There is a group of islands in the temperate zone of the planet," Bill replied. "One of them is quite extensive and has what appears to be a stable zone near both a river and an ocean. That is on the southeastern tip of the island. While a scan of the island did show some fires on the northern portions, the southeast appears clear of natives. There is one anomaly, though."

"What's that?" the XO asked.

"There is a high level of neutrino emission on the planet," Bill said. "And it's concentrated in the 'civilized' areas. But the emissions are all over the place. I'm not sure what's causing it, but it seems as if something down there is a neutrino emitter."

"Neutrinos are what drive the warp," the CO said, puzzled. "They're only generated by a nuclear reaction normally, right?"

"Yes, sir," Bill said. "Fission or fusion. We get them from generating mesons out of the boson particle in the cannon. But in nature they're fairly rare and only generated by stars or nuclear reactors. Slippery suckers, too. Until the Adar came along the only detectors we had were massive. But you don't even get this sort of emission with really massive radioactive ores. As I said, sir, I'm not sure what's causing the emissions."

"But there's no apparent hazard?" the CO asked.

"It *may* indicate a high local radioactive background, sir," Bill said, shrugging. "But my guess is that the only way we're going to find out what's causing it is to go down there and find the emitters."

"Very well," the CO said. "Let's get cracking."

"I'm going to let Chief Miller handle the brief on this one," the first sergeant said. The reduced company had gathered on level two, missile compartment, at word of a new habitable planet. "Mister Miller?"

"It's another moon," Miller said. "Pretty much Earth size, gravity a bit higher 'cause it's denser than Earth. Tectonically active, deep oceans. Cold but not frozen solid. Earth standard biology type, so there might even be stuff we can eat, sort of. And it's inhabited."

"What?" Guppy asked.

"At ease!" Staff Sergeant Driscoll snapped. "Warrant officer is speaking!"

Golupski had definitely drawn the short straw on the cruise. Not only had the rest of his team been wiped out but in the reorganization he'd gotten Driscoll, who after all had nothing better to do, as his team leader. The XO's RTO, Charles "Chuckie" Seeley had been brought in to round out what was now Second Bravo.

The CO had reorganized by combining the remains of First and Second into one platoon, designated Second. The company was based on teams and the only team that had been only *partially* wiped out was Guppy's when Summerlin and Chandler were eaten by the ship-eating crabpus. All the other teams had lost all three members or been unscathed. Gunny Frandsen had been moved to Ops sergeant, Lieutenant Berisford and Gunny Hocieniec had absorbed the survivors, Alpha Team from First, and the unit moved on.

But it meant, among other things, that Driscoll was now a team leader and Guppy had to put up with him.

"Sorry, Staff Sergeant," Guppy said balefully.

"We don't have much of a read on the inhabitants," Miller continued as if there had been no interruption. "We don't have that resolution. But they're down there. Most of the indicators say that they are very low-tech but there are a large number of strange particle emissions from the planet. They may simply *seem* low-tech. The command group is working on a plan for survey and contact. That's all I've got."

"Basically, sit tight, do your missions and wait for the word," Top said. "That's all. Get back to work. Staff Sergeant Driscoll, if I could have a moment of your time . . ."

"Jacks locked," the COB said.

"Initial scans show no major life-forms in the area," Tactical reported.

"Deploy the security team."

"So how come we *always* have to be first?" Hattelstad asked.

"Just lucky," Jaenisch replied as the elevator reached ground level. "Now shut up and watch your sector."

"Got nothing, so far," Bergstresser said as the trio moved forward from the elevator, weapons swinging from side to side. "Small life-forms. Lots of those. Nothing big."

"Hold it up for full spectrum scan," Jaenisch said.

"Security, hold in place," the radio crackled. "We're getting a weird reading from the woodline."

"It just popped up," the tactical officer said, pointing at the screen. "Neutrino emissions. A lot."

"Commander Weaver, your input at Tactical please," the CO said.

"I've got the same thing, sir," Bill replied in a puzzled tone. "And it's a moving emitter. If I didn't know better, I'd say somebody had an active boson. Or maybe a nuclear reactor. But all I'm getting is neutrinos. And I think it's multiple sources. This appears to be the source of those strange neutrino emissions we saw from orbit. Whatever it is. I'd advise holding the security team in place. Other than neutrinos, I'm not getting anything else. And neutrinos aren't hazardous."

"Very well," the CO said. "Security team. Hold your position."

"Oh . . . wow," the TACO said a moment later, looking at the picture on the main viewscreen.

"Now that is . . . odd," the CO admitted.

"Go figure," Bill replied.


"Holy Hanna," Jaenisch muttered.

"What?" Bergstresser asked without turning around. "I'm getting lots of neutrino emissions from your direction and now there's some baryons. What the *grapp* is it?"

"Go ahead and take a look," Jaenisch replied. "This you gotta see."

Flying above the grass was a group of, presumably, locals. They were rotund and either wearing fur coats or covered in fur in a wild variety of colors and patterns. As they approached, Jaenisch confirmed that they were, in fact, covered in fur. The base color was mostly a light brown with darker patches on the shoulders and face but that was only a median. Some of them were nearly white with random spots of black or brown, others were nearly black with patches of lighter patterns.

Physically they resembled bipedal rodents with long snouts and small ears. Their hands were undersized and tucked in close to their bodies but they had massive hindquarters, possibly designed for hopping.

He wasn't sure how they "walked" because each of the group was riding something that looked like a broad surfboard, colored brilliant gold, that was jetting along over the ground. They weren't at equal heights, either. Some were just over the grass while others were floating along ten meters over the seed-tops.

As the group approached the armor-clad Marines it spread out, the riders hefting spears and shaking them at the trio. The spears were simple in the extreme, nothing more than long sticks with sharpened points.

"Okay, this is *grapping* weird," Hattelstad muttered. "Giant crabs I can handle. Giant acid-spitting crabs even. But I'm not real sure about giant spear-wielding, surfer hamsters."

"Command, Security Team One," Jaenisch said. "Orders?"

"They're so *cute*," Miriam squealed as the elevator descended.

"They're six-foot tall, spear-wielding hamsters," Weaver reminded her. "And just because we have a brief truce doesn't mean they won't fill you full of spears. Please be careful."

"I will," Miriam said. "But they're so *cute*! And they don't really look like hamsters. More like chinchillas. Chinchillas have opposable thumbs."

"Fine, spear-wielding surfer chinchillas," Bill said. "Just be careful."

He and Miller followed the linguist towards where the trio of Marines were lined up facing the locals. The natives had mostly grounded their boards when it became apparent that the visitors weren't going anywhere. A few of them had flown around the ship, much to the consternation of the captain, but otherwise they seemed fine with just watching for the time being.

"Lots of body language," Miriam said as she approached the trio. "The way they're moving their ears and noses seems to almost be part of their language."

"Have you picked up anything from the squeaks?" Bill asked.

"Lots," Miriam said as she strode past the Marines. "*Eegle, eegle, meek!*" she squeaked over the external speakers.

The apparent leader of the group, mottled in patches of brown over a dark coat, stood up and squeaked back at her.

This went on for about three minutes, with Miriam occasionally waving her arms, then paused. Before Weaver could react, the front of the suit opened up and Miriam stepped out wearing only the skin-tight coverall that was necessary to pilot the suit.

"*Eegle, sreek!*" Miriam said, waving to the group of locals.

"Oh, *maulk*," Weaver said. "Command, we have contamination."

"I saw," the CO said. "We also have some large forms moving in from the northeast."

"We're on it," Jaenisch said. "Hattelstad, echelon right."

"Heat forms," Hattelstad said, vectoring his cannon in the direction of the threat.

"Miss Miriam," Jaenisch boomed over the external speakers.

"We have heat forms moving in from the northeast. Please reenter your armor."

"I'm on it," Miller said, his Wyvern bounding into a trot to the northeast. "Marines, ensure local security."

Miriam squeaked at the leader and pointed to the northeast. The leader didn't appear to understand at first then gestured for two of the group to head that way. They passed the bounding Wyvern, then turned back, squeaking and whistling at the group of locals. They, in turn, began scrambling on their boards and clawing for altitude.

"She's not listening," Berg said, striding forward. He lightly tapped Miriam on the shoulder and pointed for her to get behind him.

"I'm fine right here," Miriam said. "If they get close, I'll get in my armor."

"Ma'am," Berg said, trying not to pick the silly twit up and toss her back on the ship. "The armor doesn't always work. Would you at least stand *behind* me?"

"Okay," Miriam said with a pout. She squeaked at the leader and then pointed.

"*Grapp*," Miller said, sliding to a stop at the sight of the pack of obvious predators. The things looked like some sort of dragon or giant lizard, their backs and shoulders armored in broad plates with narrow spines sticking up along their back. They were about the size of a male lion, with triangular shaped heads that appeared to be almost entirely bone and teeth. And there were eight of them.

As soon as they saw the Wyvern, they charged.

Miller knew that backing away was not an option, so he took a knee and opened fire.

Fortunately, unlike that on the crabpus, the armoring of these predators was not resistant to 7.62 mm high-velocity bullets nor were the creatures stupid. The scything fire of the Gatling gun tore into the group, splashing three of them on the ground and scattering the rest into retreat.

The locals had initially approached the pack, keeping high with their spears angled down to throw. But at the chainsaw blast of fire from the Gatling gun they turned tail and ran as well, heading for the treeline.

"*Meek, eek!*" Miriam yelled. "*Eegle neek, neek! Sccccrrkk!*"

"Do you actually know what you're saying?" Weaver asked.

"Yes," Miriam snapped. "See?"

The group of locals had paused and were now returning, slowly. The leader gestured and squeaked and two of the group flew towards the Wyvern, then outwards. They evidently found the pack and traced it as it circled. The predators had only been driven off momentarily.

"Command, Ground," Weaver said. "Can we get some more security out here?"

"On the way," the CO said. "Another set of Marines. We're going to cycle them through as fast as we can."

"Roger," Weaver said. "Miss Moon, if you could tell the locals that more of us are coming out and that it's for protection not a threat to them, please?"

"I'll try," Miriam said, breaking into more squeaks.

The group of locals came to a hover over the human detachment as Miller rejoined the group.

"Those two out there mean what I think it means?" Miller asked, following the two locals as they came around to the north and started, slowly, closing on the humans.

"I'm presuming they're tracking the predators," Weaver said. "How tough are they?"

"Pretty easy, really," Miller said. "Scary looking as hell, but a 7.62 mm takes them down just fine. Jaenisch, you get that?"

"You got automatically switched to local," Sergeant Jaenisch said. "We got it. I guess Two-Gun can't show off."

Berg ground his teeth but remained silent.

The leader of the locals suddenly swooped down, causing Bergstresser to raise his Gatling gun. It annoyed him that his first action had actually been to drop his hand towards his side.

"Wait," Miriam said as the local settled close to her and squeaked, holding out his hand.

"He's figured out that I'm the only one that's vulnerable," Miriam said. "He wants me to get on his board."

"Don't," the CO said over the circuit. "Do *not* go with them. They appear marginally friendly, but if you get scooped up, we're going to have a hard time tracking you down. They can move faster than we can."

She squeaked and pointed, then pointed back at her armor.

The local squeaked at her, then jumped off the board, offering it to her.

"Holy *maulk*," Bill said. "Security, priority is to ensure the survival of the local. Is that clear?"

"Clear, sir," Jaenisch said. "Bergstresser, Hattelstad, close on the local and ensure his protection."

"I don't know how to ride one of those things," Miriam said nervously.

"Figure it out, fast," Bill replied. "They apparently don't want you back in armor. We'll go with that for now if you can get up to altitude."

"Okay," Miriam replied, stepping on the board. "Whoa!" she shouted as the board rapidly ascended then banked. "Hey, this is *fun*!"

The two Marines had stepped over to the local and then forward, between him—and the local was definitely a "he"—and the threat.

"*Grapp* this," Miller muttered. "Command, permission to exit armor."

"Warrant officer, if you exit armor you will be required to maintain one month quarantine," the CO pointed out. "That means you'll still be in quarantine after we get back."

"Understood, sir," the SEAL replied. "I think it would be useful for purposes of local contact."

"Agreed," the CO said. "Permission granted."

"Oorah," Miller said, hitting the release on his armor and stepping out. The fresh air felt wonderful after over a month on the boat. It seemed like the clearest air he'd ever breathed. However, he didn't have much time for sight-seeing. He quickly opened up the bail-out pack on the armor and donned his body armor, grabbed a pair of combat glasses and pulled out an M-10.

"*Eegle meek*," he tried to squeak as he walked over to take a position by the local leader and slid on the glasses. "Whatever the *grapp* that means."

"*Eeg, eeg, neek*," the local responded, looking the SEAL up and down. "*Neek ga-srreeee*."

"Yeah," Miller said, rubbing his head. "*Ga-sree.* I hope I didn't just insult his mother."

"There they are," Jaenisch said.

»       »       »

The heat forms were evident in the combat glasses, even through the screening vegetation. Miller lifted the M-10 to his shoulder and got a good solid position.

"You better get ready to *ga-sree*," he said to the local.

"*Neek, sreeeeee*," the local responded, dropping his spear to hip level and crouching. "*Meee, snaaa*." The local lifted his nose and sniffed aggressively.

"Not sure if I smell 'em or not," Miller said, sniffing. There were just too many unfamiliar smells. Strangely, he wasn't sure he was getting *any* scent from the local, even though they were in touching distance. Maybe a sort of mustiness, but that was about it.

The pack had paused at what Miller figured was its charging distance. It probably thought it was out of sight.

"Should we open fire, sir?" Sergeant Jaenisch asked.

The question was over radio but it was transmitted to the SEAL's earplugs.

"Negative," Miller said. "Wait until they are in view. Pick your targets. I get full left. You take left center, Two-Gun right center, Hatt full right."

The pack broke cover just as he finished and he targeted his chosen beasts, firing three-round bursts into the chest region. The M-10 didn't have the authority of one of the Gatlings, but the 7.62 mm rounds punched the first lizard center of the target zone, and it stumbled to its knees, then rolled over, kicking in death throes.

The rest of the pack had been stopped just as cold, Jaenisch getting two in one sweep of fire and Berg, Weaver and Hattelstad each getting one.

"*Yeeee!*" the local shrieked, holding his hands to his ears and squeaking in what certainly sounded like curses.

"Sorry about that," Miller said, reloading quickly. "Yeah, they're kinda loud."

# 25

## The Frumious Neenion

"The biggest problem with this world is that I can see the possibility of cross-contamination," Julia said, shaking her head. "This biology and human is so close it's *scary*."

"How's the sampling going?" Weaver asked as the biologist squatted down and scooped up a sample of dung.

"We're buried in data, as Dr. Dean would have said," Julia responded, sealing away the sample. "If this world was terraformed, it was a *long* time ago. Lots of speciation, multiple families, deep soil, complex ecosystem. Well, just the difference between those predators and the locals shows that. This isn't a simple world by any stretch of the imagination. Most of it's going to have to be sorted out back on Earth. I'm just sampling and checking for potential cross-infections. I've been pumping air and water from the surroundings to the rats and mice, but it's really pointless. Our two biggest guinea pigs are over there," she said, gesturing with her sensor pod.

Miriam and Miller, backed by the three suited Marines, were cross-legged in the center of a group of the locals. The locals had started a fire, butchered most of the predators and were now having a barbeque while talking with the SEAL and the linguist. Mostly with the linguist, who seemed to be absorbing the language like a sponge.

"How's it going?" Weaver asked, striding over to the group.

"Well," Miller said, shrugging. "She's apparently established the name of the local tribe, that the name for 'other' is enemy, but they're willing to accept that we're not here to take their land and that the name of the predators is Sreee. That's all I've got. Cop a squat if you're any good at languages."

"They don't seem too freaked out by our armor," Bill said. "Or the ship."

"She's working on that," Miller replied. "They've apparently got a legend about flying ships. They also have a legend that flying ships are good but when they arrive, the 'Demons' return. We're not sure what the Demons are or why they're associated with the flying ships. But the association seems to be that the Demons don't come *from* the flying ships, they're just a result of them. Basically, they're saying we're welcome for a bit but then we need to leave."

"Interesting," Bill said. "There's a crate of trade goods coming down from the ship in payment for our stay. Tell Miss Moon to pass on that we're going to be here just long enough to look around, then we're leaving."

"She already did," Miller said. "Anything else, Obi Wan?"

"No," Bill said, chuckling. "There's enough security down that I'm headed back to the ship. I guess we won't be sharing any syrup any time soon."

"Yeah, get that cycled through to me, will you?" Miller replied. "But, what the hell, when I'm stuck in quarantine at least I've got cute company."

"Is it just me or does this place *really* make you want to pop your armor?" Guppy asked.

"There with you, pard," Chuckie said. "This is sweet. I mean, the grass looks like *grass* if you know what I mean."

"Just because it looks like grass, it doesn't mean it won't kill you," Staff Sergeant Driscoll said. "Keep the chatter down and keep an eye on your sectors."

"Staff Sergeant, with all due respect," Chuckie said formally, "we are watching our sectors. There is not apparent reason to maintain radio silence and there is no other way to pass the time than talking."

"And I gave you an order, PFC," the staff sergeant said. "Are you questioning my orders under combat conditions?"

"No, Staff Sergeant," the former RTO said.

"Then shut up."

"Hey, Dris," Sergeant Jaenisch said, walking over. "See anything?"

"You will refer to me as Staff Sergeant Driscoll, Sergeant Jaenisch," Driscoll said. "And if we had observed any movement we would have reported it."

"Okay, Staff Sergeant Driscoll," Jaen replied. "Excuse me for asking. I was just wondering, though, if you'd detected any neenion emissions."

"Neenions?" Driscoll said.

"A tertiary quark junction," Jaen said, sighing. "You have read the manual on neenions, right? Because they can cause failure of your quantum subprocessors. We were getting some neenion twitches from your direction. All your suits are a hundred percent, right?"

"I haven't gotten any red lights," Staff Sergeant Driscoll said.

"Okay, but keep an eye out for neenions," Jaenisch said seriously. "You might want Lurch to check your systems when we get back."

"Thanks for the heads up, Sergeant," Driscoll said.

"No prob."

Chuckie cut his transmitter and walked over to Guppy, leaning his armor into the lance corporal's. By making contact between two sets of armor it was possible, barely, to communicate.

"What the *grapp* is a neenion?" Chuckie yelled.

"There isn't any such thing as a neenion!" Guppy yelled back.

"Thought so!"

"PFC Seeley, get back into position!"

"Sorry, Staff Sergeant," Seeley replied, quickly turning his transmitter back on. "I was doing a neenion check on Lance Corporal Golupski's armor!"

"Oh."

"Well, while slightly out of sequence I would say that that was a successful mission," the CO said to the after-actions group.

The ship was back in orbit, having suffered no casualties and gathered reams of data. They'd also bought one of the flying boards, which was now carefully tucked away. Where the natives had gotten them was still a mystery, but the leader had been more than willing to give one up in return for a crate of steel hatchets and machetes. He'd tried to hold out for one of the M-10s until Miriam got across to him that the "magic" was strictly limited and he wouldn't be able to recreate it.

"We picked up a mass of data," Dr. Beach said. "I'm inclined to agree with Dr. Robertson that most of it is going to have to be analyzed on Earth. There is one anomaly about the locals though. Dr. Robertson?"

"We caught a number of small animals, including some which are essentially mammaloform, as are the locals," Julia said, frowning. "And I was able to gather a hair sample from the natives. The problem is, while the cellular biology of the two groups is *close*, it's different enough to make me wonder. Miss Moon, did you get any sense that the locals might not be native to this world?"

"No," Miriam replied over the video screen. "They have legends of flying ships, but no legends of having come from off-world. But I didn't get deeply into their legend structure and something like that . . . Well, there are *human* legends that have been taken to be evidence of extraterrestrial impact on *humanity*. But nobody really believes them."

"Ezekiel's Wheel," Dr. Robertson said, nodding. "The Nazca Lines, I understand. But . . . did they say anything about special food needs?"

"Sort of," Miriam replied. "They ate the *sreee*, but they also ate some sort of vegetable or fruit. I just assumed they liked a balanced diet or they picked it up on the way."

"More likely, it's a necessity in their diet," Julia said. "I am fairly certain, based on the biology, that the 'locals' are lost star-travelers that found a planet that was close enough to survivable for them to stay. Castaways or maybe a failed colony. There was one plant I found that was closer to their genetic structure than the dozens of others we've found. I haven't been able to gene-type everything, though. For all we know, some of the small mammals may be exotics that came with them. Anyway, that's the one anomaly and I'm not stating it as a given. It might just be extreme genetic drift. I will say that they are closer to this biology than humans are, and humans are close enough that I feel quarantine is fully justified. Sorry, Chief."

"No problem," Miller said, sipping a bulb of cola. "I knew it was going to be quarantine when I opened the suit. I just felt . . ."

"It was a great help," Miriam said. "I appreciate it. They were more accepting with a warrior present. They knew I wasn't one," she added with a laugh.

"Miss Moon, can you describe the control method of the flying board?" Dr. Beach asked.

"Not really," Miriam said. "Except it's like telepathy. I just got on and thought 'up' and it went up. From there on I just sort of . . . flew it and it went where I wanted to go. Ever used a Segway?"

"Yes," Everette said, chuckling. "I even took a nose dive on one."

"Well, the board was like that but more so," Miriam said. "You just lean and it banks. Think where you want to go and it goes. It might be very subtle reading of body clues but . . . We are not *locals*. So it is able to read both our body clues and those of the locals."

"How do they produce them?" the CO asked.

"They don't," Miriam said. "New ones turn up from time to time. They just find them while hunting. But rarely. Most of them are handed down over generations. They don't know where they come from."

"So the next step, if I've read the manual right, is to make contact with a civilization," the CO said. "Get to work looking over the possible candidates. I'll give the science team two days to assimilate their data, then we'll meet again. Among other things, that will give maintenance time to do some work on systems."

"There may be some neenion contamination," Staff Sergeant Driscoll said as Lurch opened up the armor.

"Damn straight there is, Staff Sergeant," the armorer said, sighing and waving a blinking box over the interior circuits. "I'm going to be deconning this thing all day. Look, I've got to pull the motivator circuits; could you get somebody to run down to engineering and ask them for a can of ID Ten T decontaminant?"

"Hell," Driscoll said. Top had pulled his whole team off on another detail as soon as they got back to the ship. The Wyvern bay was deserted except for himself and the crip. "I'll go get it. I Dee Ten T, right?"

"Thanks, Staff Sergeant Driscoll," Lyle said, grimacing in pain as he crawled into the suit. "My back is really acting up."

Driscoll, cursing under his breath, went to the far end of the compartment and opened up the hatch to the mid level. Dogging the heavy hatch behind him, he climbed down the ladder to the bottom, opened the next hatch, dogged it behind him, climbed down and then headed over to the hatch to engineering maintenance. Which was locked on the other side.

"Hey," he said, hitting the intercom. "I need some cleaner."

"Who's there?" one of the crew asked.

"Staff Sergeant Driscoll, Second Platoon," Driscoll said. "I need some ID Ten T decontaminant."

"*Maulk*, we don't keep that *here*." The hatch was opened to reveal a short, hairy mechanic. "The locker for that's up by the torpedo room. Ask Red. But you're going to need radiation gear."

"What?" the staff sergeant asked, his eyes blinking.

"Stuff's radioactive as hell," the machinist's mate said, sucking his teeth. "You're going to have to suit up."

"We're going to put radioactive stuff in my suit?" Driscoll asked, confused.

"Hey, welcome to the Space Marines," the machinist mate said, leading him into the compartment. "The radiation and the neenions counteract each other. Your suit will be clean when they're done. Heck, if we could figure out a way to generate neenions, we'd have a way to decontaminate anything. Unfortunately, they're only found around buttumium and there's no way to, like, bottle 'em."

The machinist mate had gotten out a heavy rubber suit complete with respirator.

"You're probably gonna want to strip to put this on," he said. "It's a hot mother*grapper*."

"How do I get to the torpedo room?" Driscoll asked when he had the, yes, hot suit on.

"First, you're gonna need the tongs," he said, handing over a set of heavy metal tongs. "They're to carry the ID Ten T container. Now, to get to the torpedo room, you're going to have to pass through the conn. First, go up to the third level in Sherwood Forest . . ."

The giant gas giant above, the blue and white planet they circled, reflected light from the gas giant lighting up the clouds below . . .

Weaver never tired of the sight. So even though it was late in his shift and he should be doing paperwork, he was sitting in the CO's chair staring at the forward viewscreen when there was a buzz at the hatch to the bridge.

He looked over his shoulder and his eyes widened as the COB passed a man wearing a full rubber decontamination suit into the conn. The man walked through to the far hatch, passing tactical and pilot as he went, then exited.

"COB," Weaver said. "I have to admit I'm new to this game . . ."

"He's going up to the torpedo room for some ID Ten T decontaminant, sir," the COB said solemnly.

"ID Ten T?" Weaver said, nodding. "What's it used for?"

"Neenion particle contamination, sir," the COB said. "It's radioactive, thus the suit. And the tongs, sir. Don't forget the tongs."

"Uh, huh," Weaver said. "Think the CO is awake, yet?"

"Should be, sir," the COB said. "And had his first cup of coffee."

"And I'm guessing he'd like to see this, wouldn't he?"

"That would be my guess as well, sir," the COB said solemnly.

"ID Ten T, huh? Neenions. Why not weenions?"

"A bit obvious, sir," the COB said reproachfully.

"You must be Red," Driscoll said angrily, when he *finally* reached the designated area.

"They said you wanted . . ." Red paused and gulped. "The ID Ten T decontaminant."

"If you don't mind," Driscoll said, trying to rein in his anger. He was angry and it had been a long walk, and climb, to here.

"Okay," Red said, pointing to the locker and backing away. "It's in there."

"Great," Driscoll said, pulling open the locker. The only thing in it was a glass flask filled with a red glowing liquid. "How in the hell am I supposed to carry this on a ladder?"

"Carefully," Red said, stepping through a hatch. "Drop that and break it and it'll flood the whole *ship* with radiation."

"*Grapp*," Driscoll said, carefully lifting the container out with the tongs. "Why in the *hell* is it in *glass* then?"

"Oh, and it will probably eat a hole in the ship," Red said

from around the corner. "It's one of the strongest acids known to man."

"*Grapp* me," Driscoll whined, carefully backing around and heading back to the missile room. "Can you help me with the hatch?"

"Not on your life. Specially not on mine."

"Neenion contamination, huh?" the CO said, leaning *way* over in his chair as the staff sergeant passed.

"Yes, sir," Driscoll said nervously.

"Drop that in my ship and you're going to be breaking rocks for the rest of your life."

Driscoll finally made it back to the missile room and cautiously set the container down on the deck.

"Great," Lyle said, picking it up and sloshing some onto his hand. "This is just the thing."

"Wait!" Driscoll said. "That's radioactive!"

"Yeah, but the neenions counteract it!" Lyle said, cheerfully rubbing some onto the surface of the motivator module. "See?" he continued, taking a taste of his finger.

"Tastes like . . . sugar water," the armorer added, grinning. "Try writing it out with the *number*, Staff Sergeant Driscoll. I-D-1-0-T."

"Oh, you son of a—" Driscoll said, ripping off the respirator. "I'm going to . . ."

"You're going to what, Staff Sergeant?" the first sergeant said, coming around the side of the missile tube and leaning up against it.

"Top, I cannot believe that you have—" Driscoll said, furiously. "This is an insult to my dignity as an NCO!"

"Walk with me, Driscoll," the first sergeant said, waving towards the far end of the compartment. "Walk with me, as the Disciples once walked with the Lord God. And perhaps open up your ears . . ."

# 26

## Define "Demon"

"I don't see how we can do a humble approach," Dr. Beach said.

"The manual calls for making contact away from major civilization," the XO pointed out. "Appendix Sixty-Seven."

"We *could* set down well off position and march overland to make contact," Dr. Beach said. "But that would have us contacting peripheral leadership. If we're going to make serious contact with these civilizations, determine their real technological and social advancement, we'll need to contact primary leadership. I'd say that a reasonably close approach to one of the major cities, while it has issues, is a better choice."

"Like riots," Captain MacDonald said. "Crowds. Attack by local military forces or mobs."

"Our orders are clear," the CO said. "We're to make contact with civilization on the planet. Somebody that can speak for a sizeable body if there's no world government. We're not to become involved in wars but we are to assess the political and military structure of the governments. So landing on the peripherals is out, whatever the book says."

"There's a bunch of cities," the tactical officer said.

"First Sergeant Powell," the CO said. "I would like your input."

"I can only extrapolate from human civilizations, sir," Top said.

"But, historically, contact like this would, in general, be better suited for a growing society. Indicators of physical growth in cities would be what I would look for. Such societies are already adjusting to societal change associated with that population growth. While they are going to be more volatile, in general they are more able to accept change. There are exceptions, of course. London didn't really start to regrow after the Black Death for some time and yet underwent a Renaissance. But, in general, it's the way to steer."

"And while that will potentially increase the security threat," Captain MacDonald said, "it's unlikely that there will be anything we can't handle. As long as Miss Moon agrees to remain in her armor."

"Then I have a suggestion," Miriam said. She and the chief were back on videophone. "The first city we've spotted. I was looking for some of the same indicators and it gives evidence of recent growth."

"Okay," the CO said. "I'd say that's our target. Captain MacDonald is in charge of determining the landing zone. Think ability to contact and security."

"What do you got, Top?" MacDonald said, looking up from the computer screen.

"Interesting suggestion, sir," the first sergeant said, laying a sheet of paper on the desk. "This spot is located about six klicks from the outer edge of the real metropolitan area. It's a large manor that seems to be part castle. Broad lawns, so they apparently like the same sort of stuff we do, which is interesting. Most important . . ."

"Those look like defenses," the CO said, pointing to spots. "Is that a trenchline?"

"That, sir, is a ha-ha," Top corrected. "A deep ditch designed to keep the riff-raff out. This, in fact, looks very much like their version of Buckingham Palace, just when the duke of Buckingham still owned it. Some interesting indicators to be drawn from it. The fact that all serious defenses have been eradicated indicates that the area is free from external threats. Lots of ship traffic. I think Miss Moon hit the jackpot."

"I was looking at this thing," the CO said, pulling out a similar printout. It showed an open plain and a very large hill apparently composed entirely of granite.

"I saw that as well, sir," the first sergeant said uncomfortably.

"And you have objections," the CO said. "It's certainly defensible. And if we need to make a quick getaway . . ."

"As you say, sir," the first sergeant replied.

"Say it, Top."

"First, sir, there's the fact that there is no development," the first sergeant said. "There's no indication that even when this area was castellated, and there's significant indicators of previous castellation, that any occurred on that hill. So they deliberately chose not to build defenses on it. That could indicate anything from instability to taboo to religious reasons. Second, sir, it's a long damned walk. Communication with the ship will be difficult if we end up entering the city. And in the worst possible scenario, fighting our way back to the ship will be difficult or impossible. Those are my objections, sir."

"And they're good objections," Captain MacDonald said, frowning. "I'd thought of the second one but not the first. Very well, First Sergeant, Buckingham Palace it is . . ."


"To arms! To arms!"

"What *is* my son shouting about, Sreen?" Lady Che-chee asked as her footman entered the room. The normally phlegmatic servant was showing clear signs of agitation in his demeanor, his ears twitching most distressingly.

"Mistress," Sreen said, his nose flickering open and closed. "There is a . . . thing on the lawn. It appears to be a greater metal Demon."

"The Demons are here?" Lady Che-chee said, rising to her full height of nearly two meters. "Bring my sword and have the pups evacuated immediately."

"Yes, mistress," Sreen said, backing out of the room.


"Nice reception," Jaen said as he stepped out of the elevator.

The locals had lined up confronting the sub, which had landed on the broad lawn of the manor. The building had fewer windows than a similar structure on Earth, but otherwise was remarkably similar. There were two long wings centered on a main "hall" that had clear signs of having once been a small fort or castle.

Drawn up by the heavy front door were, apparently, the defenders. Two were in plate armor and holding swords. They also were standing on a pair of the golden surfboards. It descended from there to a local that had to be a young teen holding a butcher knife. Most of the locals were holding short spears. No firearms, no bows and sure as hell nothing that could penetrate Wyvern armor.

The threesome deployed then, as instructed; Jaen marched forward, halfway to the "reception committee," laid a heavy casket on the ground, then backed up.

"Be interesting to see what they think of the bait," Berg said just as one of the armored guys lifted off on his surfboard. The action apparently was not agreed upon by the other, larger, armored figure who raised an arm and squeaked at the other.

Despite the apparent imprecations, the figure swept down and took a spear from one of the retainers, then swept around to face Jaen.

"Oh, *maulk*," the team leader muttered.

"Do *not* fire," the CO said. "Just take it."

The local hefted his short lance and then barreled forward, gaining speed rapidly until he could plunge the weapon, hard, into the team leader's chest.

Jaen, who had planted one foot behind him, didn't even rock from the blow. The spear shattered.

The local, clearly infuriated, came around for another run holding his sword.

"If that's a monomolecular edge it's gonna sting," Berg noted.

It wasn't. The local nearly lost his grip on the sword, which was clearly ringing like a bell in his hand, but he stayed in the fight, whaling away on Jaen's armor as the team leader took the blows stolidly.

"Sir?" he said. "Any suggestions?"

"Cha-chai! Get back here this instant!" Lady Che-chee shouted. Her son had recently joined the cavalry regiment and thought himself quite the warrior. Given that Lady Che-chee had started life as an almost penniless ensign and risen to the peerage, she knew what "warrior" meant.

And the visitors were clearly uninterested in attacking. They had no obvious weapons, but those suits of armor alone made them a weapon. She could see no air gaps, no way for them to breathe. Just masses of metal, perhaps even metal *things* like the *chak-chak.* The legends spoke of such, but she had never expected to see the day. Of course, the legends also said that where the metal things went, there went the Demons.

Cha-chai had ignored her, as was too frequently the case lately, and now snatched a spear from the gamesman and charged the leader of the trio. Aware that it could mean war at any moment, Lady Che-chee took a stance and prepared to draw. But the spear shattered upon the armor and the armored figure didn't even rock.

And now the young idiot was attacking with his *sword*!

"That was your grandmother's!" Lady Che-chee shouted. "If you break it I will so shave your coat you young snot!"

"Sir," the first sergeant said.

"Go," Captain MacDonald said. "Diplomatically, please."

"For values of diplomacy," the first sergeant replied. "Miss Moon, I need your input. I'm reading the body language of the other armored figure as annoyance at the smaller one's antics."

"I agree, First Sergeant Powell," Miriam said, grinning over the video link. "The younger one is acting a bit like, well, a headstrong young nobleman. And the larger would be either his father or a senior retainer."

"Yes, ma'am," the first sergeant said. "That was my read as well. So. Two-Gun, can you get the sword away from that local? Without harming him?"

Lady Che-chee didn't want to make the situation any worse by approaching. No matter how diplomatic you were about it, being approached by an armored Mother was intimidating. But she realized she was simply going to have to go over and stop the young idiot before he got someone killed.

Just as she was about to step off, one of the armored figures solved the situation for her. It reached over and first took Cha-chai's wrist in its claw, firmly but not violently. It was apparent, however, from her son's struggles that it was an immovable hold. Then the armored figure took away her son's sword. He handed it to the leader, gently and carefully, then fumbled for a moment and removed her son's helmet.

Afraid that he was going to kill her headstrong son, Lady Che-chee drew her sword and lifted into the air. But before she could even approach, the figure simply held the helmet in one hand and closed the hand, turning the helm of finest Mee-reean steel into a lump.

Then he handed the lump back, respectfully. The sword followed.

"Mother," Cha-chai yelled, hovering his *chak-chak*. "I believe they wish to speak to *you*."

Berg watched as one of the servants stepped over to the case and, after fumbling with the closure, looked inside. His chittering was unintelligible but he was definitely excited and Berg noticed him slip one of the gems into the belt that was his only clothing.

The gems were "real." They were manufactured gemstones, virtually worthless on Earth but indistinguishable from the real thing. There were also some small bars of gold. Gems and gold might or might not have local value. They'd have to see.

The helmetless local swooped down and reached into the case, removing one of the sapphires. He looked over at Jaen and chittered something, tossing the gem in the air.

"Mother," Cha-chai called. "I do believe my promotion is paid for. As are my gambling debts."

"What?" Lady Che-chee said. "*All* of them? Bring it over here."

Cha-chai and the gamesman brought the chest over and she looked in it and nodded.

"Tribute," she said. "But for what? Ruining my lawn? Or the endless trouble their presence is going to cause? Surely not to prevent us attacking them. Nothing we own could damage that ship; even rocks from a trebuchet would do nought much more than dent it."

Two more of the suits of armor were descending in the glass room. How any glass, though, could support the weight of those suits was beyond her. However, they stepped out and walked over, passing the threesome who then redeployed to either side and slightly back. Bodyguards, then. She supposed it was wise to send guards first in a situation where you knew nothing of the locals. She could overlook the insult and it was not as if they were even beginning to treat with each other. Sumar knows she had done enough reconnaissance of enemy positions in her time.

The two new suits, which were colored a sky blue with a black dome on top, stopped a few paces from her. Then she got the shock of her life as the suits opened up along an nearly invisible seam and two of the occupants stepped out, causing a great shout amongst her retainers.

She, everyone, had been expecting Cheerick. But they were not! Except upon the head of one they were furless. Shiny black bodies, like *sgraga* that caught in the fur! No, those were *clothes*. Close fitting and showing odd lumps like large pustules on the chest of the smaller one! Their legs moved oddly. Their faces were so *flat*! They were *revolting*!

But she quelled her urge to vomit at the sight as the larger, nearly furless, one turned to the rear of the armor and began removing gear. She had thought it might be more presents, but it was not. A cuirass of some strange gray metal, a helmet of same, a harness. She caught a glimpse of ropy scars as the clothing moved aside. A warrior. So who was the smaller?

When the warrior was properly armed, the smaller came forward and made a strange arm movement. It was similar to one the island tribes used, a sign of parley.

"Lady Che-chee," the smaller one said, her small nose twitching. "Know language not. Learn must."

"You are the interpreter," Lady Che-chee said, her ears twitching in agreement. "I would speak with your mistress."

"Would speak . . ." The interpreter paused. "Understanding not." The rest was an unintelligible squeak that had, yes, the lilt of the islands.

"I would speak to your leader," Lady Che-chee said. "I would speak to your lord. I would speak to your master. I would speak to your mistress."

"Lady Che-chee speak master," the interpreter said, pointing to her head. "Master speak, I speak."

"She has a demon in her!" Cha-chai shouted.

"Silence!" Lady Che-chee shouted. "You will not shame me by this display. All but my armsmen, return to your duties!

"Now, interpreter, what is your name?" Lady Che-chee asked.

"Miriam, Lady Che-chee."

"Mrn-mreem," Lady Che-chee said. "Your master here."

"Master there," Miriam said, pointing at the ship. "Speak me, speak him."

"Why will he not come out and treat with us properly?" Cha-chai said angrily.

"Not know say," Miriam said. "Master ship. Not come out."

"I will not treat with an inferior," Lady Che-chee said bluntly. "Get your ship off my lawn."

"Wait," Miriam said, holding her hand to her head. "Wait."

"She refuses to talk to me," Miriam said. "Very proper, seems to know what she's doing, she's negotiated before. But she's unwilling to talk to an inferior. Probably *because* she's negotiated before."

"Try to get more language," the CO said, looking around at the command staff. "Try to explain that I cannot exit the ship. I don't even have a Wyvern, which is something that needs to be changed. Tell her that I will send a senior deputy."

"I guess I'd better go get my Wyvern on," Weaver said, standing up.

"Captain MacDonald, you go, too," Spectre said. "Take Top as well."

"Yes, sir."

"Lady Che-chee," Miriam said. "Talk others? Language learn? Explain?"

"I will permit that," she said, looking at her son. "Cha-chai . . . No. Sreen!"

"Madame?" the footman said imperturbably. As long as it wasn't Demons, he was fine.

"Talk with this one," she said imperiously. "And bring me a drink and a chair. I'm getting too old to stand around in armor all day. A *solid* chair."

"So far, so good," Jaen said. "Okay, let's get 360 security here."

"Got it," Berg said, turning in position. "The only major emissions are from those flying board things and the ship. Nice place. I'd love to swim in that lake."

"Probably got crabpus in it," Hatt said. "How's the pow-wow going?"

"Looks okay," Jaen said. "I can almost follow the pantomime. That Miss Moon's some actress."

"She's some lady," Hatt said. "Nice voice, too."

"I sure as hell can't make some of those sounds," Jaen said. "Squeak, eak! Rats. Why'd it have to be rats?"

"Chinchillas," Berg corrected. "Miss Moon said they're more like chinchillas. Think of them that way. Or giant hamsters."

"Whatever."

"Commander Weaver," the CO said over the radio link. "You are *not* permitted out of armor."

"Understood, sir," Weaver said as the elevator opened. "Wasn't planning on it."

"Hey, Miller," he added as he approached the pow-wow. "How's it going?"

"Pretty good, I think," Miller said, standing stolidly. If he was noticing the chill he didn't show it, but they'd brought coats for both him and Miriam. Miriam was definitely noticing it in the thin body suit. She was shivering and it was beginning to affect her speech.

Weaver handed over the coats, then stood by Miriam.

"Okay, I'll see if this will work," Miriam said, her teeth chattering. "Thank you."

"You're welcome," Weaver said over the external speaker.

Miriam shrugged on the long, down coat, then turned up the heater.

"Sreee," Miriam said in Cheerick. "Commander William Weaver. Commander Beeel, shiny. Third officer of ship. Only officer has armor." Miriam tapped that.

"And must have armor to exit ship," Sreee said. "You don't have armor. Why?"

"Dangers," Miriam said. "Law. Must have special cleaning if no armor. Commander Beeel no leave armor. Speak for commander. Friend to our queen. High lord."

"This one no armor," Sreee said, pointing at Miller.

"Crazy-brave warrior," Miriam said. "Does cleaning, too. Cleaning very long. Many days."

"I will speak to my mistress."

"They have a law that they cannot leave the ship without armor, mistress," Sreee said. "Only the interpreter and her guard as I understand it may be without armor. And they must undergo special cleaning. One of the new people is their third officer, the highest officer who has armor. He sounds as if he is an officer from their court, a friend of their queen."

"Their lord has no armor?" Cha-chai interjected. "Can he not afford it?"

"He has paid for his commission to this ship," Lady Che-chee said. "I guess he sold it."

"They somehow speak to their commander," Sreee said. "I do not understand how. When I ask she points at her ear or her head, as if she hears voices. It may be they speak mind to mind."

"No," Lady Che-chee said, standing up. "The new one, he spoke aloud through the armor. It is their magic. Very well, I will speak to him and through him to their commander. Ask them, first, if their magic permits their commander's voice to at least be heard."

"Yeah, we can do that," Weaver said, looking at his controls. "No, I can't. This suit isn't equipped for retrans! Jaen."

"Sir?"

"I need one of your team over here, stat," Weaver said. "Smart one."

"Two-Gun," Jaen said. "You're up."

Berg walked over quickly and took up a position by Miss Moon.

"Set your system to retrans to the ship," Commander Weaver said. "Channel Four. The CO's going to use it to speak."

"Yes, sir," Berg said, dropping his glove and hitting the controls rapidly. "Set, sir."

"Good man. . . ."

"Hello, Chic-chic-tic Che-chee," the CO enunciated carefully. "I am Captain Steven Blankemeier of the Alliance Space Ship *Vorpal Blade* and I greet you in peace in the name of the Human-Adar Alliance."

"Whooo," he added, leaning back from the command table. "One small step and all that . . ."

"Yes, sir," the XO said. "But I think you got your lines right."

"Those are the words of my commander," Miriam said, pointing at the suit. "He speaks through this."

"Not the one in the suit?" Lady Che-chee asked suspiciously.

"No, lady," Miriam replied. "Would one of your servitors pretend to be you?"

"No," Lady Che-chee said. "Very well. Captain Beeela . . . Captain. What are your intentions, here?"

"To make peaceful contact with your people," Miriam said, translating the captain's words. "We are explorers. We are not conquerors and wish nothing but peaceful relations. We have enemies, in other places, and we seek their location. But we will not bring our war to you. Nor do we ask for soldiers or support."

"That's good," Lady Che-chee said, flicking her ears. "We have wars enough aplenty. I am not a high leader of my people. I must bring word to my queen that emissaries have arrived. I must warn you, this will cause turmoil. There is much of which we must speak but I will do so through your interpreter and your officer. Thank you for your courtesy in speaking to me directly."

"I wish I could meet with you in person," Miriam translated. "But I am not allowed by our laws."

"So I understand," Lady Che-chee said. "Sreee, conduct Miriam and Commander Beeel to . . ." She looked at the armor and blanched at the damage it would do to the floors. Not to mention that it couldn't get through any door but the main one. On the other hand, their visit gifts would more than pay for the damage.

"Conduct them to the Great Hall. Bring food and drink. And get Trik-trik ready to get me out of this *damned* armor."

"They have eaten and drunk nothing, mistress," Sreee said as Lady Che-chee entered the Great Hall.

The hall had once been the center of manor life and still had the antique sleeping niches that had been comfort in elder times. Now it was mainly used for large balls. She had managed to avoid hosting many of those but she was fairly sure that had just changed. However, depending on how this fell out, her status was either going to be raised enormously at Court or she was about to lose her head. She'd dealt with the promise of both problems before, however. And a chest of jewels and gold was certainly going to help.

"You do not care for our food?" she asked, approaching the table.

"I wish I could," Miriam said. "But we are not Cheerick. It

is poison to us. I can drink plain water. That, too, is possibly poison, but one that our chirurgeon can mend."

"Sreee," Che-chee said. "Bring some of the boiled campaign water."

"That would be perfect," Miriam said. "That I can drink. I mean no offense. You said something about the water. *Aseek*. You know of poisons in unboiled water?"

"Yes," Lady Che-chee said. "Unboiled water can cause terrible disease on campaign. Also it can make plagues worse. I only drink boiled water, wine, or water with brandy. All three prevent illness much of the time. This is ancient knowledge and much of that is wrong. But this I have tested in my time and find to be true."

"Ancient knowledge?" Miriam asked. "Knowledge handed down from old times? Is this things old Mothers speak of or written records?"

"Some of both," Lady Che-chee said. "And it is that of which we must speak. Your armor is invulnerable to our weapons, that is plain. But be aware that there may be great anger about you and your ship. We have legends and some fragments regarding great ships of metal and even metal things that walk and talk as Cheerick. But the Demons follow them."

"I hope that we do not bring them," Miriam said.

"Actually, you're late," Lady Che-chee said ambiguously.

"We first spoke to the island people," Miriam said.

"I thought as much," Lady Che-chee said. "Your arm motion, that is an island people gesture. Go on."

"They, too, spoke of the Demons," Miriam said. "What are the Demons?"

"This is not well known," Lady Che-chee said. "But if your armored people will allow you to accompany me deeper into the manor, I will show you something of them. Your 'crazy-brave' guard may accompany you."

"She wants to show me something deeper in the castle," Miriam said. "Something about these demons they keep talking about. They have the same legend. I don't think the armor will fit. She says that Chief Miller can come with me."

"Go," Bill said. "By the time anything gets by Miller we'll be there."

» » »

The room that they were led to was at the very back of the castle. The lintel of the door was very low, so low Miller had to near get on his knees, as did Lady Che-chee.

Miller paused as he started to go through and frowned.

"What the hell are those?" he asked, pointing to marks above the door.

"Demon claws," Lady Che-chee said, without asking for translation. "That is what I wished to show you."

"Damn," Miller said after the words were translated. The gouges in the limestone were nearly finger deep and nearly as wide. He could fit a finger most of the way down.

"Yes," Lady Che-chee said, apparently getting the context. "Inside I will show you more."

The room was small but well-lit by candles and lined with . . . bits. There was a tapestry, some metal workings, some pieces of armor. The latter, made of heavy bronze, were torn to shreds.

At the back of the room was another small door, very low, and made of stone and metal. Both had been heavily gouged.

"Observe the tapestry," Lady Che-chee said, gesturing.

The tapestry depicted a battle scene. A one-sided one. Cheer-ick dressed similar to Greek hoplites were being torn apart by a wave of—

"Are those Dreen?" Miriam asked nervously.

"No," Miller said, immediately. "At least none that I've seen. Similar, though."

There were several kinds of demons. In the forefront of the wave were low-slung beasts not too different from the predators they'd fought on the island. The big difference being that their skin seemed to have been hardened. Some were depicted as being killed by the spears and short swords of the Cheerick, some were slashed. But it was clearly hard to kill them.

Mingling with them and behind were bigger beasts, the size of rhinoceros, which were insectoid and beetlelike. Those were shown as being nearly invulnerable. One was spitted by a lance-wielding flier on some sort of seat. But nothing else seemed to stop them.

Behind *them*, surrounded in places by flying fighters, were bigger beasts that looked something like a low-slung dragon, complete with overlapping scales. Again, one had been injured by being poked in the mouth but otherwise was unstoppable.

In the distance, set in one corner of the tapestry, were vague figures that seemed to be flying towards the fight. Their form appeared to be unclear to the artist of the tapestry as well, simply being impressions of something that looked a bit like a long-winged airplane.

"This is a class," Miller said. "This is a class on what you can do, what little you can do from the looks of things, to stop the Demons."

"Yes," Lady Che-chee said when that was translated. "I took it the same way."

"Where did you get it?" Miriam asked.

"This home was owned, for many generations, by the same family," Lady Che-chee said. "I bought it when they had become destitute. Their ancestor was the Lady of this area the last time the Demons came. The legend is that the city had become corrupt and the Demons came to bring it back to the path of right. The writings that survive indicate that it had become, in fact, much as it is right now. That is, people were asking questions long prevented by the Church. And that, somehow, that drew the Demons."

"Oh," Miriam said, frowning.

"They are said to be drawn, as well, by made moving things, such as your armor," Lady Che-chee said. "And light that comes not from fire. But there's an interesting thing . . ."

"Yes?" Miriam asked.

"You see, there are already rumors that the Demons are returning," Lady Che-chee said. "Quite valid ones, I'm afraid. Last month, I was sent a message from Court. Two farms nearby the capital had been attacked. It was assumed, initially, that it had been by brigands. A cavalry patrol was dispatched to hunt them down. One fighter returned. Carrying this."

She opened up the small door and pulled out a large glass flask. In it was a taloned paw.

"So. The Demons seem to have returned."

## 27

## You Want Us to What?

"We didn't cause this, right?" the CO said.

"We were forty light-years away a month ago, sir," Commander Weaver pointed out.

"And we're sure this isn't just legends?" the CO asked.

"About as legendary as the Roman Republic," Miriam said. "Their written records go back several thousand years. And they have these periodic 'demon' attacks."

"Having seen the evidence up close, sir," Chief Warrant Officer Miller interjected, "it is my professional opinion that the demons are either real or very well hoaxed. I measured a couple of the gouges in the door and on the armor and they're pretty much identical. I don't know what their claws are made of, but they cut through heavy bronze like butter."

"Lady Che-chee is, besides being a soldier, apparently a bit of a scholar," Miriam said. "She's collected every fragment of information about the Demon Times she could afford. I guess it's a natural sort of thing for soldiers to be interested in. It seems like every time this society hits a Renaissance, they get destroyed. The Fall of Atlantis over and over again."

"That confirms an indicator we've seen, recently," First Sergeant Powell said. "Besides the obvious civilizations, there are several

311

that Miss Moon initially identified as 'barbaric.' The problem being that, based on the nature of some of those regions, ready access to the oceans, fertile farmland, there was no reason for it to be barbarian areas."

"Let me guess," the CO said.

"One whole continent is peppered with recent ruins, sir," the first sergeant said.

"And Atlantis falls," Chief Miller said. "That's just lousy."

"I find it interesting that there are legends of machinery but no machinery," Weaver interjected. "They even have drawings of what look like robots. Of course, they're on clay tablets. Could these Cheerick be transplants?"

"Possible," Dr. Robertson said. "Their biology *is* different."

"So how, or why, did these Demons destroy their biology?" the CO asked. "And are they a threat to us?"

"Unknown, sir," Chief Miller answered. "Based on the tapestry, none of the Demons could harm the ship. The beetles or the dragon might take out a Wyvern, though. No real clue how resistant to Gatling fire they are."

"The last thing I want to do is get into another furball," the CO said. "But we really haven't made full contact, yet. Captain MacDonald, security is going to get stretched. I want your Marines to be ready for deployment at all times. Figure out the details on that and get back to me. Obviously, any away team has to have security but don't strip the ship."

"Yes, sir," Mac said.

"XO, make sure our own security is up to snuff," the CO said. "Marines have point but they're to back them. Schedule combined ops drills."

"Sir."

"Let's establish communication with the local leaders, get a survey done and then get the hell out of here."

"With the coming of these intruders, the Day of the Demons assuredly draws near," High Priest Chik-chak hissed.

"They were here already," Queen Sicrac replied quietly, considering the missive from Lady Che-chee. The old fighter had a wonderful flare for prose. "Perhaps they are able to help us."

"Blasphemy," the high priest said, but mutedly. "There is no stopping the Demons; they are a scourge sent by the gods to punish the wicked. Unfortunately, it's become hard to decide what is wicked and what not. And in this case, the blasphemy comes *after* the Demons have returned."

The rumors had been unstoppable and before the humans ever landed, proclamations had been sent throughout Cheerick, shouted in the square and announced in the temples. The Demons had returned. Prepare as well as you can. Reserves of the Guard were called up and the preparations the priests had long sought, food and records sealed in deep caves, had begun. No one knew when the worst of the Demon wave would hit, but the queen intended that, this once, something would be left to rebuild civilization.

Now, out of all legend and historical sequence, these . . . Chrans had come with their made things. *After* the first of the Demons. It upset precedent. The queen, however, had jumped on it. The Chrans had come to aid them against the Demons.

Now, if she could just convince them of the same thing.

"Okay, call me Dr. Dean if you want, but that thing bugs the every living *maulk* out of me," Runner said, looking to the northwest.

"The hill?" Sergeant Kristopher said, planting the drill. "It's a basolith." This referred to an igneous upwelling that formed underground, then was exposed as lighter materials eroded away from it.

"Really?" Runner said sarcastically. He picked up a section of pipe and inserted it. This was the fourth core sample they'd taken and they were all coming up the same, soil followed by layers of limestone and sandstone. The region had, several million years before, been under water. There were fossils. The layers all looked right. *Normal* for this sort of region. This world hadn't been terraformed recently, that was for sure. "You're the expert? Son, there's *no* surface evidence of granite anywhere within six hundred clicks of that so-called basolith. And there's nothing for a hundred meters down. You *always* get some secondary outcroppings when you've got basolithic extrusion, but everything in the area is loam or limestone."

"So what do you think it is, Dr. Runner?"

"I dunno," Runner admitted. "And I'll even admit to missing Dr. Dean. *He* might have had a clue."

"We can ask for permission to check it out," Kristopher said. "Go over and get some samples."

"Maybe after the negotiations are complete," Runner said. "Long damned walk."

"Ask if we can borrow a cart."

"Jesus Christ!" Sergeant Jaenisch said as they reached the walls of the inner city.

Chief Miller and Miss Moon had been installed in an open carriage pulled by six-legged beasts while Commander Weaver and the first sergeant, still in their Wyverns, followed in a cart festooned with flowers and bunting. And the beasts were moving along at a nice trot, requiring the security team to trot along behind to keep up. But the run wasn't what caused Jaen's exclamation. That was the crowds.

They had already passed through the outer periphery of the city, slums really, and there had been locals there, their fur matted with filth but squeaking in apparent enthusiasm and making way for the team of cavalry that led and secured the procession. But it wasn't until they cleared the ruinous walls of the city that they hit the *real* crowds. There the cavalry had to slow, slapping Cheerick aside with their swords and squeaking curses. The roadway was packed with the locals who were throwing flowers and paper at the carriages and trying to mob them in joy.

"Well, at least they're happy to see us," Hatt said.

"They're ecstatic," Top Powell said, breaking in on the team freq. "And any group *this* happy to see a military force has military problems. Keep that in mind."

The group was effectively stopped by the crowds and some of them had broken through the cavalry and were now climbing on the carriages.

"Miss Moon, how do you say: Thank you but you must move aside?" Weaver asked.

"It's . . . can you . . ."

"PFC Berg, can you retrans from Miss Moon?"

"Set up, sir," Berg said.

"Tell the drivers to hold onto their beasts!" Weaver said. "Berg, max volume!"

"*CHEE-SHA TREEK!*" Berg's armor suddenly shrieked. "*SHA-SHA MEEK!*"

The crowd pressed back and some of the cavalry were nearly thrown as their beasts started to bolt. The formerly placid draft-beasts pulling Commander Weaver's cart tried to bolt as well, but Jaen grabbed onto the cart and planted his feet.

"Sorry, ain't goin' nowhere," he said as Berg and Hatt got a hold as well.

Chief Miller hammered the fingers of a local still holding the carriage and waved his M-10 at the leader of the cavalry.

"Go! Go!" he yelled, pointing down the road.

As the cavalry broke into a canter, the security team let go and followed at a steady bound.

*"CHEE-SHA TREEK! SHA-SHA MEEK!"*

Between the charging cavalry and the shrieking armor, they managed to pass out of the near riot, and the crowds farther down the road stood aside.

"Oh, yeah," Jaen said, panting. "This is gonna be fun."

Weaver walked solemnly down the throne room, trailing Miriam and Miller. The latter had given up his knife before being allowed in but his M-10 was slung. Nobody had apparently realized that the things on the Terran's shoulders were weapons.

The throne room was low and rather dark. He'd noticed a tendency towards less light in all the Cheerick buildings. He wondered about the evolutionary background of the Cheerick as he approached the throne.

The latter was rather ornate, but not exactly "jewel encrusted." The Cheerick definitely used jewels, though, since the queen was wearing a cloak that had them along the hem and a large necklace that had more. It might just be that they were very rare in this society.

They stopped at a balk line and a male wearing complex vestments started speaking, apparently for the queen.

"Negotiations," Weaver muttered. "This should be interesting."

"Just remember, sir," the first sergeant said. "There's going to be that one thing they really want from us. All we have to do is figure out what it is, whether we're willing to do it and how much they're willing to pay. The essence of negotiation is control. Find out what you control and what you don't and you win. I think the reception we got says it all. These people are scared."

"I'd rather be defending a scientific paper," Weaver said.

"Lots of fun, sir?" Top asked.

"Brutal."

"Brutal."

They'd managed to get the claw away from Lady Che-chee with some more jewels and the, honest, statement that they wished to examine it. Apparently the one specimen that was brought back by the patrol survivor had been distributed, packed in alcohol, to every major lord in the land.

This claw was nineteen centimeters from the "ankle" to the tip of the longest claw. Dr. Robertson picked up the thing and pulled out some material she'd borrowed from the geology lab. It was a kit designed to test mineral hardness. She'd been informed of the claw marks in the limestone so she skipped right up to glass.

"Scores it," she said, moving up to sapphire, the material of aliglass.

"Damn," Master Sergeant Bartlett said. The claw hadn't just scratched the sapphire, it had deeply gouged it.

"That's bad," Dr. Robertson said.

"Absolutely," Bartlett said. "What is that stuff? I don't know anything biological that is that strong!"

"Anything producible by machinery is producible by biology," Dr. Robertson said. "Did you imagine the Dreen?"

"No," Bartlett said. "But they also didn't make anything that strong. Their armor was based on fibrous polymers like Kevlar. That's high hardness refractory material, Doctor."

"And what is it?" she asked quizzically. "I think we're going to have to turn it over to engineering or bio to figure out. Tchar, perhaps."

"If we can get a sample," Bartlett said, picking up a diamond saw. It skittered over the surface of the material but didn't penetrate. "It's stronger than diamond."

"Yes," Dr. Robertson said. "We need to communicate that to the Marines immediately. And get this down to engineering to see if they have anything that can take a sample."

"He's the high priest of the local religion," Miriam said. "Despite that fact, he started off by stating that both the secular authorities and religious agree that the Demons were not caused by our arrival. They believe that the Demons were sent to punish this city, and possibly this region, for various blasphemies. The most interesting one I thought was 'rebellion against the crown.'"

"Divine right," Weaver said, wincing. "We need to keep a close eye on that or we might tread on a nascent democratic revolution."

"This appears to be a rebellion by some outer area lords," Miriam said. "Over taxes."

"Doesn't sound like William Wallace to me, sir," the first sergeant said.

"We need to know more about the religious aspect," Captain MacDonald said. "The high priest represents the establishment. Is there a fundamentalist strain that is a security threat? We don't need to be fighting demons on one side and Cheerick on the other."

"I can't ask that in open Court, Captain," Miriam said, then began chittering.

"I told them that we're glad that they have determined we are not the problem and that we wished to open relations with them on a friendly level."

The high priest chittered for a while, then stopped, at which point the queen stood up and began speaking.

"Oh, no," Miriam muttered as she finished.

"What?" Weaver asked.

"They're more or less willing to open up to trade or whatever we want," Miriam said. "Alliance, troops, supplies, you name it. But they want us to try to rid them of the scourge of the Demons."

# 28

## The Lady, She's a Mother

"Oh, *hell* no," Captain Blankemeier said. "One ship. Twenty Marines. And that's what's *left*. Have you seen Dr. Robertson's report?"

"No, sir," Weaver said. "I haven't downloaded recently."

The humans had, quite reasonably from the queen's perspective, asked for time to communicate with their commander. They'd been led to a room that *appeared* to be immune to eavesdropping for their colloquy. Miller and Top had checked it out and found two "sound holes" hidden behind tapestries. On the other hand, everyone in the group could subvocalize so they did.

"That Demon claw? It's an advanced composite that's going to cut through Wyvern armor. Not quite like butter, but it's gonna cut it. Not to mention—"

"Steel, sir," Bill said. "Damn. Sir, the point is, if we make a treaty of mutual respect and admiration then just *leave*, there's not going to be a government to come back to."

"And we're unlikely to be able to stop that," Captain MacDonald said. "Not with my Marines. I've seen the tapestry, Commander Weaver. That looks one hell of a lot like a Dreen wave, even if they're not Dreen."

"Sir, I'm arguing for reasons other than just knight errant, I assure you," Commander Weaver said. "I think, though, that I need to express them in person."

"Very well, Commander," the captain said. "Tell the powers that be that their request is under consideration and return to the ship. Bring the first sergeant with you."

"If I may, sir," Captain MacDonald interjected. "I'm going to send a replacement team for Two Charlie from Third. They can bring supplies for Miss Moon and Chief Miller."

"Any advance on the bio side, sir?" Miller asked. "Is any of this food safe to eat?"

"I don't think Dr. Robertson has had time to check," the CO said. "I'll ask if there's any way to advance that. In the meantime, stick with MREs, Chief Miller."

"Yes, sir."

"Commander Weaver," the CO said. "When you get back here you'd better have a pretty compelling argument why I should risk the only starship the Alliance has on what looks to me like a forlorn hope. If not, we're going to stay here no more than seventy-two hours, complete our survey and then head for Earth with the information."

"Understood, sir."

"*Vorpal Blade*, out."

"And do you have a compelling argument, sir?" the first sergeant asked.

"I don't know," the commander admitted. "But I sure hope so."

"Then remember what I said about negotiation," Top replied, smiling. "It works with commanders, too, Commander."

"You sound as if you want to stay and fight," Commander Weaver said.

"Don't have a dog in that fight, sir," the first sergeant said.

"If anyone does, it's the Marines," Commander Weaver argued.

"If I worried about where I was going to be tomorrow, or whether being there was going to get me into a fight, or killed, I would have gotten out of this job a long time ago, sir," Top said. "Stay or go, that's a discussion for you and the CO and the Old Man, sir. Don't care one way or the other. A Marine goes where ordered and faithfully performs his duties. That's the whole point of the motto, sir."

"Okay, now I've seen some weird *maulk* . . ." Runner said.

"Like armored crab octopuses?" Staff Sergeant Kristopher said.

"Or are you talking about shipwrecking gravity waves? Or regions of space that cause up to be down and right to be up? Or maybe partially terraformed worlds? Layers of oil in gas giants?"

"All of that," Runner said. "And it's not exactly oil but . . . Oh, never mind. Damn, I wish Dr. Dean was here—"

"What is it?" Kristopher asked, walking over to the master sergeant's station.

"Seismic activity," Runner said, pointing. "Okay, P waves from a distant earthquake. Deep one, too. Surface quakes in mountain ranges, got that. Got some S waves coming from that mountain range east of here. This is probably that big-ass volcano we saw . . .

"But this is what's getting me," he continued, pointing at a series of small indicators and zooming in on them. "They're pinpointed near that big rock. And they appear to be moving, slowly. They're real faint, though."

"What the *grapp*?" Kristopher said. "I've seen something like that before . . ."

"I'm glad you have, cause it's got me stumped," Runner said. "Where?"

"I cannot for the life of me remember," Kristopher said. "I seem to remember being told to filter it out. But I can't remember where or why. But it wasn't any big deal, I remember that."

"Oh, great," Runner said. "On *Earth* it's no big deal. Well, I'm going to kick it up to Dr. Beach."

"I don't recognize it," Dr. Beach said, frowning. "It's certainly interesting, isn't it? But it's not at a level that would normally be called seismic. It almost looks like truck traffic."

"Frequency is wrong," Runner said, bringing up a pop-up and sorting through the list of known low-impact seismic events. "This is truck traffic. Low-frequency rumble. It's close to small-tube magma movement. This . . . I don't have anything like it."

"Too bad we lost Dr. Dean," Dr. Beach said. "I know you didn't get along, but—"

"I *tried* to stop him from going that way, Doctor," Runner said. "It was a professional failure on my part that he died. And I also recognized that we needed him. This is only one example. That hill over there is another. I keep thinking that if I could figure out how a basolith appeared without any secondary indicators I could determine what *this* is. But neither of them make sense."

"Keep an eye on it," Dr. Beach said. "If it is some sort of slowly moving mini-fault, we don't want any damage to the ship."

"Especially since the nearest rumble is less than a kilometer away."

"Tough day, Weaver?" the CO asked as Commander Weaver entered his office. Weaver had thrown on his uniform over his blacksuit but his hair was still plastered with sweat.

"Long one, at least," Weaver said. "I hated leaving Miller behind. He's like a right arm."

"So I'd like your argument for staying," the CO said. "I feel I owe you that. But be aware that I'm pretty much set on leaving and letting D.C. decide. Among other things, I feel it's over my paygrade to set up long-term treaties."

"Understood, sir," Bill said, rubbing his forehead. "My first argument is the one that I stated. The records of these people indicate that demon break-outs tend to occur when they get too advanced or something along those lines. Maybe population density. They don't know what causes it and we don't either. But they're here, now, and if we make a treaty with this group and then leave it's a waste of paper. They won't be here when we get back."

"Got that one," the CO said. "And while I feel for them—"

"There's a PR aspect, sir," Weaver said, frowning. "Even in the black community. These guys are *cute*. If we cut and run and leave the poor little rodents to be eaten by demons . . . Sir, that's going to look like *maulk*. Especially if we run without so much as contact with the demons. 'Oooh, big bad *Vorpal Blade* is scared of some widdew demons?' I'm not saying that should be a factor that causes you to accept casualties, but it's a factor. One I only thought about on the walk back. And when we do, eventually, go white . . . It's gonna look even worse. Especially since we or somebody *will* be back and see the aftermath."

"So you're saying I'm damned if I do and damned if I don't," Spectre said. "That I can lose my career fighting a pointless battle and losing troops or by cutting and running and letting the poor little chinchillas die."

"Taking Miss Miriam as a pool of the eventual white PR reaction, sir," Weaver said, "I would guess 'crucified' is more likely in the latter case."

"Great," Spectre said. "But there's a better reason, I hope?"

"There are too many questions, sir," Weaver said. "And I'm not talking about pure curiosity, here. I'm talking about things that are just bugging the *maulk* out of me. The boards. Where in the *hell* do *they* come from? They are tech that is advanced on Adar. I've tried the one we've got out and they really *do* seem to read your mind. And we're not even Cheerick! I want some more just so we monkeys can tear them apart and be baffled. The Demons. I'd say they are some sort of created species, like the Dreen, but very focused. What is their *purpose*? How are they created? *Where* are they created? If we leave and come back after this society is destroyed, we're just going to have to start all over again. And we'll need to find one that is just about as advanced to have any luck with using local support. Even if we go back just to ask for reinforcements, we're going to get held up. Committees, commissions, boards, every idiot in the black community, and they are numerous, sir, trust me, is going to want to add to the reports and recommendations. State is going to get involved and that means two months of reports going back and forth for addendum and amendment.

"Right here, right now, sir, you have more authority than any captain since the sailing days. Go back and it's going to be two generals and an admiral arguing over sandwiches. Maybe at far remove they can make a better decision, sir, but by the time they decide to come back, maybe with more firepower, it's going to be too late. Those are my arguments, sir."

"And more responsibility than any CO in history," Spectre said. "This is the *only* spaceship we have, as I have repeatedly pointed out. If these Demons are bad as they seem, we could lose it."

"Not . . . if it's off the ground, sir," Bill said. "At least, it *reduces* the likelihood."

"Take off and hold in orbit?" Spectre said. "Drop down to replace troops from time to time?"

"Yes, sir," Bill replied. "Actually, it's not really necessary to get into geosynch. It actually won't even be an orbit. It is more like a hover in the region of the atmosphere known as near space. It will require continuous piloting to keep the ship over Cheerick City, but it can be done. You could even stay lower in atmosphere than near space but then it really is like flying in the wind. Commo shouldn't be a big problem as we'll only be at altitudes a little higher than a U2 flies. High data rate commo might require a better ground station though."

"Leave one platoon on the ground," the CO said, nodding. "If they need support, we can drop anywhere to provide it."

"And you can engage with the lasers, sir," Bill pointed out. "Those will stop an assault of Demons, sir. They're designed to take out *ships*."

"'Fire phasers from orbit, Chekhov,'" Spectre intoned. "Heh. Let me think about it, Weaver, but those are all cogent points. Dismissed. And get a shower."

"Yes, sir," Weaver said, grinning.

"We've had the distillers running full time, so go ahead and get a *Hollywood* shower," the CO said, referring to just letting the water run. Normally, a shower was spray on water, soap, rinse.

"Thank you, sir."

"Jesus Christ," Guppy said as soon as the three exhausted Marines entered the compartment. "You heard about these *grapping* Demons, right?"

"I've been following Commander Weaver around for the last sixteen hours," Jaen said, hopping in his rack and stripping off his skins. "But we weren't exactly privy to the discussions."

"That Adar down in engineering's trying to figure out what the claws are made out of," Seeley said, rolling over. "But they tested it on a piece of *grapped* up Wyvern armor and it cut right through it. Not easy or anything, but it could cut right through it."

"Fine, we do our survey and then get the *grapp* out," Berg said, rolling into his own rack and slipping his skinsuit into a bag with a nannie pack.

"The Cheerick asked if we'd stay and help them," Seeley said. "Captain MacDonald's against it. There's not enough of us left for one thing. But Captain Blankemeier has the final word. Commander Weaver's meeting with him right now."

"What's he think?" Berg asked.

"I think he's supporting staying," Seeley said. "I only got what I've got from Pearson." The latter was the CO's radioman and could occasionally pick up solid info, "straight poop," instead of the rumor that was the normal stuff of the bay.

"I think he's off my Christmas card list," Hatt said, lacing his fingers behind his head. "We took enough of a beating on Runner's World. He's probably got an argument for it, but . . . I'm about ready to get back to the World and chill. Hell, even on deployment you've got more security than we do doing this *maulk*."

"We're Marines," Sergeant Jaenisch said. "We go where the CO says and we kill whatever the CO tells us to kill. And that's pretty much the deal."

"Semper *Grapping* Fi, Sergeant," Hatt said. "In that case, I'm gonna get some rest. Because, you know, the CO might decide we need to fight an army of unstoppable Demons tomorrow."

"In which case we say 'Aye-aye' and we kill Demons," Jaen said. "End of story."

"We're staying," the CO said, looking around at the gathered scientists and officers. "Sort of. Commander Weaver had several cogent arguments to advance. But we're not going to be stupid about it. We've got the materials to set up a base camp. As soon as that is installed, we're going to lift the ship and hold it in near space. Designated science personnel and a platoon of Marines will stay groundside to secure the survey. In the event of Demon attack, we will assess the possibility of being of use to the locals. If we cannot do anything about it, we will pick up all personnel and *leave*. However, as Commander Weaver pointed out, we have *lasers* on this ship. Those, right there, should be able to stop a Demon assault wave. We'll have Miss Moon request a basing area near the palace. That will permit us to support to the last moment. Captain MacDonald? Comments?"

"Works for me, sir," MacDonald said, nodding. "I don't want to lose more Marines, obviously, but on the other hand . . . Hell, sir, I hate to run from a fight."

"Oorah," the first sergeant said.

"XO?"

"Escape from Saigon if it comes to it," the XO said, nodding. "Let's hope nobody gets photos this time." The pictures of helicopters picking up the last personnel from the American embassy in Saigon were some of the worst from a PR perspective of the entire war.

"We can, quite literally, do the same thing with this boat," the CO pointed out. "One day to get negotiations done and then we'll drop the materials for the base. Captain MacDonald, you will remain on the ground. We'll drop from time to time to rotate the platoon."

"Yes, sir," MacDonald said.

"We will remain for no more than two weeks," the CO said. "We don't have consumables for more. Dr. Chet?"

"Yes, Captain," the doctor rumbled.

"I understand that you took over food testing from bio," the CO said. "Any advances?"

"Oh, many," Dr. Chet said. "So far, most of the foods I've found are consumable by animals. They have no useable vitamins in them, but they have many of the same sugars and peptides as Earth foods. There is one problem, though. There is a possibility of long-term side effects. I would not suggest permitting the food to be eaten without widespread testing. Food allergies is another issue. Those, however, can be dealt with. Things like prions cannot. If food is eaten, I would suggest that people stick to the grains and fruits. Less possibility of prion poisoning. Miss Moon has reported eating some of the fruit that I cleared with no ill effects. And she is . . . finicky."

"Tell her next time to ask *me* first," the CO said. "Okay, come up with a list of acceptable consumables. We can get protein and sugars from them, right?"

"Oh, yes," Dr. Chet said. "All the same amino acids as Earth and the same simple sugars. Benefits of a Type One biosphere. And they, of course, can eat us. But no vitamins. At least, none that I've found so far."

"XO, if we take on local foodstuffs, how long can we stay?"

"Until we run out of parts, sir," the XO said. "About two months at a guess. Depends on what breaks first. And there's always duct tape. The sub service proverbially runs on duct tape."

"We're due back on Earth before then," the CO said. "And we don't want to be overdue. It would cause too much concern. Very well, prepare to drop a ground base. See if we can get some cleared fruits at least. Some fresh food would be welcome."

"I'll coordinate with Miss Moon on both, sir," Captain Mac-Donald said.

"Anything else we need to discuss?" the CO asked, looking around. "Commander Weaver, head back to the palace and pass on the plan. Let's get cracking."

"No indicators of Demon activity?" Lieutenant Souza said.

The ship did have one intel specialist, a Navy seaman who

had been compiling all the information about the Demons that was available. Jeff Waggoner had been a very busy boy.

"No, sir," the seaman said, pushing his glasses back up his nose. With his crewcut and large ears his head looked like nothing so much as a giant vase. The Coke-bottle glasses and tiny office scattered with paper simply completed the look that defined the "Intel Geek." "I've only got two indicators of Demon activity and those distant from our position. Our sector appears to be clear of Demon activity at this time, sir."

"So the boat should be clear of Demon activity for at least two days?" Lieutenant Souza said.

"Unless indicators change radically, yes, sir," Waggoner said, pushing his glasses back up.

"Commander Beeel is a *male*?" Lady Che-chee asked.

She had returned to Court shortly after the first meeting and after a brief meeting with the queen had become the primary liaison with the humans. In that role, she was trying to impart some aspects of Cheerick society on Miriam while being shocked and dismayed in what she was discovering about humans.

"Why, yes," Miriam said. "Most of our military is male. There are females in it, many, and some of them of fairly high level. But it is still a primarily male profession. When we were in the islands we encountered an all-male party and your son is a warrior, isn't he?"

"Well, yes," Lady Che-chee said. "But he's a *warrior*. He will never be a *commander*! Males are far too flighty. I mean, look at his silly display when you landed! I had come to understand *you* were a female and your bodyguard is a male, but I thought that natural."

"What are you talking about?" Chief Warrant Officer Miller asked.

"Male-female relationships in Cheerick society," Miriam said delicately, then turned back to Lady Che-chee. "Chief Miller is a bit more than my bodyguard. I know nothing about war and would not begin to think I do. He is not only a very famous warrior on our planet but one of the ship's senior advisers on ground combat. The Commander Weaver is a male, the ship's captain, Captain Blankemeier is a male, and even the person I referred to as our queen is, in fact, a male. For now. It is possible that the next will be a female. We rotate our highest position every four years."

"How do they learn their jobs?" Lady Che-chee asked, aghast. "It takes at least that long for a queen to become accustomed to her position! Most of her decisions in her first four years are *awful* if she doesn't listen to her advisers."

"They serve in lesser capacities prior to that job," Miriam said. "And . . . they are not born to it. They are chosen by the full body of the citizens in a process called democracy. They contest for the job and then are voted upon."

"So they, too, are warriors," Lady Che-chee said. "The best warrior is not necessarily the best leader, miss."

"Clarification," Miriam said, grinning. "They don't *physically* fight for it. They give speeches, participate in debates, things like that. Some have been, as you would call it, warriors, others not."

"Your society is very confusing," Lady Che-chee said.

"As is yours," Miriam said. "So only females can be leaders?"

"Once they pass through the Change, yes," Lady Che-chee said. "Before that, they are Breeders. Only Mothers can be leaders."

"The Change?" Miriam asked.

"Young females are only Breeders," Lady Che-chee said. "We are . . . very dumb. They can barely speak, but when you are a Breeder you hear and remember much. Families such as mine, in fact, instruct their Breeders despite the fact that at the time they understand very little. Then when we stop breeding, we go through the Change. It's a very strange time. Suddenly, things begin making sense. Or make less sense. It is said there is nothing more intelligent than a Mother just post-Change nor more stupid. I know that was how *I* was. My Mother was a Lady of a small farm, my father a priest. I was instructed in many arts as a Breeder but didn't understand them until I passed the Change. There was no position for me so my Mother obtained a commission for me in the queen's forces. All of my lands accrued from my service with the queen and other positions I took over the years. But all of that was after the Change."

"And your son?" Miriam asked.

"He was kept by my Mother and father until he grew large enough to obtain a commission as well," Lady Che-chee said. "By then I was a general and prepared to retire. He has been posted to one of the cavalry regiments. That was shortly before I purchased the estates. He is a *sheshar*, a junior cavalryman. Most of the soldiers are males, the officers are all Mothers. I know of only two males considered both wise enough and fierce enough to be officers and they are both very low rank. Good fellows, but not someone you'd make a general."

"I see," Miriam said, trying not to grin.

"Okay, I need some of that translated, obviously," Miller said. "I can tell when there's something somebody doesn't want to tell me."

"It's sort of complicated," Miriam said, still trying not to grin.

# 29

## *Now* You Think of That

"Third's going on initial deployment," Sergeant Jaenisch said. "They'll be on the ground for two weeks with the science team, then we'll drop for two weeks. After that, we have to go home. The boat's running short on spares and our $CO_2$ filters are about shot."

"Sounds good to me," Guppy said. "Let *grapping* Third take the heat this time."

"I *heard* that, Guppy," Sergeant Samson caroled from down the compartment.

"First and Second took a hammering on Runner's," Tanner pointed out. "Time for us to earn our pay."

"Hey, we were on Runner's too," Lance Corporal Revells said.

"Yeah, and Two-Gun saved your ass," Sergeant Jaenisch said. "This time, though, you're on your own."

"We're going to be dropping a Barrett for the SEAL chief," Revells said. "That should take care of any old demon."

"Anybody asks *me* about it on the after-actions report," Tanner said, "I'm going to recommend bigger guns. Screw these damned 7.62 mm Gatlings."

"And rocket launchers," Sergeant Samson said, making a "whoosh" sound. "And claymores."

"The ship needs a cannon mount, too," Revells said.

"Yeah, and we need a tank while you're at it," Hatt said. "Couple of F-18s with JDAMs wouldn't be turned down. Make that a carrier. Oh, wait, that won't *fit*. Where, exactly, are we going to put a cannon on the ship?"

"We can put it in the bunk area for one platoon," Guppy said, gesturing at the empty bunks. "*Plenty* of room there," he added bitterly.

"I'd rather have the troops," Jaen said. "But I agree on the heavier firepower. We definitely need .50 calibers. 7.62 mm just don't cut it."

"We've got 'em," Sergeant Samson said sarcastically. "Old Two-Gun will always save the day!"

"Sergeant, with all due respect," Berg said. "Take a flying—"

"Third Platoon!" Gunny Hedger said. "Get your ass down to the missile bay! We need to prep load out!"

"On the way, Gunny," Samson caroled. "Hold that thought, Two-Gun. I'm interested to see how it ends."

"How were you going to end that without ending up on report?" Sergeant Jaen asked. "Because if you were going to end it the way I *think* you were going to end it—"

"'Take a flying jump on a squealing chinchilla,'" Berg said. "What did you *think* I was going to say, Sergeant?"

"We appreciate your offer, Commander Beeel," the queen squeaked. "I understand that you must return to your homes soon. But if the Demons attack, we are united in defense, this is agreed?"

"Agreed," Bill said through Miriam's translation. "We normally try to coordinate with local forces in something like this, but we are hampered by language. But in the event of attack, we will respond. We do need some things, however, to remain. Our doctor has determined that some of your food is partially edible. We cannot survive on it, but we have had no fresh food for some months. We would like to get some food from you. We also would like to establish a ground base near the palace so that we can help in the defense of your city. So we will need a spot of land. And it will be dug up because we intend to build a small fort for defense. We will put tents in there that will allow us to come out of our armor. We will put some of our ground forces in that fort. Some will remain on the ship. It will then withdraw into the air. From there it has weapons that can fire down to attack the Demons and also drop the remaining Marines in places where they are needed."

"This is a wonderful ability," the queen said. "But can they not use boards?"

"We do not have boards, Your Majesty," Weaver said. "We are, in fact, interested in how they work. But until we understand them, we must use the ship."

The queen had brought up one of her commanders to stand equal with the high priest on her other side. She waved him down and there was a whispered colloquy before she turned back, her nose wrinkling.

"They have fourteen boards they're willing to let us use," Miriam said. "In fact, if all goes well, we can keep them."

"Go for it," Miller said. "Hell, the Wyverns might be able to drop from orbit on those things."

"We don't know if they'll take Wyverns," Weaver said. "We need to experiment. But, yes, Miriam, offer her our thanks."

"General Chuk-tuk also points out that we have a disused barracks," the queen said. "It is based on an old fort. You might wish to look it over and see if you can make of it a sanctuary for your fighters."

"Thank you, Your Majesty," Weaver said. "I will communicate that to my commander."

"We will meet in privy counsel at sunset," the queen said. "Please discuss this with your commander and if you must use open space, by that time we will find it. We appreciate your willingness to aid us in our time of need. Though we do not have your wonderful devices, we Cheerick are strong, able and courageous. Never will we forget your aid, win or lose."

"Thank you, Your Majesty," Bill said, bending over as far as he could in the armor. It was as close as he could get to a bow.

"There's no place to effectively drop the ship on palace grounds," Weaver said. "The commander of local forces, though, is preparing a cart caravan. It will bring out some fresh food and pick up the materials for the base. In the meantime they suggest staying here with Lady Che-chee."

"What about this fort?" Captain MacDonald asked.

"It's in good condition," Bill replied. "I'm not sure if we can perfectly seal it, though. And we'll have to decontaminate the interior."

"We can always use ID Ten T decontaminator," the CO said, blank-faced.

"That's only effective on neenion contamination, sir," the first sergeant said.

"What in hell is a neenion?" Captain MacDonald asked.

"Never mind," Spectre said, grinning. "Okay, Captain, I would suggest taking your boys to the barracks and seeing if we can decontaminate and seal it. If Dr. Chet clears it for occupancy, and if there's enough room for gear, you can move in there."

"We'll leave Second Platoon in place and take Third," Captain MacDonald said. "When's this caravan arrive?"

"This afternoon," Bill said.

"Make sure that food is *thoroughly* decontaminated," the CO said. "I'm not going to sit in quarantine for a month because the med board says we violated quarantine. No matter *how* much fresh fruit is involved."


"Oh, this is quite wonderful," Dr. Becker said, looking at the astronomy laboratory attached to the palace. "It takes me back," he added, looking at the lens-grinding area.

"We believe we saw your wonderful ship floating above," Master Jadum said. "Journeyman Agoul actually spotted it first. He has very good eyes."

"He must have been using this," Dr. Becker said, peering through the lens of the telescope, which was about a sixteen power but so distorted as to be nearly opaque. "But you don't have optical coatings. Hmmm . . . I think I remember some very low-tech optical coating recipes from when I was in high school. Those, alone, will double the clarity of this scope. And if you add a mirror, a clear one, you can double your focal length. But using a bigger aperture diameter is the key . . ."

"I'm not sure I can translate all of that," Miriam said.

"Of course, my dear, sorry," Dr. Becker said. "And what's this? An electric spark generator?"

"We are just beginning to explore these properties," Master Jadum said enthusiastically, pointing to the complex arrangement. "This has some of the same properties as the puffiness from fur in winter."

"Yes," Dr. Becker said, nodding. "And with a bit more tinkering and by hooking it up to, oh, a water wheel, you can have full-scale power generation. Electric lights, even . . ."

"Dr. Becker," Chief Miller said. "We haven't been using flashlights around them since they say that is one thing that always brings the Demons."

"But they're already here," Miriam said. "So it's not our flashlights that are causing them."

"True," Becker said, then frowned. "Is it the light or the . . ."

"Oh," Miriam said, her eyes flying wide. "Electromagnetism?"

"Radio signals," Becker said, his face going white.

"Particle emissions?" Miriam whispered.

"You mean it's just the electricity?" Miller said. "These things track in on *electricity*? Like, you know, *the generators on the boat*?"

"If we're right, the boat is a giant *smorgasbord* to these things," Becker said.

"But the boat's in orbit, right?" Miller pointed out.

"Chief Miller," Miriam said, hoarsely. "Do you remember the tapestry?"

"The . . . Yeah," Miller said, frowning.

"Those figures in the corner," Miriam said rapidly. "The ones that looked like fighter planes? What if they can *reach* orbit?"

"Marine One, Marine One, this is SEAL One . . ."

# 30

## Okay, So Sometimes It *Is* Two-Gun Mojo

"Mother," Cha-chai said, calmly.

"Yes, my son," Lady Che-chee said, not looking up from the report she was writing. The Chrans might or might not be friendly. So far, all seemed well. However, the queen and General Chuktuk required daily reports on their activities. Unfortunately, Lady Che-chee had no real idea of what such activities as driving spikes in her lawn actually meant.

"I know that I became somewhat overwrought when the Chrans arrived," the young Cheerick said. "However, I believe it would be wise for you to look at the spaceship."

Lady Che-chee looked up at the male, then turned to look out her window. She turned back quite calmly then pointed her muzzle at the ceiling.

"TO ARMS!"

"What the hell is that noise?" Sub Dude asked, yanking on the nut to get it to break free.

"You're gonna break it off," Red warned. "Then we're gonna have to back it out."

"Hand me the damned liquid wrench, then," Sub Dude said. The two were trying to get a recalcitrant diesel engine to work.

The CO had powered down the ardune reactor to cut down on both heat production and ardune use. The latter was very expensive fuel. So the diesels had to be run to keep the ship going and one of them had quit. So, Gants and Red had been dispatched to fix that little issue. After which they had a list of "honey-dos" that was longer than their arm. It didn't help that the damned things were nearly in the bilges. "If the CO would just open up the ship and vent it, we wouldn't even *need* this thing."

"I'd rather fix the engine than spend a month in quarantine," Red said, frowning as he handed over the liquid wrench. "I dunno. I hear it, too."

"Well, I could do with a nice breeze on my face," Sub Dude said, just as there was a gurgling sound underfoot followed by a blast of air.

"You just got one!" Red yelled, shaking his head. "Damn, my ears are ringing!"

"Hit the alarm!" Michael said, backing away and looking down through the grating underfoot. "HOLY *MAULK*!"

"INTRUDER ALERT! INTRUDER ALERT!"

Military personnel learn to count a "day" as the period from one sleep to the next. Naps do not count. Berg's "day" therefore, had been somewhere on the order of twenty-two hours long. His "night" might not count since he had only been asleep for three hours. And it was sodden sleep. He'd run back and forth to the palace twice, helped Third Platoon with their load-out, taken in supplies and had to work on his Wyvern for two hours. He was a bit tired when he finally hit the rack.

But when his eyes flew open his actions were practiced and he had his skins out of their wrapper and on before he really woke up. The Marines had learned to sleep in them. You could leave them on under your uniform *or* in the Wyverns. They even made halfway decent pajamas. But his had been rank, so he'd "laundered" them with a nannie pack.

They were still a tad ripe as he pulled the top over his head. But you put up with it. Welcome to the Space Marines. Talk all you will of heavier firepower, *his* suggestion was going to be two sets of skins, minimum.

"SECOND PLATOON, GROUND MOUNT!"

On went the trousers and the bunk opened up as he snatched

at his boots and slid on his top at the same time. He could seal both on the way to the armory.

"THIS IS NOT A DRILL!"

It took him until he'd cleared the sleeping compartment for that one to sink in.

"BREACH IN CONTROL SECTOR! ALL TEAMS TO DEFENSE STATIONS!"

"Holy *grapp*," Hatt muttered as they reached the doors of the gear station.

"DRAW LIVE ROUNDS! BRAVO TEAM TO AUXILIARY DIESEL COMPARTMENT!"

"Is it the *grapping* Cheerick?" Sergeant Jaenisch asked as he dropped into his seat and mounted his gear.

"How the *grapp* do I know?" Staff Sergeant Driscoll snapped. "It's probably neenion contamination." The staff sergeant was having a hard time getting his gear on and Jaen stood up and slapped it into position.

"Well, if it is, you're our neenion expert, Staff Sergeant," Jaen said, slapping him on the shoulder. "But you need to get into your spot, with all due respect."

Staff Sergeant Driscoll lifted his M-10 out of the rack, then looked over at Guppy and Chuckie.

"Guppy," he said. "You've got point."

"Got it, Dreen-Man," Guppy said, darting out of the compartment. "Follow me!"

"Did he just call me Dreen-Man?" Driscoll asked as he cleared the compartment.

"Yes, Staff Sergeant," Chuckie said, jacking a round into his grenade launcher. "And your point?"

"Nothing," Driscoll said. "Just trying to make sure I know my team name."

"Demons!" Sub Dude shouted as the three Marines reached the hatch to recycling. There was banging on the far side of the hatch and then a scratching. "They just ripped their way up through the bottom of the hull!"

"*Grapp*," Guppy said, backing up.

"Out of here," Driscoll said. "We've got it. Chuckie, grenade through the hole as soon as they dig through. Guppy, frags if it clears. I'm going to stay on the M-10."

"Got it," Chuckie said, flipping the safety off his grenade launcher. "Keep it open for me, Dreen-Man."

"I'll do that little thing, Chuck," Driscoll said, taking position so he was peeking around the corner of a reinforcing member. "Command, Two-Alpha. Reported Demon breach. We are about to engage."

"Roger, Two-Alpha."

"DEMON BREACH IN AUXILIARY PLANT! ALL DEFENSE TEAMS TO POSITIONS!"

"Demons," the CO said. "Pilot, lift us. Lift us now."

"Sir," the pilot said. "Two minutes to warm up the drive."

"Engineering, Conn," the CO said. "Get that drive up. We need to get off the ground!"

"Roger, Conn," the Eng said. "Warming up the ball. Ninety seconds to full power."

"Lieutenant Berisford," Spectre said. "Status?"

"Reported Demon breach in auxiliary engine spaces," Berisford said, panting. "Two mechanics mates were working in there when they broke through but our guys made it out. Two-Alpha is holding the corridor but the Demons dug right through the hull so I'm not sure they're just going to stay in corridors."

"Roger," the CO said, hitting the enunciator. "Seal all watertight doors. Report any suspicious sounds to conn. Demons in recycling. Engines warming. I intend to break contact with the ground as soon as the engine is up, then clear the ship."

There was a boom in the distance followed by a rattle of gunfire.

"All hands stand by to repel boarders."

"Ma'am," Runner said, handing Mimi a pistol. "That's only for if they make it past us."

The mission specialists had gathered in the missile room and were busy donning their Wyvern armor.

Mimi nodded and slid the pistol into a holster inside the Wyvern armor.

"I hate to say this, but I don't think they'll be able to kill me," Mimi said, gesturing with her chin to Tuffy.

"Wish I could say the same, ma'am," Runner said, stepping back into his armor and shutting the hatch. The barrels of his

Gatling spun for a moment then slid to a halt. "And I hope like hell I don't hit any of the damned missiles."

The Demon had a heavy triangular beak that seemed to be made of the same thing as its claws. The head appeared, first, tearing at the heavy duty steel of the hatch as if it were cardboard.

"Chuckie," Driscoll said.

"Fragments are going to bounce back," Chuckie pointed out.

"I know that, Marine," Driscoll said. "Fire. Guppy, duck."

The grenade caused the Demon to turn aside for a moment, but immediately after it went back to ripping, if anything with more fury.

"*Grapp,*" Driscoll said. But as the opening widened he could see a bit of shoulder. And that didn't seem to have the same armoring. He fired a burst and was rewarded with a splash of red. "Chuckie, more. Pour 'em in."

Chuckie fired off the rest of his five-round clip on slow fire and managed to blow the Demon back from the door.

"Guppy! Now!"

Guppy had been sheltering in a hatchway to the side. He stepped out and tossed a frag through the door, then pulled another off his belt and pulled the pin. Just as he did, the Demon lifted up into the opening and slid through, biting through the Marine's shoulder. Its beak slid right through the refractory ceramic armor as if it were unnoticeable.

Golupski screamed and dropped to his knees but didn't drop the grenade. Instead, he thumbed the spoon off the grenade and thrust his arm up into the Demon's half-open mouth.

"Eat this mothergra—" he said then slumped, blood spurting across the companionway.

The Demon bit down, ripping the arm off just above the elbow, then blew across the opening as the grenade detonated.

"Chuckie," Driscoll said, firing at a half-seen form in the compartment. "Grenades."

"Reloaded," Seeley said, darting forward then dropping to a knee. He pumped two grenades into the compartment, to screams of anger within, then another Demon humped its way into the opening. The grenade he'd just fired bounced off the armored head of the beast and ricocheted into the compartment.

"*Grapp!*" Seeley said, dropping to the ground.

The grenade bounced off the overhead and landed on his back, detonating on contact with the carbon boride armor.

"*Behanchod!*" Driscoll shouted, stepping forward and pouring 7.62 mm fire into the beast in the opening. It ignored the rounds sparking off its head, tearing at the hatch to make a larger opening.

"Get Chuck out of here," Gunny Hocieniec said, dropping to one knee next to the staff sergeant.

".308s bounce the *grapp* off," Driscoll said, grabbing the wounded grenadier and dragging him back.

"Noticed," Gunny Hocieniec said.

"We put grenades in there but I'm not sure if it's working," Driscoll said, getting the wounded Marine to the end of the corridor. A Navy corpsman grabbed the grenadier and threw him across his shoulders in a fireman's carry.

"It's not," Gunny Hocieniec said as the Demon tore open the hatch.

There were more of them than just that one coming through, a wall of claws and beaks. They had no trouble climbing along the companionway, top and sides, their adamantine claws giving them solid purchase in the steel.

Head and chest were armored in the same material as the claws, but the shoulders were vulnerable. Between Driscoll and Hocieniec they managed to drop three of the beasts, wounded if not dead, before the creatures got to them.

"*Grapp* me," Hocieniec said thrusting his rifle into the throat of the beast and levering it up. But its claws ripped through his armor, flaying him open even as he got the weapon planted in its belly and fired a burst. "Dreen-ma—"

Driscoll fired a burst on full rock and roll, breaking the plate of one beast and dropping it in a puddle of red. But two more snatched him at almost the same time. He blocked with the M-10, only to see it bitten in half.

"*Grapp* you!" he shouted, reaching down and ripping out the pins on all four of his frags. "Eat *ma*—" The rest of what he might have said was cut off as one of the beasts ripped out his throat.

"Conn, Two-Alpha is down," Lieutenant Berisford said. "Containment is breached. We're trying to stop them in corridor . . ." There was a burst of fire and the circuit went dead.

"Lifting now," the pilot said. "Max G."

"Where are the other Marines?" the CO asked.

"Two-Bravo is securing engineering," the XO said. "Two-Charlie is at the door of the conn."

"What's the word on—"

"Conn! Conn! Security Team Four! We can't stop these things! They're headed for—"

"Team Four is in the mess," the XO said.

"Conn, Team Nine. We've got them stopped in the Torpedo Room. We welded extra cover on the hatches and they just turned away. Torpedo Room is holding."

"Conn! Team Six! They're coming up! Headed right for control!"

The firing could be heard through the deck, coming closer.

"Only *how* many indicators of alien activity?" Torpedoman Joseph Olbinski screamed, firing his shotgun at the charging Demons. A member of the sub's security team, he was trying to hold the corridor directly beneath the conn. And losing.

"There wasn't *anything* in the area!" Jeff Waggoner shouted, the 9mm rounds from his MP-7 bouncing off their armored forequarters.

"I *hate* intel!" Olbinski screamed as the first Demon reached him.

"Conn!" Waggoner shouted into his comm. "Demons at . . . urk!"

Then it was cut off.

"That was missile control," the XO said. "Right under us."

"Get the Marines *in* here," the CO said. "If these things can tunnel right through steel, I want to have security *inside* the compartment."

"Aye, aye," the XO said.

Runner watched as the Demons ran past and then shook his head inside his armor.

"Ain't that a thing?" he asked as they started ripping at the door of engineering. There were seven of them, ugly beasts like bulked up Komodo dragons. But from the scores in the deck and the way they were tearing at the door, their bite was much worse than their bark.

"Kris, you thinking what I'm thinking?"

"Yep."

"On three," the master sergeant said. "One, two . . . three."

The 7.62 mm Gatling guns fired almost simultaneously. While the 7.62 mms might bounce off the forward armor of the beasts, they had no problems with their thickened skin, ripping three of the Demons to shreds in less than a second.

The remaining four, however, turned towards the Wyverns and rounds started skipping off their fronts. One had been hit in the withers and its back legs were shattered, but it continued forward.

"Spread," Runner said, ducking backwards around a missile tube.

That started a game of cat and Demon in the missile compartment as the Wyverns ducked in and out around the tubes, fired at Demons and ducked back. The team had fought similar actions before in countless "games" and they worked well together. They dropped the Demons before one came near any of them.

"I wonder if we can get them to *all* come to us?" Kristopher said.

"Oh, I think there's gonna be plenty for everybody," Runner replied. "Engineering . . ."

"Remember," Lady Che-chee said, donning her gloves and taking a spear from one of her retainers. "They are only vulnerable on the sides. And they can *jump*."

"Yes, Mother," Cha-chai said.

"Bi-lateral sweeps, just as they teach you at the regiment," Lady Che-chee said, donning her board. "Strike, then return for another spear. Get them chasing us while the Breeders and pups are evacuated."

"Yes, Mother," Cha-chai said, sighing.

"I think you'd better start saying *Colonel*, sonny," Lady Che-chee said. "Right, Sergeant, you take left, I'll take right. For the Regiment!"

Josh Lyle looked up from his workbench at the scrabbling under his feet and sighed.

"You just *had* to get busy in here, didn't you?" the armorer said, walking over to the rack on the wall. He considered it, finger on lips, for a moment. *7.62 mm skipped right off, eh?* He plucked a weapon from the rack and pulled out a pre-loaded magazine.

The Demon's head poked through the deck much as a newborn alligator opens an egg. And the squeal that came from it had a similar sound, if much deeper. One deep-set red eye rolled and spotted Lyle. Then a claw came ripping up through the steel, opening the hole.

"Really?" Lyle asked. "You really want to get busy in here? People never learn."

He lifted the "modified" carbine to his shoulder and settled the laser pointer just below the eye.

"Let's see how you like this."

The .50 caliber scramjet round barely had time to accelerate before it hit the Demon's head. While it didn't punch through, the head snapped sharply to the side. Whether it was the snapping of the Demon's spine or the fact that the deck had cut half way through its neck that killed it, Lyle wasn't sure. But he'd take that as a kill.

"Next?"


Berg took a spot by the CO's chair. It gave him all around views of the conn compartment. He noticed that all the conn personnel had strapped on side arms but he didn't think .45s were going to do much good. The COB had his in a two-handed grip, pointed at the rear hatch.

"Son, why do you have two pistols strapped on your sides like a gunfighter?" the CO asked calmly.

"Sir, that's PFC Berg," the XO said just as there was a scrabbling at the rear hatch. "The one you signed the award authorization for."

"So you can fire two guns at once?" the CO asked as a Demon head appeared in the ripped-apart hatch.

"No, sir," Berg replied, drawing both pistols. "Only one."

"Oh," the CO said as the Demon's head became fully visible. "Pilot, elevation?"

"Holding at Angels Nine," the pilot said.

"Engineering?" the CO said, punching the comm.

"Engineering," the Eng answered. "We're holding. The SF team took out the Demons that were attacking us."

"Conn, Tactical. I have eyeballs on the Demons that were

attacking on the ground. There's a large cluster of them on Lady Che-chee's lawn . . ."

"Open fire with Laser Two," the CO said as the Demons tore through the door. "Engineering, Tac, in the event Conn is taken out, try to maintain the fight. Good luck."

As the first Demon's head punched through the door, Berg looked for a vulnerable spot. The whole head and front was armored, but just under the jaw it flexed. He faintly heard firing around him but he ignored it, waiting.

Finally, the thing lifted up to tear at the top of the opening and he fired one round. The demon's head nearly blew off as it flew back in a welter of crimson.

"Damn, boy," the CO said, holding up his smoking pistol.

Another Demon immediately took its place but the next problem was on the starboard side of the hatch, low, where Demons were tearing through at deck level. One was squeezing its way through the hole and Berg noted another flex point at the juncture of shoulder and neck.

"I'm just going to stop bothering," the CO said as the Demon began convulsing in the opening.

The Demons had broken all the way through the door and for the next few seconds Berg sort of lost track. All he could recall was beaks and claws and muted shots like everybody was using silencers.

He came back to reality when the CO touched him on the shoulder. Both of his pistols were smoking, both were locked back and there were eight dead Demons in the compartment. One was right at his feet. It had been shot three times in the back.

"Hey, I'm pretty sure I got one," the COB said. "Two rounds in the side."

"Yeah, I think that's yours," the CO said. "The rest appear to be PFC Berg's here. You can put the guns down, now, son."

Berg automatically holstered the right, reloaded, holstered the left and reloaded the right.

"Compartment is clear of threat, sir," Sergeant Jaenisch reported. "Two-Gun, you okay?"

"Fine," Berg said, suddenly shaking his head. "What just happened?"

# 31

## Could Be Worse, Could Have Been Us

"*This* is unusual," the queen said, looking at the three armored suits. Weaver had explained to Miriam that with the report from the *Vorpal Blade*, she could get in her suit or she could stay in the barracks and he would try to explain what was happening through pantomime.

"Your Majesty," Weaver said. "We have a report of a Demon breakout that has attacked our ship. It has lifted to avoid further attack, but Lady Che-chee's manor is under assault. We intend to support her, but at this time we need to expect—"

There was a scream in the distance and the guards on the door of the audience room shifted stance.

"Commander Weaver, Marine One. Three-Charlie reports Demon breakout near the main entrance of the palace. They're coming up through a hole in the ground."

"Roger," Weaver said. Over his external pickups he could hear the fighting spreading. "Your Majesty, if there is a more secure spot . . ."

"Your Majesty!" General Chuk-tuk said, coming through the doors on a board. "You need to retreat! The Demons are here!"

"I will do no such thing," the queen said, rising to her full two meters of height. "Bring my armor!"

347

"No *time*, Your Majesty," Chuk-tuk said, just as one of the low-slung beasts came through the door.

"BACK!" Miller boomed, cycling his Gatling gun.

7.62 mm fire from the M-10s might have bounced off, but the laserlike fire from the Gatling gun spun the creature around and splashed it across the doors as mush.

Weaver cycled on his own and the two strode forward, covering the door as the ceremonial guards clustered around the throne.

"That was a small group," Miller said as they finished off the Demons. "Where are the rest? And where is this tunnel?"

"They zero in on electromagnetism," Miriam said. "Which means *we* were probably the targets. The only other source is the barracks and the science arboretum next to it."

"Uh, oh," Weaver said. "Marine One . . ."

"We're rather busy at the moment, Commander," Captain MacDonald said calmly. "The Demons seem rather bent on entering our quarters."

"They zero in on electromagnetism," Weaver said. "The suits are primary targets."

"Well, then you'd better get away, hadn't you?" MacDonald said.

"What about you?"

"Don't think that's an option at the moment . . ."

"Die *behanchods*!" Lance Corporal Clay said, plastering the hole with cannon fire.

The problem was, the Demons just kept coming. Already they'd broken through in two more places, digging around the initial hole. And there didn't seem to be any end to them. They were piled up around the holes like dead ants at a poisoned hive. When the hole got blocked they'd dig through their own dead or dig around.

"Poison," Clay said. "There's an idea. Next time, we need VX."

"Claymores," PFC Jonathan Smith said. "*Grapping* artillery."

"Air support," Staff Sergeant Rocco said. "*Grapp*. Gunny Hedger. Doesn't the ship have lasers?"

"Got one, Mother!" Cha-chai called, swooping up to avoid the bouncing Demons.

"Bloody good, Son!" Lady Che-chee called. The Demons had stopped coming out of the hole once the ship was gone, but quite a few remained on her lawn. "Time to refresh our weapons, boy!"

"Mother?" Cha-chai called as he swept past where the retainers were holding spears up for the warriors. "Why is the lawn *smoking*?"

Lady Che-chee was wondering that herself. It was a small patch and it looked as if a volcano had started on her lawn. More of those damned Demons?

"Wait," she said, holding up her hand as the smoking spot suddenly swept to the side, cutting one of the Demons in half. It appeared to pause again then, suddenly, all the Demons were severed, many of them into pieces.

"What just happened?" Cha-chai asked.

"I think we just saw a demonstration of our friends' weapons," Lady Che-chee said. She was impressed less by the power than the precision. There were narrow lines of burned grass across the entire lawn. And they were perfectly spaced.

"Right," the CO said, satisfaction in his voice. "Head for the palace."

"Dr. Beach, you need to get to the upper floors," Gunnery Sergeant Hedger said. "These things are digging up through the ground. They could break in here at any time."

"Very well," Dr. Beach said. The stairs were wide enough, and sturdy enough, for his armor. The Marines had made the climb. But it looked . . . difficult. "I'll just head up then, shall I?"

"If you please, sir," the gunny said.

"Digging up through the floors?" Dr. Beach said, putting his foot on the stair, gingerly. "That's interesting."

"Yes, sir," Gunny Hedger said. "If you could possibly hurry, sir."

"Digging . . . digging," Beach muttered, taking cautious steps. "Digging . . . *mining*!"

"Yes, sir, I suppose it could be called . . ."

"No!" Beach said. "That's it! The seismic readings! They were mining indicators!"

"Is this really important, because . . ."

The gunny had stayed down in the lab, to cover the scientist's retreat. So he saw the head of the Demon pop through the floor immediately.

"Dr. Beach, if you would please *run* now?"

"What?" Beach said, turning to look and sliding to the side. "Aaaaah!"

"*Maulk!*" Gunny Hedger snapped. "Dr. Beach!"

The Demons popped up through a half dozen holes and swarmed the scrabbling armor.

"It's important!" the scientist screamed. "Tell Runner! The readings! Aaaaagh!"

"*Grapp*," Hedger said, backing up the stairs and filling the room with lead. "We have breakthrough in the basement! Dr. Beach is KIA!"

". . . Demons have broken through in the basement," Captain MacDonald said. "They've also breached the lower doors. We've three KIA, including Dr. Beach."

"Hang on," Spectre said. "We'll be overhead in ninety seconds. We'll clear the courtyard then exit the building and we'll deal with the Demons in there."

"Roger, sir," MacDonald said. "I'm sure we can hold ninety seconds . . ."

"Oh, no, you don't!" Sergeant Samson said, firing down the stairs at the wave of Demons scrabbling up it. "You want some?"

The Gatling fire smashed the Demons to the side, spinning them to where their more vulnerable flank was exposed, then blasting them apart. But more and more were pouring up the stairs, climbing over the bodies of their dead.

"There's too many of them!" Tanner screamed, pumping grenades into the room. When they hit a Demon dead center they'd kill it, but the light fragments barely slowed them down. Some of the Demons had guts hanging down but they just kept coming.

"We can hold them, Marine!" Samson screamed. "Just hold your position! We can—"

"Sergeant!" Revells screamed as the rock floor under the sergeant's armor gave way, Demon claws scrabbling at it.

"Aaah!" Samson said, dropping into the hole. "*Behanch—*"

"Sergeant!" Tanner yelled, firing grenades down into the hole.

But the fire taken away from the Demons on the stairway let them charge up and Tanner was covered in a wave of bodies.

"Gunny! Second level's down!" Revells yelled, backing towards the stairs. "I need cover!"

"*Grapp*," Gunny Hedger said. "Alpha, cover Revells' retreat." He paused for a second then nodded. "Bartlett?"

"Here, Gunny," the master sergeant said. He was covering Dr. Robertson, who wasn't even in armor for *grapp*'s sake, on the top level.

"Dr. Beach said something," Hedger said. "About readings. He said Runner would know what he meant. Something about mining and readings. That's all I got. He thought it was important enough, it was his last words."

"Not 'oh, *maulk*' or '*grapp* me'?" Bartlett said. "I've got it. I'll try to retrans it to the ship. Because it don't look like I'm going to be telling him in person."

"We'll hold 'em," Hedger said. "We've got the stairway covered and . . . Aaaaah!"

"Dr. Robertson, did you get that?" Bartlett asked.

"Yes, I did," the biologist said. "And, no, I don't know what it means."

"All teams," Lieutenant Mark Van Groll said calmly. "They're coming up through the floors. Second level is—" The platoon leader of Third Platoon was cut off in mid-sentence.

"*Grapp, grapp, grapp!*"

The Marines were boiling up the stairs and taking positions around the room.

"They're tearing through the floor!" Revells yelled. "They're—" The stone floor under him erupted and he dropped into the hole, screaming and firing his Gatling at the monsters that were tearing at his armor.

Captain MacDonald looked out the window at the courtyard. No joy, there; it was covered in Demons. As he watched, a beetle-like head erupted, looked around, then most of the courtyard punched up as the massive beast surfaced.

There was, however, a roof below. It wouldn't hold the Wyverns, but . . .

"Dr. Robertson," the captain said, holding out a hand. "How well do you jump?"

Clay felt the ground under him give way and he shook his head.

"This is a *grapped*-up place to die."

"No *maulk*, man," PFC Smith said, turning to present his back.

The two went back to back and as they dropped they stayed together, arms locked. The Gatlings didn't need arm controls, being controlled by eye movements.

The Demons had stacked on top of each other to tear at the floor and the two descending Wyverns knocked the pyramid over. The Demons just scrambled back up and started tearing but the two Gatlings tore into them, ripping them to shreds. The two suits of armor were still against a wall and for a moment they held the horde off.

Then one of the ripped Demons pulled itself forward, its guts trailing on the floor, and ripped up into Clay's armor.

"Sir, if I may," Top said.

"Go for it," the CO said.

"Join arms if you will, sir," Top said. "Bartlett! Roberts! Marines! Circle up, face out!"

The Demons were coming up the stairs as well and when Staff Sergeant Rocco tried to retreat from the door they swarmed him.

"Concentrate fire on that, please," Top said, even though he was facing the other direction. "Right, now, *hop!*"

Two hops was all it took and the overstressed floor gave way.

There were Demons waiting on the level below, but when two tons of rock and fourteen tons of Wyvern dropped on them, they weren't doing much fighting.

The group not only fell through that level but the one below and, floor by floor, into the basement.

"Right," Top said, clambering out of the rubble. "Down the hole."

There was still a trickle of Demons coming out of the hole, but most of them seemed to have been in the upper floors. Quite a few of those had fallen with the group, but they were in a daze from the rocks and fall, those that weren't killed by it, and the group finished them off, then darted to the hole.

"Top, this is where they're coming from," the CO pointed out.

"And there is a rather large one in the courtyard, sir," the first sergeant said. "But we will fight our way to the courtyard, then hunker down. How long until the ship gets here?"

"Mac, you still there?"

"Some of us, sir," the captain said.

"We're on sight. Clearing the courtyard . . . now."

"We're going out of commo," MacDonald said. "But we'll be back in a moment."

"Bailey, Holland, you have point," Top said.

"Roger that, Top," Corporal Chris Bailey gestured for his rifleman then got down on elbows and knees. "Let's go, Holley."

"This really sucks," PFC Holland said, squeezing into the narrow tunnel next to his team leader. Immediately, he saw a Demon headed for them and bit down on his fire circuit, blowing it to pieces. They were big pieces, though. "How we getting through *that*?"

"More power," Bailey said, firing his Gatling and ripping up the Demon even more. "Now we push."

"Bartlett, Roberts, you've got back door," Captain MacDonald said.

"Roger that, sir," Bartlett said. "You first, Garrett."

"No arguments," the staff sergeant said, backing into the hole.

A Demon dropped from the upper floors and Bartlett blew it against the wall, then started backing into the tunnel.

As he did, a rock rolled aside and a Demon reached out with one claw, ripping into the back of his Wyvern, severing his ammo feed and piercing the back of his armor.

"*Grapp*," Bartlett said. "Gun's down and I've lost containment." He turned his head and *saw* the claw ripping into his armor.

Another and another dropped from the still uncleared upper floors. The two Demons approached the trapped SF master sergeant cautiously, but he couldn't fire.

"Right," Bartlett said. "Gary, you well back?"

"What are you going to do, Ed?" the staff sergeant asked.

"Just get the *grapp* out of here," Bartlett said. "I'm going to close this *grapping* hole. Get *way* the *grapp* back."

» » »

"Top Sergeant, we gotta move!"

"We're moving as fast as we can," First Sergeant Powell said. "Why do we have to move faster?"

"Because this place is about to blow!"

Smart people in the military are a joy and a pain. The problem is that military life creates a great degree of boredom. And smart people try to find ways to become unbored. Certain types of smart people play practical jokes. Others act up. Still others, though, tinker.

Master Sergeant Ed Bartlett was a tinkerer. So when he'd gotten a Mark V Wyvern, he had tried to discover *everything* that a Wyvern should and should not do.

One of the things he discovered, and told no one else, was that under certain very precise conditions, the americium reactor on the Wyvern could be forced to do things other than engage in controlled reaction. It was a very "hot" reactor, the radioactive material very pure and very finely packed. It was, in fact, right on the edge of being a nuclear bomb, rather than a nuclear reactor.

And in certain circumstances it could be forced to change its mind.

The term is "sub-critical reaction." The bomb was below the yield of any weapon in the nuclear inventory. Only a very little bit of the americium could be forced to enter unrestricted chain reaction. But a very little bit of nuclear explosion is a lot of explosion.

"Whoa!" the XO said as the converted barracks blossomed up and outwards. "What the *grapp* caused that?"

"Command, Tactical. We just got a nuclear spike from the location of the palace."

"I'm pretty sure we didn't issue any special munitions down there," the CO said. "We didn't issue any special munitions, right?"

"I'm sure we would have noticed, sir," the XO said.

"Mac, you there?" the CO said. "Talk to me, Mac."

"Sort of!" Captain MacDonald said.

The narrow tunnel had blossomed out into some seriously

*un*narrow tunnels. And the big beetle that *had* been in the courtyard had reoccupied them when it felt its armor getting singed by lasers.

Now the Marines surrounded it, pouring fire into the thing. Which its armor was shrugging off.

"Aaah!" Corporal Bailey screamed as one of the thing's claws caught him and flung him across the thirty meter wide room. He slammed into the wall and slid to the ground, his armor limp.

"Check fire!" Top shouted. "Holland! Wave at it!"

The Marine lifted both his hands and cut in his external circuit.

"Yo! Ugly! Over here!"

The massive beetle spun in place and considered the Marine for just a moment.

That was all the time that Top needed. He dropped to his wheels and slid under the beetle's rump, then pointed his Gatling upwards and opened fire.

The beetle jumped up at least ten feet, then landed, spinning again, stamping inward to try to kill its tormentor.

But the first sergeant wasn't having any of that. He stood up abruptly and jumped himself, bringing the Gatling down as he entered the blown-open cavity and grabbed the sides.

He swept the inside of the beast until he felt its knees buckle and drop. At that point he was trapped *inside* the beast but he had pretty good spatial awareness.

"Top!" Holland screamed. "Top! Are you okay?"

"Just peachy, Holland," the first sergeant said, blasting out the mouthparts of the beetle and crawling out. "Kind of a strange day, I'll admit. You?"

"How are we going to get them out of there?" the XO asked.

"Hmmm . . ." the CO said. "We still got that hole in the bottom of the ship or have we patched it, yet?"

"There's a team getting ready to put a patch on now, sir," the XO said.

"Tell 'em to hold up."

"Yeah, Top, I think I'd call this a strange day," Holland said as he tied the fast-rope around his Wyvern.

"Welcome to the Space Marines," Top said, holding out his arms.

"Everyone in place?" Captain MacDonald asked. "Right. *Vorpal Blade*, you can lift at any time."

The remaining Marines and one SF staff sergeant lifted off the beetle's shell and upwards into the light, dangling from the bottom of the ship.

"We lost a lot of people," Holland said, looking back at the smoking hole where the barracks used to be.

"Could be worse," Top said as they STABOed eastwards. "Could have been us."

# 32

## Is This a Good Time to Panic?

"Okay, we're out of here," the CO said as soon as Weaver entered the compartment. "These things track in on electromagnetism. We're just a big attraction to them. Wherever we go, they'll follow."

One by one the groups had been picked up as the *Vorpal Blade* scoured the area of surfaced Demons. Weaver, Miller and Miss Moon had been plucked out of a running gunfight; Dr. Robertson had been pulled off the roof of a building. The ship had then lifted to hover at ten thousand feet while the meeting took place. The agenda was obvious. Everybody living was aboard and it was time to leave.

"Sir," the XO said uncomfortably. "I agree that we need to leave. However, we've got major damage throughout the ship. We're not exactly air-worthy at the moment."

"Then the Marines go in their bunks and we run like hell," the CO said.

"Very well, sir," the XO replied, nodding. "It's only about eighteen hours to Earth. But we're definitely not *sea*worthy. We're going to have to land out at Dreamland."

"Sir, if you'll give me a moment," Dr. Robertson said.

"Doctor, I appreciate your input—"

"This may be important," the biologist said. "Runner?"

357

"Sir, I think everyone has noticed this hill," he said, keying up a map of the local area.

"Yes, Master Sergeant," Spectre said, holding onto his patience.

"I believe it is the source of the Demons," the master sergeant said. "At least locally."

"Say again," the CO said.

"We were picking up odd seismic activity, sir," Runner said, walking to the computer screen. "It was coming from the direction of this hill. The hill looks like a basolith, a granitic extrusion. But it has no secondary indicators of being one. There should be more granite around and there's not. Then we were getting those seismic readings, moving towards us and the city. I couldn't figure out what they were. Dr. Beach did, just before he died."

"Tunneling," Weaver said.

"Yes, sir," Runner said, shaking his head. "It sounded sort of like mining, but not exactly, so I didn't pick it up. But it was these *things* heading for us and the city."

"They started coming out because of the electrical experiments the Cheerick scientists were conducting," Miss Moon said. "When we got here it just moved up the date of the first attack."

"Why are they attacking electricity?" the XO said. "And why not one of those boards?"

"Unknown, sir," Weaver said, leaning forward and looking at the screen. "Captain, we're beat up and need repairs. If we can stop these things, at the source, we can get those repairs, here, *and* save these people."

"Commander Weaver, we've got, what? Ten marines left?" the CO said, exasperated. "And you want to send a forlorn hope?"

"No, sir, I want to *lead* a forlorn hope," Weaver said. "I want to know what is under that mountain. And I want to have a culture to come back to. The boards take the weight of armor. We can drop from right here and take out that facility. Enter one of the tunnels, put an ardune warhead in it and that's all she wrote."

"You want a special weapon," the CO said wonderingly.

"I was thinking one of the torps, sir," Bill said. "Actually, I was thinking two; one for backup. There's a way to adjust them to be selective yield. We can do this, sir. Now that we know the source of the Demons."

"Captain, Tactical. We've got some boards coming up from the ground."

"I don't know why we're even talking about this," the CO said.

"We've got eighteen Marines shooters, sir," MacDonald said, turning back from a quiet conversation with the first sergeant. "We are, of course, at your disposal."

"You *want* to do this, Mac?" the CO asked in disbelief.

"Payback, sir," MacDonald said, stone-faced. "I left a bunch of good boys down there. Lost more up here while I was running for my life. Hell *yes* I want to take them out, sir."

"Nuke it from orbit," the XO said. "Only way to be sure."

"Granite's tough stuff, sir," Runner said. "It would take a full-yield ardune system to be sure of cracking it. Probably why it's *made* of granite. Take it out and you're pretty much going to take out the city."

"And if we pop one inside?" the CO asked.

"The granite's going to absorb most of it," Bill said. "Trust me on this, I've done nuclear design. Granite that big, less than fifty kilotons? It's going to shatter it and *maybe* toss some around. Not much. And ardune's pretty clean stuff. Not even much fall-out."

"Captain, sorry, Tactical again," Lieutenant Souza said, nervously. "It's Lady Che-chee, the queen and some of her guards. They're getting pretty close."

"Tell the COB to get a party up on the sail hatch," the CO said. "I'll receive her there."

"Okay, okay," he continued, looking at the group. "If you really want to do this, Mac, you can do this. But you need to leave *soon*. Get every clerk and jerk in armor. We don't have enough boards, though."

"Some arriving, sir," Bill said. "And I suspect they're going to be willing to loan us some . . ."

"This is a bold plan, Captain Blankemeier," the queen said.

Most of her party was clearly overwhelmed by the ship. But the queen along with Lady Che-chee and General Chuk-tuk just as clearly refused to appear surprised. The queen had allowed the captain to escort her to the wardroom, disdained the apologies for the conditions and then listened, carefully, to the translation of the plan. Actually, it couldn't really be called a plan. The synopsis. The outline. The guess.

"Can you not leave?" the queen asked.

"Our ship has sustained damage," Spectre admitted. "We could run home, possibly, but we'd rather repair damage first and . . ."

"And . . . ?" Miriam asked.

"Just translate it as closely as possible," the CO said.

"And you don't care to run away with your tail down," the queen said, her nose pulling back.

"That too," the CO admitted.

"Why do you tell me?" the queen asked.

"First of all, the weapon we are going to use is going to do damage beyond the mountain," the CO said. "We could strike the mountain from space and remove the threat entirely and with no danger. But that would destroy your capital as well."

"You have weapons that powerful?" General Chuk-tuk asked. "And yet you fight on the ground."

"Different needs, sir," Commander Weaver said.

"Yes, we do," the CO said. "But by putting it *in* the mountain, it will do less damage. Less, not none."

"I see," the queen said, nodding. "The Demons will wipe us out entirely. Do it."

"Yes, ma'am," the CO said. "We also need three or four more boards. We're going to drop all our remaining Marines from up here."

"You have them," the queen said. "I will lead this force."

"No you will not," General Chuk-tuk said. "You will remain safe on this ship. *I* am your war-leader. *I* can be lost. You cannot. Your Daughter is still a Breeder—"

"I am your queen—"

"Ma'am," Weaver cut in. "The general's right, you're not. Don't go gettin' your fur in a fluff. And, General, with all due respect, I think you should send Lady Che-chee. She's younger, fitter and less important than you while still being of high enough station that you have participation."

"Are you sure you want me to translate that?" Miriam said.

"What did he say?" the queen squeaked imperiously.

"You won't like it," Miriam said, then translated.

The queen flicked her ears indignantly as General Chuk-tuk smoothed her whiskers in satisfaction, then squeaked in laughter when the general's nose went back in a snarl.

"Yes," the queen said, still squeaking in laughter. "The commander has it. Lady Che-chee, do you accept this quest?"

"With delight, Your Majesty," the Lady said. "But we must make haste. The Demons seem to have retreated for now, but they will be back."

"Agreed," the CO said. "My Marines are suiting up now. Commander Weaver, defer most tactical decisions to Captain MacDonald. I hope we all agree that the ground commander is Commander Weaver?"

"Agreed," Lady Che-chee said. "Your Majesty, could I take a contingent of guards?"

"Ten," General Chuk-tuk said. "No more."

"Problem," Miriam said. "I can't be in two places at once. None of the Cheerick, that I'm aware of, speak English. Someone is going to have to translate on the boat and someone is going to have to translate on the ground."

"We try Ekish," the queen squeaked. "Ko fit."

"Miss Moon is not a fighter," Commander Weaver pointed out.

"Is fit," the queen squeaked. "Ko."

"Miss Moon?" the CO asked.

"I think I have to go with the ground force," Miriam said, standing up. "I'll meet you in ten minutes in the Wyvern bay."

"I think she's going to go panic," Miller said as she left the room.

"I think *I'm* going to panic," Weaver said.

# 33

## We Got Bandits!

"Keep the links straight!" Berg said. "If there's a kink, the gun will jam."

"Got it," Sub Dude said, straightening out the chain of rounds. "Have fun."

"This is *not* my definition of fun," Berg said, resetting his gun controls. On the last test they had been running about a degree off parallax. Most of this was probably going to be short-ranged, but . . .

"Holy *maulk*," Hatt said quietly.

"What?" Berg said, looking around. His eyes went wide, though, at the sight.

It was hard to describe, even to himself, but Miss Moon had changed. Something in the walk, the face. Subtle but impossible to miss. She strode across the compartment, ignoring the looks and the sudden cessation of movement and walked up to Berg.

"Two-Gun," she said, looking up at the towering PFC. "My Wyvern needs a gun. And I need someone to carry it."

"Yes, ma'am," Berg said, popping to attention. All the "mission specialists" rated officer rank, but nobody really treated them that way. Until now. "I'll be right back."

When he got back, Marines were falling all over themselves to ready the linguist's Wyvern. Two were loading ammo, another was checking the traversing mechanism, a fourth was doing a check of the circuitry. Miriam was standing watching the activity with her hands behind her back.

Berg mounted the Gatling, nodded at her, then returned to his own system.

He hadn't noticed Lurch follow him back from the armory but as he started to enter his Wyvern, the armorer walked up with two pistols in his hands.

"You forgot your real guns, Two-Gun," Lurch said, holding them out.

"Gatlings have done it so far, Lyle," Berg said.

"Take the guns, Two-Gun," Top said, walking up. "I'll mount them."

"If you say so, First Sergeant," Berg said, getting out. "I'll mount them. Lyle, I need my reloads."

"We've done some dumbass things in our time, buddy," Miller said, settling his Gatling in position. "But this about takes the cake."

"I dunno," Weaver said. "I sort of thought almost blowing Earth off the map was worse than this."

"I said dumbass," Miller replied, checking the traverse mechanism and running the feed into place.

"It's not *that* bad," Weaver said. "They're not attacking right now. The tunnel could be clear. Besides, Runner found an entrance not far from the mountain. Couple of hundred meters and we're in."

"These things tunnel like there's no tomorrow," Miller pointed out. "Which means they're going to be coming out of the walls."

"You're such a pessimist," Bill said, grinning and pulling himself into his Wyvern. "What, you want to live forever?"

"Absolutely," Miller said, lifting himself into place. "Got a problem with that?"

"No," Weaver admitted. "But I also know how much you love derring-do."

"God," Miller muttered as he closed his suit. "I could be doing flower arrangements right now."

"Surf's up, people!" Top yelled, standing at the edge of the open air lock.

The elevator could be moved up and out of the way and it had been. The Marines were about to drop through the resultant hole.

"I cannot *grapping* believe we're doing this," Hatt said.

"What?" Berg asked. "Preparing to assault a mountain full of monsters that just wiped out half our company? Or getting ready to drop from nearly orbit on golden antigravity surfboards?"

"Yes!"

"Marines, this is the CO. Get this one done and we're home free. Two days and we're back in the World. Good luck and Semper Fi."

"Oorah!" the first sergeant shouted. "On the Bounce, Marines!"

His board lifted up and he dropped into the rushing wind.

"Go!" Captain MacDonald shouted. "Go! Go!"

"What the hell is 'On the Bounce'?" Hatt asked.

"Oh. My. God," Berg answered, grinning inside his suit.

"Top read that book, too?" Jaen said. "Cool."

"What book?" Hatt snapped. "What the hell?"

"Just shut up and drop, Marine," Jaen said. "On the Bounce!"

"What the hell is that?" the tactical tech asked.

"What you got?" the tactical NCOIC said.

"Neutrinos," the tech answered. "Lots of them. From the southeast about two hundred klicks. Wait . . ."

"Boards," the NCOIC said, easily. "I've got the contact on radar."

"But those are *big* signatures," the tech pointed out. "And the neutrino count is way higher than that many boards."

"Going visual," the NCOIC said, punching controls for one of the tactical scopes. "And . . . zooming."

"What?" the tech said, looking over at the NCOIC who was frozen at the scope.

"Conn! Tactical! We got bandits at ten o'clock!"

"Ooo-RAH!" Berg shouted, the nose of the golden surfboard pointed at the ground.

The surface must have generated some sort of sticky field. He'd started out fighting the thing but as the first sergeant nosed over and hammered it towards the ground, he had to follow.

He wasn't sure if the thing was reading subtle clues from the armor or if it was actually reading his mind. But it was one *hell* of a ride. He could see the hole below, like a dark eye in the middle of a plowed field. He also noted that it was blazing with apparently random particles. Those Demon things might be biological but they had some sort of high tech basis.

"Next time," Hatt said, passing him and giving him a thumbs up, "we drop from *orbit*!"

"Oorah!" Berg shouted, again, speeding up to catch up to the cannoneer. "Last one to the LZ buys the first beer when we get back!"

"You're on, Rookie!"

"What in the hell are those?" the CO said, looking at the scope. "Are those . . . dragonflies?"

The species had a superficial resemblance. They had long, vaguely torpedo shaped bodies, four long wings and compound eyes. They were also brightly colored, mostly blue with flashes of red, especially on the eyes.

"I don't know, sir," the XO admitted. "But everything around here but the Cheerick has been pretty unfriendly."

"The hell with this," the CO said. "Tactical. Lase them."

"Laser locked," the weapons operator said.

"Fire," Souza replied.

The front rank of the oncoming hoard of dragonflies blazed bright orange at the laser fire but kept coming.

"Did I just see what I think I saw?" he said.

"Was that some sort of *shield*?" the XO replied.

"Pilot, back us up into space," the CO said. "XO—"

"ALL HANDS! ALL HANDS! GENERAL QUARTERS! PREPARE FOR DEPRESSURIZATION! MAN GENERAL QUARTERS STATIONS!"

As he said that the group blazed red and beams of energy began slamming into the ship.

"Pilot!" the CO yelled.

"Heading for orbit now, sir!" the pilot said.

"She backs up as fast as she goes forward," the CO said. "Keep the lasers on target! Tactical, as soon as we're out of atmosphere, hit those things with an ardune torp!"

» » »

"Marines," MacDonald said. "The ship is under attack. Hopefully, we can stop that by taking out this mountain. The importance of what we're doing just went up."

"*Maulk*," Berg said. The ground was coming up, fast, so he flared out, taking the gees with his knees, and settled next to the large hole.

It had probably been made by one of the beetles, but if so the beast was nowhere in sight.

"Okay, Marines," Captain MacDonald said. "By the numbers. Two-Charlie . . ."

"Sir," Gunny Frandsen said. "We're getting low on privates. Why don't I take point?"

"Lead on, Gunny," the CO said. "Everyone stay off the radio as much as possible. It's liable to attract these things."

Frandsen dropped into the hole, followed by Berg, Hattelstad and Jaenisch. They stayed on their boards since the drop was over thirty meters.

"Keep your eyes and ears open," the gunny growled, looking around. There were several tunnels branching off from the hole, but only two big enough for one of the beetles. One was headed towards the city so . . .

"Heading left," Gunny Frandsen said.

The tunnel bent almost immediately, then dropped sharply downward. Gunny Frandsen slid down the slope carefully and negotiated another bend as it bottomed out. The tunnel twisted like it had been made by a snake. Just around the corner the gunny stopped at the sight of one of the smaller Demons. It was lying on the ground, its head propped on crossed forearms, and appeared to be asleep.

The gunny reached down and pulled out a bush-axe. He'd carried one ever since he was a teenager doing survey work in the arctic.

Sneaking was not impossible in a Wyvern when the floor was reasonably flat. And this one had, clearly, been flattened by the feet of quite a few Demons. It was even easier on the boards.

The gunny silently slid forward until he was looming over the Demon, then slashed downward, severing its spine.

He levered the big axe out, wiped it on the Demon, tracked right and left with his Gatling then waved the team forward.

» » »

"Sir, the hull is overheating," the XO said. "We're up to a thousand degrees on the rear edges."

"And they are gaining on us," the CO pointed out. "We'll chill as soon as we can. Right now, we're fighting for our lives."

As the ship left the atmosphere, it could speed up. But, apparently, so could the dragonflies. Their wings had retracted and now projected as thin canards, tilted up and down and glowing faintly blue. And the laser fire hadn't reduced. The sonar-dome was melted through and the forward torpedo room had had to be evacuated, the torps jettisoned before they exploded.

"What's the atmosphere outside like?" the CO asked.

"Less than one tenth of a percent, sir," Lieutenant Souza answered. "We should be able to survive a short-ranged hit."

The problem was that the dragonflies had closed to within fifty klicks. The ship probably could survive an ardune strike that close, but they'd taken enough damage.

"Fire ardune torp into the center of their formation," the CO said. "Evasion course Charlie."

"We'll have to turn," Lieutenant Souza said. "Otherwise the torp's liable to slam into us."

"Pilot, prepare for skew turn," the CO said. "Rear torpedoes ready?"

"Ardune torp up on four," Lieutenant Souza replied.

"Prepare to fire on four," the CO said. "Pilot, skew turn!"

The ship pivoted in space, continuing in the same direction but briefly presenting its rear to the oncoming dragonflies.

"Fire!" the CO shouted as the torpedo came to bear.

The skew had thrown off the fire of the dragonflies so the torpedo made it out of the tubes and, following its programming, went "up" from the ship and then forward towards the enemy.

"Fire lasers when they bear!" the CO said.

The laser to laser battle began again. By bearing on just one of the dragonflies with both lasers they'd found they could burn through its shields after a few minutes of continuous fire. Doing that, they'd dropped a few. But there were over fifty in the swarm and while their lasers were not particularly powerful, *they* concentrated, too.

"Forward torpedo room breached!" the XO said.

"Good thing we launched all the torps," the CO said. "Or we'd be in a right pickle about now."

At that moment the torpedo dropped into the midst of the enemy formation and detonated in a flash that shut down all the visual systems.

"All *right!*" Spectre shouted. "Eat quarkium you dragonfly bastards!"

"Wait," the XO said, then let out a sigh. The area of effect of the warhead had been enough. Nuclear weapons don't propagate in space the same way that they do in atmosphere. In atmosphere, besides the immediate blast area effect there are various effects from atmosphere. The blast gets propagated by compression waves, destroying far beyond the "totally destroyed" area of the actual blast.

In space, there was no way to do damage much beyond where the blast spread. But in this case, the dragonfly formation had been entirely in the blast zone. None of the dragonflies came out the other side.

"Tactical, what do you have on the scope?" the CO asked.

"We had to shut the radars down, sir," Lieutenant Souza said. "Otherwise we would have lost them to EMP. We're coming back up, now."

"I don't see anything," the XO said, looking at the visual scope. It had only shut down temporarily, to prevent "blinding" the CCD camera.

"Come on, Tactical," Spectre said impatiently.

"Coming up now, sir," Lieutenant Souza said. "Stand by . . ."

"Nothing there," the NCOIC said. "Spread the scan."

"Opening up on spread scan," the tech said, then gulped.

"Oh, *maulk*," the NCOIC said.

"Conn, Tactical."

"Go."

"We have five . . . six . . . increasing groups of bandits approaching. They're coming from all over the world, sir."

"How far?" Spectre asked.

"Nearest is about two hundred klicks, sir, approaching from zero-one-eight mark minus five."

"Pilot," Spectre said. "Get this tub out to warp point. Then punch it for 60 AU from the sun. We've got to chill."

"Aye, aye, sir," the pilot said, backing away from the planet.

"The Marines are on their own," the CO said, shrugging. "Let's hope they can figure out a way for us to come back. If not, we'll be back some day."

"Yes, sir," the XO said.

"Damn this planet."

"Conn, Tactical."

"Go."

"I've been doing some computations, sir," Lieutenant Souza said. "We're deep inside the grav well of this Jovian. I don't think we're going to reach warp before we're swarmed."

"Lieutenant, you've got two torp tubes and four SM-9s at your disposal," the CO said. "Do something about that."

# 34

## Beachhead

Berg passed four kills for Gunny Frandsen before the latter's luck ran out.

The tunnel had descended deep into the earth, the walls changing from stabilized earth to limestone, then back upwards. As they abruptly changed to granite and he negotiated another of the snaking turns, Frandsen stopped and then started to backpedal.

"Dra—" he shouted over the team net. Then a head snaked around the corner and snatched the armor off the board. With a crunch that echoed through the tunnel, the gunny's armor crumpled like a beer can under a foot and splashed bright red.

The head of the dragon was twice the size of a suit of armor and armored itself with heavy overlapping plates. The head was bright red, shading backwards through purple to a blue body with red highlights on shoulders and hips.

That was about all that Berg noticed as he opened fire with his Gatlings. But as he had halfway come to expect, the rounds bounced off the bullet head of the thing, which slithered forward fast and low, snatching Sergeant Jaenisch off his board and crunching again.

"JAEN!" Berg shouted, his hands dropping to his hips. "Hatt! Back, back!"

"*Grapp* you!" Hatt shouted, backing slowly as he pumped grenades at the thing. The explosions were damaging some of the plates on the thing's head, but they weren't penetrating. Whether Hatt was cursing Berg's suggestion or the dragon wasn't clear since he was the next to go. The dragon snapped him off the board then hammered him back and forth on the granite walls.

Berg fired three of the .50 caliber rounds in various spots, juncture of the neck and shoulder, throat, leg. All three sparked off the refractory armor of the beast.

Then it was his turn as the beast charged down the granite tunnel. Its maw opened and for a moment all he saw was teeth and tonsils. Then he opened fire with all three guns.

The thing was *fast*. It was on him before he could trigger more than two rounds from each pistol, but he was biting down on his fire clamp at the same time and looking right down the thing's throat.

The 7.62 mm rounds chewed into the back of the beast's mouth, ripping the soft flesh but not stopping it; the thick bone on that portion of the head caused them to do no more than embed in flesh. It was hurt but nothing the Gatling could do was going to kill it.

The .50 caliber rounds, however, punched through the bone. One buried itself in still more bone in the thick skull of the beast. Another ricocheted down and out, punching a hole in the bottom of the monster's mouth. The third ricocheted down its throat, lodging deep in the neck of the beast in a spot that would, eventually, kill it.

The fourth, however, punched through a thick ridge of bone, then struck the beast's backbone, cracking a vertebra and severing its spinal cord.

The dragon dropped ten feet from Berg, its mouth still thrashing open and closed and its body thrashing. But it had no voluntary control over its limbs, which rattled in convulsions, shaking the refractory walls of the tunnel and causing rocks to drop from the ceiling.

"*Grapp* me," Berg muttered, sliding forward on his board and emptying his pistols into the thing's head. He stayed up near the ceiling, avoiding the clashing teeth, until it finally gave a shudder and died.

"We're blown," Captain MacDonald said. "Move up the pace. Alpha Team, point."

"*Grapp, grapp, grapp,*" Berg muttered, reloading.

"Are you sure it's dead?" PFC Wangen asked as he flew past. As he said it, the thing convulsed again, shaking down more rock.

"It's as dead as I can make it," Two-Gun said, jacking a round into the chamber of the converted rifle.

"Two-Gun," Top said. "Close up behind Bravo Team."

"Aye-aye, Top," Berg said tiredly. He didn't look at the bodies of Hatt and Jaen as he passed. The Marines made a big thing of leaving no wounded or dead behind. But there were times when it just wasn't feasible to try. Maybe, if any of them survived, they could pick up Hatt and Jaen. If they could get the armor cut off.

If any of them survived this *grapping* madhouse.

"Contact!" Staff Sergeant Sutherland shouted.

"We're up to nineteen contacts," the Tac NCOIC said.

"Fine," Lieutenant Souza said, tapping at his computer.

"Closure rate is forty kkps on the nearest. Ten minutes until we are in range of their lasers."

"I can see that," Lieutenant Souza said. "Just keep an eye out for new tracks. I'll send over the fire spread as soon as I'm done with it."

"Yes, sir," the chief petty officer said.

The smaller Demons fell in windrows to the fire of the Gatlings as the Marines pressed forward. Alpha Team had formed a stack with the two Gatling gunners low and the grenadier high. Any of the Demons who survived their assault were being picked off by Bravo.

But there was one problem.

"I'm clocking out!" Wangen screamed.

"Bravo, move forward," Lieutenant Berisford said. "Alpha, prepare to pass Bravo forward."

"Aye, aye, sir," Sutherland said. "Wanker, split right and *lift* . . ."

The two lower boards separated and lifted, maintaining fire, as Bravo Team came in low and under them and took over fire.

"Sir, there's light up ahead," Staff Sergeant Sutherland reported. "And increased particle emissions, mostly mesons."

"Roger," Lieutenant West said. The platoon leader was just

about the last officer left in the company except for the CO. "Commander Weaver? We've got meson emissions ahead."

"Could mean anything," Weaver said. "Let's see what's up there."

"Demons are discontinuing assault, moving forward," Staff Sergeant Sutherland said, then gasped. "Sir . . . I'm not sure how to evaluate this."

"This is my suggestion on spread, sir," Lieutenant Souza said, shooting the plan over to the CO's station. "It should take out the closest seven groups. But after that, we're out of ammo. And the trailing four, unless one closes on the bursts, are going to catch us short of warp point."

"Best we can do, Lieutenant," the CO said calmly. "We'll try to hold them off with the lasers until we can escape."

"Yes, sir," Souza said, knowing full well that was pissing in the wind.

"You have control over missile weapons systems," the CO said, reaching over and inserting his key. One turn was all it took to open up the long-range missiles.

"Very well, sir," Souza said. "Load all torpedo tubes. . . ."

The cavern was high and round, looking very much like a natural bubble in the rock. It also appeared to be a dead-end. And its contents were anything but natural.

"Is that Dreen fungus?" Weaver asked, looking at the round patch of mossy substance that seemed to be rippling as if from some unseen wind. It was located on the east wall of the chamber, about twenty feet across and flanked by strange protuberances that looked something like fungi.

"Wrong color," Chief Miller said, flicking on his white-light flash. The chief had outfitted himself not only with a Gatling, but with one of the remaining .50 caliber rifles. "I think it's got to be some sort of door. All the Demons we passed couldn't have come out of this chamber."

"Yeah," Weaver said. "But how do we open it?"

"Why open it?" Miller asked. "Set the damned munitions here and blow the chamber. That should stop the Demons."

"I know how to open it," Miriam said, sliding forward on her board. "And we need to."

"Why?" Miller asked.

"Because we have to know where the door goes," Miriam said cryptically, then squeaked on the external speakers.

Lady Che-chee slid forward on her own board and looked at the strange material. She squeaked at Miriam, who gestured forward.

Lifting slightly, the Lady flew over the Marines deployed in front of the moss and hovered between two of the protuberances, right at arm's length. She took off her gauntlets and, reaching out, placed one palm on each of the fungi.

The moss began rippling harder, then drew back, revealing . . .

"It's a *grapping* gate," Miller whispered. "*Grapp* me."

. . . a Looking Glass.

"So we pop the damned bomb *through* the gate then get the hell out," Miller said. "That gives us two weeks to get something better done." The ardune weapon would destabilize the gate for at least that long.

"The ship was under attack by aerial forces," Weaver said. "They didn't come from this facility. This is just a gateway to the local area. What's through there is the link to other areas, most likely."

"Then we toss *both* bombs through the gate," Miller said. "Full yield. Since it's not local, I don't give a *maulk what* it destroys."

"No," Weaver said, looking at the gate. "We need to find out where the Demons are coming from. You don't get it. The Cheerick was the key to opening the gate."

"How do we know?" Miller asked. "We didn't have one of the Marines try."

"Because Cheerick *arms* are shorter," Miriam said. "The distance is right for a Cheerick Mother. This facility, these Demons, they have something to do with the *Cheerick*."

"Look," Miller said. "You're the boss. We're going to go wherever you say. But I guarantee the other side of that gate is a world of hurt."

"It might also be the key to saving the ship," Weaver said. "And this world. Captain MacDonald."

"Done with your council, sir?" the Marine asked.

"We're going through the gate," Weaver said. "Send one man

through. Have him report back if the immediate other side is survivable . . ."

"Two-Gun."

"Yes, Top?" Berg said, both pistols and his Gatling pointed at the Looking Glass.

"You get the honor of finding out what is on the other side of that gate," the first sergeant said. "Your job is to enter, determine immediate threat level, then open up a beachhead for follow-on. Do you understand your mission?"

"Clear, Top," Berg said.

"Stand by . . . Aye, aye. Two-Gun. Take that beach."

"Oorah!" Berg shouted, hefting both pistols and charging the gate at a run. "SEMPER FI!"

# 35

## Stand My Ground

*Stand my ground, I won't give in*
*no more denying, I've got to face it*
*won't close my eyes and hide the truth inside*
*if I don't make it, someone else will*
*stand my ground.*

"Stand My Ground"
Within Temptation

"Third group, down," the Tac NCOIC said. "Fourth group . . .
They're scattering, sir."

"Let them scatter," Souza said as the SM-9 detonated. The
explosion was far enough away that the screens didn't blank. This
deep in space there was limited EMP from the explosion so the
radars didn't even cycle down.

"That got most of them," the Tac tech said. "Nine of the fifty still
functional. No, two of those are banking off and heading back."

"Vampire Five detonating," the Tac NCOIC said. "That group
didn't scatter and bandit group twelve was close alongside. We
got a piece of them."

The radar screen was cluttered with the oncoming dragonflies.
They clearly didn't fear space and they were *fast*. Their acceleration

in space was nearly twice that of the *Vorpal Blade*, worse than in air. There was no way the ship was going to make it to the warp point before at least five of the bandit groups were on them. And any one could probably destroy the ship at close range.

"Conn, Tactical," Souza said. "Recommend rotate the ship to bring the lasers to bear . . ."

"There's a ledge," Berg said, as soon as he was through the gate. The words were said through gritted teeth as he instinctively clamped down on his bite-trigger, turning a group of three Demons into paste. "The room's . . ."

He paused as he adjusted to the scale. Before he could continue his report, First Sergeant Powell was at his side.

"Holy smoke," Powell said.

There was quite a bit of that. The chamber was *massive*, so large that Berg couldn't see to the far side. A giant bowl lit by a bright spot near the center top that was hidden behind wreathes of vapor, it was lined with more of the blue fungus. But what the fungus was extruding . . .

There were thick lianas that dangled pods. One of them, fortunately about two hundred meters away, popped before his eyes, dropping a Demon onto a ledge similar to the one he occupied. The young Demon, nearly full sized but clearly shaky on his legs, toddled to a nearby pool and began to drink.

Larger pods moved sluggishly, revealing the figures of beetle Demons and dragons. There were, fortunately, far fewer of those, but the Demon pods . . . there were *thousands* of them.

And up near the ceiling, there were pods that sprouted other things. Drying their wings under the actinic light were things that looked like giant dragonflies with blue bodies and red compound eyes. Most of those looked recently hatched, but a few were older and already buzzing around near the ceiling.

Scattered along the walls and floor were Looking Glasses, hundreds of them.

The worst part, though, were the already birthed Demons. The chamber was packed with them. Dozens of beetles, at least nine dragons and *hundreds* of the relatively "smaller" Demons that had wiped out most of the company.

And they all turned to *look* at the small cluster of armor gathering on the ledge.

"Uh, oh," Chief Miller said as he exited the gate.

"Whoa!" Weaver said as he entered the area. "Well, ain't *that* something. You were right, Miller. Let's set the bombs and get the hell out of here."

"No," Miller said, pointing. "Wrong. Under the light."

The cavern was so overwhelming, Berg had missed it. Right at the center, nearly half a kilometer away, was an arrangement of fungus that seemed to have no functional purpose. There were just arms of fungus, bending inward. And at the center was a black globe.

"Oh . . . *maulk*," Weaver muttered.

"So, rocket scientist," Miller said. "What happens if you drop a bunch of unique quarks into a Chen Anomaly?"

"I haven't the foggiest," Weaver admitted.

"Me neither," Miller said. "But my guess is it's bad."

"What the hell do we *do*?' Weaver asked.

"We take Colonel Che-chee down there," Miriam said, suddenly at his elbow. "And she goes into the anomaly."

Berg had splattered the nearest Demons, but there were others not much farther away. They had apparently gotten over their own shock at the appearance of the Marines and a group of four charged the armored Terrans. Weaver, Berg and Miller blasted them without really thinking about it, but others were coming, including from above them.

"Whatever we're going to do, we need to do it *now*," First Sergeant Powell said.

"First Sergeant," Weaver said. "Leave one team behind to hold this gate. Get everyone else out of here, now!"

"Bandit group eleven closing to laser range."

"Open fire with both lasers when they bear," the CO said. "XO, get ready for more damage."

"Aye, aye, sir," the XO said, rolling his eyes. Most of the forward section of the ship was open to atmosphere, the tough steel of the sub slagged into molten ruin. Not only were they missing their sonar but he and the CO no longer had a berth. One more solid hit and tactical and the conn were going to be eating laser fire.

"Time to warp point?" the CO asked.

"Two minutes," the pilot said.

» » »

"Dragonflies at nine o'clock!" Staff Sergeant Sutherland shouted as the flies dove on the group.

There were only six of the things capable of flight, but one had already taken out Wangen with an unexpected burst of what looked one *hell* of a lot like a red-light laser coming out of its eyes. The group of humans and Cheerick had scattered, jinking through the air to avoid the flies' fire as they charged the facility at the center of the cavern.

"Top!" Berg shouted. "You've got one on your tail!"

"Well get it off of me!" the first sergeant replied, then cursed. "Oh, the hell with this," he said, spinning in place and firing to the rear.

The 7.62 mm rounds flew to the side of the fly then tracked back, ripping into its face.

"Oorah," the first sergeant said, spinning back around. ".308 takes them out."

"Two-Gun, scissor!" Corwin shouted, zooming left. A dragonfly banked to engage him and came right into Berg's sights.

"Scratch two!" Berg said then ducked as a board nearly knocked him off his feet. "Watch it!"

Sergeant Cha-chai barreled onward, then reached up and swept back, ripping off the wing of a dragonfly that had been closing on Berg.

"Thanks, Cha-chai!" Berg yelled over the external speakers.

The last fly was shot down by First Sergeant Powell and the group of humans and Cheerick charged onward. The flies were fast but they weren't maneuverable in the confines of the cavern, the only thing that had kept casualties down.

However, they were going to have to land. And the monsters on the ground had been following their progress hungrily.

"Lady Che-chee," Miriam said, flying alongside the old warrior's board. "I need you to take my hand. We are going into that black ball."

"Very well, Miss," Lady Che-chee said. "Together we shall triumph over any enemy."

"I'm not sure there's an enemy on the far side," Miriam said. "But we shall see . . ."

"Burn-through!" the Tac tech shouted. "Laser One is down! Laser Two is down!"

"Nothing more we can do here," Lieutenant Souza said, standing up. Even through his space suit he could feel the heat from the lasers that were lashing the hull. "Chief, evacuate the compart—"

The lasers from group fourteen finally burned through the steel of the hull and lashed the compartment, ripping through the targeting system, the tech and Lieutenant Souza.

"Everybody out of the pool!" the NCOIC said to the remaining radar tech. "We are *leaving*! Conn, Tactical, we are *down*."

"Engineering, Conn!"

"Tchar, Captain," the Adari said, nursing the neutrino generator. The room was hotter than a summer day at Edenasai and the neutrino cannon was glowing the bright white of a metal in a melt. "We took a blast in Engineering. Eng is down."

"Tchar, we need more speed! We're getting hammered."

"I'm giving it all I can, Captain!" Tchar said, just as another blast of laser fire penetrated the most protected compartment on the ship and a heat spall popped off the cover of the cannon. "She's coming apart!"

"Deploy," Captain MacDonald said as the group landed. The area was clear of the fungus, except for the strange overhanging growths. It was just bare rock, more granite, raised in what would be called a dais if it wasn't so natural looking.

The Marines fanned out as the smaller, faster Demons closed.

"Hold this ground," Weaver said as Miriam and Lady Che-chee stepped off their boards. The Royal Guard interleaved themselves with the humans, drawing their long swords and raising their shields. "We have to *hold*!"

"The enemy is on my right . . ." Top said.

"The enemy is on my flank . . ." Captain MacDonald continued.

"The enemy is to my rear . . ." Lieutenant Berisford finished.

"*I HAVE THEM RIGHT WHERE I WANT THEM!*" the entire group of Marines chorused.

"Open fire!"

"Conn, Tactical, we are evacuating this compartment!"

"Pilot, rotate the ship," the CO said. "Get some of this fire spread!"

Three of the groups had closed, coming in not only from

straight on but also from the sides, slashing the *Blade* with laser fire. The ship had breaches in every compartment and was bleeding air and water into space. Even if they could make it into warp, they might not be able to limp back to Earth as damaged as they were.

"Rotating!" the pilot said as the air suddenly jumped about two hundred degrees.

"Hit on the sail!" the XO said. "It's . . ."

The lasers from the dragonflies burned through the sturdy metal of the ship, ripping into the conn and into the XO.

"Breach in conn," the CO said into the comm. "Damage parties to the bridge."

He looked over at the blasted remnants of the XO and worked his jaw.

"Now I gotta train a new one."


"Eat *maulk* and die!" Pearson screamed. The CO's RTO carried the extra burden of the long-range communicators and thus less ammo. So his counter was dropping fast as the Demons came on in seemingly unending waves. "I am so gonna—"

Despite the fire of the Marines, the Demons were breaking through, and one managed to get its teeth in the Wyvern's leg, ripping it out from under the Marine.

"*Behanchod!*" Pearson shouted as the Wyvern toppled. There were Royal Guardsmen on either side and one cut down, killing one of the Demons that swarmed the armor, but they could barely keep the Demons off themselves.

"Die you mother*grappers!*" Pearson screamed, waving his Gatling back and forth as the Demons ripped into his armor. As a Demon face appeared in the opening, he spit at it. "I'll eat your soul and—"


"Oh," Lady Che-chee said as they stepped through the anomaly.

The far side was a small room, almost bare except for a pile of the blue moss. And the skeleton lying on it.

"We need to move her," Miriam said, picking up a bone. "Quickly. Then you have to lie down there."

"How do you know this?" Lady Che-chee said, reaching onto the dais and sweeping most of the bones away with one broad motion.

"I don't know," Miriam said. "I just have a knack. Please. Hurry. More than Cheerick could depend on this."

"Pearson's down," the first sergeant said to Chief Miller. "Can you fill the gap?"

Miller had lifted his board up and was carefully engaging the approaching beetles with his sniper rifle while occasionally providing supporting fire with his Gatling. He looked over at the gap, where a Royal Guardsman was being ripped apart, and dropped down.

"Got it," he said, sliding forward, then casually stepping off the board. Two bursts cleared the Demons in the hole and he strode into it, firing his Gatling into the mass of Demons, then switching to the rifle to fire at an approaching dragon. "Gotta *love* a target rich environment."

"One minute to warp," the pilot said. He wished he could wipe his face. Even through his space suit the compartment was hot as hell.

"Come on, baby," the CO said, patting the hull. "Hold together . . ."

"I just lost power!" the pilot shouted. "We're drifting. Drifting fast, but drifting!"

"Burn through in engineering! Drive down!"

"That is *not* holding together!"

"*EEK!*" Lady Che-chee squeaked.

"What is going on?" Miriam asked.

"I have a hard time telling," Lady Che-chee said. "I can see . . . everything."

"Can you see how to control the Demons?" Miriam asked. "Especially, are there any in space, near the planet?"

"I . . . yes!" Lady Che-chee said. "I think . . . yes . . ."

"Couldn't we wait to patch these until *after* the battle?" Sub Dude asked, slapping a sheet of heavy steel down on a hole in the hull.

"I wish," Red said, just as the steel blasted backwards, melting even as it moved.

"*Maulk!*" Gants shouted, trying to jump back just as the gravity cut out. "Blow this for a game of soldiers!" he continued, float-ing in midair.

"*Grapp*," Red said, his hand on his arm. "I think one of those melted pieces hit my suit." Air and red could be seen escaping between his clutched fingers.

"Hang on, Red," Gants said desperately, trying to reach any-thing that he could bounce off of to get to the injured teammate. "Just hang *on*."

"HOLD YOUR GROUND!" First Sergeant Powell shouted as Captain MacDonald was picked up by a dragon and killed with a single crunch. "HOLD!"

The perimeter had shrunk to a tiny handful with their backs practically to the anomaly. The Demons were up on the dais and they'd been joined by their bigger brethren.

"Die you *grapp*tard!" Berg shouted, firing both pistols and his Gatling into a beetle's mouth. Even the .50 caliber rounds were sparking off of the beetle's mouthparts. And when it opened its mouth, it was going to close on his armor. "GRAPPING DIE!"

As he screamed that the beetle suddenly stopped, then backed away.

"Okay," Berg said, lifting up on his bite-trigger. "Running away works."

All of the beasts were backing away, retreating to the edge of the room even as the Marines continued to fire.

"Cease fire!" Top shouted, looking around.

Lieutenant Patrick West was dead, his armor ripped open by Demons then crushed in the jaws of a dragon. Staff Sergeant Sutherland lay on the dais surrounded by a wall of Demon bod-ies. Holland was just . . . in pieces.

Top, Berg, Seeley and Corwin were the only Marines left stand-ing. Besides the Marines there were two Royal Guardsmen, one with a ripped up leg, Commander Weaver and Chief Miller.

The latter's smoking Gatling tracked from side to side as the Demons settled in a distant ring around the Marine contingent.

"That's right, you'd better run," Miller said, holding his rifle over his head. "SEALS RULE!"

"Actually, I think the Cheerick rule," Miriam said, stepping out of the anomaly. "Right now, I'm trying to figure out how we explain to the captain that the dragonflies are going to tow him home."

# 36

## This One Time Off Cygnus Alpha...

"It's a planetary defense system," Weaver said, looking at the plans.

The "anomaly room" had contained more than just the control dais. There were metal plates with complex formulas, schematics and a strange language.

The entire assembly had been packed back out by the remaining Marines and Royal Guardsmen. The dead Marines from the battle were carried out on the backs of dragons. Remarkably tame dragons that followed the orders of Lady Che-chee like so many dogs. The whole procession had ended up in the palace along with the officers from the ship.

"It might even be a system designed to fight the Dreen," he continued. "The big chamber is where the weapons are forged. But why do they track in on electrical signals?"

"Want a guess?" Miller asked. "Somebody gained control of it during a war between Cheerick. Or maybe the last guardian of it set it to the simplest thing she could imagine, knowing that any enemy would use electricity."

"But now we know what it is truly designed for," Lady Che-chee said, looking at the plans. "Yes, I saw all of this on the bed. Also I could see how to stop the Demons attacking."

"And towing back the ship," Chief Miller said, looking over at Captain Blankemeier and grinning. "That was a hell of a sight."

"You should have seen it from my perspective, Chief Warrant," the CO said bitterly. "There we were, dead in space. All of a sudden, the flies stopped firing. Great. Then they grab onto the ship and start towing it back to the planet. Ever seen a wasp pick up a spider it's taking home to feed to its young?"

"Hmmm . . ." Bill said. "Lady Che-chee?"

"Commander Beeel?"

"Is there a way you could get one of those guys to fly over to your estate? While the ship's being worked on I think we need to take a look at it."

"Ahem," the CO said. "Might I point out to you, XO, that the *duty* of getting this ship functional is *yours*?"

"Understood, sir," Bill replied, straightening up. "There are others that can take a look at it. Permission to have a brief discussion with First Sergeant Powell and Chief Miller before I get into reconstructing a half-destroyed ship sufficiently to make it spaceworthy back to earth?"

"Permission granted," the CO said. "But make it short."

"It actually *does* look like a dragonfly, doesn't it?" First Sergeant Powell said, walking around the grounded . . . thing.

The "dragonfly" was about twelve meters long from what looked like a feeding tube to the end of its abdomen. However, it had no segmentation and no antennae, its legs were extremely stubby and instead of having a head, thorax and abdomen it had three sections not nearly as well delineated. The junctures were thick, unlike an insect. The two sets of wings were also separated by a short, indented, section where the thorax would be.

"More like a solfugid that's evolved to fly," Dr. Robertson said, circling in the other direction. "But the similarity is interesting."

Three of the beasts had been directed to Lady Che-Chee's estate and now rested on the front lawn. In deference to the Mother, who had done the directing, the group had waited until she returned to begin their examination. But she had just arrived and now stepped off her gravboard.

"Solfugid?" Berg asked.

"About the only kind you might know about is a camel spider," Dr. Robertson replied. "But they're found in various places."

Lady Che-chee looked at it and flipped her hands a few times, chittering something.

"She thinks it's pretty but she's not sure of its use," Miriam said. "Neither am I."

"Well, for them, ground support," Powell replied. "Fire those lasers down on enemy troops and you're going to win about any battle."

When that was translated Cha-chai spat out a sentence and wrinkled his nose, at which point his mother apparently dressed him down with a few pungent squeals.

"Cha-chai thinks that's an unsporting way to fight," Miriam said unhappily. "Lady Che-chee pointed out that all war is unsporting or it's not war. But she's still unhappy about the idea."

"The system was created to defend your planet," First Sergeant Powell said, nodding. "Apparently by long gone Cheerick. Using it against other Cheerick would be . . . unethical. However, there's another reason we're finding out what we can do with it." He walked over to the thorax area and laid his hand on the indented part.

"I was looking at that," Dr. Robertson said. "That looks very much like . . ."

"A saddle," Powell replied. "I think this probably won't work, but . . . Berg."

"Top?"

"Up on the saddle, Two-Gun."

"Thought you were about to volunteer me," Berg said, but he strode over and hopped up on the dragonfly. "Gee-yap," he said, kicking his feet. "Nada, Top."

"Think up or fly or something, like a board."

Berg got a look of concentration on his face, then shook his head. "Nada."

"Okay, Miss Moon, could you ask Lady Che-chee if she would be willing to volunteer her son for the same exercise?"

"Okay," Miriam said, then started talking. It took a bit to get across but finally Cha-chai walked over and climbed on the seat. Almost immediately, the dragonfly took off.

"How high did you tell him to go?" Powell asked as the dragonfly climbed upwards.

"I just asked if he could try to fly it," Miriam said desperately. She chittered at Lady Che-chee for a moment, then shrugged.

"Lady Che-chee says that when you go high on the boards, it is noticeable that you get thinner air. He should stop then . . ."

"Let's hope," Powell said, picking up the mike of the long-range radio. *"Blade, Blade,* Marine Seven."

"Go, Marine Seven."

"Do we have any radars left?"

"Hold one." There was a pause. "Tactical is maintaining a watch using the weather set. They've *blaged* it up for tactical but it's not great. They said a bogey just went up from your location."

"Roger. Can we get a read on its altitude, please?"

"Stand by."

"Marine Seven, Tactical. Bogey is at angels thirty and ascending. What is the situation, over?"

"Shit," Powell muttered, then keyed the mike. "Tac, be aware that a local is riding the bogey. Apparently it is now an out of control fly since he's got to be out of air."

"Roger, will advise. Bogey is maintaining rate of climb and attitude. Passing angels forty. Velocity is Mach One Dot Three and increasing. Passing Fifty. Passing Sixty. Marine Seven, be advised this looks a lot like an extra-atmospheric mission, over."

"Roger."

"Passing ninety. Bogey One is now officially extra-atmospheric at Angels One Zero Five. Speed decreasing. Leveling off at Angels One One Six or close. This is the wrong radar for this, Marine Seven, but that looks to be it. Bogey sure *appears* to be under positive control. Bogey is beginning reentry. Looks to be headed to your location."

"Thank you, Tac," Powell said. "If there's any major change, let me know."

"Glad to help. You said somebody was *riding* this thing?"

"Roger."

"Then they just took a ride into space."

Cha-chai was hooting fit to die as he landed the dragonfly and hopped off. He ran around squeaking for quite some time before his mother could get him calmed down.

"What's he saying?" Powell asked.

"Most of it's incoherent," Miriam replied, smiling. "The one part I'm getting is 'The World Is Round!'"

» » »

"We're sure about this?" the CO asked.

"The dragonflies are controllable by a pilot, much like the boards," Bill replied tiredly. He'd been working nonstop trying to get the ship spaceworthy. Having this on his plate as well was a bit much. But he knew it was, arguably, as important. "They maintain not only a defensive screen but one that traps a bubble of air. And, somehow, they process it as well. At least as long as they'll fly. Lady Che-chee sent one out as far as she could. It eventually died. We're not sure how far out that was since we couldn't track it. But they *do* eventually give up. But the good news is, this trip, all the casualties, they just got worth it."

"You've lost me," Spectre said. "I like the Cheerick and all, but I'm still dreading the board of inquiry on this one."

"Don't, sir," Bill said. "I'm surprised that you, of all people on this boat, can't see the implications, sir. A vehicle with an onboard weapons system controllable by a pilot that has extra-atmospheric capability and a range of at least two super-Jovian diameters, probably farther. Think about it, sir!"

"Can you say 'space fighter?'" the CO said, finally grinning. "Holy *maulk*, Astro!"

"Exactly, sir," Bill replied. "My first thought was about the future. A space navy with dragonflies for fighters flying off of carriers. But they're even useful for *us*. Think about a group of flies, if we can figure out how to 'feed' them, attached to the *Blade*. We can use them to recon planets, sure. But even more important, if we get into a fight we can use their shields. Just have them fly between us and fire."

Spectre suddenly snorted and shook his head.

"Oh, I'm in agreement, Commander Weaver," the CO said, still shaking his head. "But have you thought about the picture?"

"Excuse me, sir?" Bill said, a bit befuddled.

"Giant, laser-beam-shooting-out-of-their-eyes dragonflies flown by *space* hamsters," the CO pointed out. "Can you imagine the manual on *that* one?"

"Chinchillas, sir," Bill said with a sigh. He could, indeed, imagine the manuals, and the meetings and the reports and the meetings, and oh, my, GOD the meetings on that one. "Space chinchillas."

"Well, I'm sure the chief of boat's seen something weirder," the CO said with a grin. "But not much."

# EPILOGUE

## Heart of a Dragon

"Sergeant Bergstresser, by order of the Commander in Chief of the Armed Forces of the United States, I hereby award you the Navy Cross for valor above and beyond the call of duty during classified missions of the highest importance . . ."

Berg kept his eyes on the flag as the secretary of the Navy pinned the cross to the front of his dress blues. A cold front had swept through the Norfolk area, bringing slashing rains followed by cold, clear skies and winds that rippled the stars and stripes like a whip. The secretary had already read off a list of posthumous awards that had taken nearly an hour, one by one handing them out to grieving women who, for now, could not be told how their sons, brothers, spouses had died. All Berg could do was flex his jaw as the list went on and on.

Less than a mile away in a covered dry dock a shattered submarine was being crawled over by technicians. The *Blade* was damaged but not done. Already the planning was in the works for the next mission. To go where no sub had gone before, into wonders and terrors untold.

Finally, the interminable ceremony was over. The group broke up and Berg wandered towards where he'd parked his Jeep.

"Hey, Two-Gun," Gants said. "Where to?"

"Leave," Berg said. "Headed home. How's Red?"

"They're fitting a prosthetic today," Gants said, dropping in to step beside the much taller Marine. "He's talking about trying to get back on duty."

"Hell, with as much damage as the sub took, he could be ready for duty before we go back out," Berg said.

"You're going?" Gants asked, sucking his teeth.

Berg stopped and looked up at the sky. It was midday so not a star could be seen, not even the "evening star" of Venus. He hadn't even thought about his response. He had been asked to "volunteer" again and had given an equivocating reply. But looking up at the cold blue skies of Virginia, he had no question in his mind.

"I'm a Marine," Berg answered. "I go wherever the Corps sends me."

"Hey, Two-Gun!" Miriam said, walking up and putting her arm through his.

"Hello, Miss Moon," Berg said, looking down at the slight linguist. She'd changed again, back to the whimsical creature they'd all come to know and love. "How are you doing?"

"Cold," Miriam said, despite being bundled up in a heavy jacket. "Where you going?"

"On leave," Berg repeated. "Home, I guess."

"Right now?" Miriam asked.

"Doesn't have to be," Berg said.

"Shiny. You. Me. Dance club. Now."

"Works," Berg said, grinning. "See ya, Sub Dude."

"Take care," Gants said, walking over to a busty redhead and a couple of kids. "See ya when I see ya."

"Where is home, by the way?" Miriam asked as they walked off.

"West Virginia. Hey, you *were* talking about a country and western club, right?"

"Do I *look* like I was talking about a country and western club . . . ?"

*Too Hot. Always too Hot now. But surely, someday, it would be Cold again. And then it could Be.*

"Okay," Bill said. "Good news."

He hung up the secure phone and looked over at Miller.

"The shipwrights are done with their survey," he said as the SEAL, very much against regulations, sipped a beer. "Six months to repair all the damage. On the other hand, we're going to get various upgrades."

"Glad to hear that," Miller said, setting his beer down. "What about you?"

"What about me?" Weaver asked.

"You going?"

"Oh, hell, yeah," Weaver said. "They're not sure if I'll keep the XO slot or not. But, yeah. You?"

"You ever think about fate?" Miller asked rhetorically. "Mimi told me that Tuffy couldn't explain exactly why I had to be along. Was it my pointing out that there was an anomaly in the room? Was it the couple of times I kept Miriam alive? She figured it out when nobody else did. What? That mission? The next? Mimi won't say. So do I have to go on, theoretically, saving the universe every time?"

"Do I?" Bill said. "Every day we wake up and we get faced with all these choices. Sometimes they're clearly big, yeah. But there are always choices. And every day we have to figure out which one is going to save our personal universe. So which one you gonna choose, Big Boy?"

"Face it," Miller said. "You just want to find out what we run into next."

"Well, that too," Bill said, chuckling. "It's a big old universe and we've hardly scratched the surface. Don't you?"

"Oh, hell yeah," Miller admitted. "Wouldn't miss it for the w . . . universe. But this time, I'm taking some more flowers. And a bigger *grapping* gun . . ."

> *Proud and so glorious*
> *Stand here the four of us.*
> *Our souls will shine bright in the sky.*
> *When united we come*
> *to the realm of the sun*
> *With the heart of a dragon we ride!*
> "Heart of a Dragon"
> DragonForce

# AFTERWORD

## On Writing Science Fiction

I rarely, these days, look at reviews on Amazon. As a fellow author puts it, "they are the slush (the unsolicited and mostly unreadable manuscripts) of reviews." There are rare, very rare, nuggets of brilliance in them and the "Top Reviewers" are generally very good. The rest, however . . . Sigh. One must shovel a great deal of muck to find a diamond. I have no patience for reading slush and less for Amazon reviews.

I did, nonetheless, read some of the reviews of *Into the Looking Glass*, the prequel to this novel. And I, as usual, had to shake my head. Especially at one reviewer (now made semi-famous and immortal) who thought it was a good book but "there was too much science in it."

Two words: *Science* Fiction.

*Looking Glass* was a very strange book that came from nowhere. It had no precedents in my thought processes. But as I wrote it I became very happy. Because strange as that novel was, it had some serious science in it. I am not a scientist but I grew up with science fiction. Indeed, much of what I know about physics and astronomy comes not from classes (of which I've had few of the former and none of the latter) but from reading the "greats" of science fiction.

When pressed by my publisher to create a series from *Looking Glass* (which I'd intended to be a stand-alone), I realized that I had a golden opportunity to write some serious SF. Not aliens creating a pretext for a world war. Not a science fictionalized "boat book" (a term of art about a young man exploring a world new to him). A real, old-fashioned, can-you-handle-your-astronomy-straight-up? science fiction series. Nobody but *nobody* has said it better than Gene Rodenberry. *"To boldly go where no man has gone before."* And, along the way, impart a modicum of science to the uninitiated. (While avoiding as much balonium and make-*maulk*-uppium as possible.)

I knew that much of that was beyond me. I am neither an astronomer nor a physicist (as noted). I'm a former grunt with some background in biology and geology who likes SF. To do it, I needed a scientist, specifically an astronomer and physicist, to do the "fiddly bits."

Thus I enlisted Doctor Travis Taylor, Ph.D. For those who find "Dr. William Weaver" unlikely, a snippet from Dr. Taylor's bio:

> Travis Shane Taylor is a born and bred southerner and resides just outside Huntsville, Alabama. He has a Doctorate in Optical Science and Engineering, a Master's degree in Physics, a Master's degree in Aerospace Engineering, all from the University of Alabama in Huntsville; a Master's degree in Astronomy from the Univ. of Western Sydney, and a Bachelor's degree in Electrical Engineering from Auburn University. He is a licensed Professional Engineer in the state of Alabama.
>
> Dr. Taylor has worked on various programs for the Department of Defense and NASA for the past sixteen years. He has been a guitarist with several hard rock bands, the 2000 Alabama State Champion in Karate, is a nationally recognized mountain biker, SCUBA diver, private pilot and is worshipped and adored by legions of female fans since he looks like a cross between Tom Cruise and a young Richard Dean Anderson.
>
> (Okay, I added that last bit. ☺)

So much for "Yeah, like there's really a redneck physicist who mountain bikes for fun . . ."

From my point of view, the mission of SF was handed down from the greats. Science fiction, speculative fiction, however you wish to say it, has the mission of looking at current theory and taking it beyond the realm of the currently possible. To push the boundaries and think about what *could* be out there. Whether that is in macrocosmic space, looking at what planets might look like beyond our solar system, or in the microcosmic, looking at what particles might *really* be doing and why, in biology extrapolating and questioning the ethics of bioengineering in all its manifestations, SF is now and always has been about pushing the boundaries of the known and striking out into the unknown. To speculate, not to prove. What ifness to the nth degree. And maybe get some bright young guy to invent some of this stuff thus making my job harder. What, you don't have a communicator? AKA a flip-phone?

While, of course, hopefully having a cracking good storyline and some characters people like.

Whether we succeed in our mission, to boldly impart some of the most advanced ideas in quantum theory and cosmology to the uninitiated, to enlighten and entertain, to develop a spark that blossoms into the flame of reality, or not, the mission is worthwhile. And maybe Doc will eventually get me to understand what a fermion is and why it's important.

Alas . . . I have the mind of a fourteen-year-old male. Whenever I even *write* "fermion" I get an image that is anything but cosmological . . .

☺

John Ringo
Chattanooga, Tennessee
August 2006

# On the Particle Physics in *This* Work of Fiction

Thought I would add my two cents in here as well. There is an awful lot of talk about particles and such in here so I thought a quick description of the fundamentals might be useful. But then again, it might just be damned confusing. But if I were going to give the Space Marines a one- or two-page summary of particles they should keep up with I'd do it with the following information.

Known fundamental particles that can't be broken into smaller particles are:

Fermions:
  Quarks: up, down, top, bottom (sometimes called beauty), charm, and strange
  Leptons: electrons, muons, tau, and the three flavors of neutrinos which are electron neutrino, muon neutrion, and tau neutrino

Bosons:
  Gauge bosons: photons, W+, W-, Zo, and gluons
  Other bosons (theoretical and possibly gauge): Higgs and the graviton (although I personally don't hold a lot of stock in the graviton)

Now, these are the fundamental particles that can't be made smaller by splitting them or smacking the hell out of them or anything else. It is these particles that in some combination or other that make up all the matter and interactions in the universe. Well, if you don't like the graviton we have to consider gravity from some other approach like strings or membranes or spacetime fabric or—oh hell, let's leave it at that for now.

Fermions are normally the ones that make up matter and stuff and the bosons are the ones that do the interacting or make up the so-called "forces" in nature that we hear about. The four forces are gravity, electromagnetism, weak, and strong forces.

And here is how they work.

Gravity works through the graviton (remember this is debatable as gravity can be described quite well with Einstein's General Relativity, but most particle weenies won't admit that. Einstein. Need I say more? Probably, but that'd take all semester).

Electromagnetism works through the photon, which accounts for radio, microwaves, terahertz waves, infrared, visible light, ultra-violet, x rays, gamma rays, and anything higher energy than that. This theory also explains the interactions of electrons and the electric and magnetic fields and is refered to as quantum electrodynamics or QED and is the field that Richard Feynman is most famous for. Humanity really, and I mean REALLY, understands QED. Or at least we think we do.

The weak force works via the W and Z bosons which were predicted by Abdus Salam, Steven Weinberg, and one of my idols, Sheldon Glashow. These guys won a Nobel prize in 1979 after the bosons were finally measured to exist in a particle collision experiment. The study of the weak force interactions is known as GWS theory for the founders. Sometimes it is apparently called quantum flavordynamics but I've never actually heard that used out loud by anyone. It is the weak force that allows for the color of gluons in a neutron to change and therefore allow it to decay into a proton. Interestingly enough, the process requires another field from which the heavy W and Z bosons can gain mass and hence we have the Higgs field (sometimes we'll hear Higgs mechanism). You see, the interaction between the electro-magnetic boson (the photon) and the weak force bosons (W and Z bosons) requires a middle man to transfer various properties including mass as the weak force bosons are heavy and the photon is massless. This middle man is the Higgs boson, which by the way has never been measured no matter what drunk particle physicists might claim.

The strong force uses the gluons and describes the way that particles in a nucleus of an atom (protons and neutrons) are held together. The study of the strong force particles is known as quantum chromodynamics or QCD. QCD was championed by Frank Wilczec, David Politzer, and David Gross who shared a Nobel prize in 2004 for their theory. The strong force governs hadrons, which are particles made up of quarks and gluons. The hadrons contain baryons, which are fermions made of three quarks (with gluons holding them together), and mesons, which are made of two quarks (again with gluons holding them together). These gluons have colors of red, green, or blue and don't forget the anticolors. Seriously, I'm not making this *maulk* up! When one of these gluons changes color is when there are neutrons decaying into protons as described above in the weak interaction description.

Finally, know this, in this book we mention a new set of "make believe" bosons that are connected and when manipulated properly allow for travel from one to another. This idea of Looking Glass bosons is not unlike at all how the Higgs boson transfers the effect of mass from an all encompassing and permeating field (the Higgs field or Higgs ocean) between the massless boson and the massive bosons of the electromagnetic and weak fields. It is possible that as we understand new ideas in modern physics we will uncover some similar mechanisms that will allow for "gate travel" as Ringo and I describe in this book. On the other hand, we could have just made all this *maulk* up.

"Doc" Travis S. Taylor
Harvest, Alabama
August 2006